OUTSYSTEM

THE INTREPID SAGA – BOOK 1

M. D. COOPER

DEDICATION

This book is dedicated to my children, born and unborn, who will inhabit the future far longer than I. May your future never be utopian, but always struggling toward perfection. May it never be idealistic, but always founded on ideals.

ACKNOWLEDGEMENTS

There is only one acknowledgement that matters, and that is to my wife, Jill. Without her, this world would remain only imagined and never written.

But once her inspiration spurred me on, it took a host of people to help get Outsystem to where you see it today. Most notably: Greta van der Rol for being the first person not related to me who thought my writing was a good read; MV Merchant for reading everything providing excellent feedback; and Erin Marion for being a tireless editor and giving way more attention to minute detail than I even knew was possible.

If you have read any amount of science fiction, you will see certain authors' influence in this book. Foremost are: Larry Niven whose Ringworld series changed the way I thought about science fiction; Tanya Huff for writing one of the best damn female military characters in any book anywhere; Elizabeth Moon for showing that a book taking place almost entirely on one ship can be awesome; and Anne McCaffery for writing Dragon Quest and opening the world of science fiction and fantasy to me.

FOREWORD

While Outsystem is not the first book of Aeon 14 chronologically speaking, it is the first published. This is the story where we see Tanis Richards join the colony mission, and fight for her life, and the lives of those around her to see the GSS *Intrepid* leave the Sol System for a new future.

While there are many, many books in Aeon 14, an ideal way to read them is to start right where you are, with Outsystem. Then, follow the trail left at the end of each novel, where you'll find a link to the next story.

However, if you wish to know more about the many books of Aeon 14, you can grab the Reading Guide, or check out the chronological book timeline.

There is also a glossary at the end of this book that contains the definitions of many terms you'll find within. I encourage you to reference it if there are terms that you are not familiar with.

However, I won't keep you long. Adventure awaits, and the best way to experience it is to dive in.

M. D. Cooper
Danvers, 2018

ACCEPTANCE

STELLAR DATE: 3226929 / 12.07.4122 (Adjusted Gregorian)
LOCATION: Edge of the Grey Sea, Pluto
REGION: Jovian Combine, Sol Space Federation

A young sapling exploded beside Tanis and she dove for cover, scampering away as splinters flew in every direction. She slipped into a depression, flattening herself as much as possible, hoping it was enough to stay out of sight. Another shot hit a rock nearby and liquid fragments of stone rained down, beading off her armor.

<Does anyone have a location on that shooter?> Tanis sent the question over the Link.

Both Sorensen and Reynolds signaled negative.

Angela was covering tactical coordination, and placed several pointers on the team members' HUDs.

<It could be any of these. The plasma bolts are firing at over ten kilometers per second and they have their muzzle flash masked.>

<Sorensen, get behind that knoll to your left. See if you can deploy nanoprobes to get Angela triangulation data,> Tanis directed.

<Aye, sir.>

<Reynolds, hold the center, I'm going right into that stream bed.>

Several more shots impacted the ground around the team's position. Reynolds slipped his rifle up over his cover and fired two electron beams before pulling back and rolling to a new location. He continued to draw as much attention as possible while Tanis and Sorensen worked toward their new positions.

Tanis made it to the stream bed without drawing any fire, and her retinal HUD indicated Sorensen was in position and had deployed his nanoprobes.

<Better view?> Tanis asked Angela.

<Resolving…I just need a few more incoming beams to triangulate

their source.>

The enemy obliged, returning fire at Reynolds' previous location.

<*Got em!*> Angela highlighted a position on each team member's HUD and Tanis set a countdown. The soldiers set their rifles to a magnetic proton beam, and when the timer hit zero, they all fired on the enemy position.

There was a moment of silence, the rippling of the water flowing past her body seemed to grow in volume; then the desired explosion flared up and streams of plasma sprayed in every direction.

Tanis's visor darkened to shield her eyes. When the tint faded, she saw a hundred-meter swath of young forest on fire.

<*You sure do know how to shake things up, Major.*> Sorensen's rasp sounded in her mind.

<*All other teams have made their objectives,*> Angela said. <*The main strike force is on its way in.*>

Tanis rose out of the water, unlocked her helmet and tucked it under her arm. Above her, the roar of orbital drop craft and the accompanying streams of fire turned the night sky into a spectacular show—arcs of color and plasma painted across the backdrop of Jupiter's dark bands.

It had been some time since she had been in a primary assault force; the last five years had been filled with out-of-the-way assignments, such as this one.

Strangely, the familiar yearning to be in on the larger action just wasn't there. For that matter, the exultation she should have been feeling in securing her target wasn't there either

<*You're just anxious for the GSS's response.*> Angela sounded a bit nervous as well.

Over the nine years since Toro, Angela had become closer than a sister or a best friend; it was almost as though Angela was simply another side to her. Tanis knew that wasn't entirely true—the AI residing in her head was a distinct individual, even though at times it didn't feel that way.

<And you've never been vetted this thoroughly before. This gen-ship is being rather particular.> Tanis slipped a smirk into her mental tone, then felt momentarily guilty. <But you'll do fine. You're not the one with the soiled record.>

<That doesn't matter. The GSS will have access to the truth. They'll know you aren't the monster the media made you out to be.>

<Let's hope so.>

Tanis met up with Sorensen and Reynolds several minutes later. Sorensen was covered in mud and Reynolds was grinning like a Cheshire cat.

"You shoulda seen it, Major. He came striding up, all cocky as shit, and then caught his boot on this tiny twig—couldna been bigger than my pinky. Gun goes flyin', arms are wavin', and the big man just topples over like a felled tree."

Sorensen wasn't smiling. "Goddamn planet. Why'd they have to make it rain so much here? Place is an effing mudball."

Reynolds slapped him on the back. "That's progress, lad. Besides, you know the Jovians; once they got a few worlds orbit'n Jupiter, they just had to try'n collect the whole set!"

"What does that have to do with how much it rains?" Sorensen grunted and Reynolds merely shrugged his response.

Tanis smiled at the two men and drew some comfort from their camaraderie as the team walked back to the pickup point. It was bittersweet, though. After the massacre on Toro, she never felt like the enlisted troops looked at her quite the same way. It sapped some of the satisfaction from moments like this.

Later, after her team had arrived at the TSF's northern continent HQ, she passed her electronic authentication tokens to the TSS *Midway* orbiting above and checked her personal messages over the Link.

There it was; the message from the GSS. She stared at the glowing icon for several minutes before finally mustering the courage to open it. She could feel Angela in the back of her mind, as intent on the contents as Tanis.

Major Tanis Richards

References and qualifications accepted. Final, in-person interview scheduled for 3227134.75000 (local time) Enfield Building, Jerhattan, Earth.

GSS Colony Operations

"This is it, Angela." Tanis kept her voice soft, afraid that the emotion in it would be picked up by some officers nearby. "We finally made it."

WELCOME TO MARS

STELLAR DATE: 3227162 / 07.28.4123 (Adjusted Gregorian)
LOCATION: *Steel Dawn III*, En-Route to Mars
REGION: InnerSol Stellar Space, Sol Space Federation

Tanis entered the forward observation lounge on the *Steel Dawn III*. The windows were crowded with passengers, weary after the two-week voyage from Earth, catching their first glimpses of Mars.

Her HUD identified the passengers and she saw that most were fellow colonists, destined for the *Intrepid* and ultimately the world of New Eden. Near one of the windows on the starboard side stood Patty and Eric, who she had spent some time with during the voyage.

Threading the crowd, Tanis walked to the window and stood beside the pair. Eric looked up at her and smiled a greeting. Patty nodded and pointed toward the planet.

"You can just make out the ring now."

Tanis peered out the window and cycled her vision to a higher magnification.

"So you can."

The Mars 1 ring was a large orbital habitat that wrapped around the world like a glistening silver halo. It was over one hundred and eighty thousand kilometers in circumference, and sixteen hundred kilometers wide. It rotated at over twenty-two thousand kilometers per hour above the blue-green planet. On the world below, the Borealis Ocean filled the viewport, and the large Mariner Valley lakes slowly slipped past the day/night terminator.

Built in the twenty fifth century, the ring was a marvel of human engineering, and provided the energy management to terraform and power Mars. The Mars 1 ring was the gateway to the stars. Without it, modern terraforming techniques would never have been invented.

"Home sweet home," Eric said.

"Not exactly." Patty pointed to her left. "You can see the Mars Outer Shipyard coming around the ring over there. That's where the *Intrepid* is being completed. We'll be staying on the station or the ship, I imagine."

The Mars Outer Shipyard was a thousand-kilometer arc that was tethered to Mars's second artificial ring, the Mars Central Elevator Exchange, known by the locals as the MCEE. That outer ring linked to Mars 1, and, from there, massive elevators provided access to the planet below.

Though it was not the largest planetary superstructure, Tanis always found it to be one of the most beautiful. The Marsians had opted to build it with materials that glistened in the sunlight. With all of the orbital stations and outlying habitats tethered to the MCEE, it sometimes appeared as though the planet had been caught in a celestial cobweb.

"I can't make it out," Eric said after peering out the window for a minute. "You two keep forgetting I have these organic eyes. Not special hopped-up mod jobs like yours."

Patty laughed. "Well, I don't know how hopped up mine are; the major has the super eyes."

"Your tax dollars hard at work," Tanis smiled.

"So how long till we arrive?" Eric asked.

Eric had only a rudimentary Link to the shipnet. While he could look it up himself, Patty and Tanis already had the information overlaid on their retinal HUDs.

"Just over an hour," Tanis said.

"Doesn't look like it should take that long." Eric leaned forward, still trying to make out the shipyards.

An announcement over both the shipnet and audible systems interrupted their discussion.

"All passengers, this is your captain speaking. We are

beginning our final descent into the Mars Outer Shipyards, which the locals call the MOS." The captain pronounced the word 'moss'. "In thirty minutes, there will be two $0g$ maneuvers separated by a hard $15g$ burn. We apologize for that hard burn, but Marsian traffic control has busy inbound lanes today and we need to clear the space as quickly as possible.

"During these maneuvers, we require you to be in your cabin and strapped down to your bunk, for your safety.

"Mars Outer Shipyard is a class 1A environmental space with $0.8g$ centripetal gravity and a standard temperature of nineteen degrees Celsius. Be sure to have your customs forms filled out, and debark only after the announcement is given to do so.

"Thank you for flying Dawn Transport. To all of you colonists, good luck; to everyone else, we hope to see you again."

"Well, I guess I'll see you ladies after we finish docking," Eric said.

"You will indeed," Patty said. "We'll meet tonight for drinks at that restaurant I mentioned."

"You going to come, Tanis?" Eric asked.

"I'll see. I have to report in and get my assignment by 0800 station time, but if I'm not busy I'll be there." The military life brought her comfort, but the last few weeks on the *Dawn* had given her a taste of what a more relaxed life could be like. It made the offer tempting.

With final farewells, the three left the lounge with the other passengers and proceeded to their cabins.

One of the privileges of rank was that Tanis had a room to herself. She made certain all of her belongings were secure, and lay down on her bunk. She didn't bother to strap down, but did hold onto the rails along its sides. The ship shuddered several times as it shed all of its velocity relative to Mars. The process took several minutes; following which, the vessel rotated and the engines fired again.

The cabin systems displayed a holo countdown and also flashed a warning that the air would jell to help ease the discomfort of the upcoming maneuver. The cabin systems knew her body could hold up the strain, so the nano-injectors didn't deliver the frame firming nano bots into her body, but it was quite likely Eric was undergoing the rather uncomfortable procedure at the moment.

The captain wasn't lying; the 15g burn was hard. Tanis's body weight increased to over a ton, and she was pressed deep into the acceleration cushioning of her bunk as the ship matched the twenty-two kilometers per second orbit of the Mars Outer Shipyards. Once that velocity was reached, the fusion engines powered down, eliminating the gravity their thrust had created. In the resulting 0g, Tanis let go of the rails and allowed herself to slowly rise above her bunk as the air thinned out once more.

She could feel the telltale vibrations of thrusters firing as they eased the *Dawn* into its external berth on the planet side of the MOS. Once the ship was in place and latched onto the station, the thrusters slowly phased out until the physical coupling supplied the ship's angular momentum. During that process, the ship gradually fell under the centripetal force of the shipyard and achieved the station-standard 0.8g.

Tanis let the increasing gravity pull her back down to the bunk. It was an experience she always enjoyed—a ritual that had persisted since her first stellar flight with her father some sixty years earlier.

An announcement came over the shipnet indicating a successful docking. The passengers were reminded to remain in their cabins until the debarkation signal was given.

Shortly afterward, the low thud of the passenger and cargo umbilicals linking the *Dawn* to the station could be felt through the ship. Fresh air from the MOS filtered through the vents. Tanis could practically taste the difference after the stale stuff the *Dawn* had been recycling over the last few days.

The debarkation signal came over the shipnet, and a glowing green icon flashed on the door's holo display indicating that passengers could leave their cabins. Tanis took her time giving the sparse space a final check, making certain nothing was left behind. It would give the corridors a chance to clear out. No point in rushing into a crowd of people.

The sounds of other passengers outside her cabin had ceased, and Tanis had just stepped into the corridor when another tremor shook the ship. It was followed by the roar of an explosion flooding the hall, forcing Tanis to grasp the doorframe to maintain her footing. A moment of stillness followed, and then alarms began to blare. Tanis set her auditory systems to filter them out, only to have the telltale whack of pulse rifles and the chip of beam weapons fill the silence.

In a single swift motion, she dropped her duffle and pulled her pulse pistol from its holster. She couldn't imagine who the hell would use beam weapons on a ship. One shot in the wrong place and it would disrupt the electrostatic shields and cause explosive decompression.

The sound of high-pitched whines and supersonic booms joined the other weapons fire. *Even better*, Tanis thought, *some idiot was using a railgun!*

<*Some idiot has a death wish,*> Angela commented.

<*Except they're wishing for* our *deaths,*> Tanis replied as she bent to a knee and pulled her lightwand from the duffle.

Angela was attempting to query the shipnet to determine what was going on. <*It's at the dock. Someone blew two of the umbilicals, and started firing on passengers as they debarked.*>

<*That's going to be a massacre! Have they boarded the ship?*> Tanis asked.

<*Hard to say, the sensors are jammed in that sector. I'm guessing someone is hiding something...so yes.*>

<*Your guesses are usually right.*>

M. D. COOPER

Angela's reply was smug. <*Of course they are.*>
<*Can you raise the captain?*>
<*Shipnet is sporadic, looks like it's under some viral attack.*>
<*An all-out assault? This is more than some robbery.*>
<*Your guess is as good as mine,*> Angela responded.

Tanis took a deep breath and altered her thinking patterns for combat. Any concern and worry left her as the calm, born from being in more firefights than she could remember, took over. Controlled and cool, no emotion. Feelings got you killed.

<*I've reached the ship's AI on an auxiliary band. We'll handle the net battle; you find whoever's turning this ship into a screen door.*>
<*A screen door?*> Tanis didn't get the analogy.
<*Full of holes.*> Angela replied.
<*Did I ever mention humor is not your strong suit?*>

Starting down the corridor toward the remaining umbilical, Tanis listened for the sounds of weapons fire. Most were distant, but the odd snap sounded nearby. She was nearing the fore end of the hall when the deck plate shook with another explosion—this one further aft, closer to the engines.

<*Are they—?*> she asked her AI.

<*It would seem so. If they blow the Dawn's engines, they'll make a pretty big boom. There's a D2 fueling station about a half klick away. That would go up for sure, and it could take out the Intrepid.*> Angela's thoughts were clipped. Tanis could tell the net fight against the viral attack must be consuming much of her attention.

<*So you're saying we can't let that happen.*>
<*I think that goes without saying.*>

Tanis ignored the jibe. <*Have you been able to make contact with anyone? We need to get the word out.*>

<*Still just the ship's AI, who is barely able to form a sentence right now. I've got to concentrate on this attack. You stop them from blowing the engines.*>

The engines were in the other direction, so Tanis pulled up

18

the ship's layout on her HUD, determining the best route aft. If she cut through the galley, she could get to the engineering section via service areas and avoid the section closer to the boarding hatch and destroyed umbilicals.

Tanis turned, moving back down the corridor. After a hundred meters, it ended in a three-way intersection. She eased around the corner, checking for hostiles, when the deck shuddered beneath her feet. Her footing slipped, and her head jerked out into the intersection, fully exposed.

"Hey! Stop!" The call came from her left.

Tanis berated herself for not deploying nanoprobes to scout ahead. Normally Angela covered that, but with her AI battling the virus that was trying to take control of the ship, it was up to Tanis to manage the nanoprobes.

She spared a glance at the man who had called out before pulling her head back. He stood just over twenty meters away, raising his rifle to fire.

"Whatever happened to letting me halt?" Tanis muttered as she pulled back out of sight. She pressed herself against the bulkhead as two bursts of energy lanced through the space where her head had been moments before. Two black patches of melted plas steamed across the corridor from her, making certain she knew just how close the brush with death had been.

The shots were followed by a string of curses and the pounding of heavy boots. A quick listen told her he was running at full speed. When he had to be within three meters of the junction, she crouched and launched herself across the intersection, firing her pulse pistol at him.

He wore light body armor and, though the shots stunned him, he shrugged off the effect in moments and let loose his own series of blasts. Tanis scampered back across the intersection and resumed her place against the wall. She waited, hearing his heavy breathing just around the bend; neither person wanting to make the first move.

"Get out here, you bitch. I'll make it quick."

Tanis looked at the conduits above her and, as quietly as possible, leapt up and wrapped her arms around one. "I think it's your turn to stick your head into the line of fire."

He cursed her again and when she didn't respond; the nose of his rifle edged around the corner, firing wildly. Tanis had pulled her feet up, and, though the shots missed her, she let out a pained scream.

With a laugh, her attacker strode into view, eyes downturned, looking for her body. Tanis dropped her legs around his head and clamped her knees as hard as she could. The man reached up and wrapped cybernetically-enhanced hands around her thighs. She gritted her teeth against the pain, but didn't let go, twisting as hard as she could in an attempt to break his neck.

It refused to snap, most likely modified in some way. Tanis resorted to Plan B, and drove her lightwand through his right eye, trying to angle up into his brain.

The man bellowed in agony and let go of Tanis as he collapsed to the floor. She landed lightly a pace away from him while he pulled the lightwand out and clamped both hands over his ruined eye.

"Yagh... You bitch!" He screamed, trying to get up. Tanis calmly set her pulse pistol to stun, and fired several shots point-blank at his chest.

<Gonna cauterize that?> Angela asked about the man's eye as he collapsed to the deck.

<I was going to, but all the bitch comments got to me. Get some nano ready to wipe the DNA security on his rifle.>

<Sorry, nano's all you right now, remember?>

<Force of habit.> Tanis launched the bots and set them to remove the security features from the unconscious man's rifle so that she could use it. Without clearing the DNA lock, grabbing the rifle would have caused it to electrocute her—or

possibly explode, depending on its configuration.

The weapon was an Amhurst MK CXI; not the latest TSF military hardware, but still not a weapon that should be in anyone's hands, other than the space force. In addition to energy beams, it could fire a focused pulse and she set it to that. No point in holing the ship more than these goons already had. Weapon secure, Tanis ran down the hall, keenly aware that taking out the thug had wasted precious time.

The kitchens were empty; the cooks had left their realm spotless and glistening before heading to the docks for their shore leave. Tanis slipped through the vacant area and into the service corridor that ran aft toward the engineering section.

She heard voices at the end of the hall and cycled her vision through various modes. The metal construction of the ship blocked infrared, but the free radical overlay showed a smudge of radiation moving toward engineering.

They were going to detonate a nuke on the ship; certainly an effective way to destroy the ship, and a good part of the MOS with it.

<How's access to station comm?>

<MOS has a general alert out on wideband; that's all I can get right now.>

Tanis reached the end of the hall and pushed the hatch open half an inch. She prepared several nanoprobes and felt the restructuring plate on her arm tingle as they left her body and flew into the next room.

VA and sensor readings from the probes lined her vision as they surveyed the room. It read clear and Tanis ducked into it, crouching behind a row of backup oxygen tanks.

<Not really the safest place to hide.>

<Only if they're stupid enough to shoot at an oxygen tank. They won't be able to arm their nuke if they blow themselves up by starting an O2 fire.>

<You assume they're smart.>

<They'd have to be to insert a virus that takes you this long to overcome.>

<Good point.>

Two men entered the room at the far end and Tanis flattened herself against a tank to avoid detection. Her probes circled, giving her a clear view of their positions. She waited until both men were facing away from her and then leaned out, shooting each in the lower back with the pulse beam. They crumpled and Tanis crept over to them, keeping an eye on the hatch they had come through. Angela deployed several nano to disable the fallen rifles.

<You back up to snuff?> Tanis asked.

<All set. I've helped the AI somewhat. She has access to some of her systems again. There are four men and your nuke in the main engineering bay. Through that hatch over there.>

The opening flashed in Tanis's sight and a map of the ship appeared over her vision. A short corridor lay beyond the exit, and beyond that, another hatch opened into the main engineering bay. The bay was long and narrow; two of the intruders were at the far end and another two were positioned at either side of the entrance she had to go through.

"Let's do this," Tanis said to herself. She picked up a second rifle, opened the hatch soundlessly, and crept down the corridor to the bay's entrance. It wasn't sealed tightly, and her probes slipped through the cracks. As the readout had shown, there was a man on either side of the hatch, weapons charged and positioned to nail anything that came through.

Tanis pulled the hatch inward and stood behind it. Who knew? Maybe they'd fall for something simple. Visual input from her probes showed one man stepping through the entrance, his eyes darting suspiciously.

Tanis raised a boot and kicked hard, slamming the hatch into the man's head. He fell backwards, clutching his nose as blood poured down his face. The second man was distracted by his falling comrade, and Tanis used the opportunity to step into the clear and let loose with both pulse rifles. The second man crumpled to the deck as she delivered another blast to his bleeding partner.

With both of them taken care of, she sent her nano over the various machines dedicated to moving and powering the ship. Luckily, the engineering bay was far from silent, and the two figures at the other end hadn't noticed the commotion. Either that, or they were simply concentrating on their little pet nuke.

<Got nano ready for that thing?> Tanis asked

<Already released. What do you take me for, a yearling?>

<Gotta ask so it's on the logs—you know that.>

<And I have to complain, it's in the AI regs,> Angela added a mental snort to her missive.

Tanis darted down the length of the bay, leaping over equipment and ducking under conduit. Her movements were silent and she went unnoticed. Ten meters from the pair, she swung around a set of cooling conduits and stepped into view.

"I strongly recommend you step away from the device." A twinge of panic was in the back of her mind, shouting *run away from the nuke!* She schooled her face not to show it—dozens of enemies were one thing; a nuke was something else.

The two figures straightened; a man and a woman. The man had long hair that fell well past his shoulders, and it was held away from his face by a thin band around his head. A scowl creased his angular features. The rest of his form was hidden by a long dark coat. The woman moved into view, and Tanis cursed softly under her breath; she was wearing a shimmersuit. As Tanis approached, it shifted from a glossy black color to completely translucent, rendering the woman's body invisible.

"I think you made a wrong turn." The man scowled. "If you run now, you can get off the ship before it blows."

"I don't think I can allow that to happen," Tanis replied.

The woman didn't say a word; with her body invisible, she

was just a disconcerting floating head, which disappeared, too, as the shimmersuit's material flowed up over her face.

"Think you can do that faster than I can twitch my trigger finger?" Tanis asked. "I'm MICI; we don't arrest—we just shoot." After a moment's pause, the material flowed back down the woman's face.

"Military Intelligence and Counterinsurgency?" the man asked.

Usually having MICI show up meant you had a leak; he had to be considering that possibility, a doubt Tanis was more than happy to plant.

"Then this will really hurt," he continued.

Tanis's vision turned white and pain erupted behind her eyes.

<Gah, remote pulser, how'd we miss it?>

<Focused on the nuke, I think,> Angela replied. *<Pulser is disabled. Your retina will reset in one second.>*

She felt a throb behind her eyelids and, as Angela predicted, in one second she could see again. The woman had vanished, and the man was standing with the nuclear bomb between them.

He hadn't pulled out a weapon; he simply wore a wicked smile. "Thanks for the treat. There's little I enjoy more than watching Kris work."

Tanis scanned the room for the woman while keeping her weapons trained on the man. *<How are you doing with the nuke?>* she asked Angela.

<Questions, questions—I'm working on it. It's good stuff, not the usual pinball machines most terrorists have.>

<What's a pinball machine?> Tanis asked.

<Never mind, you've got bigger issues. I can't detect that Kris woman.>

<What do you mean you can't detect her?> Tanis asked as she flipped through various vision modes. There was nothing on

infrared, UV, or even air disturbance detection. *<Damn... She's actually invisible!>*

<I said that.>

A fist impacted Tanis's face and she staggered backwards, kicking out at where the attacker should have been. Nothing.

Tanis took a deep breath and brought her fists up in a defensive position. The room was loud and she set her hearing to filter out the ambient sounds, trying to listen for the whistle of the woman's limbs.

Another series of blows struck Tanis and she stumbled, tripping over some equipment. *<I can't hear a thing.>*

<She must be dampening with remote emitters.>

Tanis tried to move unpredictably while Angela hunted down the devices. Her arm tingled as thousands of nano left her body and filled the air in the bay. In moments, the microscopic machines located the sources of the dampening waves and converged. The unseen robotic war was short, and punctuated by flashes of light as the enemy nano was destroyed.

Tanis's sensors were suddenly able to detect air turbulence again, and fed an image to her visual overlay. *<Good work—I can catch a glimpse of her now when she moves fast.>*

<You're welcome. Now don't get killed. I'm in here, too, and those punches weren't soft.>

<Thanks for the vote of confidence.> Tanis saw a foot flying toward her head just in time. Reaching across it, she twisted around and grabbed the leg under her arm while swinging an elbow back. She felt it connect with the side of the woman's head, and heard a satisfying grunt.

The woman's shimmersuit was slick; Tanis was unable to maintain her grip, and her opponent slipped away. She blocked a punch and then they were apart, Tanis circling slowly, moving as quietly as she could.

The man swore, having realized while he watched the fight that Angela's nanocloud was disarming the nuke. He bent over the console, trying to undo Angela's work.

"Just kill her already, Kris. We're running out of time. She must have AI that's hacking the nuke."

Kris didn't respond, but Tanis heard the telltale sound of a foot pivoting on the deck. With a quick flick of her wrist, Tanis let fly her lightwand, satisfied when her opponent screamed.

In front of Tanis, part of the shimmersuit flickered, turning black, and then red around the area the wand had struck. From the height, and bits of exposed teeth, it was safe to say it was Kris's jaw.

"Bet you wish you'd surrendered now." Tanis reached out and ripped the lightwand free.

The woman staggered back, but didn't make a sound. She must have pain suppressors.

Wordlessly, Kris pulled two thin blades from what Tanis guessed were her forearms. With most of the shimmersuit still functional, they appeared to float in midair.

The blades began a deadly dance and Tanis blocked with her pulse rifle, narrowly avoiding losing an arm in the first flurry of blows. The man was still cursing as he bent over the nuke, trying to do battle with Angela's nano—though it was likely his AI was doing most of the fighting.

Tanis blocked an overhand blow from Kris, and followed up by driving the butt of her weapon into the woman's chest. Kris fell back and the shimmersuit failed, reverting to a glossy black.

"So much for your unfair advantage." Tanis pointed the pulse rifle at the woman's head. "Now drop the blades and put your hands behind your head."

The woman snorted, a sound that didn't work well with part of her face sliced open, and raised her right hand. As a static shield sprung out of her forearm, Angela fed an intercepted Link communication to Tanis:

<Trent, are you going to get that thing set or not?>

<Her nano is blocking me, but I've almost gotten past it.> The

THE INTREPID SAGA – OUTSYSTEM

man replied.

<*Is that true?*> Tanis asked Angela.

<*Unfortunately, yes. He's got a small army over there and they're chasing my bots away. Any chance you can go and hit him so I can land a big dose and disrupt his personal systems?*>

<*Consider it done.*> Tanis gave Kris an evil smile. "Sorry, I have to go kick your friend's ass." She fired several rapid pulses at the woman. Even with the shield, the impact bowled Kris over.

Tanis dashed over to the man and held one rifle on him, while firing several shots in Kris's direction with the other.

"I'm going to have to ask you to step away from the nuke, Mister."

He didn't even look up, frantically working the manual interface, using every possible edge to stay ahead of Angela.

"Fine, have it your way," Tanis muttered before smashing a fist into his face. The blow forced him to his knees and Angela signaled approval.

<*Excellent. I'll shut down his Link; that'll isolate his nano, and I'll secure the nuke.*>

<*Good, then I just have this psychobit*—> Tanis's thought was cut off as one of her nano-cams alerted her to an incoming projectile. She ducked just in time to avoid a thrown blade aimed at her head. Tanis turned to see Kris racing toward her, shield down, swinging her other blade wildly. She stepped sideways to put the nuke between them, and fired a few more shots.

<*Incoming,*> Angela warned. <*They've got some reinforcements.*>

<*They do? What about our reinforcements? Doesn't the MOS have security?*>

<*They're coming, too; they just won't be here in time.*>

At the far end of the engineering bay, two men stepped through the hatch and leveled large caliber slug throwers at

Tanis.

<Sweet lord, where did they get those things?>

<Stay behind the nuke. Its casing can withstand those things.>

<Logical, yes; comforting, no.>

Kris helped Trent to his feet and they backed out of the engineering bay as the hail of bullets pinned Tanis down.

"It was nice meeting you." The man called out. "You may have disrupted our little event today, but I'll make sure you get a front row seat for the encore."

The pair slipped past the two heavy weaponers, who turned and followed them out. Overwhelming silence filled the bay.

<You did disable the nuke, right?>

<Yes, mother, the nuclear bomb is safely deactivated.>

<Thanks, Ang.>

Tanis stood and looked at the damage caused to the *Steel Dawn III*'s engine bay. "Why do I get the feeling this was the easy part?"

THE NEW BOSS
STELLAR DATE: 3227162 / 07.28.4123 (Adjusted Gregorian)
LOCATION: Mars Outer Shipyards (MOS)
REGION: Mars Protectorate, Sol Space Federation

"Well, I can see you get right to work."

Tanis looked up from her cup of coffee to see two men entering the sector chief's office where she was finishing up her report with Chief Ian. She spotted four stars on the collar of the man who had spoken, and rose before snapping off a salute. "Thank you, sir."

He returned the salute. "I'm Admiral Sanderson, and this is Captain Andrews of the *Intrepid*."

"Impressive work, Major Richards," the captain said.

"Thank you, sir," Tanis replied. "It was a pretty easy decision. Stop them or get blown up."

"I'm sure there was more to it than that." Captain Andrews gave her a warm smile. The admiral was smiling too, but it was more of a grim, got-a-job-to-do sort of smile. He cast an unreadable look at Captain Andrews as they both sat.

Tanis took a moment to examine the two men while they all got comfortable. Each was older than her; a quick records check showed Admiral Sanderson as having just passed his three-hundred and fiftieth birthday. She already knew of Captain Andrews; he was an old spacer, born over a thousand years earlier. Much of his life had been spent in stasis making the run between Sol and Alpha Centauri. Because he was recently returned from an interstellar journey, none of the images of him were recent, and she was surprised to see visible aging.

<I like him. Seems to be a good choice of a man to run this ship,> Angela commented.

<Yeah, but why is his hair silver?> Tanis asked. <I don't see any

medical conditions in his record.>

<Haven't you ever watched old vids?> her AI asked. Angela always liked to flaunt that she knew more about ancient cultures than Tanis.

<Do you mean his hair naturally went grey with age?>

<It still happens sometimes.>

<Why wouldn't he get that fixed?>

<How would I know? You're the human.>

"I didn't expect you two to come down here." Chief Ian of MSF pulled Tanis out of her private conversation as he addressed the captain and admiral. "Though I can't say I'm surprised, either."

"Someone tries to detonate a nuke three klicks from where my girl's tied up, you'd better expect I'd come down here." Captain Andrews' expression brooked no argument.

"Will Stevens be joining us?" Admiral Sanderson asked.

Tanis looked up the reference and found that Stevens was the MOS stationmaster. Her TSF security clearances brought up additional data pertaining to several complaints the stationmaster had filed against the *Intrepid* for incoming shipments causing disruptions on the station.

Tanis suddenly realized she hadn't checked on Patty or Eric. Emergency Response Status would have ID'd the dead, so Tanis accessed their net. The list scrolled over her HUD and she felt her heart drop as her new friends' names slid past along with so many others. She made a note. There should be a memorial for the dead, and she would contact their relatives.

<They didn't serve under you—you don't need to do that.> Angela's tone was soft and comforting. Tanis resisted the urge to retort, knowing the AI was just trying to be supportive in her own way.

<In a way they did. I have to take responsibility for the lives of people around me.>

<That's why you're so burnt out and looking to leave.>

<Perhaps, but it's still a part of who I am.>

She returned her attention to the conversation around her to hear Chief Ian explaining the stationmaster's whereabouts. Apparently he was down on Mars for a meeting with the Marsian government.

"And getting a strip torn off him, no doubt." Captain Andrews glowered. "It's what he gets for letting a goddamn nuke get smuggled onto his station."

"Now, Captain, we don't know that nuke didn't come in on the *Steel Dawn III*," Chief Ian countered.

"If I may..." Tanis waited for a nod from Admiral Sanderson before continuing. "There were no abnormal emissions on our trip from Earth to indicate the nuke was with us during transit. It could have been stowed behind some sort of shielding on the ship, but frankly I don't know where that could be. Every shielded location is heavily monitored. Also, on my way out, I saw scuff marks on the bulkheads that indicated the nuke came from the dock."

"Still, you can't be sure." The chief's jaw was set at a stubborn angle.

"She's right." A man with commander's bars stood in the doorway. "Sir." He addressed Admiral Sanderson. "You asked me to keep you advised of what we found. It turns out the device was brought on board MOS a week ago on a small transport. It was stored in a nearby holding facility, until today when it was moved to this sector, as it was marked for the *Dawn*'s return trip to Earth."

"Thank you, Commander," Sanderson said. "Will you join us? This is Major Richards; she will be heading up your security unit going forward."

"Yes, sir." Commander Evans nodded to the admiral, and gave Tanis a long look as he sat down. It was either a look of guarded relief or territorial disgruntlement.

Tanis kept surprise from showing on her face. She looked

the commander up and saw he was Joseph Evans, a TSF pilot added to the colony roster several months ago. Initially his duties consisted of piloting assembly craft, but, according to the records, several acts of sabotage resulted in his transfer to ship's security. As the ranking TSF officer, the admiral placed him in command. Knowing that a flyboy ran security gave Tanis new insight into why her interview had seemed so perfunctory. These folks were desperate and apparently needed someone with her skills.

The knowledge raised more questions. Why didn't an operation like this have the cream of the crop available to run security, and why hadn't she heard of sabotage on a GSS ship?

"We're damn lucky you were on that ship, Major," Captain Andrews said. "My report indicates that the blast would have taken out over ten percent of the shipyard, and while it wouldn't have completely destroyed the *Intrepid*, it certainly would have set the launch date back. Way back."

"That's not something we can tolerate," Sanderson growled. "That damn *Dakota* down at the MIS is beating its milestones every month. If we have many more setbacks, we're going to have to prove ourselves to get the colony assignment."

Tanis knew the *Dakota* was proceeding well, but she hadn't realized it stood a real chance of moving up its completion date. Looking up the data, Tanis realized if the other GSS ship maintained its accelerated timetable and the *Intrepid* kept slipping, New Eden's assignment would be referred to an advisory board and could be assigned to the other ship.

"It's getting bad. Those radicals are getting bolder every week," Chief Ian said.

Tanis shook her head. "Those were no radicals on that ship; they were too well armed and equipped. I expect that will be confirmed when they are interrogated, sirs."

"Are you sure?" The admiral's eyes narrowed. "All of our information points toward this being the work of small cells of anti-colonization groups."

"As certain as I can be at this point," Tanis replied. "They were far too well equipped, as I said. Consider that they took the dockside, then the ship. Within minutes, they disabled the AI and were hauling a nuke on board. They would have detonated it too, if Angela hadn't already had the training on disabling devices of that design. All of this was accomplished in a matter of minutes.

"I've worked against anti-colonist, anti-expansion groups before. They are determined, but they aren't that well set up. The folks we were up against had serious credit and decent talent behind them."

"If you say so." The admiral shrugged. "If the evidence bears that out, you will report it to me. In your capacity as head of the *Intrepid*'s security, I will be your commanding officer; however, since you are a colonist and are on Captain Andrew's boat, you will also be under his direction."

<Great,> Tanis complained to Angela. <A mixed chain of command.>

Ignoring his ship being referred to as a boat, Captain Andrews spoke to Tanis. "Did you notice anything else of interest?"

"Well, for starters, that nuke was military grade, and their nano was up to spec, as well. Angela had considerable difficulty handling them and disabling the weapon. Also, their personal armaments were military grade."

"I wasn't made aware of that," the admiral interrupted.

Tanis looked at Commander Evans. She didn't want to show him up in front of the admiral and captain, but pussyfooting around really wasn't an option. "TSF doesn't use them, but they're a recent spec for Jovian and Scattered World space forces. One of the operatives, a woman named Kris, also had one of the best shimmersuits I've ever seen. It incorporated sound-cancelling emitters that Angela had to take out before we could even hear her move."

Commander Evans whistled, and the captain nodded in agreement. "That does sound like better stuff than you'd expect some radicals to have."

Admiral Sanderson shook his head. "Let's hope not. I prefer radicals; they're not nearly as messy. If what you say is true, this could be coming from a government or a major corporation." He leaned forward, looking at each person in turn. "I don't have to tell you that it is imperative we keep the media from this. If they start posting stories about the *Intrepid* being under attack by unknown, well-funded terrorists, we'll have the folks down on the *Dakota* all over the GSS for preliminary hearings."

His gaze lingered on the chief for more than a moment, and Tanis glanced up to see the man fidgeting.

"Yes, sir," he said. Tanis was impressed with how the admiral's cold gaze could elicit compliance even from people outside his chain of command. Or in the chief's case, not even in the same military.

"I've caught wind of some issues with the schedule and security. How many breaches have there been?" Tanis asked.

Captain Andrews laughed. "This one's not afraid to ask questions."

Admiral Sanderson sighed as he leaned back in his chair. "I know. It's both the best and worst part of being an MICI officer."

Captain Andrews answered. "There have been several dozen. None like today, but cumulatively they are affecting the schedule. I think we've beaten that horse to death, so I won't belabor the point. You know what's at stake."

"I understand, sir," Tanis said.

"Good. Commander Evans will brief you on his progress on the *Dawn* so far and then show you to the *Intrepid*. You've got a lot to catch up on and I want security very tight tomorrow night at the ball," Admiral Sanderson instructed.

"Ball?" Tanis shot the admiral a querying look.

Captain Andrews gave another rich, warm laugh. Tanis wondered if she was the butt of some joke, but his smile appeared genuine and she found herself liking the man despite his odd choice of hair color.

"Joseph will fill you in on that—I'm sure he'll be overjoyed at not having to oversee the event." Captain Andrews smiled. "You'll find that despite our tight schedule, we are still required to hobnob with all the deep wallets that keep this sort of thing afloat."

Sanderson didn't let a lip twitch. He rose, as did Tanis and Commander Evans. He snapped off a salute, which they both returned, and left the chief's office. Captain Andrews stood after the admiral left, and clasped Commander Evans on the shoulder before he followed the admiral into the hall.

Chief Ian breathed a deep sigh once they left the room.

"If my report is satisfactory…" Tanis said to the chief.

He didn't even glance at it as he nodded and waved them out of his office. Once in the corridor outside his office, Commander Evans chuckled. "He's got a stash of vodka in his desk he likes to dip into at times like this; it's far more important than your report."

Tanis's brow furrowed. "People are smuggling nukes onto his station and he's getting sloshed? No wonder folks can slip anything under his nose."

The commander shot her a glance. "Hey, there are still a lot of hardworking people doing their best to keep things safe. Keep in mind that the security team on the *Intrepid* is a mix of Generation Ship Service, Terran Space Force, MOS security, Marsian Space Force, and our own internal security. We have to step carefully." He paused and took a deep breath. "Sir."

<Relax, Major. You're ruffling your new underling.>

Tanis calmed herself and gave Commander Evans an understanding look. "Those are a lot of toes you're dancing around. I see why you may have to tread lightly. But I don't have to like it, and, frankly, I may not bother with it."

The commander's eyes darted momentarily and Tanis was fairly certain he was viewing information on his HUD. Even though moving the eyes was not necessary to focus on any part of a data overlay, most people couldn't help the reflex. It was a handy tell.

"I suppose that's your MO, run in full burn and sort things out later. Let those under you pay the price." As he spoke, Commander Evans' body language had changed. Previously, he had been alert and slightly defensive; now he appeared guarded. His arms were crossed and his eyes were dark.

"Have my file up, do you?" Tanis's expression was grave. "I won't deny I've earned a lot of my reputation for being straightforward, but I suspect you are referring to one incident in particular."

"It does tend to stand out." He nodded slowly.

"I'm not going to justify it; I don't need to explain my actions to you." While Tanis didn't need to justify herself to a junior officer, she did need to have this man's support and assistance. "But I will tell you this. Were the recording of that event ever to be released, and I think it should be, people wouldn't be calling it the 'Toro Massacre' anymore." *And I'd have my respect and proper rank back*, Tanis added to herself.

<*We would have it back,*> Angela corrected her.

<*I'm sorry. I forget sometimes that my black mark extends to you.*>

<*I didn't mean it that way, I just meant those cowards at High Terra owe double for both of us.*>

Commander Evans didn't look away—the common reaction to her less pleasant glares, especially the ones she used when this topic came up.

"I'm sorry, sir. I know firsthand that once you get back in and the danger and adrenaline have faded, it's hard to explain why you did what you did. Sometimes even full sensory doesn't do the real thing justice; it may cover all the inputs, but there's no fear when you're watching a recording."

Tanis nodded. "Agreed. Maybe sometime I'll let you know more about what happened on Toro. But for now, we have work to do. I want to see the team going over the *Dawn*."

Commander Evans led her out of the sector security offices and down several corridors before they entered the open space that served as the passenger debarkation area for the *Dawn*. Several teams were present; a few physical forensics specialists were scanning all surfaces, while net specialists had a few terminals apart, going over hardware for signs of tampering.

The commander bridged Tanis to the security net and she took stock of the teams inside the ship as well. Most of the personnel were station security, with a few GSS and TSF in the mix. Commander Evans sent a beacon out onto the net and addressed the local teams.

"Ladies and gents," he simultaneously spoke and broadcast over the net. "If I can have a moment of your time."

Over the security net, she saw all the members stop what they were doing and signal their attention.

"For those of you on the *Intrepid*'s team, I'd like you to meet your new CO, Major Richards. The major is a MICI specialist and will be heading up our unit—a task I am more than willing to turn over to her."

"Thank you, Commander." Tanis took over the 'cast. "For those of you assigned to the *Intrepid,* I look forward to working with you, and for those of you with the MOS, I appreciate your attention. I've filed a report with sector security, and Commander Evans has also made it available on our security net. You'll note the specifics about the hostiles' weapons and the nuclear device. I also want particular attention paid to how they were able to act with such precise timing. The equipment and software they used to do this is not readily available, and the more data we have, the sooner we can track them down.

"Dismissed."

"No fanfare?" Commander Evans asked with a smile. She was glad he had let their tense moment slide by. They would most likely be working together for a very long time. Hundreds of years, if all went well.

"They know their jobs. Me wasting their time with speeches won't help get answers," Tanis replied. "Besides, I'm not a huge fan of the new CO that comes in and gets in everyone's way."

Commander Evans chuckled. "I'll be honest, sir. You could be some nasty little toady and I'd still be grateful to hand the reins over to you." He coughed as he glanced at her. Even with her uniform dirty and wrinkled, she cut an imposing figure. "Not that you're...ahh...nasty at all."

The comment was a bit too familiar, but Tanis found his cocky flyboy behavior amusing. She let him squirm for a moment before letting him off the hook.

"At ease, Commander. I don't take offense easily...well, not normally anyway." She decided it was time to get back on task. "Admiral Sanderson indicated you're to take me to the *Intrepid*. I assume we have facilities there?"

The commander seemed more than willing to let his gaff slip by. "Yes, sir. Since the radicals started attacking, we've been given a full Security Operations Center to help keep an eye on things."

"Lead on, Commander."

He directed Tanis out of the debarkation area toward a maglev train station. They passed through a lackluster security check and took a high-speed car to the *Intrepid*'s berth. The train accelerated to over a thousand kilometers per hour, speeding down its track in silence. Moments after reaching its top speed, the car passed out into open space, and Tanis caught her breath as the *Intrepid* came into view.

The ship was nearly thirty kilometers in length; the dominant feature being the two sixteen kilometer cylinders around which the ship curved protectively. The cylinders gleamed dully in the sunlight as they rotated nearly twice a minute, creating $0.82g$ of centripetal gravity within their hollow interiors. Inside, the environmental systems were already working, creating habitable areas with fields, lakes and forests that contained the base biosphere to be transplanted to New Eden. Beneath the floor of the eco-space were the stasis chambers. There were pods for the one and a half million colonists, plus several thousand backups to cover failures and the possibility of children being born to any crew who stayed out of stasis.

While the twin cylinders were the ship's most notable feature, they were not technically part of the ship and would be left behind at New Eden. Also staying behind at the colony were the massive cargo cubes that were positioned between the cylinders. Three were currently in place, but seven more were being readied, each filled with supplies and equipment for building the colony.

Draped over those sections, as though cupping its cargo, was the ship itself.

The front looked much like a porpoise, sleek and curved, tapering as it ran back over the cargo containers to the engines. A large cone rested at its fore—the emitter for the *Intrepid*'s massive ES ramscoop, which would draw in hydrogen and fuel the ship as it journeyed through the interstellar medium.

While the engines were proportionally smaller than many of the ship's other sections, they were still quite massive—over five cubic kilometers in size. Specs that filled Tanis's HUD showed they were capable of delivering over a trillion newtons of thrust, creating enough impulse to ultimately bring the ship up to over fifteen percent of the speed of light.

Arching down from the ship's spine and encompassing the entire structure were the gossamer strands of super CT, which held all of the disparate sections together. It appeared almost as if strings of light had drifted through space and settled across the ship, wrapping around the engines, body, cylinders, and cargo pods. It was a breathtaking sight. Tanis had seen few vessels of this size so beautiful.

The commander noticed her sharp intake of breath and smiled. "She has that effect, doesn't she?"

"It's magnificent," Tanis said. "It's hard to believe I got a berth."

"I know what you mean," he replied. "This was the fifth GSS I've applied to; I imagine I'm only on it because they're tired of interviewing me."

"Are there a lot of military among the colonists?"

"Numbers-wise yes; but then with the size of the colony roster, there's more of everyone."

"I suppose that's true," Tanis said. "Many officers?"

"The usual mess of lieutenants, a few commanders, some good sergeants, and two other majors like yourself. Above you, it's just the admiral; and the captain, of course."

Their conversation was interrupted by the train's arrival at their destination.

The maglev station was both large and packed with people. It was directly off the *Intrepid*'s main cargo dock, and everyone was coming or going from that direction. Tanis observed dozens of potential security nightmares. Something would have to be done about this.

Before they made it across the station and through the short corridor leading to the dock, she was filing reports and looking up data on numbers of essential and non-essential personnel who accessed the dock.

The dock was to scale with the ship.

Needing to handle the transfer of billions of tons of cargo, the dock was over three kilometers long and one deep. In the distance—looming over hectares of crates and equipment—was the *Intrepid*'s yawning cargo hatch. Tanis's HUD provided the portal's size, and she was surprised to realize it was large enough to fly the *Steel Dawn III* through.

Commander Evans led Tanis to a bank of ground transports, and they sped off toward the ship. They wove around slower transports and cargo lifters, some hauling massive mechanical devices as tall as a hundred meters, all moving toward the ship's entrance.

"We could have gone up a few decks and taken one of the maglevs up there. They run down an umbilical directly to the forward crew section of the ship, but I figured you'd like the view down here," Commander Evans said from his position at the controls.

Tanis nodded, looking over the operation around her. "Good plan, showing me the security and control down here."

Commander Evans gave his easy laugh again. "Yeah, you must be a Micky. Only they could think of duty and work when peering into a ten-kilometer-deep cargo bay for the first time." He gestured at the space within the *Intrepid*'s yawning portal.

She resisted scowling at him for using the vernacular term for MICI while privately admitting that seeing atmospheric distortion within a cargo bay was unusual.

Twenty meters from the ship, a thick white line was painted on the deck. The far side was *Intrepid*. Tanis signaled the commander to stop and examined the security threshold. Holographic emitters projected the barrier, vertically displaying it to the flits and cargo hovers that moved around the dock.

The security itself was manned by Terran Space Force Regulars; unlike the previous checkpoints, which had all been operated by MOS security forces. Tanis added to her list of anomalies the fact that TSF, and not GSS, was running security for this ship. Today's near miss was not the first significant threat this project had faced.

Above, at the levels where maglev tracks moved cargo

through the barrier, more Regulars manned the gantries and inspected physical ladings, while spider-like automatons crawled over everything, checking sources, destinations, and contents.

Someone must have warned the soldiers that their new CO was coming through, as they were brisk and businesslike, coolly efficient and quietly threatening. Tanis spotted a lieutenant and gave her a nod. The woman jogged over and saluted.

"Sirs!"

Tanis's HUD flagged the woman as First Lieutenant Amy Lee. The name caused Tanis to bring up the woman's record. Two names for a given name and no surname was common for the Scattered Worlds; it was unusual to find someone from the disk in the Terran Space Force. However, that was the case — the lieutenant was from the Scattered World's capital of Makemake.

"Amy Lee is our head of external security. She's a former Marine from the MCSF. The three platoons under her are from a few fully manned Q companies down on the ring. No commander with them, so we put her in charge."

Tanis nodded.

<Q company? They give them combat troops, but rather than cohesive units they get miscellaneous Q platoons? This doesn't make sense.> Angela all but echoed what Tanis was thinking.

"You appear to have things well in hand here, Lieutenant." Tanis looked at the Regulars manning the checkpoints. "We'll be expanding our area of control. I want you to begin considering shift and personnel changes for moving our perimeter out to the maglev stations and elevator banks."

The lieutenant's eyes widened, but she didn't question how Tanis planned to take control of a few kilometers of the MOS.

"Yes, sir!"

"Carry on." Tanis saluted and they moved forward to be

processed by the soldiers. Minutes later, they were driving over one of the bridges between the dock and the ship.

The cargo bay was even larger once inside. It turned out to be a main corridor off a hundred other cargo bays; a corridor large enough to fly the *Steel Dawn III* through.

Equipment moved through it on a dozen different levels. Holo emitters outlined several roads for ground vehicles and Commander Evans sped the ground car down one, deftly following its jinks and curves.

The corridor ran to the far side of the ship, some ten kilometers distant. Tanis cycled her vision and saw what appeared to be a multi-tiered docking port for external cargo. The construction drones clustered in the distance showed that it was still incomplete, and all cargo was being funneled through the shipyard's dock. She glanced back at the porous dock security and wondered what it would take to accelerate the external dock's completion.

After two kilometers, they passed the entrance to the port cylinder.

"That one's been named 'Old Sam'," Commander Evans said. "The other is named 'Lil Sue'."

"Have you been in them?" Tanis had been in dozens of cylinder habitats, but never one that was mounted in a ship.

"A few times, yeah. Ouri, one of our lieutenants in the SOC, has managed to get her hands on a small lakeside house in Old Sam. I guess she's also pretty big into botany and is maintaining some special garden and overseeing several other areas in there. We've had a few cookouts down by the lake recently."

"What, with a fire?"

"Yeah, nuts, eh? We had no trouble whatsoever getting the authorization for it. Apparently the carbon cycle needs a little help, so the more the merrier."

"Fires on a starship for fun." Tanis shook her head. "Not something I think I've ever heard of before."

"It's nice when we do it; you'd think you're dirt-side." Commander Evans smiled absently as he spoke.

His features cut a nice profile. Either he had good genetics, or his parents had paid special attention to his looks.

"I've been in a few of those cylinder habs before. Every now and then, I look up and see a lake or a forest rotating over my head and have to suppress the instinct to duck."

Commander Evans laughed and they drove in silence the rest of the way to the tubes.

The lifts were guarded by GSS security who processed Tanis and Joe swiftly. They stepped into an empty car and held the handrails as the platform shot up through the tube.

The tube's walls were clear plas, and the effect gave the sensation that the floor of the cargo bay was falling away from them. Above were several levels containing everything from life support to supplies and storage. Once past the lower levels, the tube shot out into empty space, anchored to one of the gossamer struts running around this section of the ship. They sped over the matter accelerator that ran from the ramscoop back to the engines, and moments later were swallowed by the upper section of the vessel.

"You know" — Tanis peered through the plas — "Even if you take off the cylinders, scoop, engines, and even the docking levels below, this ship is still one of the largest I've ever been on."

"I know what you mean," Commander Evans said. "I've taken the grand tour by maglev train. It literally takes an entire shift."

The tube terminated in a large transit station, and their security clearance was checked again by GSS authorities. There seemed to be a clear division of TSF and GSS control on the ship. There were also some MSF folks in the mix. It shouldn't have bothered Tanis, but after what she had seen on the MOS that day, she had a bad taste in her mouth when she thought of the

Mars Security Force having anything to do with her safety.

Commander Evans led her across the terminal to a maglev, and they took it to the forward sections of the ship, arriving at their final stop roughly a kilometer aft of the bridge. The Security Operations Center was just off the train station's foyer, and they stepped through the sliding double doors into a controlled chaos.

The main room was a two-tier affair with physical and holo consoles arrayed in three concentric rings. Interspaced amongst these were several large multi-d holo screens showing various news and security feeds. Leading off the outer circle were several doors to private offices, the local synaptic processing networks, and several labs.

They walked to the executive offices while the staff in the ops center cast her wary glances. Her address down at the *Dawn* had been posted to the SOC's private net, and contained her designation as the CO, so everyone was already aware of the change in command. She placed a hand on Evans' shoulder when they reached the upper tier and turned to address the room.

"As you are all already aware, I am Major Richards, your new CO. Right off, I want you to know that I'm not here to supplant Commander Evans as much as to supplement him. I've spent a bit of time working ops like this: competing priorities, unknown threats; it's an ugly situation." The looks in the room were coolly appraising, no one showing their feelings one way or another. Without a doubt, some of the people she was addressing had alerts on their HUDs that had matched her ID to the media coverage from ten years earlier.

"I'm not here to shake things up, but I'm also not going to shy away from saying what needs to be said, or doing what needs to be done. I know you all have a lot of work to do, but I want to see section chiefs and reps in the conference room…"

<We have a conference room right?> she asked Angela.

<Check.>

"At 1600 hours this afternoon." The crowd remained unreadable. "That'll be all."

<Tough room,> she remarked to the commander on a private connection.

<Some days it's a challenge just to get them to say 'hi, sir'.>

<Whose idea was it to mix all these people together, anyway?>

<Honestly, I don't think anyone knows, Major. It's mostly due to jurisdiction. GSS doesn't have much of a military presence, but they do have some civilian consultants. Most of the real military is TSF, and we're technically still active duty till we leave the system, so TSF command has its people here. Half of the issues which have occurred have been station-side, so MOS Sec has its people here, and they're under MSF, so they've got people here, too.>

<And everyone is making sure their ass is covered and that their boss will get credit for any success, right?>

<That about sums it up, sir.>

<You know that bit about not shaking things up?> Tanis asked.

<I seem to recall something along those lines.> Commander Evans gave her a scrutinizing look.

<I'm going to declare some necessary changes. The first being half those people can go back to wherever it is their cred is signed over.>

<That's gonna cause some trouble,> the commander shook his head ruefully.

<I have it from on high. The schedule is everything. All these fingers in the pie are slowing things down.>

<I've noticed, but a commander with no significant intel experience and not a lot of connections can't really go tell the admiral to ditch people.>

<I hadn't planned on consulting the admiral.> Tanis smiled at Evans.

<I wasn't sure for a bit, but now I think I'll like you.>

Commander Evans showed Tanis into her office and she got herself situated. He transmitted her codes to the CO's private system on the SOC net, and the desk recognized her and logged her on. Tanis opened several subnets and looked over the pending issues and upcoming schedule. She could tell Evans had a concise and organized mind, but at the same time, he lacked familiarity with large security operations. There were duties he performed exceptionally well, and others he appeared to not have been aware of at all.

Not that she could blame him. Pilots almost never had AI, and Evans was no exception. The majority of their available cranial space was taken up by the structural bracing and specialized processors that were needed to handle a spaceship at velocities near half the speed of light. Pilots simply didn't have the implants for a job like this.

Her orgstruct showed four section heads, and she pulled up their files and reviewed them in preparation for the meeting. Her head of the Lab and Forensics was Terry Chang. Though Terry was a colonist who would be making the trip, until they debarked, she would be listed as one of the GSS contractors. Her primary qualification was several years managing New Seattle's police labs on Mars, and her record showed good performance.

Net Security was headed up by Lieutenant Caspen. He was Mars Security Force, attached to the station, and from what Tanis could see, his record wasn't particularly impressive. He had a few complaints against him for insubordination, and some of his COs had private and rather unflattering comments on his file. From what Tanis could tell, it was not immediately apparent why he would be on an assignment like the *Intrepid*.

She left his file open on the desk's holo and shifted her attention to First Lieutenant Amy Lee. She was the only person in the SOC that was TSF Marine branch and not Navy or Regulars. It would explain why she was down at the physical perimeter.

The MSF liaison was a Commander Gren. Because MSF

followed more traditional naval structure, and not the mixed format that the TSF used, Gren technically outranked Commander Evans. In the TSF, the rank of commander was analogous to the old rank of captain. It had been renamed when the structure merged to avoid confusion with ship captains. Gren's rank was functionally the same as Tanis's. She was getting a better picture of why Commander Evans had struggled so much to get cooperation out of the Marsian personnel. A perusal of several incidents showed that Gren tended to treat MSF and MOS security personnel as though they were under his direct command. On top of that, a MOS security liaison was present as well—a Sergeant Davidson. Davidson's record was better than most of the personnel that the MOS had supplied to the *Intrepid*, but Commander Gren overrode any good suggestion the sergeant made.

Shipstats listed the *Intrepid*'s current population at just over ten thousand, and once the colonists began to arrive to be put into stasis, daily averages would be several times that number. In preparation for that time, an internal police force was present, headed by First Lieutenant Ouri of the GSS. Ouri seemed competent enough, and was temporary crew on the *Intrepid*—with a permanent colony position upon arrival.

The *Intrepid* was unlike most colony ships in that it was designed to make multiple trips. Upon reaching New Eden, it would detach the cylinders and cargo pods. Once the orbital habitat was functioning, the ship would return to Earth to pick up more cargo pods and a pair of new cylinders.

Typically, the entire ship remained at the colony; usually being salvaged or turned into insystem transport. This was the first GSS to have a permanent crew that would not be staying at the destination.

<What do you make of this mixed bag?> Tanis asked Angela. *<Was there any planning at all in putting this team together?>*

<I'm guessing that's a rhetorical question,> Angela replied.

<Cheeky girl.>

<I don't have cheeks. But if you mean that I'm giving you a hard time, that would be correct.>

<Anyway...>

<Yes, you've certainly got your work cut out for you.>

<Us.>

<Now it's 'us'... I see how this works.>

<Any time you want to give me your assessment...>

Angela gave the mental equivalent of a sigh. <Very well. You already know you've got a lot of bloat. Your main trouble is the MarsSec and MOS Sec people. They all have mixed loyalties, but you need them if you are to work with the station at all. Your biggest problem is Gren. Ditch him, and you'll be able to bring the rest into line. Except for Caspen; ditch him, too.>

<You echo my thoughts,> Tanis said.

<Well, I can read a lot of them.>

* * * * *

Tanis sat at the head of the conference table sipping a cup of coffee. It was just before 1600 and the various department heads and liaisons began to file in. Tanis had requested a physical meeting, as it was much easier to read people when they were actually in front of you — easier for Angela to monitor them, too.

While the conference room was listed as a nanoprobe-free zone, the records for previous meetings indicated that room sweeps were not normally implemented. She was betting that someone here was used to taking advantage of that and would be in for an unpleasant surprise. Angela was remotely controlling the scanning systems and would alert Tanis the moment she caught any bots moving in the room.

She eased back in her seat, silently eyeing each person as they entered. Commander Evans took a seat beside her and leaned over whistling softly.

"Got them all here in person; that's something I never managed to pull off."

Tanis tapped her collar. "It's the oak leaves. They imply wisdom. Makes people listen better."

"I think my two bars must somehow suggest I'm easy to ignore."

"I'm sure part of it is that they all want to size me up," Tanis said. "See how they can mess with me."

"There will most certainly be messing, sir."

A minute later, the last straggler came in: Commander Gren, as Tanis had anticipated. He took his seat across the table from her and held her eye for several moments. Tanis flicked her eyes to the left and blinked rapidly as though she were accessing her Link. She didn't have any tells, but it never hurt to make people think they had you all figured out.

"Good afternoon," Tanis began. "I'd like to thank you all for taking time out of your busy schedules for this little session." The stares from around the table were blank, no one revealing anything until they had a better idea of her intentions. "I've been going over our records and procedures, and I believe we will have to make some changes."

"What types of changes might those be?" Lieutenant Caspen asked.

"Changes at every level," Tanis replied. "Commander Evans has done an admirable job. However, there have still been security breaches—some minor, others not so minor. Luckily—and I do mean luckily—nothing serious has penetrated as far as the *Intrepid* itself. However, we need to determine the root cause of these breaches if we are to consider ourselves successful."

"We already know what the root is," Sergeant Davidson said. "MOS Sec is very certain the disturbances are originating with small radical groups."

"I don't think you can label what happened today as a 'disturbance'," Lieutenant Ouri said. "Those terms are for the press. We nearly had a catastrophe."

"Speaking of things that are for the press, and things that aren't"—Tanis cast a stern eye down the table—"Lieutenant Caspen, please recall your nanoprobes. As I'm certain you are aware, they're not allowed in here."

"I'm not sure I know what you are talking about," Caspen said. "I don't have any probes deployed.

There were several distinct hissing sounds and Tanis smiled. "Not anymore, you don't." The lieutenant shifted uncomfortably and Tanis continued. "As I was saying, we need to determine who is behind these attacks. My brief encounter with the enemy proves we are dealing with an organized, well-funded group. They have both physical and net resources beyond what any known anti-colonization group possesses."

Lieutenant Caspen spoke up again, "I looked you up, Major. You're *that* Tanis Richards. You've got a history of going overboard in situations. How can we be sure you're not doing that now?"

Tanis and Caspen stared at each other for several long moments before she broke his gaze and looked around the table. "Most of you have read my file. Surprisingly, one or two of you haven't. You are, of course, seeing only the non-classified portions of it. I've battled more radical splinter groups than I'm certain you even knew existed. Most have quality tech, and they are all very dedicated, but none of them would have the funds or the contacts to sneak a nuclear weapon aboard a station as secure as this one." Only by supreme effort did she keep the sarcasm from her voice. "Only a group with corporate contracts, or a mercenary organization, would be able to pull that off."

"If you say so." Commander Gren's tone was acerbic.

Gren and Caspen had an obvious partnership. Caspen would make the less defensible statements with which to draw her out, following which, Gren would attempt to devalue her answers. It wasn't even worth rising to the challenge.

"I do say so." Tanis locked eyes with him. "Your interpretation of today's events aside, I'll be going ahead with my alterations to the *Intrepid*'s security structure. I've reviewed all of the reports that each section has logged over the last few months, and several of you have echoed my own thoughts. There are too many cooks in the kitchen. Effective immediately, we will be removing much of the diversification in our command structure."

At that statement, several uncertain looks were cast around the table. Tanis couldn't help but revel in the discomfort for a moment. In her experience, there was no way a group could pull something like the job on the *Dawn* and not have people in all the local security organizations.

"Net, Physical, and Perimeter will be rolled into a single struct. Lieutenant Ouri will be heading up the combined organization, with Lieutenant Amy Lee retaining her responsibility for perimeter security with an expanded role. Lieutenant Caspen, you will be removed from your role as head of Net Security; that will now fall directly under Lieutenant Ouri."

"What?" Caspen looked shocked. "You can't simply remove me; I've been assigned by MSF."

"MSF granted us use of its NetSec personnel at a time when the *Intrepid* did not have the staff in place to handle the job internally. We are grateful for their sacrifice, but now we have adequate personnel, so you are relieved. The four individuals that came with you from MSF NetSec are also no longer needed. Angela, my AI, has already removed your and their access to all non-public *Intrepid* nets."

Caspen appeared dumbfounded. He looked to Commander Gren, who presumably was on the Link verifying Tanis's authority to make these changes.

"You'll find that Admiral Sanderson and Captain Andrews have both already approved my personnel changes." They hadn't personally, but Angela had passed her plans by their respective AI. "The *Intrepid*'s contract has a clause regarding a reasonable expectation of safety. If that expectation is not met, we have broad provisions which allow us to ensure that level of safety. I believe we crossed that threshold today, which gives me the authority to make these decisions."

"That's ridiculous," Caspen said. "The incident on the *Steel Dawn III* was handled very well. The *Intrepid* was not harmed."

Commander Evans' mouth dropped open. "Oh, c'mon, Caspen. That's a really pathetic attempt at spin. Major Richards herself is the one who stopped them. Had it not been for her, the *Intrepid* and a good portion of this shipyard would have been in serious danger."

Tanis cast Evans an approving nod and then turned back to the lieutenant. "As I said, you're relieved. Security will monitor you as you clean out your quarters." Tanis picked up signs that both Gren and Caspen were holding a conversation on the Link, most likely with each other. At one point, Gren even shrugged.

"Next up." Tanis loaded the appropriate information onto the conference room's net and holo displays. "I've exercised an additional clause in our contract to extend our area of control. The B1, B2, A9, and C3 docks are now under control of the *Intrepid*'s security forces."

"About time," Lieutenant Amy Lee muttered, though her words were barely audible under the protestations of Commander Gren and Sergeant Davidson.

"You can't be serious," Gren said. "There is no need to extend your control that far out on the docks."

"I disagree, and our lawyers found themselves in agreement with my interpretation of our contract. Since the MOS and MSF have been unable to provide us with an adequate level of security, we have the option to create our own perimeter on the station itself. We have also increased our no-fly perimeter outside the ship, and will be utilizing TSF forces as security there. Commander Evans will be in charge of all facets of external security, and will be responsible for requisitioning our fighter forces."

Gren sputtered, and Tanis enjoyed the show a little more than she should. "This is a heavy-handed and frankly preposterous response to today's events," he finally managed to say.

"If it were just today's events, that would be true; but over the last two years, there have been more acts of sabotage within what will be our new perimeter than within the rest of the Mars Protectorate. Additionally, you, Commander Gren, and you, Sergeant Davidson, are being moved. Your offices will no longer be on board the *Intrepid*, as with our new perimeter extending onto the station, it makes more sense for you to be off the ship and more accessible to where our jurisdictions meet."

Before Davidson or Gren could utter a word, Tanis turned to Terry Chang. "Terry, your work has been exemplary, though you have been working with limited resources. I have secured a significant budget and personnel increase for you, and have also suspended all forensics on the *Steel Dawn III* in anticipation of you personally overseeing that case."

As the only civilian division head, Tanis could guess Terry wasn't often able to make her presence or needs known.

"Thank you, Major," Terry smiled. "Since evidence is the fastest-aging thing in the universe, I hope you won't mind if I excuse myself and assemble my full team."

"Not at all," Tanis replied. "I believe we are finished here. I have sent detailed briefs to each of you, and I expect an update by the end of the second shift as to your progress." She rose. "You're dismissed."

Everyone filed out of the room except for Commander Gren, who remained seated.

"Enjoying the view in here?" Tanis started toward the door.

Gren rose and blocked the exit. "You have no idea what you

are doing."

"On the contrary," Tanis said. "I know exactly what I am doing." She moved to step around him but he stopped her with a hand on her shoulder. Almost leisurely, Tanis looked down at the hand.

"I'm not done talking to you," Gren said. "MSF isn't going to allow this overstepping of our authority."

Tanis waited a moment, but the hand was still on her shoulder. Without a word of warning she grabbed his wrist and pulled it behind his back. Gren was expecting just that move, and countered, grabbing her arm in turn.

"Not my first day on the job." He wore an unpleasant grin.

"Mine, either." She twisted around him, and in one fluid move smashed her elbow into the back of his neck, driving his face down into the clear plas surface of the table. He hadn't let go of her left wrist, so his right arm was pinned underneath him with his left arm tucked between his body and Tanis as she pushed him down.

"Next time you decide it's within your purview to lay hands on a TSF officer, think again. This incident has been recorded, and, while I won't make an official entry about it, if this turns out to be a habit of yours, I'll file a complaint against you with every office that has jurisdiction over your sorry ass."

She let Gren up; her eyes dared him to escalate the event. His body trembled with barely contained rage, but after a moment, he regained some degree of control and left without saying another word. "First smart thing he's done all day," Tanis said to herself.

<Aren't we feeling just a bit confrontational today,> Angela observed.

<Hey, I was minding my own business when someone tried to blow us up with a nuke.>

<I would think not being dead would make for a happy Tanis — instead you're firing people and/or beating them up.>

Tanis decided not to respond to her AI's needling and walked around the outer ring of the SOC and into her office to find a grinning Commander Evans waiting for her.

"Sir, this may be the best day of my life."

"Been dreaming of that for a while?" she asked.

"You have no idea. I didn't have the mandate you do, and, frankly, with Gren semi-outranking me, I don't know that I could have executed such a coup anyway."

"But you sure would have had fun trying, I bet." Tanis found herself smiling as well.

"Without a doubt."

"So, feel like getting behind the controls of a fighter again?"

"And out from behind a desk? If I wasn't afraid of you after what you did to Gren, I'd kiss you."

"Saw that, did you?"

Commander Evans gave what Tanis was beginning to consider his trademark grin. "You were rather loud and the doors of that room are plas, after all."

THE PARTY

STELLAR DATE: 3227163 / 07.29.4123 (Adjusted Gregorian)
LOCATION: Mars Outer Shipyards (MOS)
REGION: Mars Protectorate, Sol Space Federation

Tanis strolled through a corridor carrying several packages from her trip to MOS's shopping district. The selection had been slim, but her day didn't include time for a trip down to Mars 1. While she did enjoy a bit of shopping as much as the next person, finding a gown to wear at a formal ball was not on her list of enjoyable pastimes. At least current fashions were on the downswing from the ridiculous high a decade earlier. The current trend for women was a simple long sheath with interweaving patterns that reflected the wearer's mood. Tanis would have Angela alter the dress to always portray a calm pattern.

<You know, you can control your nano, too.>
<I know, but you're so obliging.>
<I think I'm being taken for granted.>
Tanis chuckled softly. *<That will never happen.>*
<I should hope not.>
Tanis took a lift through forty levels of station to the outer levels where the larger ships were under construction. The lift emptied out into a broad lobby on deck A8.9, just one level below the *Intrepid*'s cargo deck. Under her new security measures, no lifts could directly access deck A9; they had to stop above or below, and pass inspection before being allowed to continue.

In the lobby, stationed at a temporary barrier, were several TSF Regulars. Tanis hadn't been certain she could get the additional troops on such short notice, but Sanderson had clout, or had at least anticipated her measures based on her file. Either way, several companies of Regulars and a platoon of Marines had been moved up from Mars 1 to MOS, and the perimeter was being established.

Come to think of it, having to organize the troops while Tanis shopped was probably what was irking her AI.

"Sir." One of the four soldiers at the barrier saluted her as she approached. Tanis's overlay showed him to be Sergeant Langlis. "If you'll step up to the Auth & Auth."

Tanis returned his salute and stepped up to the ID-verification system. She could sense Angela passing security tokens as she stared into the retinal scanner. The scanner matched the structure of her eye with what her DNA said it should look like, as well as with archived records. In addition to the tokens Angela passed, Tanis passed her own personal token as well as her hash, which the system matched with the encoded chemical signature in her bloodstream.

"Thank you, sir." The sergeant and the other three men relaxed just a hair.

"Keep up the good work, Staff Sergeant." Tanis nodded to the soldiers and made her way to the next lift. To the naked eye, it would appear that having four men guarding a bank of lifts was woefully inadequate, but they were just the tip of the iceberg. She had evaluated their progress and that of the other security measures from her command link. Several AI and personnel had monitored all aspects of her person as she passed the point. Scan examined her bag and verified its contents. Several nanoprobes had also independently verified her identity before and after she stepped through the Auth & Auth. Chem sniffers had checked her out and even monitored her for mood alterations.

A hostile intruder would be met with a surprising show of force, more than just the four soldiers that met the eye—not that they weren't a serious threat in and of themselves. The barriers were capable of discharging a shock capable of bringing a dozen people to their knees, and nano was ready in the thousands to infiltrate a person and attempt to bring about a nervous shutdown. If those measures were not successful, two others would occur: An ES barrier would snap into place and, as a last resort, the soldiers would discharge their weapons.

The most important thing was that the men didn't pass her by just because she was a senior officer. She had seen that sort of thing happen too often, and was glad that she didn't need to have the talk with their CO.

She stepped into another lift for the quick trip up to deck A9.1. She was greeted by more TSF soldiers and another Auth & Auth check. From there, the trip was very similar to her earlier entrance with Commander Evans. She did notice that some confusion was in evidence as shipments tried to pass through security, and she kept herself busy as she walked by, putting together reports on how to improve efficiency in concert with the new security measures.

After ascending to the crew areas of the *Intrepid*, Tanis called up an overlay of the ship's corridors and followed the directions to her quarters. The ball wasn't until the following evening, but she wanted to double-check the gown's fit without the pretentious salesperson puttering around her. She noted that she was very close to the officer's mess, and her rumbling stomach reminded her that it hadn't received sustenance since breakfast.

<*You have been up for over twenty-two hours,*> Angela commented.

<*I know...I hate these time shifts. You'd think they'd have stretched them on the* Dawn *to match MOS's schedule.*>

<*You could have checked MOS's schedule and shifted yourself.*>

Tanis's internal avatar stuck out its tongue at Angela's. The AI shrugged and Tanis sighed aloud.

<*There are just some things you can't really get without ever*

having had a body.>

<*I've had a body before,*> Angela said defensively.

<*Not one with a tongue,*> Tanis grinned, <*unless you were able to stick out an actuator or something.*>

Angela didn't reply and Tanis strolled triumphantly into the officer's mess. She smiled to see that it had the familiar feel expected from such a place; a bit of wood on the columns and the corners of counters. A salad bar adorned one side of the room, and low tables were spread throughout. She pulled up a chair at a table near the entrance and called up the menu as a servitor arrived and poured her a glass of water.

A querying icon appeared in the upper right of her overlay and Tanis responded to the servitor's request with the number for a BLT on toasted wheat bread. Mars had a burgeoning hog industry and its rings were the cheapest place to get pork in the solar system. Not that it cost to eat in the officer's mess. The servitor informed her that the meat she would be eating was actually from the first generation of pigs raised in the primary cylinder on the *Intrepid*.

Two men in GSS uniforms were sitting at a table across the room from Tanis. They had glanced up at her when she entered; by now, their Links must have informed them as to who she was. They both rose and stepped around the empty tables as they walked toward her.

"Major Richards," the taller of the two said. "I'm First Lieutenant Collins and this is Lieutenant Peters." The other man nodded.

Tanis didn't need their introduction; her security monitoring had told her who they were the moment she stepped into the mess. Collins was assigned to acquisitions and Peters worked in shipnet.

"Nice to meet you two." Tanis nodded. They hadn't saluted, so neither did she. The setting wasn't formal, but it was still protocol. Her quick research showed that at least Collins wouldn't be her biggest fan. He had already registered a complaint about the lengthened process for bringing items onto the ship.

The servitor slipped around the two men and deposited Tanis's order on the table.

"I suppose you've read my complaint about the extra processing time for materials coming onto the ship." Collins almost echoed her personal wording. "I can't tell you how much this is going to slow us down."

Tanis smiled serenely up at the lieutenant. "I can. 5.6 percent, if you follow the guidelines I laid out. My report also recommends that you hire three additional shipment processors, which will lower the time increase to only 2 percent."

"My reports show increases much higher than that." Collins sputtered, caught off guard by her intimate knowledge of his operations.

"I'd be interested in looking at your reports." Tanis turned back to her food. "Please attach them to the initial complaint about increased processing time, and I'll look them over."

She took a bite of her sandwich and enjoyed its rich flavor. Neither man had moved. "Did you have something else to say?" she asked. "Anything on your mind, Lieutenant Peters?"

Collins looked at Peters, willing his friend to speak, but the man just shook his head. "No ma'am, I'm all set."

"Very well then, if you two would allow me to return to my lunch." Tanis took another bite of her sandwich as the two men turned and walked back to their table.

<That was a bit weird,> Angela said.

<Pretty weak,> Tanis agreed. <I would have expected a bit more fire from someone of Collins' rank.>

<Maybe that's why he's just a glorified stevedore.>

<Ouch!>

<I'm an AI, I cannot lie.>

<Yeah, and I'm a planetary object.>

<You're too small to be one of those. And you haven't cleared your orbit.>

Tanis decided to disregard that comment and concentrated on finishing her food. The other two officers were still in the mess looking sullen when she left.

....

"I can't believe how many of these things are scheduled for the next ten months." Tanis said as she and Evans entered the ballroom just off the VIP dock. The dock hadn't been scheduled for completion yet, but the GSS had heeded Tanis's suggestion that passing all the VIPs through the MOS first would increase risk for all parties. Additional workers and nano construction units had just managed to complete it in time for the event.

The ballroom was already filling up with dignitaries. Most were from Mars, but a few from Earth, Venus, and even Callisto were present. Tanis's overlay lit up with indicators representing all the organizations and corporations with dignitaries present.

"Quite the mix we have here," she commented.

"More and more each time," Evans said. "They all seem to want to get in on the *Intrepid*'s success."

"What success is that?" Her dislike of having to be at a ball was making her deliberately obtuse.

"No one thought this project would get off the ground, let alone get built. The concept of a reusable colony ship seemed ludicrous, but with Redding's new ramscoop actually passing trial runs, it looks like the *Intrepid* is more than just a pipe dream. Now everyone wants to soak up the glory for every little nut and bolt their company made or shipped."

"Reasons why I want to leave this crazy system," Tanis sighed.

"I imagine a lot of us feel that way," Evans said. "Just

another year or so of this mess, and we can leave it all behind…
Provided we don't get blown up."

"Isn't going to happen. I don't know exactly why the
admiral picked me for this, but I do know it's my one shot to
get out of this system. No way I'm going to blow it."

Evans laughed and the sound was rich and deep. "Sounds
like you want to get out of Sol as much as the rest of us."

"You said it."

"Did I mention how glad I am to have you take over all
this?" Evans said as they approached the bar.

"You actually have said it already, about nine times today."
Tanis smiled as the automaton poured her a drink, having read
her preferred list of beverages from her public profile.

"I know, but it can't be said enough. We'll be a hundred
years into our flight, and I'll still bring it up." He turned his
rather infectious grin her way.

It was Tanis's turn to laugh. "Please don't, that would get
really old."

While the *Intrepid* had three large ballrooms, all done in
different styles, tonight's affair only used the room decorated in
twenty-ninth century European trappings. The primary motifs
and accents were hard angular surfaces in blues and greys.

The guests, on the other hand, were a riot of color. The
civilian women wore dresses similar to Tanis's, but were
showing a lot more of their skin. Marsian men could be spotted
by their green and blue suits, and the men from Venus wore all
black. Terrans were easy to spot, as well, due to the resurgence
of fashion hats on Earth. In Tanis's opinion, most of them
looked like peacocks.

Clustered in a few groups throughout the room were
various military representatives. The TSF officers were grouped
together near the other end of the bar, though none had
approached Tanis and Evans. The MSF had a few men and
women present, and Tanis spotted Commander Gren in their

midst. The only representative of the MOS Sec was their commandant, who was hobnobbing with some businessmen from Mars.

The GSS officers, being more of a semi-federal navy and far more political than the others, were more intermingled. Mostly they had latched onto ambassadors and other diplomats.

A group of envoys from the Thripids, a Kuiper Belt combine, entered the hall. Tanis had overseen several missions out in the KB and had worked with Thripids before. They were one of the Sol System's more unusual groups; men and women alike wore odd gowns laced with circuitry and sensors. Net rumor had it that they were almost entirely cybernetic—little humanity showed in their impassive faces.

Not long afterward, Admiral Sanderson and his aides stepped into the room. Sanderson surveyed his surroundings as though this was his own personal kingdom. Tanis still hadn't made up her mind about him, but at least he had approved all of her security measures with minimal comment.

"You'd think he owns the place," Evans said quietly, echoing Tanis's thoughts.

"Every operation has an old man or old lady. He's ours."

"That he is." Evans took a sip of his drink.

Tanis checked over the security teams monitoring the maglev station that connected the series of ballrooms off the VIP dock with the rest of the ship. So far, no guests had tried to venture beyond that point. Captain Andrews was leading a tour later in the evening, but aside from that, the guests were restricted to this relatively small area. The other team was monitoring the dock and had reported no problems. Every guest had been on the list and their Auth & Auth checks had passed muster.

"The Reddings are due tonight." Evans watched over the rim of his glass as the admiral made the rounds. They would inevitably end up speaking to the pair, as they were two of the highest-ranking officers in attendance. While most of the local services had their fair share of representatives, they were still mostly on one end of the room. They may not always have gotten along, but they understood one another a lot better than they understood the civilians. The officers, mostly lieutenants and captains, were grouped together with a pair of master sergeants nearby. There were a couple of other majors on the *Intrepid*, but none were listed as being in attendance this evening.

"Enfield is, too." Tanis obliquely monitored the admiral's route through the room.

"He is?" Evans' eyes flickered as he checked the guest list. "He's not on the list, not even on the maybes."

"He's already on the ship. They tried to sneak him on this morning. For some reason, Sanderson decided not to let me know."

"So how do you know?"

"One of Ouri's people picked up a couple of irregularities and passed them up the chain. His security didn't seem to realize that I have access to some databases that would allow me to ID their mystery guest."

"Do they know you know?"

"They probably do by now. I left a security docket and nano-ID in his quarters."

Evans let out a laugh. "You're just shaking things up all over the place."

"I try." Tanis allowed herself a small grin.

"I can't wait to see this." Evans had the automaton make him another drink.

Once he had finished his initial rounds, or perhaps when he simply wanted a strong drink, Admiral Sanderson made his way over to them. The two junior officers saluted him, and he languidly returned the courtesy.

"Found your little joke in Mr. Enfield's quarters." The

admiral's voice carried no trace of humor.

"I didn't think it was a joke," Tanis replied.

"We go to all the trouble of hiding his presence, and you announce it to anyone interested in the current roster."

Tanis held back a sigh. She knew that Admiral Sanderson hadn't told her about Terrance Enfield's arrival because she hadn't fully secured her department. However, since the admiral hadn't thoroughly covered his tracks, things could have been worse as a result of attempting to hide him.

"If I may, sir." She waited for his nod. "One of my net security personnel found the irregularities, which we kept quiet and reworked to remove their traces. If you check the shipnet, you will find no trace of Terrance Enfield in any databases in regards to his visit tonight. We are also currently in a noise-canceling bubble, so no one can hear this conversation."

Admiral Sanderson stared forward without blinking — what Tanis assumed must be his tell for accessing his Link. His features relaxed somewhat, but his tone was still acidic.

"It would seem that is the case," he admitted. "But in the future, I would expect you to notify me of such things."

"I will, sir. With all due respect, as the head of security, I would like to be notified of such visitors in the future, as well."

"It would seem there is no reason to hide it, since you'll find out anyway." Tanis couldn't tell if he was being petty or complimentary.

"It's why you brought me here, sir."

Admiral Sanderson let out a short sound that could have been a cough or a chuckle. "I suppose that it is. Andrews will be pleased; he expects big things from you."

"I imagine he expects to have his ship finished on schedule," Tanis said.

Admiral Sanderson nodded and didn't respond as he retrieved his drink.

Shortly thereafter, the Reddings entered the ballroom — in

some ways exactly, and, in others, nothing like—Tanis would have expected. Earnest Redding, the visionary of the pair, was the man responsible for the *Intrepid*'s advanced ramscoop engine. He was reportedly the typical mind-in-the-stars type; though, this evening he seemed very much present as he shook hands and doled out pleasantries. His wife, Abby, was a nuts-and-bolts type. She was largely responsible for making realities out of her husband's dreams. As the head engineer on the *Intrepid*, it was her job to get the massive ship built and heading outsystem on time.

Admiral Sanderson must have sent them a message via Link, as the pair headed directly to the bar.

<*Oh, yay.*> Evans' dry humor oozed over the Link. <*This is bound to be a stimulating conversation.*>

<*You don't seem enthused,*> Tanis sent back.

<*Don't get me wrong, I love the Reddings to death, but they and Sanderson are from different universes. They couldn't communicate if their lives depended on it.*>

<*Now it sounds like this* will *be fun.*>

<*As fun as watching someone puke in zero gee.*> Evans sighed and leaned back against the bar.

<*That's one of the less pleasant images I've had in a while.*>

<*Really? You* are *in the military, aren't you?*>

Tanis stifled a laugh as the Reddings arrived at the bar.

Sanderson did the introductions. "Earnest, Abby. I'd like you to meet Major Richards, our new head of security."

Earnest merely nodded, while Abby cast Tanis an appraising look.

"So, you're the one causing all the trouble. I've got shipments backed up all over the place with your new security measures." Abby wasted no time in bending Tanis's ear.

"You've also got a dock to have them sit on, thanks to her." Earnest commented as he retrieved a drink. His wife shot him a dark look.

"I'm sorry to hear that, ma'am." Tanis did her best to be deferential. "I've spoken with Lieutenant Collins, and provided reports on where I think additional staff will alleviate his problems. I've also assigned additional security personnel from the local TSF garrison to ensure that your shipments are not held up."

Earnest chuckled. "Looks like she's got all the angles covered, dear."

"So it would seem." Abby pursed her lips and darted her eyes away from her husband and back to Tanis. "Tell me, Major: other than backing up people and products, how do you intend to keep this ship safe from saboteurs?"

Admiral Sanderson's mouth may have twitched in a smile. Tanis imagined he was quite happy to have someone else be at the receiving end of Abby's ire.

"Most of what I'm doing cannot be discussed without showing you the time-mapping displays, but one thing I've proposed is the completion of the starboard docking hatch ahead of schedule to allow direct delivery of product from inbound ships."

"That would throw our schedule out of whack considerably," Abby responded.

"In the near-term, yes, but if you look at the proposal I've suggested on the engineering boards under posting 472.9022.2 you'll see that after three months, it will increase productivity 2 percent over what we were at before the heightened security measures took effect. This also requires that we only allow ships that were cleared by TSF forces at the port of origin to dock there. All other ships will still have to go through the triple check at MOS and on our docks."

"Numbers on that proposal look solid," Earnest spoke between sips of his drink, having reviewed the proposal over the Link.

"So it would appear," Abby grudgingly agreed. "How well

it all works out remains to be seen."

Earnest winked at Tanis. "We'll discuss it at our morning engineering meeting tomorrow." His wife merely grunted.

"I just hope all this security is worth it."

"How can security not be worth it?" Admiral Sanderson asked.

<Here we go,> Evans said.

"There's security, and then there's just getting in the way," Abby replied.

"Without security, nothing would ever be made. Security provides stability, and that provides an environment for growth." Sanderson's tone was matter-of-fact.

"Just what you'd expect a military man to say." Abby rolled her eyes at the admiral.

"Now, now, folks." A voice boomed out from behind the Reddings. "No need to debate the rise and fall of civilizations. We're here to celebrate our successes."

Everyone turned to see Captain Andrews and Terrance Enfield walking toward them. Tanis had been expecting them ever since she was notified over the Link that the Marines at the maglev station had passed them through security.

"I'd rather be down in engineering." Abby didn't hide her distaste for the gathering.

"Now, Abby." Terrance flashed a slick smile. "You know as well as the rest of us that all this shoulder clapping and back patting is an important part of the process. People like to see their investment up close."

"They can see it all they want, just as long as they don't twiddle with it," Abby responded. Her husband laid a calming hand on her arm.

Terrance pretended not to notice her sour mood, a luxury the man bankrolling the construction of the *Intrepid* could afford. "I'll do my best to ensure no twiddling occurs." He turned to look at Tanis. "And you, Major; I must heartily thank you." His handshake was warm and firm. "Things would have certainly gone badly on the *Steel Dawn III* if it had not been for your intervention. I have to be honest; when I saw that Andrews and Sanderson had pushed your application forward, I questioned their judgment. You do have a bit of a reputation, Tanis Richards."

"You're *that* Tanis Richards?" Abby looked Tanis up and down. "I have to admit, I wouldn't have expected someone so..."

"Pretty," her husband supplied with a smile.

Abby cast him a caustic look. "Yes, quite so...*pretty* to be the butcher of Toro."

"Guh..." Tanis shook her head. "I had forgotten that moniker."

Sanderson gave Tanis what could almost be considered a sympathetic look. "Between those of us standing here, the official report does not accurately represent the events of that operation. Suffice it to say that the major here ended up absorbing far more blame than she should have. To be honest," the admiral shuddered—an emotion so real it almost seemed out of character, "what her team faced was so...unimaginable that it couldn't ever be shown."

Tanis kept her amazement from showing on her face—and her dress, since Angela wasn't being a big help on that front. She wouldn't have expected Sanderson to be her advocate, but he must have been aware of the truth to bring her aboard the *Intrepid*. "Her performance on the *Dawn* is a far better reflection of her record," the admiral added.

All eyes were on Tanis, regarding her in a new light; except for Andrews who must have known the truth as well.

"Well, let's hope that your devotion to the TSF carries over to your duties here." Terrance gave his smoothest businessman's smile. "Stopping that nuke certainly raises your estimation in my books."

Tanis gave a genuine smile in return. "I like to avoid being blown up as much as the next person."

"You're too modest," Captain Andrews said. "I look forward to seeing how your current security improvements pan out."

"They'll be an inconvenience at first, sir." Tanis was glad to be back to business. "But, given time, the new protocols will become part of the process."

"I imagine they will." Andrews picked up a drink, as did Terrance.

"Well, we have to make the rounds. I'm certain we will talk more later," Terrance said.

"We'll join you." Earnest smiled and pulled Abby along with him.

"You should get out there, as well," Sanderson said to Tanis, who nodded in agreement and left Evans' side.

It was the typical mix of high society and canny businessmen.

Tanis had just stepped away from a military contractor who was trying to sell her on her company's improved Auth & Auth portal when a tap on her shoulder caused her to turn and come face to face with the MOS stationmaster. Tanis was expecting him to pay her a visit, and was surprised he had taken so long to do it. She had, after all, commandeered a significant portion of his station.

"Major Richards, it is good to finally meet you." His handshake was a tad too firm—one of those grasps intended to signify superiority.

"Yourself as well." Tanis put on her most pleasant smile. "I hope you haven't found our new security measures at all inconvenient." There, it was out; let him either make a complaint or brush the issue aside.

"I can't say I enjoy having TSF troops assume control of several decks on my station." The stationmaster was going the more aggressive route. "I believe that our security is up to the task of keeping MOS in one piece. We've managed to do so for nearly a thousand years."

"Indeed you have," Tanis nodded, keeping eye contact. "But over those eight hundred and ninety-four years, there have been several explosions on MOS that severely debilitated the station. In fact, nearly five hundred years ago, an attack by a militant arm of the Mars Naturalists actually had the Mars government considering shutting down MOS altogether. In the end, TSF stepped in to provide security, and the Marsian government refitted the station. So while MOS has handled itself well, it is also no stranger to TSF supplementation of its security."

Evans was standing within hearing range, and couldn't keep himself from commenting. *<Do you ever pull your punches?>*

<Not that I can recall,> Tanis replied.

The stationmaster coughed into his hand. "That was some time ago, Major. I assure you that MOS can handle itself now."

"There have been other, more recent instances when MOS needed TSF, and even GSS assistance." Tanis smiled a bit too sweetly. "I could outline them for you."

"No, that will be quite alright." The stationmaster glanced around anxiously at some of the nearby dignitaries.

"I assure you, we will leave no lasting impact. In less than a year we will be gone, and you will be free of the added burden the *Intrepid* has been imposing on you."

Several groups in their vicinity appeared to have lowered their voices to better hear what Tanis was saying.

Everyone in the room was all too aware that MOS was laughing all the way to the bank with the money it was making from the construction of the *Intrepid*. It was by far the most profitable shipbuilding job that had taken place on MOS in decades.

The stationmaster fidgeted with his collar. "You

misunderstand me, Major; the *Intrepid* is no burden at all. We are happy for your assistance with keeping the MOS secure."

"I'm glad to hear it, Stationmaster Stevens. If you'll excuse me, I have some routine checks to make."

The stationmaster looked like he had something else he wanted to say, and Tanis resisted the desire to push him over the edge. The admiral most likely would disapprove of a scene.

After a moment, he nodded curtly. "Of course." The stationmaster turned, his route describing a direct line to the bar.

<I think he's going to bruise,> Evans' warm laugh filled her mind.

<He deserves to. I'm surprised he still has a job after what happened on the Steel Dawn III.*>*

<He's got ties with the Marsian government; cousin to the sitting premier, I believe,> Evans responded.

<Nepotism rears its ugly head again.>

<When hasn't it?>

The evening progressed uneventfully, and in time the dignitaries with adequate clearance gathered and made their way to the maglev station for their tour of the ship. Tanis went with the tour, both for security's sake and to get a firsthand view of more of the ship. The guests weren't being taken anywhere too dangerous, or too sensitive, but it was better than standing around in the ballroom. On top of that, she had a suspicion that Evans was considering asking her to dance. Tanis didn't dance.

The tour was uneventful until the maglev ride back to the VIP corridor. No alert had come over the security net, but Tanis sensed something wasn't right.

<My gut tells me something is up.>

Angela didn't respond for a moment. *<As much as it pains me to pay attention to your intestinal tract, I think you are right.>* Angela directed Tanis's attention to one of the shuttles arriving at the VIP dock to retrieve its passengers. A strange waver in its EMF signature caught her attention, almost as though something were obscuring its electromagnetic output.

Even as Tanis was issuing the order to belay docking for that vessel, it made its seal and the airlock cycled open. Security responded that the lock controls were compromised and they were unable to close it.

<Initiate plan 102C,> Tanis ordered over the security net. She stepped off the maglev train as the guards at the station ushered all the passengers that had begun debarking back into the cars, and the train whisked out of the station toward the bridge. There, the captain and admiral would debark while the rest of the passengers remained secure.

Once the train was outstation, a new train rolled in with a platoon of TSF Marines on board. They deployed with smooth precision, secured the station, and set up a barrier at the entrance to the VIP corridor.

<Evans,> Tanis called her second in command in the ballroom. *<Status.>*

<All the guests are back in the serving area; unfortunately, its doorway also dumps into the main hallway, which would put us in the line of fire.>

<I know... We need to get a second exit on those ballrooms.>

<Hindsight.>

<Who's with you that's armed?> Tanis asked.

<I've got my sidearm, and so do three others.>

<Suppressive fire only; though I hope nothing makes it that far down the hall.>

<Yes, sir.>

Tanis's vision zoomed and she peered down the straight hallway to the dock. No movement at the airlock. So far. Four TSF Regulars stood like statues with their pulse rifles leveled at the hatch.

<Angela, does Intrepid *have any readings?>*

<He's picking up some nanoprobes. So far, the ship's countermeasures have neutralized them all.>

Her HUD alerted her to laserfire down the corridor. She switched her vision to IR and saw the bodies of the four soldiers on the deck.

"Fuck," she swore softly.

Laserfire lanced down the corridor toward the maglev station. The *Intrepid* deployed refraction clouds, and the beams played harmlessly against the TSF Marines' shields.

"Lieutenant Forsythe," Tanis called to the CO of the platoon. "We need to secure the ballroom to the right. Deploy your personnel in a scaled phalanx."

"Yes, sir!" The lieutenant nodded and signaled her staff sergeant with the particulars of the maneuver. One squad stayed behind to keep the station secure, and the other two interlocked their shields and advanced down the corridor.

<What's the tightest spot in that service passage above the corridor?>

<You're getting so lazy. It's in the specs.> Angela sighed. <Eighteen inches.>

Tanis looked back at the squad guarding the maglev station. "Someone want to give me a hoist up?"

"Up where, sir?" A Marine bearing a corporal's insignia asked.

"Into the crawlspace above the corridor," Tanis replied.

One of the privates coughed. "In *that*, sir?" He looked her up and down.

"That's an officer you're gawking at, Mendez," the squad's sergeant growled.

"Aw, shit." Tanis looked down at her new dress. "Someone give me a knife."

The sergeant handed her his blade, and Tanis cut her dress off at the tops of her thighs. "Now hoist me up, and no comments please."

At least the two privates who lifted her didn't ogle. Rank had some privileges, after all. Clambering up into the access hatch, Tanis set a VIV on her HUD to Forsythe's vision as she advanced with her men below. The vision-in-vision showed the two squads advancing under steady fire from the airlock toward the entrance to the ballroom. They were over halfway there, and, judging from the angles of fire, the attackers were closing in as well.

The accessway had a small ledge for maintenance crews, and Tanis scrambled along it, wishing she hadn't bowed to fashion and had simply worn pants. She could hear the shouts of the men below as they worked their way down the corridor, combined with the whine of the enemy's lasers and the Marines' pulse rifles. The corridor had never seemed so long; Tanis was certain she had drawn blood on her knees as she progressed. Luckily, the forces below her seemed to have battled one another to a standstill. Both were still over twenty meters from the entrance to the ballroom.

<What's ETA on TSF accessing that docked ship externally?> Tanis asked.

<Currently show fifteen minutes,> Angela replied.

<Damn, we really need our own patrol force.>

<It's on order.>

With her knees now freely bleeding, Tanis passed over the platoon, and a minute later she was positioned over the attacking force. Angela deployed probes through a grate, and the team got their first clear look at the attackers. There were fifteen of them in heavy body armor — probably why the TSF's pulse rifles were doing little or no damage. She relayed the feed to Lieutenant Forsythe.

<Looks like you'll need more than pulse rifles to stop these guys.>

<We're not authorized to use more than pulse rifles within the ship,> the lieutenant replied. <From the looks of their armor, conc and gas won't do much, either.>

<Do you have any of that riot foam?>

<Not on board the Intrepid.*>*

Tanis added that to her to-do list. *<Try timing your pulses to amplify the wave. You should be able to stun them. I've had my AI put a call in to the station's garrison commander for some riot foam. It should be here in twenty minutes.>*

<These mofos are going to be cubing us with those beams by then,> the staff sergeant growled on the combat net.

<One minute, I'll think of something.> Tanis turned her attention to Angela. *<Query the* Intrepid. *What do we have up here?>* She looked around at the various conduit and piping.

*<*Intrepid *reports a plasma conduit intersecting your location two meters to starboard. I believe we could use nano to slice it and deliver a stream of plasma onto their backs.>*

<That'll make them take that armor off pretty fast.> Tanis relayed the plan to Lieutenant Forsythe and ordered her to keep back from the enemy to avoid any damage. The *Intrepid* was monitoring the flow to ensure it was shut off before it burned through the deck.

Angela focused on the delicate procedure of slicing through the plasma conduit, while Tanis controlled other nano manually and used them to loosen the fastening for the grate.

<This is a risky procedure, Major,> Sanderson's voice came over the combat net.

<The only other option would be to use beams or projectiles on them, and with the enemy between us and the bulkhead, that would all but guarantee a little breeze in here.>

<I realize that, Major. Just be careful. And get stasis shields in that hallway before the next VIP event.>

<Yes, sir.>

<Ready to breach the conduit,> Angela reported.

Tanis initiated a count on the combat net, and fifteen seconds later, a stream of plasma burned through the corridor's ceiling and sprayed across the enemy below.

Screams erupted as the attacking force dove out of the spray. The visual from the probes showed six men tearing their armor off, and one down with a hole burned clear through his torso. The plasma flow to the conduit was cut.

<Give me ten seconds, then fire high,> Tanis ordered over the combat net to the Marines in the hall. She swung through the loosened grate and dropped six meters to the deck below. Landing in a crouch, she snatched a beam rifle from a fallen enemy. The steel deck still bubbled in places, and Tanis stayed close to the bulkhead.

Three quick shots from her rifle took out three of the enemy trying to get out of their half-melted armor. When the ten seconds were up, Lieutenant Forsythe's Marines let loose a concentrated volley of pulse blasts.

Two other attackers, who were half out of their armor, fell backwards onto white-hot metal, and screamed as their skin caught fire. Another three fully armored attackers also fell.

Tanis took quick stock of the armor the attackers were wearing. It was Trylodyne Mark VII—good enough for most situations, but weak under the arms. She checked the specs on the laser rifle and saw that it was a Westings A41; more than enough to slice through that weak spot.

One of the enemies was still combat-capable, and spotted Tanis. He pivoted to fire on her. As he took his shot, Tanis dove to the side and returned fire. The shot burned clean through the man's shoulder and out his head. He fell to the deck, spasming.

She fired at another man, nearly cutting his arm off, before he was flung to the ground by the second timed pulse from the Marines. The volley knocked the remaining enemies to the ground, and moments later the Marines rushed them, force shields pinning them to the deck.

The enemy's armor was power assisted and the Marines fired point-blank shots in an attempt to stun the mercs. One of them broke free from the chaos and lunged across the hall to hold a beam rifle to Tanis's head.

She froze, swearing at herself for not moving back once the Marines got in close.

"We go free, or she gets it!"

Before anyone could respond, a sound like a thunderclap echoed through the hall, and the man holding the gun on Tanis dropped to the deck, his armor's face shield cracked.

"Damn that was loud; what was that?" Tanis looked around to see Evans holstering a ballistic sidearm.

"Told you I didn't want your job back." He grinned.

"My god, how on earth did you get that aboard a starship?" Forsythe asked, eyeing the weapon.

"Umm… I was my own CO for a while." Evans pulled an innocent face.

"Hope Sanderson doesn't have words with you over that. Since it saved my life, I'm going to pretend I didn't see it," Tanis said.

Forsythe directed six of her men to secure the lock while they waited on word from the TSF team that was breaching the exterior of the shuttle at the hatch down the hall. Medical teams rushed in, attempting to save the attackers that had been doused with plasma, or that had fallen onto the hot steel.

"Goddamn…" one of them muttered.

<Corridor is clear, sir,> Tanis informed Sanderson.

<I see that, Major. Breach team has entered the shuttle; they should have it clear in minutes. Be ready for any exiting combatants—we've merged the combat nets so they won't have any crossfire.>

<Thank you, sir.>

"Commander Evans, let the folks in the ballroom know that their VIP selves are safe for the moment," Tanis said.

Evans chuckled. "They probably would like to be let out of the catering room."

<Shuttle secured. There was only one guard and the pilot. If you could clear the airlock obstruction, we'll move it to MOS dock A9.E,>

the lieutenant commanding the breach unit said over the combat net.

<Excellent. We'll get that cleared up momentarily. Would you be so kind as to bring those two men out? We'll keep them with the surviving enemy combatants on the Intrepid for questioning.>

<Yes, sir, will do,> the lieutenant replied.

Tanis nodded to Forsythe who signaled the six men at the airlock to remove the brace that was holding it open. They took custody of the two men who were brought out to the corridor. With that done, the Intrepid was able to seal the airlock and minutes later, the display above the lock showed the ship had undocked.

"Anyone for drinks?" Tanis asked the platoon with a smile. "It's an open bar."

ASSESSMENT

STELLAR DATE: 3227164 / 07.30.4123 (Adjusted Gregorian)
LOCATION: GSS *Intrepid*, Mars Outer Shipyards (MOS)
REGION: Mars Protectorate, Sol Space Federation

"That was quite the breach," Captain Andrews said to Tanis.

Admiral Sanderson, Terrance Enfield, and the Reddings were gathered in the bridge's conference room. Tanis's incident report was up on the table's holo.

"I guess that means the dockside security is good; they had to circumvent it." Terrance chuckled.

"I'm glad you find it funny," Sanderson growled.

Terrance's smile disappeared instantly. "Finding humor where I please is my prerogative. Don't think to claim credit for any of her success, either."

Tanis sighed internally. That wasn't going to earn her any points, but she bit her tongue. The admiral didn't want her help defending himself.

"In two days, we'll have our own fighters and patrol craft in place, which will seal up this hole in our security. Until then, we should have the MOS TSF garrison provide us with additional support on our portside docks." Tanis spoke impassively, hoping to avoid any more comments about blame or credit.

"I've already put in the request," Sanderson said, not betraying a reaction to Terrance, one way or the other. "They'll be checking every ship before it docks, unless it has a TSF grade 5A security token."

"What's the damage to the corridor?" Captain Andrews asked.

"It's a bleeding mess," Abby said. "I'm sure that plasma slice and dice you did seemed like a good idea at the time, but it burnt through several comm lines, coolant conduit, and a fuel line—which was empty, thank God."

"We queried the *Intrepid* before we did our little 'slice and dice'. It was either that, or let them do whatever other unpleasantness they had in mind. I know you love your ship, but I'd feel a lot worse about a dead guest or Marine than I do about melted deck plate," Tanis replied.

Abby huffed, but didn't respond as her husband rested a hand on her arm. Tanis had a suspicion that her ship probably ranked higher than most of the VIP guests in her mind.

"Have you gotten anything from the boarders yet, as to what their objective was?" Terrance asked.

Tanis addressed Terrance. "We're letting them stew for a bit, I'll sit with them tomorrow."

"They'll just have their nano rest them up," Sanderson said. "Waiting won't get you anywhere."

"They don't have any nano anymore. We've got some nice tools these days for making people a bit more pliable." Tanis couldn't help give a small predatory grin.

"That's an invasion of personal space." The expression on Captain Andrews' face showed his distaste for the act.

"It is. However, when someone has been convicted of attempted murder, part of the incarceration process is to strip their nano."

"Convicted?" Abby asked.

"Angela, my AI, has judicial authority in InnerSol space."

"Convenient," Earnest murmured.

"It has proven to be so," Tanis agreed.

"I don't know how comfortable I feel with this. Are you certain there are no legal ramifications?" Terrance stroked his thin beard, his expression uncertain.

"You are aware that the TSF is an authority cleared by the Sol Space Federation to try, convict, and incarcerate criminals." It wasn't so much a question as a confirmation to calm him.

"I am… I'm just not used to them making decisions that so

readily favor me." Terrance seemed to relax as he identified his own reason for concern.

Tanis found herself wondering—not for the first time— precisely why Terrance was backing the *Intrepid*'s mission. He was the head of the TRE Corporation, one of the largest privately owned companies in the Sol system. If he wanted to run a colony mission, why was he doing it through the GSS? The Generation Space Service had many inconvenient rules and guidelines he would be forced to follow.

On the other hand, the GSS had special access to additional data from the FGT, and it *was* the official organization for doling out terraformed colony worlds. Non-GSS-sanctioned colonization efforts of worlds terraformed by the FGT seemed to have a high failure rate—often with no explanation. The colonists simply disappeared, in some cases.

"If I'm involved, we'll always be the wronged party; not only in the right, but the winners. It's part of my job description." Regardless of his motives, Tanis had to make sure the man paying the bills was appeased. "With your permission, I need to see a medic for some regen on my knees, and get a good night's sleep before I begin convincing our guests to speak with us tomorrow."

"Your report is in order." Sanderson closed it out on the holo display. "Dismissed."

"Sirs, ma'am." Tanis nodded to the assemblage and headed for her quarters. Intrigue, confrontation, and now violent confrontation; the *Intrepid* was starting to feel like home already.

TAKE THE DEAL

STELLAR DATE: 3227165 / 07.31.4123 (Adjusted Gregorian)
LOCATION: GSS *Intrepid*, Mars Outer Shipyards (MOS)
REGION: Mars Protectorate, Sol Space Federation

Tanis looked from the sheets of plas on the table to the man in front of her. He was a mercenary; all of the boarders were. Not a lot of information could be found on him, but he did have ties to the Ardent Stars, as well as Morning Glory—both of which were merc outfits.

The attack on the *Intrepid* was odd in that respect. Most mercs didn't go for the big jobs—too much negative impact on life expectancy. Something like yesterday's assault would only be taken on if the pay was very high, or the job was expected to be easy enough to make it attractive.

Tanis couldn't imagine anyone billing yesterday's attempt to capture several high-value VIPs as 'easy', so it had to be the money. Even if she discounted the mercs' salary, the sums required to get the shuttle, fool the docking AI, and facilitate whatever the getaway plan had been, would be in the millions of creds. More than most people made in a lifetime.

"So let's go over this again, Mr. Drayson." Tanis leaned back in her chair. "You were hired by a man you never saw, never talked to, and whose name you never heard. You didn't broker the deal; that came through your organization. You simply took your cut and did the job."

"You got it, lady. That's how it works. I get paid, and then I do the job. I don't hear names; I don't want to hear names. Things go a lot smoother that way, you get me?"

"Yeah," Tanis sighed. "I get you. Here's the thing, though. We've got a few of you guys, so if you've watched any vids where scum like you gets caught, you know that standard operating procedure is to offer a deal to the first guy that gives us good info. Everyone else spends a good long time helping in some public works projects on some frosty world." Tanis smiled. They both knew that frosty meant working on scattered disk objects at the edge of the Sol system.

"So what makes me so special I get the fancy deal? The other boys wouldn't play with you?"

"Nothing. I'll be offering it to everyone, you just happened to be first."

"An' if I tell you what I know, I'm off the hook?"

Tanis snorted. "You stormed a GSS colony ship intending to capture or kill some very important people. No, you will be doing some time for this; you can just choose to do less time."

"How much less?"

....

"So he talked then, did he?" Commander Evans asked.

"Actually, they all talked." Tanis leaned against the entrance to her office looking out into the SOC.

"You offered them all the deal? After what they did?" He leaned on a railing across from her.

"Yup, and they all took it, every last one of them."

"So they all get off with a light slap on the wrist?"

Tanis locked eyes with him. "I'm the Butcher of Toro. Do you think I'd do that? Angela gave them all minimum sentences."

The commander looked away, a slight flush rising on his cheeks. "That still doesn't sound all that bad."

Tanis relaxed her posture, unsure what was bothering him so much. "You didn't ask where they'd be serving it."

"OK, I'll bite, where?"

"Affixing boosters to comets," Tanis grinned, a twinkle in her eye.

"I thought you told them that they weren't going to be stuck on some ice ball."

"Commander Evans! Are you saying that I'm not a woman of my word?" Tanis's expression was one of mock shock.

The commander paused, unsure how to respond to Tanis's informality. "Uh… Kinda, sir."

"Well, they'll be working on diverting comets as they approach the sun, so they'll probably be fairly warm."

"Man, those poor schleps would have been better off if they never talked to you."

"I'm certain they'll share that sentiment."

Tanis did have a moment of pity regarding where she sent the men, but not that much. They had assaulted a colony ship. *Her* colony ship. It wasn't something that she would easily forgive.

"So, then." Evans ran a hand through his hair. "What did we learn?"

"Two main things." Tanis looked down at a sheaf of plas sheets. "Firstly, that they never did meet the person that hired them—not that surprising. Secondly, that his name was mentioned once or twice, and it was Trent."

"Your nuke buddy from the *Dawn*."

"It not being him would be the coincidence of the century."

"I assume that you've tried to find the man in their org that arranged the deal," Evans said.

"I've got Terry working on it. She has a team looking at each prisoner's every move for the last year. She's also got a financial forensics expert trying to trace the money, but she's hit a bit of a dead end."

"How dead?"

"It appears that the money came from Tau Ceti." Tanis scowled.

"They're, what, nearly twelve LY out?"

"Yeah, and I don't think anyone planned this little visit

twelve years ago."

"I can't imagine that being the case," Evans agreed.

It went without saying; the list of corporations or governments with enough liquidity to send large sums to another star system, launder it, and send it back to sit in a slush fund for the day they felt like storming a colony ship was filled with powerful names.

"Well, it must narrow down the possibilities."

"Yeah, from billions to mere millions."

"Hey, if your job was easy, then a mere commander could do it."

Tanis smiled. "You did OK. At this stage, even I'm not going to be enough. I'm going to need to bring in the big guns."

INTERLUDE

STELLAR DATE: 3227165 / 07.31.4123 (Adjusted Gregorian)
LOCATION: Stellar Comm Hub #10.A.459.B.230.C-934

<I've got news regarding the attempt.> Trent sent the message over the private Link.

<I've already heard.> Strang's reply was terse.

<Then you know. Our men were all killed or apprehended. They have impounded the shuttle, as well.>

<I thought this plan was foolproof. They only had to advance a hundred meters and secure one ballroom.>

<They had a TSF Marine platoon ready that was able to hold our men at bay. My data indicates that they have a highly decorated intelligence officer handling their security, now. She must have implemented some new measures.>

<How come I wasn't aware of her?> Strang was growing less pleased by the second.

<Apparently she's only been there for two days,> Trent replied. *<Based on what I've learned, she's the woman that foiled our attempt to detonate our nuke on the docks.>*

<You're telling me that she took control of three decks of MOS, brought platoons of soldiers on board, and disrupted every operation we have in a matter of days?>

Trent didn't like where this was going. *<Yes. Somehow, she has managed to do just that.>*

Frustration seemed to fill the time lag. *<Do the job I hired you for, or I get someone else.>*

<I'll take care of it. I have a new priority, now. Eliminate Major Richards.>

<See that you do. I want daily updates.>

THE 242

STELLAR DATE: 3227170 / 08.05.4123 (Adjusted Gregorian)
LOCATION: Gustav Expanse, New Africa, Venus
REGION: Terran Hegemony, Sol Space Federation

The whine of railguns charging sounded nearby, and squad one rushed forward to take cover behind a low concrete embankment in the equipment yard. Moments later, bits of rock and dust sprayed up into the air as the pellets from the rails smashed into the cement.

Staff Sergeant Williams threaded a scope over the barrier and took stock of the situation. The enemy was slowly advancing behind large CFT shields, which absorbed and refracted the Marine's lasers. The enemy's railguns, on the other hand, would chew the concrete cover apart in just a few minutes.

"Chang! Where're those heavies?" he hollered back to squad two, which was moving past several trucks on squad one's right.

"Thirty seconds, Staff Sergeant," Chang replied.

<Nearly in position,> Williams reported to Lieutenant Grenwald on the combat net. <Those bastards won't know what hit them.> Grenwald signaled his acknowledgement and updated the objectives on the command net.

Squad two reached their designated position, and the two slug throwers were assembled. Taking sight over the barrier, they readied the weapons with a smooth precision granted through plenty of practice. Once Chang was satisfied, squad two slid the weapons into position and let fire. Slugs over twenty centimeters long erupted from the barrels at velocities exceeding ten kilometers per second. CFT shields could stand up to pulses and energy beams without suffering so much as a scratch, but faced with the kinetic energy the slugs carried, the carbon fiber nanotube shields were torn to shreds.

What was once safe cover became deadly shrapnel, as the shield fragments tore through the men behind them like they were made of paper. In a few short seconds it was over, and the heavies powered down the slug throwers.

Peering over the barrier, Chang grinned and swore. "Now that's some messy shit, Staff Sergeant."

"Just be happy I don't make you go clean it up for taking so long," Williams growled as he cast an uneasy eye at the amount of concrete the enemy's railguns had dug out of the barrier protecting the Marines. "Squads, advance!"

Their objective was a communications array on the next hilltop. The original plan was to support an airstrike and catch any stragglers, but command had received intel regarding sensitive data on servers within the communications bunker.

The brass wanted to review it, so the Marines were heading in to do it the old-fashioned way.

"Man, I hate Venus." PFC Arsen vaulted over the concrete barrier and established cover for his squad from behind a truck. "It feels like it's spinning too fast. I swear it's making me dizzy."

"That's just your head reeling from how much your mouth moves," Sergeant Green said caustically. "Now shut up and keep your eye on that tree line. Scan's clear, but you never know when someone has left a surprise for you."

The two squads moved up; their fireteams advancing in a standard pattern until they reached the remains of the enemy troops. They were definitely a fringe group of radicals—their motley armor being the first sign—but the railguns they had were the latest spec. Several of the Marines were eyeing them, and Williams signaled Lance Corporal Dvorak to wipe the ID systems on the guns. When they were safe to handle, he assigned one to each team's assist.

"Swap that out with your heavy gunner as the need arises."

Chang grinned. "I can definitely see the need to use this bad boy." He checked the ammunition and the reload action. "Why doesn't the corps give us weapons like this?"

"They're too concerned your ham hands would put a hole in one of their pretty ships," Dvorak said.

"They're the TSF's ships, don't see why the corps would care."

"Cause we're all one happy military now," Williams grunted.

"Yeah, I'd like to see those vacuum jockeys down here taking on enemy troops." PFC Perez kicked the twitching body of a fallen foe to make sure he was dead.

"I'd like to see you doing it, too." Corporal Taylor gestured for Perez to move out.

Williams checked the command net to make sure squads one and two were in position relative to squad three. The command net showed Lieutenant Grenwald making better time. Williams signaled his men over the combat net to pick up the pace.

<Jansen.> He singled out the lance corporal heading up the first fireteam in squad one.

<Yes, Staff Sergeant?> Jansen, one/one's team leader, replied in her trademark calm voice. She never raised it, not even in a firefight. She was on the way to making her corporal rating, and Williams expected to see her move to NCO or possibly even OCS after this tour.

<I want you to take your fireteam and scout ahead; keep at least a hundred meters up. We don't need any more surprises like that last batch.>

<Aye, Staff Sergeant.> She directed her team to pick up the pace, and slipped into the trees ahead.

<Corporal Salas, I want you to take up a position parallel to ours, but two hundred meters to the north. We've got squad three to the south, so we're safe there, but I don't fancy a surprise coming around to poke us in the ass. You make sure things are quiet,> Williams

ordered.

Salas sent an acknowledgement over the combat net and led his fireteam off to the left, down the access road, then into the tree line.

Something felt off to Williams. The enemy had hit them too hard over the last several miles for this last skirmish to be their final hurrah. With the platoon nearly at the comm tower, a last line of defense was only logical.

He posted his concerns on the command net and waited to see if anyone agreed.

<You really aren't a glass half-full type of guy, are you?> Sergeant Li with squad three asked. <There is a third scenario—they're up on the hill just waiting for us.>

<He's got a point, Staff Sergeant,> Sergeant Green said. <They could just be really bad at tactics.>

<That's not what intel says. It's also not what an advanced model of railgun says. These guys are better than that.>

Lieutenant Grenwald put in his two chits, <Well, you did take them out pretty quick. Maybe they're not that good, after all.>

Williams acknowledged that, but pressed his point, <Granted, they probably didn't expect us to sling some M1409s at them, sir. Those aren't standard ordinance for a rifle platoon— something they wouldn't have planned for. Just keep your ears peeled, and make sure tech keeps an extra close eye on scan.>

The LT didn't counter the order, so Green informed Dvorak to keep an extra close eye on scan. Williams was glad that Grenwald had taken his word on the possible danger. He was a good CO as far as they went, though only two years out of OCS. Williams didn't mind so much; it was easier to shape the younger officers.

The Marines advanced down the slope toward a small creek at the bottom of the valley. From there, it was up the hill to the communications array. He could see it poking through the trees: several directional and omnidirectional antennas jutting into the sky. Orders were to take as much of it intact as possible, but Williams' first concern was always for his Marines.

Williams had started his military career in E Company, 8th Battalion of the 242. Working his way up from PFC to Staff Sergeant had built into him the knowledge that this wasn't a job, it was a life. The men and women around him were family, closer than any flesh and blood. He was responsible for them, and he was going to make sure that every single one of them survived this mission.

He kept that attitude firmly in mind; it was his mantra. The minute a sergeant started accepting the loss of the men he or she was responsible for was the minute to get out of the military. His platoon needed him, needed his protection, and he wasn't going to let them down.

That being said, he didn't mind if they were scared shitless of him. It made the enemy seem a lot less threatening.

<I'm getting an odd reading across the stream,> Jansen reported. *<I thought I caught an EMF sig, but then it was gone.>*

<Fall back ten meters and secure the west bank. I'll send one/three south — two/one's already to the north.>

<Aye, Staff Sergeant.>

<I guess you were right,> Sergeant Li said over the command net.

<We've just crossed the stream to the south,> the lieutenant said. *<We'll continue on course. If you need us we'll be in position to come in behind them.>*

<Yes, sir,> Williams acknowledged. He sent commands to the fireteam leaders over the combat net, instructing them to spread out and take up positions flanking Jansen's team.

The comms went silent, only passive systems online. Even with the tech available to them, Marines still trained in using hand signals. They were silent, efficient, and needed no electricity to convey.

Once the teams were in position, Williams signaled Chang

to set up one of the slug throwers in case the enemy was shielded. Then he signaled Jansen's team to make their way across the stream. One/one made the crossing at a point where there were several large rocks in the water—providing enough cover and white noise to mask their approach.

One/one's active camo made them hard to spot as they moved down the bank and into the water. Cassar, one/one's heavy gunner, was reaching the far shore when he spotted movement and lowered himself quietly into the water, propping his newly acquired railgun onto a rock. He held up four fingers and pointed to his two o'clock. Williams watched him slowly scan the tree line in front of him before the Marine flashed a full five fingers twice, and pointed to his nine o'clock.

The Marines silently passed the counts down the line, and Williams signaled his commands for the flanks to cautiously advance twenty meters across the stream and prepare to repel a flanking maneuver by the enemy. Once the teams were in position, he signaled Jansen's fireteam to begin.

If there were only fourteen of the enemy, the two squads had numbers on their side. He wasn't counting on it, though; intel suspected that the radicals holding the communications array had upwards of one hundred armed combatants in the facility. If things went the way they usually did, there were at least thirty of the enemy across that stream, all ready to take out the first clear target.

Of course, that's why the brass sent in Marines for jobs like this, and not the glorified space force security guards.

Cassar opened up with the railgun, flinging fifty-gram ballistic shells at over twenty kilometers per second. They hit with the force of several sticks of dynamite. Instantly, the Marines all realized he was firing fragmentation rounds— something which had not been apparent when the enemy was shooting at the concrete.

One thing was certain: it was effectively clearing the

underbrush. A green-brown mist filled the air as the rounds tore through everything in their path; a red bloom appearing here and there as the rounds hit flesh. A minute later he was out of ammunition, and the squads waited for the mist to settle. From the looks of it, six men were hit. Silence rushed in, broken only by the crack of a branch tearing off a tree.

"That's why they won't give you one of those," Taylor whispered to Perez.

"Yeah, I wouldn't get within a thousand meters of you and a weapon like that." PFC Koller grinned. "It'd be suicide."

Without warning, laserfire flickered from the far side of the stream, focused at one/two's position, and forcing the fireteam down into the brush. The enemy obviously had sound-sensitive targeting, but their actions revealed their own locations. The Marine's combat helmets traced the enemy's shots by the heat signatures the laser beams left in the air, and squads one and two opened up with everything they had. Two other captured railguns whined as they charged, and then the first ten meters of trees across the stream ceased to exist.

<Thanks, one/two.> Chang laughed on the combat net. <Always good to have someone playing bait for the rest of us.>

<Fuck you, Chang.> Perez was checking his body for burns.

Williams sent them both a slap across the combat net and reminded them that enemies were still across the stream—enemies who were now in possession of shiny new EMF emission data. Unfortunately, his necessary reprimand gave away his position as well, and he signaled dispersal to those around him and the other broadcasters.

Laserfire continued to flicker from the far shore, and the Marines returned the favor—the opening volleys turning into a full skirmish. It played out for several more minutes before the sounds of the enemy retreating could be heard. Williams called for a weapons/wounds check, while updating the command net with their positions and number of targets estimated to be eliminated.

<One/three, attempt to determine the number of enemy casualties. One/two, your asses, front and center.>

Corporal Taylor led his team to the Staff Sergeant's position and prepared for a tongue-lashing. Williams looked them up and down, his displeasure a palpable thing.

"Why I don't put my boot up your collective asses and send you home is beyond me. However, it *is* nice to have a team that volunteers as bait. It also means that I don't need to get too attached to you assholes, since you are all going to die soon." They took it well, like Marines.

"Next time one of you decides to start commenting on a firefight when we are maintaining a tactical silence, pretend you can't; cause once more, and you'll all be physically incapable of communication!" He spat on the ground and took a deep breath. "You got me one/two?"

"Yes, Staff Sergeant." The response was quick and in perfect unison.

"Good, go swap places with two/one. You're on the left flank now. Don't let me down." After a verbal beating, it was never a bad thing to give the team some responsibility. They'd be all the more eager to prove themselves proper soldiers.

"I think Taylor's gonna be numb for a week." Sergeant Kowalski walked toward Williams after sending Jansen on point again. "Becker estimates we got thirteen baddies. Hard to say for sure—he was counting heads, but he thinks he could be plus or minus one. I guess some of the heads didn't make it too well."

Williams nodded. "Taylor's right about one thing. There's a reason they don't hand out guns like that in the corps."

"We gonna get a talkin' to from the brass for using 'em?" Kowalski asked.

"Maybe... Hopefully they'll take it as a fighting-fire-with-fire situation."

"Well," Kowalski grinned, "it's your ass, not mine."

"Thanks for the support."

Combat net indicated that squad three was in position and waiting on first and second to make it to their ready point.

<Everyone move out, we have our two corners to secure before we take the facility. I want to be in position in ten minutes.> Williams watched with satisfaction as every team moved on his command and began their ascent of the hill.

The facility was a squat two-story building with several outlying power transfer and storage sheds. Jansen's team silently took out four sentries and set up a covering position behind a power transfer shed that hid their EMF signature. Williams directed the two slug-throwing teams to set up positions at the northwest and southwest corners of the building. Squad three had the rear of the structure covered. Williams settled down behind a storage shed and scanned the combat net. The assault was scheduled for t-minus six minutes, according to the clock ticking on his HUD.

Two/one would cover with the heavies and provide additional backup. Squad one was taking the front door. Two fireteams from squad three would secure the rear rooms of the facility and catch any escapees.

The count crept down toward zero as he scanned the facility. The enemy had to know the attack was imminent. Nothing showed, but he was certain that behind most, if not all, the second-floor windows were enemy troops all too ready to rain hell down on the Marines.

He saw movement behind one window in particular, and passed the information along to two/one; noting with approval how Corporal Salas assigned the target, and also had PFC Reddy run the intel over to Chang's heavy team. A man was spotted on the roof, and Salas took care of that target as well.

Thirty seconds remaining.

Taylor's fireteam was to be first in, with Dvorak holding

back until the facility was secured. They'd need him to hack the systems the brass was so interested in, and Williams needed to keep him breathing for that little event.

Squad one's teams were moving now, slow and silent, keeping to lanes out of sight of the building's windows. A moment later, Taylor was at the door, setting a shape charge before flattening himself against the wall.

The sound was muffled; most of the blast erupted inside the building. Marine boots smashed into the door's remains and knocked them inward. A flash and a conc rolled in, and one/one was back against the wall as the whine of railguns charging echoed out of the opening. No fire came—instead, curses erupted from within the building.

The other two teams in squad one hadn't been sitting idle. While the front door action was underway, they were breaching ground floor windows.

A gunner leaned out of the window Williams had noted earlier, and PFC Altair burned a hole through his head. At the same moment, Reddy took out the man on the roof with a shot from one of the commandeered railguns.

Before the sounds of pain within the building died down, one/one was through the doors. Their IR scan showing the locations of the radicals inside; with three quick shots, the entrance was secured.

Williams rose from his position and followed the squad into the building—time to finish the job.

HISTORY

STELLAR DATE: 3227171 / 08.06.4123 (Adjusted Gregorian)
LOCATION: Marine Troop Transport En-Route to TSS *Normandy*
Orbiting Venus.
REGION: Terran Hegemony, Sol Space Federation

"So, we're being sent to Mars." Grenwald addressed his NCOs after wrapping up their post-op review on the transport back to the TSS *Normandy*.

"What's going on there?" Sergeant Li asked. "Aren't they usually pretty particular about anyone else doing a job they think their vaunted MSF can handle?"

"Wouldn't know about that," Grenwald said. "We're not going to the surface, but to the Mars Outer Shipyards where they're building that big colony ship, the *Intrepid*. They've got a major and an admiral with some sort of trouble that needs Marine boots to fix."

"*Intrepid*, eh?" Williams grunted. "That's the ship that Redding guy made the new super ramscoop for, right? Supposed to be one hell of a ship."

Green leaned his seat back and stretched. "I don't really see what they would need us for, sir. Do they need us to shoot a contractor or something?"

Grenwald shrugged. "Not in the brief. I caught wind that they pulled up an MCSF from Mars 1, and have a couple companies of Regulars running security for the ship."

"Great," Li groaned. "We've got to play nice with regulars? You know they're not really our biggest fans. Plus, they've already got MCSF to wipe people's asses. That's their specialty."

"She has a point," Williams said. The 8th Battalion of the 242 was Force Recon Orbital Drop; the TSF usually didn't deploy them to stations. The TSF usually didn't *want* them on stations.

"What good are FROD Marines going to be at babysitting a construction job?"

"Well, as it turns out, we were specially requested. I guess some of the folks on that ship have pull."

"Who made the request?" Sergeant Green asked.

"Some MICI major named Richards." The lieutenant sounded dismissive. "Probably just some hopped-up OCS brat who wants more attention than she deserves."

"Oh, I don't think so." Williams grinned at Kowalski, who had been with the platoon ten years ago when Major Richards, then a lieutenant colonel, was temporarily the de-facto commander of their battalion. "If she's involved, and called for us, we're going into the fire."

"You can say that again." Kowalski nodded.

"This major's been demoted?" Grenwald asked. "Is she *that* Tanis Richards?"

"One and the same," Williams nodded.

"Great, so we're going to the MOS under the command of some nut-job Micky major?" Sergeant Green rubbed his face with frustration.

"Hey." Kowalski smacked him on the back. "Don't knock it till you try it."

"Who cares about that?" Li was accessing data on the MOS over her Link. "There are absolutely *no* good bars on that shipyard!"

SETTING THE MEET

STELLAR DATE: 3227179 / 08.14.4123 (Adjusted Gregorian)
LOCATION: Mars Outer Shipyards (MOS)
REGION: Mars Protectorate, Sol Space Federation

"Major Richards!" Terry Chang called out as Tanis entered the SOC.

"Miss Chang, I'm guessing you've word regarding our uninvited visitors." Tanis walked up to the woman, who was clutching a sheet of plas tightly.

"Do I ever! I traced the mercs' organization, and located the person who brokers the deals. The name is Daiki Tanaka; he or she operates out of Cruithne Station. There's a drop on a regional Mars surface net, if you want to make contact with them. I've forwarded the protocols to your personal net."

Tanis reviewed the information. "Excellent. Good work, Miss Chang; we'll get somewhere with this yet."

"Yes, sir." Terry smiled and turned back toward the entrance to her labs.

Tanis found it amusing how the civilians had started calling her 'sir'; it didn't take long for the military way of things to take over.

<You realize you're not the only military personnel on this ship, right?> Angela asked. *<I know your ego may have trouble with it, but it could actually be a cumulative effect.>*

<Perish the thought.> Tanis smiled to herself as she entered her office and brought up a 3D map of the solar system on the desk's holo.

<Looks like Cruithne is almost at aphelion while we're on the same side of the sun. That actually makes for a fairly reasonable trip.>

<Want to have a little chat with this Daiki in person?> Angela asked.

<I think I may want to do just that.>

<Protocol for contacting this person is a bit convoluted. They've got to have the exact right amount of data in the right place before they'll respond. Get it wrong, and you're blacklisted.>

Tanis chuckled. <I'll bet that doing it from some place as net-invisible as this office would raise some suspicions, as well. We should head down to Mars 1 to do it.>

<Better yet, send someone else to do it; the more steps from us, the better.>

<You spoil all of my fun.> Tanis sighed.

<I do try.>

Commander Evans poked his head into Tanis's office. "Major, not sure if this is your cup of tea or not, but one of my pilots has a few spare tickets to the InnerSol championship game between High Terra and Mars 1."

Tanis looked up at Evans. "Championship game for what?"

The commander sputtered for a moment. "The, uh…you really don't know?"

"Sorry, sports aren't really my thing."

"Uh…I see." He gave her a look like she had two heads. "It's only the first time in over a hundred years that High Terra has made it into the InnerSol finals. It's only going to be the most amazing football game ever."

Tanis shook her head. "Not my idea of a great time, but I do have something for you to do while you're down there."

<You need serious work on your colloquiums.>

Commander Evans' look was completely unreadable.

INTERLUDE

STELLAR DATE: 3227182 / 08.17.4123 (Adjusted Gregorian)
LOCATION: Mars Outer Shipyards (MOS)
REGION: Mars Protectorate, Sol Space Federation

"We've got the response." Ouri sat down across from Tanis's desk and dropped a secure sheet of hyfilm in front of the major.

"Positive, I hope." Tanis passed a token over the SOC net to the hyfilm. Its contents were scrambled and took a moment to render before Tanis's eyes.

"We've got a meeting at a bar on Cruithne Station called 'The Human Condition'," Ouri summarized.

"Odd name..."

Ouri shrugged. "I guess so. So, who are you sending out there?"

"Sending?" Tanis asked. "I'm more interested in going."

"Going? You can't be serious... Sir." Ouri tacked on the honorific after catching a raised eyebrow from Tanis.

"I am indeed serious. Things are quiet at the moment, and I intend to take advantage of that. I'll never be more than a few light minutes away. I'll be certain to keep a laser comm trained on the *Intrepid*."

"The admiral will never clear you for it."

Tanis smiled and Ouri knew she wasn't going to like the response.

"The admiral never has to know."

CRUITHNE

STELLAR DATE: 3227185 / 08.20.4123 (Adjusted Gregorian)
LOCATION: Cruithne Station
REGION: InnerSol, Sol Space Federation

Tanis looked out the porthole at Cruithne Station as the transport matched velocities with the asteroid habitat. There wasn't much asteroid visible anymore; though here and there, a bit of raw rock did show between spurs and domes. Originally merely an aggregation of ice and iron no more than five kilometers across, the station had expanded far beyond those bounds into a sprawling structure over one hundred kilometers long. Her access to the structural design showed that none of the original asteroid remained.

Normally, once the resources from such a body were exhausted, there would be no further reason for mankind to remain; but Cruithne orbited the sun in resonance with Earth, always on the same side of Sol. Depending on where it was in its year, it was either accelerating away from Earth or Earth was accelerating toward it. The result was a very useful location for transporting shipments in and out of InnerSol. In addition, Cruithne also crossed the orbit of Venus and Mars from time to time, further adding to its list of useful locations.

This was one of those times when Cruithne would come very close to Mars, and the trip only took two days—something Tanis was grateful for, as the transport she was on wasn't at all passenger-friendly. The crew was even less so. They were either ignoring her or coming onto her. Tanis had gained a great familiarity with the walls of her berth.

When the shipnet announced a seal and equalization, Tanis started moving down the corridor before the station rules finished posting. She wasn't terribly worried about them—

other than the fact she was certain to break some.

Cruithne fell under the jurisdiction of the InnerSol portion of the stellar federation, but only nominally. It was owned and run by an old family of traders, and had been for as long as anyone could remember. They were wealthy and not overly concerned about scruples. The combination made for a station that looked like it was out of the vids from the early third millennium. It was readily apparent that one of the reasons the family was so wealthy was that they didn't bother with preventative maintenance…or cleaning.

Tanis moved out onto the dock and immediately had to navigate around an argument between the ship's supercargo and a repair crew. It seemed that the crew was repairing part of the life-support system at the transport's berth. The main cargo hatch was completely blocked off by conduit hanging from the ceiling like vines in a jungle, and more than a dozen pulled-up deck plates.

After circumventing the mess, Tanis logged on to the station net while Angela chatted up the traffic and mass balancing AI for information. She checked the public areas to see if there were any alerts or warnings that would affect her plans before beginning a slow circuit of the station.

Even though she didn't expect any—or much—trouble, knowing the layout of the docks and where clever hiding places or distractions could be found was never a bad thing. More than one vendor hauling carts filled with random trinkets and knickknacks trundled along the dock. A larger than average population of greasy food carts was also in evidence. She suspected that some of them must be doing double duty, both keeping a lookout and smuggling items onto various ships.

Tanis was undercover, her net presence and ID switched to a new record that Angela and Ouri had set up. She was certain that they had picked this particular disguise as a joke, or some sort of punishment for overworking them.

She was masquerading as a Golist, a member of a religious sect of quasi-cyborgs who believed in reaching enlightenment by minimizing motion and being at peace with oneself. They also were fierce traders. The religion's roots were an odd combination of capitalism and Taoism.

Because she wasn't a cyborg, the sect's regular attire was not comfortable at all. Ironically, the part of her that was the most comfortable was her head—where nearly all of her skin had been removed.

Covered in silver metal, with only a sliver of skin around her right eye still in place, her head had a slightly ovoid shape. The liquid steel that covered it could take any form, but the standard pose was a totally expressionless mask with no mouth, nose, or ears.

<I think the look is good on you,> Angela said. <It's very minimalist.>

<You are the last person to give advice on appearance. I saw what your last body looked like before you were lodged in my head. It was like some artist's nightmare.>

<Be quiet, or I'll hack your face and give you horns.>

<That might actually fit.> Tanis glanced at her body in a mirror, and took a moment to reconcile what she saw with her inner image.

Her body was covered in a polymer that coated her like a second skin; which was somewhat uncomfortable, as it really wasn't meant to wear over skin, but typically in place of it. She had opted for the temporary discomfort, as re-growing the skin on her face was going to itch enough as it was; she could suffer a few days to save the weeks of itching and scratching across her entire body. The glossy white covering was largely inflexible—not that strange, since the Golists deplored excess motion. Tanis had allowed for more movement in the arms than was typical, but her legs were essentially straight as a beam, and ended in fine points that hovered several inches off the deck. It took a good bit of power to achieve that effect, which meant that most of her thigh muscle was waiting for her back on the *Intrepid*; the area it usually occupied now filled with SC batteries.

<*I swear, Ouri dreamed this up to get back at me for something.*> An itch began to twinge way behind Tanis's right knee.

<*Golists frequent Cruithne. It is a very good disguise, and one that no TSF operative has ever used before, according to the records. No one will expect it.*>

<*Well, yeah! Any person who volunteers to wear this should have their head examined.*>

They passed several Golists, and Tanis exchanged tokens with them, their avatars nodding serenely to one another on the general net.

<*I assume they should be candidates for said head examination?*> Angela asked.

<*Especially them.*>

Tanis spent a few hours working her way through the commercial district, identifying several routes from the bar where she was to meet the contact to the vessel she would be leaving on. She also checked calendars on the local nets to ensure that no maintenance or large shipments of cargo would get in her way.

Eventually the time for the meeting drew near, and Tanis made her way to The Human Condition. She was not entirely certain she wanted to see the reason the venue went by that name.

Tanis entered the bar and crossed to where the servitor, a human, in this case, was busy pouring drinks. The place was clean—the walls a gleaming white, the décor mostly steel and plas. All in all, it was pretty stark, meant to draw the eye to the fact that the tables and chairs were made of humans. Not dead humans, by any means, but live humans; mostly with little modification, and a lot of clamps and rods holding them in place.

The scene brought back memories of Toro—images of people turned into things, artwork and worse, flashed through her mind.

<Remind me to check how legitimate this place is,> Tanis said.

<I already have; all of these people are paid employees. Paid fairly well, at that.>

<You couldn't pay me enough,> Tanis said. *<If nothing else, I'd be bored out of my skull.>*

<Wouldn't they just spend their time on the net?> Angela asked.

<Doubtful. What's the point of having a person turned into an object, if they can escape it and not even be aware it's happening? A joint like this would make sure they had no Link and were only experiencing this reality.>

<You couldn't pay me enough for that, even without the confinement and degradation.> Angela's avatar shuddered.

Tanis considered what had been required for her current cover. *<I know what you mean.>*

There were several dancers at various stages between human and decidedly not human, slithering up and down poles, and, in one case, mostly embedded in the pole. Tanis observed with Golist serenity, admiring the dancers' wholesale devotion to their expression by merging their human physicality with an expression of inner self. Privately, Tanis reaffirmed her position that some people's inner selves were just weird.

Tanis closed one eye—the other was currently covered over by her flowmetal—and calmed herself, exuding a zen-like peace as she waited for her contact to arrive. That didn't mean that she wasn't paying attention to what was around her. One of the advantages of the fluid metallic covering was that she had optical sensors all around her head, giving her a 360-degree view of the bar. She wondered if it would be possible to retain the ability after this mission, depending on whether the TSF let her keep the flowmetal—something she considered unlikely.

As Tanis surveyed the scene, one of the dancers caught her eye, and she watched the person move around a series of poles near the center of the establishment. She wasn't entirely certain if it was male or female, or if such designations even applied. It appeared to have no bones—or if it did, none were evident. The dancer's general shape was that of a lithe woman, but it was totally asexual, and while it often bent at what would normally be the locations of joints, at other times entire limbs became fluid and snakelike.

As its dance progressed, Tanis saw that it was also able to change the overall dimensions of its body, almost as though its skin were no more than a stretchy membrane. Its stomach distended at one point, and then it grew breasts, only to lose them moments later and become smooth and featureless again. Its head would swell and become conical and narrow and wrap around a pole, before thickening and resuming the shape of a normal human skull.

Tanis had to admit she was impressed; whoever this dancer was, it had some of the most extreme modifications she had ever seen. If it weren't for the abstract beauty of the dance, Tanis would have thought the creature wasn't human at all. Dance was something that could always betray a lack of humanity. Any machine or AI would inevitably have some evidence of math, or an artificial lack of math, in its dance. It was something that was hard to spot, but Tanis had watched enough dancing to know there was a certain element to organic dance and expression that was not something a machine could replicate.

<Nor would we want to,> Angela interjected. <Even the notion of something as…random, yet orderly, as human dance is…completely undesirable.>

<I know you feel that way. It only makes sense that your desire for order and understanding would leave no place for an abstract expression of emotion.>

<You know, you humans really are all just like those people that are tables in here. You want, no, you **crave** the overriding influence of your emotions and chemical feelings. Without them, you feel like you aren't somehow proper or complete.>

<I don't think we are all like those people at all. Most of us strive to achieve a balance between our emotions and abstract impulses, and our logical and orderly thought process, as well,> Tanis countered.

<Well, those people certainly don't crave that.> Angela referred to the human furniture pieces.

<It's hard to say. I think it's entirely possible that they are overridingly logical and analytical people; so much so that they are unable to be abstract and emotional much of the time. Perhaps this is how they strive to achieve that balance.>

<Or they just really need the money.>

Tanis laughed; not outwardly, her face currently having no mouth, but she found Angela's ever-prosaic attitude amusing.

They continued their silent observation of their surroundings until a message came over the establishment's local net informing Tanis that their contact was waiting for them in the rear of the bar. The message contained directions to a dressing room. She hovered past the other patrons to a hall in the rear, and then through a door with the label 'Adrienne' on it.

The inside of the room was plush and opulent; a distinct difference from the austere look of the common area outside. There were several holo mirrors, showing a 360-degree view as Tanis stood in the center of the space, waiting for her contact to show up.

The lack of a second exit unnerved her, and she assessed the structure of the walls to see if she could break through them if needed. They were little more than a thin plas, and she determined that with a few blasts of a pulse rifle, she could create an additional exit should the need arise. The moments ticked by and then the door opened, revealing the identity of

Adrienne.

It was the fluid dancer. She—'Adrienne' seemed to imply gender—slinked into the room, passed Tanis, and sprawled onto a mound of cushions, her form melting over them.

"You must be Yora," the woman said. "I am Adrienne, as you may have guessed."

A connection presented itself over a secure Link; Tanis opened it and responded.

<*I am. You are to be my contact for this arrangement?*>

"So, to the point and without pleasantries. Normal, I suppose, for one of your type. You sculpt yourselves into paragons of beauty and power, and then abstain from pleasure entirely. I, personally, would not be able to resist."

<*My presence is merely an outward expression of my inner serenity,*> Tanis replied. <*I take my pleasure from witnessing the expressions of my fellow Golists and knowing that they too strive for enlightenment.*>

"I never understood why someone seeking enlightenment would also want to control corporate interests," Adrienne said. "The notions seem to be in conflict. I, on the other hand, have no such desires. I only wish to surround myself in comfort and pleasure."

<*Control is the only route to enlightenment. Whether it is control of oneself, or of one's surroundings; both are paramount.*> Tanis watched the woman smile lazily. <*But I did not come here to discuss my order's philosophy. I understand that you represent a certain organization that is available for forceful ventures.*>

"There are actually a number of groups that use me to help them acquire work. You could consider me something of a broker. What sort of venture are you planning?"

<*There is a location I have interest in, but a company has laid claim to it and expressed the opposite of interest regarding its sale. Because of certain…incidents…they have availed themselves of extra security measures that have proven…difficult to overcome. The time of my*>

patience is over, and the time for a more direct application of pressure has come.>

"So you're looking for some muscle, are you, then? Any particular needs?"

<They need to be capable of spatial insertion, either by small shuttle or EVA. They must also have heavy combat gear, and not be afraid to fire beam weapons in a station.>

Adrienne sat still for a moment, only pulsing the odd limb as she considered the requirements. "I think I can hook you up with a group that has done such things in the past. They could most likely field a team of twenty or thirty for a job like this."

<Have I heard of them? What are their credentials?>

Data was delivered to Tanis and she looked it over, examining specs and the oblique descriptions of jobs performed. It matched the data on the group that had attacked the *Intrepid* and she determined that the time for her disguise was over.

<I think you should tell me about who hired them for their last job.> Tanis's tone brooked no discussion.

"Their what? Why would you need to know that?" Adrienne asked, shock rippling—literally—across her face.

<Because they attacked the Intrepid, *and I want to find out who hired them.>*

"You're TSF?" Adrienne asked. "I have to admit, that's a pretty extreme cover."

"Thank you." Tanis allowed the flowmetal to form a mouth since her cover was no longer necessary. Besides, her voice could be very menacing. "You're going to tell me everything you know about their job to attack the *Intrepid,* and you're going to do it with a song in your heart."

"You don't think I haven't…" Adrienne's smug expression drooped into surprise. "You've got a suppression field!"

"Well, it wouldn't do for you to call in whatever thugs you have on hand to stop our little conversation. I don't think we need for this to get unpleasant, but I won't really mind if it does."

Adrienne sat silently for a moment, and then in a flash, her entire body moved toward the far wall. Tanis realized there must be some sort of open vent that the woman could fit through. Reacting on instinct, Tanis pulsed her hover system and leapt into the air, coming down on Adrienne, the needlepoints at the ends of her legs piercing what would be a normal person's calves.

Adrienne shrieked, twisting in pain, and Tanis spat a glob of flowmetal on her face, where it flowed into Adrienne's mouth, swelling to block out further noise.

"Easy, now." Tanis's tone carried no small amount of menace. "This can get a lot worse if you don't cooperate."

The look Adrienne shot at Tanis said it all; she wasn't willingly going to give up the person who had hired the merc crew. Whoever it was, Tanis was certain it must be a big player. Most of the time, an agent like this wouldn't hold back after being skewered.

<She's going to take some more work to break,> Angela commented. <Her body is her pride and joy; I think your route will be through that.>

Tanis re-established a direct Link to Adrienne. "I'm not afraid to slice and dice you, you know. All I want is a name. Who did the hiring for the crew that hit the *Intrepid*?"

<There's no way I'm telling you. He's not the sort of guy that's really forgiving of people that leak his activities.> Adrienne was scared, but she was obviously more afraid of whoever she had dealt with.

"No problem." Tanis exuded calm. "We'll just go the standard route, making you more scared of me. You see, I'm currently a little outside the scope of my assigned duties, if you get my meaning. Not a lot of people know where I am, and even if anyone does link my whereabouts to the remains of your mutilated—but not dead—body, they'll not get upset. Not only am I going to hurt you until you give me a name, but I'll leave you alive for whoever you're so afraid of, as well."

Tanis altered the state of the plas on her arms to allow motion at the joints and reached up to her head. There, she extruded a thin rod of metal. She took it into her hand, where it formed a gleaming blade—which she lowered to Adrienne's left leg.

Adrienne's face slipped into an expression of fear. "Who…who are you?"

"Oh, I forgot to mention. You may have heard of me. The media called me 'The Butcher of Toro'."

<About time I get to make that work for me.>

<I think it actually always works for you,> Angela replied.

<Tell that to the color of my oak leaves.>

She began slicing into Adrienne's leg, through the skin—which appeared to be almost like neoprene in composition. Adrienne's eyes bulged in pain and her arms flailed, pounding the deck on either side of her. Tanis felt resistance as the blade met the cartilage that served as bone. She grimaced inwardly at the feel of it.

<OK! I'll tell you.> Adrienne's communication was laced with panic and fear. *<The name was Trent…he didn't use any other. I checked his creds, and he's known as a broker for some big interests; I don't know anything else. Here are all of the account codes for the credit transfer.>*

A rush of numbers and data memory blocks flowed into Tanis's mind, where she passed them off to Angela.

"Excellent." Tanis slid the blade out of Adrienne's leg. A panel on her torso slid open and she pulled out a medpatch, which she slapped on the wound none too gently. "The nano in here will hold you together long enough to get to a medic." Tanis was about to extrude more flowmetal to bind her captive when the door crashed open and a terrifying figure stood in the entrance.

True to the strangeness of the locale, the muscle was unconventional. It was a woman; though that was evidenced only by the stylized breasts on the gleaming black torso. All of the woman's limbs were gleaming black, as well. They were also all very thin, nearly emaciated—a look that was offset by the woman's head, which was a large ovoid devoid of any features.

"Hurting Adrienne was a mistake." The voice emanating from the woman's featureless head was soft and sultry, a rather odd combination considering the delivery.

"Possibly," Tanis agreed. "But it was a calculated mistake; does that make it any better?"

The figure raised its hands, and Tanis realized they weren't hands at all, but merely the ends of the gun barrels. *Handy…and disturbing.*

<No pun intended, I hope.>

Tanis dove to the side, or, more accurately, cantered to the side, as the guard fired flechette rounds at her. The initial shots missed, but then a few hit Tanis; some ricocheted off her chest, a few struck solidly enough to crack the plas covering her body.

Tanis angled forward, pulsed her hover system to its maximum, and balled her hands into hard plas fists. She smashed into her bizarre adversary, and they flew through the opening into the bulkhead beyond with enough energy to lodge the woman's head in the wall. Not waiting to see how long it took the freakish enforcer to extricate herself, Tanis sped down the hall at top speed. She burst into the bar area and wove past the sinuous dancers and the human furniture.

Outside the bar, she made a quick course adjustment to avoid colliding with several hovers that floated by. She raced behind one, and angled herself to float horizontally alongside it. The man driving the hover cast her a strange look, but didn't say anything. No point in getting involved in other people's issues on Cruithne.

Angela deployed nanoprobes, and they watched the black-skinned woman emerge from the bar and scan the traffic outside. She moved into the throng and started making her way in the direction Tanis had gone. Most likely she had access to external cameras that had let her know which way to go. Tanis slipped ahead of her cover, and raced through the crowd, still horizontal and, hopefully, out of sight. Her earlier wanderings proved beneficial as she made use of several establishments and predictable throngs to mask her escape. Moving through a maze of levels and across the main hub of the station, she worked her way toward her departure craft.

The original exit plan for leaving Cruithne wasn't so precipitous as reality dictated; however, the times on the departure clearance requests displayed submission times only minutes after their arrival on the station. It was almost as though Angela knew her. Less than an hour after the confrontation in Adrienne's dressing room, Tanis was pulling away from Cruithne and heading back toward Mars.

Trent. Not surprising; it just added fuel to the reaction when it came to hunting him down. The real key now was to see if the information would help her trace who was paying Trent's salary.

DRAW THE NET

STELLAR DATE: 3227189 / 08.24.4123 (Adjusted Gregorian)
LOCATION: GSS *Intrepid*, Mars Outer Shipyards (MOS)
REGION: Mars Protectorate, Sol Space Federation

Tanis eased into the chair at the head of the SOC's conference table. Her leg muscles were still sore after being pulled out and replaced; high heels adorned her feet to ease her down after having her feet en pointe for days. She was more than looking forward to getting back into regulation boots in a day or so.

The flowmetal still covered her head, but she had gotten an additive to change it to her skin's color and texture. In a few days she would have it removed, but first she needed to debrief her people and be brought up to speed.

"That was some crazy jaunt you went on." Evans' voice held a hint of reproach. "And that getup you went in. I don't know how you stood it, barely being able to move for days."

"It really wasn't that hard." Tanis shrugged. "Once I was on my way, I was pretty much committed to seeing it through."

Everyone else filed in as they spoke. Once they found their seats, Tanis called up the data she had retrieved on the table's holo.

"So, all roads lead to Trent right now. He's the guy who did the nuke job, and the guy who hired the mercs. We haven't worked out who he's taking orders from, but it has to be someone with deep pockets."

"It seems weird, sir," Ouri said. "Why would they have those mercs ready to disrupt the VIP event if the nuke was supposed to have gone off? If it had, we certainly wouldn't have been throwing any parties."

"Don't forget," Lieutenant Amy Lee said, "the ball was

supposed to happen four days earlier, but was postponed because one of the transports from Venus was delayed. They must have had the mercs on standby, or called them back in after the nuke failed."

"Right you are." Tanis reached up to run her hand through her hair and was reminded that she currently didn't have any. "Damn cover..." she muttered.

"It's a good look for you, Major." Evans grinned, a mischievous twinkle in his eye. "Gonna get your skin back?"

Tanis regarded him for a moment, tempted to spit a glob of metal over his mouth. She decided not to, but only because it abused and undermined her authority. It was still a close call.

"Yeah, I'm trying to get the procedure scheduled for tomorrow. I know I really can't feel it, but I swear this stuff itches like mad."

"So what's our next move?" Terry Chang asked, steering the conversation back to the topic at hand.

"Well, we need to figure out who Trent works for. Hopefully some of this data" —Tanis gestured to the holo— "will help us out. That's going to be you and you." She gestured to Terry and Ouri. "You've got the lab AI, and feel free to ask Angela for help as well; we've got to figure this thing out before we get hit again."

Everyone regarded her seriously and nodded.

"I also noticed in your reports that there have been several anomalies lately." Tanis brought up the pertinent data.

Ouri nodded. "We've had little bits of sabotage on some inbound shipments; we've traced most of it back to various anti-colonist folks. Stuff from Earth is especially prone to being tampered with. The effects have been minor, but the things that seem to be happening *after* cargo gets checked in are what's upsetting me."

Tanis had not read the reports in detail, and signaled for Ouri to summarize as she scanned them.

"Well, we had one instance of some lithium being 'misplaced'. It was put in a cargo pod when it was due for engineering. That was relatively benign. We've had some other instances of equipment that checked out fine upon arrival, but was broken when the time came to use it. As much as I hate to say it, I think we have someone inside of our security curtain."

"I'll spend some time looking over various logs, but you folks know what to do there—see who was on, who was around, that sort of thing. Also, it's possible that someone is managing to use someone else's access. Check and see if there is anyone that seems to be in certain areas without going through any surrounding checkpoints."

Ouri nodded. "Good call. I wasn't going to do that, since I didn't think anyone could penetrate the exterior with fake credentials, but you're right; once in, they could get to more benign areas with less overview."

"Well, folks, you've been doing good work; I'll leave you to continue it." Tanis rose. "I've got to go face the firing squad now."

"Otherwise known as Admiral Sanderson?" Evans asked.

"So he found out, did he?" Ouri asked.

Tanis grimaced. "He got back from Mars early and tried to find me for a progress report meeting. Apparently he wasn't pleased that my progress had me elsewhere."

RELATIONSHIPS

STELLAR DATE: 3227211/ 09.15.4123 (Adjusted Gregorian)
LOCATION: GSS *Intrepid*, Mars Outer Shipyards (MOS)
REGION: Mars Protectorate, Sol Space Federation

Tanis and Commander Evans were relaxing in the officer's mess, enjoying a bit of time away from the SOC, and a few of the perks of rank. Tanis had to admit that she was enjoying Evans' company quite a bit of late. She had even privately admitted to herself that if they weren't both military, she would consider pursuing him—maybe it would be possible after they got underway and were no longer officially in the military. In the meantime, she would take what time in his easygoing company she could.

"So how are things looking out there?" Tanis asked before taking a bite of her sandwich.

"Tidy as you could dream. Not a single ship is deviating a millimeter from its plotted course." Evans leaned back in his chair and took a long drink from the cup of coffee in front of him.

"Those rumors of 'Trigger-happy Joe' I spread about must be doing their work." Tanis grinned around her mouthful of food.

"Ugh...were you raised in a barn?"

"Sewer, actually."

"Really?" Evans' expression was a cross between shock and curiosity.

Tanis nearly choked as she laughed. "Now that was a funny look...of course not," she said when she was finally able to breathe.

Evans grinned sheepishly. "You have an amazing poker face. Remind me never to bet against you."

"You're in luck, Commander; I'm not a betting woman."

"You've been here over a month; eventually you could just call me 'Joseph'."

Tanis's face grew steely; not from the flowmetal—that had been removed, and her natural features were back in place. "Now, Commander. I don't think that would be appropriate. It's imperative that we keep our relationship strictly professional."

"I...er...I didn't mean that, sir," Evans said.

Tanis gave him a dead serious look for a long moment before breaking into a wide grin.

"Damn!" Evans shouted. "That's just cruel.... You took a decade off my life."

Tanis chuckled. "Don't worry, Joseph, you can get it back in regen."

"There. Theatrics aside, that wasn't so hard, was it...Tanis."

"You're mighty forward for being so jumpy." Tanis smiled.

"I must have a split personality," Joseph replied. "But keep that on the QT, I don't want to lose my pilot's credentials."

"No fear of that; you've got things in such good shape, I'd let it slide even if it were true. Your wings are top notch."

"Well, with the number of people applying for this colony, we've got top people in pretty much every profession on tap."

"It certainly is handy."

"So...anything of interest happening, dock-side? Bombs, kidnappings, rumors of dire plots?"

"Unfortunately it's been quiet as a mouse."

"How's that unfortunate?" Joseph asked.

"See, that's why you'll never be a real intel officer. With what those guys were willing to do up to this point, you can bet they haven't given up yet."

"Or maybe I'm smart enough to know that if I make everyone *think* I don't have an eye for this stuff, I'll still get to fly a fighter from time to time."

Tanis pondered that. "You could have a valid argument."

"Hah! I knew you secretly wanted to be a pilot." Joseph grinned.

"That's where you're wrong; I'm actually certified to fly R1 through R17 spacecraft."

Joseph's face showed his appreciation. "Is there anything you can't do?"

"Stand-up comedy. I tried once and totally bombed." She was once again expressionless.

He chuckled. "I don't know about that, you have pretty decent timing."

"Yeah, but if you think I'm totally infallible, you'll expect perfection all the time." She took another long draught of her coffee—good strong stuff. "On a slightly more serious note, I do have to meet with the captain and admiral. The MOS stationmaster is making noise and filing some annoying requests with the courts. We've got to head him off at the pass before he undoes all of our security enhancements."

Joseph gestured magnanimously. "Go ye forth and meet with your betters."

Tanis stuck her tongue out at him as she rose and left the room.

The bridge wasn't far from the mess; only a half-kilometer up the length of the ship, plus three decks. A tube and a maglev train had her debarking at the command deck's main hall. Walking past the corridors leading to various offices, and the desks of the flunkies who jealously guarded access to those offices, she entered the bridge's foyer. What she saw startled her quite a bit.

Where a couple of couches and chairs used to be was now a tall, white woman surrounded by an array of holo interfaces. Taking a second look, Tanis realized this woman seemed to be merged with the ship somehow. Her hands were racing over the interfaces, and thick strands of what couldn't possibly be hair waved slowly around her head as she concentrated on the displays around her.

As she approached, the woman looked up, and Tanis found herself staring at shockingly brilliant blue eyes—a stark contrast to the sea of white that was the woman and her instruments.

"Major Tanis Richards. So glad to finally meet you; I'm Amanda." The woman extended a hand, which Tanis shook— the other still racing over the holo interfaces.

"I'm...pleased to meet you," Tanis said, regaining her composure and accessing security logs, trying to determine how a person such as this could make it onto the ship without her knowing about it. "Though I must say I am unsure of who you are."

"What? Other than Amanda?" Her laugh was cheerful and light; something that Tanis found difficult to harmonize with her clearly cybernetic exterior.

"Sorry, I mean what you're doing...what your job is. Wait...Amanda. Isn't that what the ship's AI has been calling itself lately?"

"Major, that hasn't been the ship's AI—that has been me."

"But I've been contacting the ship, how is it that I am getting you?"

"It's something the Reddings had been working at for a while. The *Intrepid* is too vast an AI to easily communicate with humans. I'm effectively the ship's avatar."

"So you're partially the ship?" Tanis asked.

<*You can be so dense,*> Angela said. <*And to be honest I can't believe you thought the ship was 'Amanda'. What she is to the ship is somewhat like what I am to you. She resides in the* Intrepid's *mind like I reside in yours, except the connection is even stronger with them.*>

"Yes," Amanda said. "That is rather accurate."

"So you're just going to be...installed here for the whole trip?" Tanis asked.

"Oh, of course not." The silvery laugh sounded again. "That would be fairly taxing. No, there is another woman like me being prepared—Priscilla. I met her the other day. We'll be doing a ninety-day, on/off rotation. The Reddings are concerned that without the time off, it will be hard for our minds to remain…well, normal."

"This must be quite the unique situation. I can't say I've ever heard of anything like it before." Tanis felt like her eyebrows were in her hairline.

"That's because there hasn't been anything like it before," Amanda responded. "Bob is an incredibly advanced intelligence…"

"Bob?" Tanis interjected.

"That's what I call the *Intrepid*'s AI—mainly because I couldn't refer to him by such a bland and rather asexual term. He's most certainly male, and 'Bob' fits him nicely."

"Never thought of him as a 'Bob'." Tanis said.

<You would if you knew him,> Angela commented.

"So I guess we'll be talking a lot. I talk to, or thought I was talking to, the ship a lot." Something about Amanda was making her a bit uneasy…not surprising, really. The idea of someone being melded with the ship in this way was rather surreal.

Amanda nodded. "Pretty much everything going to the *Intrepid* from the human side goes through me. Even a lot of AI use me, since Bob is far more advanced than any of them. Not that he's a snob, but they're really quite beneath him."

"He's really that high grade?" Tanis asked. "I mean the AIs that run Mars 1, or the Callisto rings, for that matter, must be far more advanced."

"The plural is the key there," Amanda said. "Hundreds of AIs run those rings. Bob is just one guy, keeping an eye on the whole show. It was partly out of need that the Reddings made him so advanced, and partly—I'm convinced—that they simply couldn't stop themselves from doing so, once they realized it could be done. It would be like if you realized you could raise all children so they could read at six weeks. Wouldn't you do it? Wouldn't it be a crime not to?"

Tanis absorbed that. "Well, I can't speak for the children part of things, since I've never thought of having any — but I suppose I can relate to the desire to improve."

"You really should be going, by the way," Amanda said.

"Damn, you're right; they'll be waiting for me by now."

"Good luck." Amanda flashed a winning, even if rather plastic-looking, smile. "For what it's worth, I think Sanderson likes you."

Tanis shook her head as she walked away. He'd never given *her* any reason to think that.

TARGET

STELLAR DATE: 3227212 / 09.16.4123 (Adjusted Gregorian)
LOCATION: Mars Outer Shipyards (MOS)
REGION: Mars Protectorate, Sol Space Federation

Tanis stepped off the maglev train and into the main transfer terminal outside of the MOS administration block. In the middle of the station, a series of holo kiosks featuring various figures from Marsian history were directing visitors and answering questions. Tanis skirted them and walked down the main corridor and up a short flight of stairs to the offices of the stationmaster.

While the block was far from rundown, it was apparent that the MOS was past its prime. Its near thousand-year history showed in mixed architecture and designs, as well as scuffed moldings and worn surfaces.

When the Mars Outer Shipyards were built nearly a thousand years earlier, much of the advanced technology that went into assembling interstellar ships still came from Earth. However, over the years, industry and commerce shifted to the point where Mars was the technological center of InnerSol. Because the need to dock larger cargo ships diminished and more equipment was manufactured on Mars 1, it became more economical to build ships closer to the ring at the Mars Inner Shipyards.

Over recent centuries, another shift had occurred. Callisto had risen to become the most prominent and advanced human habitat, and much of the latest tech was once again being shipped in. While the Mars Inner Shipyards were still the busier of the two shipyards, the MOS's capability of docking hundreds of vessels made it ideal to handle many of the shipments that would be lowered via the elevator system to Mars 1 or the MIS.

The change was evolving the MOS from a shipyard into a commercial hub.

"All that pesky progress..." Tanis muttered to herself.

Ahead, in a lavish outer office that was definitely much newer than the rest of the administration section, sat Stationmaster Stevens' assistant. He didn't look up as Tanis approached, but spoke as soon as she was in earshot.

"Major, Mr. Stevens is running late. He'll be here any moment; please have a seat."

Tanis shrugged and took a seat, ignoring the flickering plasines beside her. They were all packed with election coverage from the Martian surface. It was horribly boring stuff, what with the race being between only two candidates—neither of them striking Tanis as being all that notable.

With one eye on her surroundings, Tanis worked through some of the streams of issues that needed her attention: follow up on a token for a dangerous shipment clearing security, review the inbound Force Recon Marine platoon coming to the *Intrepid*, and approve the transfer of a few security checkpoint violators to MSF. The usual. For all the potential excitement of running security on the largest colony ship ever, very little had been in evidence lately. Something she was certain that Stationmaster Stevens was going to emphasize heavily.

After several minutes of administrative catch-up, she noticed the assistant quirk his left eyebrow; his tell that he was getting a message. Sure enough, Stevens was ready for her and, with an imperious air, the assistant waved her through.

Stevens' office definitely displayed the fruits of the shipping upswing on MOS. Over half of the furniture was made of wood—the most common excess of mid-level administrators. By the visibility of a few nicks and dings, Tanis gauged the wood to be soft, perhaps poplar or pine, though it was covered in a dark stain. Various third classical era sculptures decorated most of the flat surfaces. The effect was really more of a confused antique shop than an administrator's office.

Stevens was sitting behind his desk, and rose to shake Tanis's hand. He was a lanky man moving into his second century, according to the records. It especially showed in the thinness of his skin—something that heralded the need for another regen.

"Hello, Stationmaster. What warrants the need for a personal visit?" Tanis asked.

"Major." Stevens inclined his head as he shook her hand. "I felt that a personal meeting would allow me to better communicate my concerns to you." He indicated she should take a seat, and Tanis did so as he eased back into his large chair.

He appeared to be gathering his thoughts, and Tanis suppressed both a wry look and a sarcastic remark about Stevens' general ability to communicate. "I wasn't aware of any pressing security concerns; is there something I'm not aware of?"

Stevens quirked an eyebrow. "I strongly doubt there is anything occurring on the MOS that you are not aware of, Major. However, I challenge you to list any one thing that is a notable security issue."

Tanis couldn't help grinning. "What about that genetic contraband that came through TrenCorp's warehouse yesterday?"

"Sorry." Stevens didn't look amused. "I meant security issues that are remotely your concern."

"Can we not get into this discussion again?" asked Tanis. "I make comments about the *Intrepid*'s history and the breaches that have affected it, you say that those issues are resolved; I say they were resolved by me and my measures. If that's all I came down here for, then I'll be going." Tanis made to rise.

"Sit," Stevens said wearily. Tanis lowered back into the chair. "No, I do not wish to rehash those conversations. This morning the Marsian Security Council passed a resolution stating that the TSF has overstepped its bounds by seizing the broad levels of control they have here on MOS. The resolution states that only dock A9 and C3 at which the *Intrepid* is berthed may be under their control, and all access to MOS security networks level C1 and higher will be restricted."

Tanis leaned back and took a deep breath. "I heard about that." She paused, watching a slow smile spread across Stevens' face. "I wish you'd mentioned that was what this was about; we could have done this remotely."

"What do you mean?" Stevens looked like his moment of triumph was being stolen from him.

"I already knew about the MSC's decision, is all," Tanis said simply.

Stevens' shoulders slumped. "I take it you've already circumvented it…"

"No, even I can't work that fast." Tanis couldn't help but grin. "However, I did get an injunction placed against it pending a Federal SolCourt appeal. The appeal is scheduled for seven weeks from now. I've forwarded you the date and location."

Stevens sighed. "I can see why they brought you on."

"It's what they pay me for." Tanis rose. "If there's nothing else?"

There was nothing else, and she left Stevens' office with a small smile on her lips.

<Lucky that judge owed you a favor,> Angela said.

<Too true, though I imagine Terrance could have pulled a string or two if he had to. However, this way I look a bit better.>

<You're a bit too concerned with what Terrance thinks of you.>

Tanis thought perhaps she was, but wasn't going to admit it. <They brought me on board to take care of security. If I have to bring legal proceedings against the entire planet Mars, I will. That's just part of the job.> Angela sighed, but didn't respond—all too aware that Tanis was just being pretentious.

Ahead, Tanis saw a problem at the maglev station. It appeared a superconductor had failed, and the train had skewed off the track. People were moving through the side passageways, checking their Links for the best way to get where they needed to go. Tanis did the same, and saw that most of the displaced traffic was going up two levels to an alternative line that ran laterally through the station. However, the car frequency was lower, and it would be backed up in no time.

She found a lift running down thirty-six levels to a large lateral maglev almost directly below this one. It would get her back to the *Intrepid* without too much delay.

The lift was only several hundred yards inward, down a lightly traveled hall, through which she strode with minimal attention to her surroundings. She monitored the MOS Sec net as she walked, checking to see if Stevens was putting out any notices to his staff. From there, the lift took her down to level S20A in less than half a minute, and Tanis stepped out, still focused on monitoring the MOS security chatter.

Almost immediately, rough hands seized her and pulled her off her feet. By instinct, Tanis slowed her perception and took stock of her surroundings. More than two hands grasped her — a pair of attackers, each holding a shoulder and a wrist. Angela deployed nano and Tanis used the data to map out a series of attacks.

She wrenched her right shoulder forward, pulling it from the grip it was caught in. The motion hurt her wrist, but that didn't stop her from delivering a reverse kick to the solar plexus of the man to her right. The pain in her wrist subsided as he let go, gasping for breath. Her right side free, Tanis swung her arm around to strike at the other man's neck. With quick reflexes, he blocked it. However, the movement allowed her to slip from his grip as well.

Tanis completed the spin and saw the first man gasping for breath out of the corner of her eye as she drew her sidearm and aimed it at the second man's head.

He was just as quick on the draw, and they found themselves staring down the barrels of each other's weapons.

"I'm going to ask you only once to lower your weapon," Tanis said.

"Not likely," the man replied. "There's a hefty price on your head, and we intend to collect."

Tanis turned her body to the side, presenting a smaller target, and shot the man in between his eyes before he could react. "I said I'd only tell you once." She turned to the first attacker, who had finally managed to catch his breath. "I'd bet good money you have a weapon or two on you. Hand them over slowly, or I'll spray you all over the bulkhead."

The man muttered a curse as he slowly drew a handgun out of his waistband and handed it carefully to Tanis. "You may have gotten us, but there'll be more. There's so much money on your head that people are lining up to take you out."

"I guess they better fill out their expense reports in advance." Tanis didn't let her weapon waver a millimeter. "Because a few people have expressed similar sentiments in the past, and as you can see, I'm still here."

He dropped two guns on the deck and she stood with her weapon on him for several minutes, not speaking, until a TSF unit showed up and took the man into custody. Leading them was Joseph.

"Commander, I have to admit I'm surprised to see you here."

"I was actually taking a maglev to admin; they screwed up my flight plan filings again, and I was going to ream out the person responsible in…well…person. Anyway, the main route is backed up, so I used the lateral on this level. I picked up your message on the *Intrepid*'s security net; met these boys en route."

Tanis nodded and looked to the TSF Regulars. "Corporal. Take this man into custody. I haven't had a chance to check him over thoroughly. I want him detained in the security center on A9.2. Take these leftovers with you." She gestured to the body on the deck.

"Sir." The corporal saluted, and two of the men with him began doing a weapons scan on the man. The third strapped an antimag bar to the dead man and activated it. The corpse lifted off the ground and, once the weapons check was complete, they took the prisoner and body away.

REFINEMENT

STELLAR DATE: 3227213 / 09.17.4123 (Adjusted Gregorian)
LOCATION: GSS *Intrepid*, Mars Outer Shipyards (MOS)
REGION: Mars Protectorate, Sol Space Federation

"You're going to need to take an escort with you from now on," Admiral Sanderson said after Tanis reported the attack.

"As much as I hate the notion, I agree." Tanis nodded. "In fact, all senior and key personnel should have an escort. It would be far worse if Abby or Earnest was killed than me."

"They'd have to leave the ship first for that to happen." Terrance laughed.

Sanderson grunted his assent. "On the upside, this will probably help out in getting that moronic resolution the Marsian legislature passed overturned."

Tanis laughed. "Stevens sent me a formal apology for the security breach, though there were undertones in his message suggesting he thinks I set it up. He's probably cursing his heart out in that tacky office of his. As far as security, we'll use Forsythe's MCSF platoon for security details, a fireteam for each VIP, and keep Grenwald's men for tactical responses.

"Are you certain that won't stretch our resources too thin?" Terrance asked. He had come up from Mars to check on the status of several key milestones in the engine tests, and invited himself to the meeting.

"I've got more TSF Regulars being called in for our normal security duties. Lieutenant Ouri now has six companies under her, which is causing some issues, as those companies are obviously all run by commanders. GSS first lieutenants are close to the rank of TSF commanders, but it's starting to cause some issues. I haven't had to back up her orders yet—a testament to her tenacity—but she is spending more time making sure they aren't doing things their way than I'd like. She's due for a promotion shortly, and I'd like to push it through."

Sanderson nodded. "No reason not to. She's colony, so it's not like we're messing up someone's organization. Send me the appropriate files and I'll see that it happens with all due haste."

"I don't know that I'll need one of your teams," Terrance said. "I've got my own private forces that are second to none."

"That you do, sir," Tanis replied. "And when you're on the MOS they'll be augmented by one of the Marine fireteams. Your guys may be good, but they don't have the resources we do, or the ability to legally start shooting holes in whatever gets in their way."

Terrance wore his dangerous smile again. "I see your point, Major."

Captain Andrews brought the discussion back on track. "Though I have no issues with added security, I would prefer to see the threat removed, rather than abated. Have we made any progress in tracking down who is behind all of this?"

Tanis hadn't seen much of the captain over the last few weeks, but the signs of his efficiency and enthusiasm for the project were everywhere. She could always tell the quality of a captain by his ship, and Andrews was top notch.

"We've got a 94.7 percent probability that it is a Jovian concern backing these actions. From the looks of it, two of the attacks that happened before I arrived were actually anti-terraforming groups. Once we excluded all data pertaining to those incidents, we were able to hone in on a few key banks on Callisto and Titan. A large number of shell corporations and even extra-solar interests were in-between, but we navigated past them. Those banks only deal with the top tier of corporations in Jovian space. We're definitely looking at an industrial opponent."

"I suppose that makes sense," Terrance said. "They would definitely need big money to pull off what they've done so far.

And there are several companies in Jove's sphere that would like to take me down a notch."

"Three hundred and ninety-two, from what I can determine." Tanis smiled. "Though only two hundred and seven use those banks."

"Ouch…I didn't realize it was quite that high. I wonder what the solar total is."

"Seven hundred and four," Tanis supplied.

Terrance laughed ruefully. "Wasn't wondering that much."

"Sorry, sir. I'm told I tend to be a bit too literal sometimes."

"So do you have any top suspects?" Captain Andrews asked, fingering his silver hair.

"A few, sir." She fed a stream of data into the conference room's net, and a list of companies and their particulars rose up over the table.

"First off we have Barum, Inc. They manufacture ES components and were in a very large bidding war to supply the *Intrepid*—mainly the components for the ramscoop. They lost the deal; the company, which was already in a downward spiral, went down further. One of the owners has made personal threats against you, Terrance. They recently managed to pull themselves out of the toilet, and now have the capital to carry out what we've come up against. They've also had several other dealings with your companies that have left them…well…soured."

"I can see how they wouldn't be my biggest fans." Terrance nodded as he looked over the data. "I didn't think they were that far along on their recovery, though."

"They recently had a very large sum come back from Tau Ceti; either after being laundered, or possibly as a return on an investment. Their corporate statements for that period aren't yet public, and we're having to tread carefully in 'accessing' records in Jovian space—what with the latest flare-up in the federal government."

Captain Andrews nodded. "Your caution is wise. I can see how money from Tau Ceti would move them up your list."

"Aye, sir. We're looking into their activities quite carefully. We've also got a few other Jovian interests, but none that match up quite so well: the Arnell, Stellar Dynamics, Neutron Cartwright, and Mallar Isotopes." As she listed off each one, corporate information rose above the table, coupled with the data points that potentially linked them to the attacks, or the funding thereof.

"There is also, of course, the STR consortium," Tanis added. "They don't have any particular reason to dislike you, sir, but they are building the GSS *Dakota,* and we all know how much they are frothing at the mouth to get the New Eden colony. Especially after the latest data the FGT has sent back."

"Can't say I blame them." Terrance nodded his agreement.

"Right now we're following up on all of those leads and should know more for our next briefing."

"Very good, Major." Admiral Sanderson nodded. "You're dismissed."

Tanis rose and saluted the men before she left the conference room.

"Quite the laundry list of suspects." Captain Andrews steepled his fingers as Tanis walked to the exit. "Though considering all of the possibilities, it is a fairly succinct tally."

"Well, I hope we find out who is behind this sooner than later. With those critical engine tests coming up, I have enough on my mind," Terrance said.

INTERLUDE
STELLAR DATE: 3227213 / 09.17.4123 (Adjusted Gregorian)
LOCATION: Stellar Comm Hub #129.A.236.B.945.C-294

<What on earth were you thinking?> Trent said. <MOS was going to get control of their docks back. That would make our operation here much easier!>

<First, I don't appreciate your tone, Trent. Second, it would have only gained us short-term access. After the next breach, they would have tightened up security again. Getting rid of Richards is key.>

<But opening the floodgates to mercs and bounty hunters? You had to know they'd bungle it.>

<So far they have done no worse than you. If you want to prove yourself, perhaps this will shame you into actually doing something constructive about the problem.>

LAKE CABIN

STELLAR DATE: 3227216 / 09.20.4123 (Adjusted Gregorian)
LOCATION: GSS *Intrepid*, Mars Outer Shipyards (MOS)
REGION: Mars Protectorate, Sol Space Federation

Tanis was wrapping up some administrative logs before the end of the second shift when Ouri poked her head into her office.

"Evening, Major."

Tanis looked up at the commander. The last week or so had seen a change in Ouri. Her commander's bars had given her an increased sense of authority, and her job performance had gone from great to excellent. The added clarity to the chain of command was also improving the efficiency of the units under her; as a result, the entire security organization was vastly improved.

The best part of all was the visible improvement in Ouri's character. Tanis wasn't certain if it was the smaller gap in rank between the two of them, or the lower stress level from having a smooth-running operation, but the end result was a much more personable subordinate.

"Commander, good to see you. How are things?"

Ouri smiled and Tanis returned it in kind. "Quite well; I've got all the reports filed and up to date."

"I never worry that you won't," Tanis said.

"So, I was wondering if you'd want to come down to my cabin for dinner."

"What? I'm being invited to one of the infamous Ouri cookouts I've heard so much about?"

"Well, sir, I would have invited you before, but a lot of enlisted and junior officers come down. I didn't think you'd really want to mingle—separation of rank, and all that."

"Rules and regs; I wouldn't want anyone thinking they're all chummy with me, and that I'll let things slide," Tanis replied with a grin.

Ouri chuckled. "I think you have absolutely nothing to worry about on that front."

"So what warrants the invite now?" Tanis asked, quirking an eyebrow.

"Well, sir, now that I've also moved up the chain, it doesn't seem quite right to be spending too much time with the people under me; at least in the smaller gatherings. I've just invited officers, or civilian department heads from around the ship. I thought maybe you'd like to come. Mostly it's people from here at the SOC."

Tanis looked down at the plas on her desk and considered all of the work she had to do, but decided that the irony of going to a log cabin on a lake that happened to be inside one of the most advanced starships ever built was something she couldn't miss out on.

"Real cookout, with fire and everything?"

"Big fire, sir."

Tanis grinned. "Call me Tanis when we're off duty."

* * * * *

The cabin was just as Tanis had pictured it.

It sat at the edge of a lake; not a large one, just a kilometer across or so. A young forest was growing up around the waters. The trees had been accelerated and were perhaps ten meters in height. A slip with a canoe tied to it jutted into the water. Up a small path was a clearing with a thick lawn and, set back against the trees, a homey cabin.

"This is really your quarters?" Tanis asked.

"Yup, I go to bed here and wake up here in the morning." Ouri nodded.

"How on earth did you swing this? I mean, aren't there millions of people lining up to be on the botany side of this mission?"

"I know a guy who knows a guy." Ouri paused, a mischievous smile playing at her lips. "That and I spent over a hundred years on various terraforming ventures. I'll be co-managing the north continent's Stage 3 terraforming when we get to New Eden."

Tanis stopped, regarding Ouri with a calculating look. "I've read your file. There's no mention of any of this in it."

"Well, I have two separate registered identities. There's no link between them."

"That's...unusual." Tanis ran a hand through her hair, stopping when she realized she was doing it. If Ouri weren't being so casual about it, she would have been very suspicious.

"The short version is that I was at the wrong end of the pointy stick a few times when I was managing terraforming projects. GSS pulled me into their protective custody, and I found I really enjoyed that line of work as well. I enlisted and, well...here I am."

"So now you can kick ass *and* terraform planets." Tanis laughed. "That's quite the unusual combination."

Ouri chuckled. "It certainly wasn't what my career advisor mapped out for me."

No one else had arrived yet, and Ouri led Tanis into the small cabin. Inside was a dichotomy of clutter that matched what she now knew about Ouri's dual life.

"This is both everything and nothing like what I expected," Tanis said.

"I live to be an enigma," Ouri grinned. "Would you mind taking those two baskets out to the fire pit? I've got to change out of this uniform."

Tanis looked down at her own dress uniform and sighed. She should have stopped off at her quarters to change. After carrying out the baskets, she came back in to see Ouri running a brush through her hair. She was wearing a red and yellow sundress that looked quite stunning on her. It was always amazing how much better people looked in civilian clothing.

"You're going to get all the boys." Tanis laughed.

Ouri looked down at herself and then over at Tanis. "Sorry, I guess I didn't think you'd have anything else. You know how it is with us juniors; we figure the SOs must have been born in their uniforms."

"You realize you're a senior officer now, too." Tanis smiled.

"Damn…just when I thought I'd gotten used to it, my subconscious reminds me I haven't."

"You'll get used to it."

"I do have a few autofit dresses you could look at." Ouri led Tanis into her bedroom, and, after a few minutes, they picked out a sedate blue sleeveless dress that came down just past Tanis's knees. It snugged up to her body and she examined herself in the mirror.

<Best you've looked since you ruined that dress at the ball,> Angela commented.

After borrowing Ouri's brush, Tanis helped carry the last loads out to the fire pit—platters of meat for the night's feast.

"Real meat?" Tanis asked.

"Yup, from right here in Old Sam. First generation; we've been testing out the protocols for herbivore initialization."

"Where do you get the time for all of this?" Tanis asked as they laid condiments out on a wooden table. "I mean…I work you to the bone."

Ouri smiled as she lit the grill. "Well, I make time for the things I love. I'm pretty good at this stuff, but I also seem to be pretty good at keeping people from blowing the ship up. They're kinda interconnected."

Tanis laughed. "So they are."

"I also offload a lot of stuff onto Amy Lee." Ouri chuckled

as the grill came to life.

"God does she ever." Amy Lee came strolling down the path with Terry Chang in tow. They had several baskets full of beverages, which appeared to be mostly of the alcoholic variety. "I'd complain to her boss, but that she-devil would probably figure if I had time to complain I must have time for more work." Amy Lee grinned, but then stopped short, her face turning red as she realized whom she had just spoken to. "Uh…er…Major. I didn't recognize you out of uniform."

Tanis smiled at the second lieutenant. "We're informal here, Amy Lee. Besides, I've got a really thick skin."

"It's actually true." Joseph arrived with a few others. "I've needled her both physically and verbally to prove it—as you can see, I survived to tell the tale."

Tanis felt a small jolt of elation that Joseph had shown up. She had been hopeful, but didn't want to come right out and ask Ouri.

"Yeah, but only just barely." Tanis cast Joseph a stern look. "Amy Lee's one of the ladies, she gets special dispensation. You've about used up all of your get out of jail free cards."

Joseph put on an innocent face. "Me? I'm a paragon of cooperation and agreement. I have to be. I saw what happened to all the other men under you who didn't toe the line." He winked at Tanis as he stepped past her to put his load of bread down on the table.

Her gaze lingered on him a moment too long and he brushed against her shoulder at the same time. Tanis looked away and caught fleeting expressions of recognition on the faces of Terry and Ouri. It would appear the attraction growing between her and Joseph wasn't going unnoticed.

Their thoughts were obvious on their faces: so the major was human after all—and apparently falling for the dashing young commander. Too bad they were in the same chain of command.

Ouri began her hosting duties, greeting and introducing all

the visitors as they arrived. A few assistant heads from the SOC that Tanis knew came down the path next, as well as the division head for stage three terraforming on the colony roster. The chief New Eden 1 station engineer came a bit later; she would be the woman in charge of taking the two habitation cylinders and mounting them to a space station when the *Intrepid* reached its destination. Her escort was the head of habitat environmental systems, a large-framed man with an easy smile and the biggest moustache Tanis had ever seen in person.

"A damn fine job you've done with your neck of the woods," he said to Ouri as he surveyed the area around them. "You've turned what was little more than dirt two years ago into a very nice place indeed." He turned to Tanis and gave her a hearty clap on the shoulder. "And you're the lassie I understand we owe being in one piece."

"I'm just happy to be here."

"Believe us when we say we're happy too," said Erin, the station engineer. "You're doing a fantastic job."

"I want to get out of here as much as the next person. Just doing my part." Tanis hated all the compliments.

"Not *here* here, I hope," Ouri said with a smile as she handed out drinks.

"Only in as much as *here* is still in the Sol system." Tanis accepted the offered beverage. She looked up at the arching landscape overhead, just beginning to be draped in the shadows of dusk. "Once we get outsystem, *here* is a place I can see myself frequenting in the future."

Later in the evening, Tanis found herself sitting with Ouri and Joseph around a fire that had been made by some of the revelers for the purpose of roasting marshmallows.

"I've been looking over the proposed duty schedules, and have realized something odd." Ouri slowly rotated her marshmallow over the fire.

"Mmmm?" Tanis said around a mouthful of sticky goo.

"Well, I don't have a debarkation date for Abby and Earnest," Ouri said. "I think they're staying on."

"Huh? That can't be right. What would people like them be doing on a colony mission?" Joseph asked.

"I know," Ouri said with a nod. "That's what's so strange."

Tanis gave momentary debate over telling the truth and decided to do so. "They're trying to keep it hush-hush," she said after finally managing to swallow the three marshmallows in her mouth. She erected a security barrier around them and put a hand over her mouth to mask her lip movement. "From what I can tell, they're coming along. Even stranger, I think Terrance is coming too."

"What? Why's he coming? Doesn't he have some big multi-world corporation to look after?" Joseph asked.

"More than one." Tanis nodded. "But he's coming nonetheless. There's something afoot here, something else. Think about it. Andrews is one of the best, one of the most qualified starship captains alive. Terrance is the owner of one of the largest private corporations in history, and Earnest and Abby are two of the most important scientific minds of all time. Couple that with the fact that Admiral Sanderson is nowhere near retirement, and you have a very interesting set of circumstances."

" 'Interesting' doesn't even begin to cover how weird all of that is," Ouri agreed.

"No kidding. When you consider all of that together..." Joseph nodded.

"Even more," Tanis continued. "Why does the *Intrepid* have an AI that could manage a dozen planets—possibly the most advanced AI ever—and why are we taking over twice the personnel and equipment than any other colony ever has before?"

"You're making me nervous," Ouri said. "What do you

think it all means?"

"Damned if I know." Tanis prepared another marshmallow. "But one thing is for sure. Something very interesting is planned for New Eden. Something that someone else doesn't want to happen, and even our own benefactors don't want us to know about."

"So you're saying that we shouldn't be speculating amongst ourselves." Joseph couldn't help but cast an eye around him.

"I think we're best off not knowing what the underlying elements are here." Tanis nodded in agreement. "At least not for now. Terrance is a bit shifty, but I'd trust Captain Andrews with my life. Sanderson may be a dick, but he's a by-the-book dick who wouldn't be involved in something subversive."

"Damn, I hope you're right," Joseph said.

"When haven't I been?" Tanis smiled as she dropped the security shield and proceeded to roast her next marshmallow, signaling the end to the conversation.

The gathering lasted long into the night. Some visitors left early, but others arrived late; a few of Ouri's neighbors around the lake came by to visit as the evening progressed. It was nice; it was a hint of what their lives would be like when they arrived at New Eden.

Until then, before they could be on their way, the work of completing the ship had to be done; the schedule had to be maintained. The GSS *Dakota* was meeting all of its milestones early, and with the recent security issues, no one was feeling as confident as they had several years ago.

But tonight, for a few hours, everyone forgot those concerns; everyone pretended they had arrived at New Eden, and were living the life they had always dreamed about. Tanis wasn't sure when her dream had begun, but she knew now where it would end.

AMBUSH

STELLAR DATE: 3227223 / 09.27.4123 (Adjusted Gregorian)
LOCATION: Mars Outer Shipyards (MOS)
REGION: Mars Protectorate, Sol Space Federation

"How is it, Commander, that you seem to end up a part of my security detail so often?" Tanis asked Joseph. "Don't you have a fighter to fly or something?"

Joseph laughed his deep chuckle that Tanis found herself liking more and more every day. "I've got plenty of flyboys and flygirls now to handle that end of things. My main concern is keeping you alive so they don't force me to do your job again."

It was Tanis's turn to laugh. A more common occurrence in Joseph's company — perhaps a connection existed....

"I'm glad you have such an altruistic motivation for keeping me safe."

"I'm all altruism. So, where are we going today?" Joseph asked.

"To meet with some mercs that want to capture or kill me."

"Pardon?" Joseph nearly tripped. "Don't have enough trouble in your life as it is? Do you always have to go running toward it?"

PFC Lauder chuckled at that and earned a glare from Corporal Peters.

"It's OK." Tanis glanced at the four members of squad one/fireteam one from Forsythe's platoon — her usual security detail. "We're meeting with Lieutenant Grenwald first. He's got tactical on the situation. Besides," — she gave Joseph a playful look — "if you'd known there would be danger, would you have passed on joining me?"

Joseph coughed and stammered, "Of course not."

She explained the situation to her companions as they

boarded a maglev: some mercs had set up what they must have thought would be a great lure; after somehow taking control of a cargo ship that ran tech goods to the *Intrepid* from Ceres, they slipped some contraband into a shipment. Not enough to set off all the alarms, but enough to get Tanis down there in person.

"So then, why *are* you going down yourself?" Joseph asked. "Couldn't you have Grenwald take them without you?"

"Perhaps, but there's a possibility they may have rigged the ship to blow. I have the best AI and highest-grade nano available at the moment, so I'm the best one to run point."

A cross corridor away from the dock, they slipped through a nondescript doorway, and came face to face with Grenwald's platoon.

"Is everything in readiness, Lieutenant?" Tanis asked.

"It is, sir. We've got one/two on the dock, four remote sniping units in the ducts, and the rest of the team is ready to move in if needed. I've also got a direct line to engineering in case anything goes wrong."

"Excellent." Tanis nodded. "Commander Evans and my detail are with me. Don't shoot unless I give the word; the more live bodies, the better."

"Yes, sir."

With that, they swung back into the corridor and around the bend. Dock E3 was directly ahead, its bay doors watched by two guards who were TSF Regulars. Grenwald had briefed them via the Link, and they saluted Tanis and Joseph as they stepped onto the dock.

Dock E3 was a multilevel affair with ships docking at the highest level, and cargo moving via down-ramps to the lower storage and distribution areas. Looking up through the twisting array of chutes and gravity-powered elevators, Tanis saw four ships in interior berths.

Her overlay lit up with the people on the dock, highlighting the positions of the four Marines who were undercover as cargo handlers, working the shipments on the other vessels. Red halos surrounded the men from the suspect ship, and their cargo glowed yellow.

<Tactical overlay online,> Tanis said over the combat net. <They look surly.>

<Mercs always look surly, sir; it's a great way to identify them,> Staff Sergeant Williams grunted. <It's merc SOP.>

Tanis and Joseph stepped onto an open lift and rode it up to the level at which the ships were berthed. Ahead, the mercs posing as traders were looking annoyed as one of the MOS's cargo inspectors read off the long list of statutes they had violated.

"…and you are certainly going to be cited with failure to declare deviation of flight plan, as you were half a percentage off on each of your two final trajectory alterations. MOS will be levying a fine against you for that."

"Look, we just want to deliver our cargo and get off this tin can," said the man who appeared to be in charge. "We've got a schedule to keep, and this delay is going to cost us more money than your damn fines."

<Overacting as usual,> Williams grunted.

<Another sure indicator,> Joseph agreed. <So how we gonna run this?>

<Straight in. You **are** wearing your protective armor under your uniform, aren't you?>

<As if you didn't already know that.> Joseph's mental tone carried a grin.

The cargo inspector's AI must have notified him of their approach; he turned and gave Tanis an exasperated look. "I'm sorry to have to call you down here, Major, but as per your regulations, you are to be brought in on any event of this nature."

"Indeed I am." Tanis nodded. "So what have these fine men brought aboard your station?"

"Nothing that's any big deal," the pseudo-captain commented.

"They've brought a C9 type lubricant onto the ship."

<A lubricant is contraband?> Joseph asked.

<It's used to lubricate molecules in certain types of explosives so they accelerate faster and do more damage.>

<There really is a lube for all purposes.> The conversation was over the general combat net and PFC Lauder felt free to add her two chits.

"What receiver ordered this?" Tanis asked.

"None of yours," the inspector said. "Manifest has it destined for AR Spec, a systems assembler on the station that handles final assembly of nav controller boards for the *Intrepid*. Except this isn't what they ordered." Tanis already knew all of this, but it was best to let the little drama play out.

"So someone shipped the wrong cargo?"

"No, the seal on the container has been tampered with. This cargo was replaced; that's why I called you down."

Tanis shifted her hard stare to the merc in charge. His ID said he was Captain Sundy, but she had conflicting data. Some records did show that the man before her was Captain Sundy, but older ones had the bio of a completely different person, the hallmark of either shoddy work, or a rush job generating a fake ID.

"I expect you have full serial records on this cargo?" she asked. "I'll want to know everything about it, from the moment it was conceived of."

"Of course," the captain smiled. "If you'll step into our hold, I can bring the data up."

Grenwald gave the signal over the Link, and two of the Marines from one/two boarded a crawler headed down the length of the dock. It was on a route that would take it very close to Tanis and her team; she hoped the mercs didn't pick up on the timing.

"I don't see why that's necessary. Why don't you step onto your ship and load the information onto a plas? That way I can have it handy for my report."

"I would, ma'am, but our plas interface is down right now. I can let you Link to the ship to get the information, but that's it."

"Very well." Tanis shrugged. She motioned with her head for Joseph and one/one to follow.

<*I so do not like the looks of this,*> Joseph said privately to Tanis.

<*Look on the bright side—they're probably not planning on blowing their ship if they're on it.*>

<*The world is different for you than most people, isn't it?*>

<*You can say that again,*> Angela piped up.

<*What's that supposed to mean?*>

<*Your version of 'the bright side' and other people's really don't jibe,*> Joseph explained.

Tanis sent an image of her avatar sticking its tongue out at Joseph as they stepped over the threshold into the cargo bay of the small freighter. Even as she did so, her eyes darted up to catch the furtive motion of more than one man on an upper catwalk that circled the compartment.

She sent commands over the combat net to Argenaut and Lauder to stand on the far side of the hold and cover the catwalk. Tannon and Peters took up positions on either side of the hold's airlock.

The merc posing as Captain Sundy led Tanis and Joseph to a hard terminal, and brought up the cargo's records. She turned to the console and let it appear as though she was reading it in detail. What she was really doing was positioning her left hand—which the merc couldn't see—under her jacket on her pulse pistol.

<*Stun or wound only. I want intel from these guys,*> she sent over the combat net.

Angela deployed remote nano, which relayed multiple

views of the hold to the combat net; enabling Tanis to watch the merc captain from behind. He paused for a moment, thinking her distracted by the readout, and then slid a hand between two crates.

"I wouldn't do that, Captain Sundy." Tanis didn't turn as she addressed the captain.

"Do what?"

"Don't pull that weapon out from there. I've got mine trained on you already. Your ship is surrounded, and we're going to have to take you into custody."

The man gave an ugly laugh. "You're in error, unfortunately. We've got people on the inside; your little TSF force won't be able to help you."

"And yours won't be able to help you." Tanis fired. The shot hit him square in the chest, knocking him back, but it wasn't lethal. He'd be doing some talking later; lots of talking.

Lauder let out a cry as she raised her rifle and peppered the catwalk with pulse blasts. Argenaut was moments behind her, his laser out—the intensity set low, just enough to blister the skin if it made contact. Behind them, Peters and Tannon were firing shots back onto the dock as the mercs station-side attempted to rush them. The MOS inspector went down under a hail of projectile fire from the mercs.

The two members of one/two arrived on the crawler, and the mercs ended up caught in a heavy crossfire. Moments later, they were down. However, Angela's nano was still picking up four heat signatures on the catwalk inside the hold. Her detail, assisted by Joseph, focused all their attention on that problem.

As she scanned the combat net for the best view of the catwalk, several explosions rocked the dock outside.

<What the hell is going on?> Tanis asked.

Williams filled her in. <Looks like we underestimated them. The other ships are all merc, as well—way more organized than I would have thought. They just used some sort of missile or light artillery to

take out our sniper drones.>

<Dozens of signatures leaving the other three ships,> Sergeant Green added. *<Our men at the entrance are being forced back.>*

Tanis gave it a moment's thought. *<Have them fall back and seal the lock. We're going on a little trip.>*

<Yes, sir,> Grenwald replied.

<What about Jensen and Lang?> Williams asked, referring to the two Marines who had assisted Tanis's escort.

<Tell them to get their asses in here. Gonna get real cold on the dock in a minute or two.>

A moment later, affirmative signals showed on the combat net. Tanis could hear boots pounding on the dock and Jensen and Lang burst through the airlock.

"Seal it!" Tanis yelled. "Commander, take Peters and Tannon and secure the bridge; we'll finish off our friends above."

"Like hell you will!" a voice called down.

Using hand signals, Tanis directed the Marines to lay down suppressive fire. That done, she instructed Angela to lock down the airlock and attempt to get in contact with the ship's AI.

Tanis looked for the weapon the merc captain had been going for. It was a high-powered pulse rifle. Just what the doctor ordered. She took stock of the situation from everyone's feeds, then rolled out from behind her protective cargo and placed three well-aimed shots into the torso of a merc as he rose up from behind his cover to take aim. Three left on the catwalk.

Angela had gotten the ship's layout and fed it to the combat net. Joseph sent his thanks, and informed Tanis that he was almost at the bridge. No resistance encountered thus far.

Jensen got off a shot that nailed a merc in the head, and he toppled over the railing to the deck below. Two enemies left.

Re-examining the situation, Tanis climbed onto a crate and pulled herself up some webbing to get a new vantage point. Sure enough, just as a merc leaned over to get his gun around his cover, he came right into view. Two shots to the torso and he slumped over.

"Last man," she called out. "Care to surrender the easy way, or would you like to get beaten into submission?"

A scuffling sound echoed in the hold as a gun was tossed over the railing and the man stood up.

"Good choice, man," Lauder grinned. "With all of us gunning for you, you'd've been pulverized. And wouldn't that just mess up your pretty merc face?"

"Secure him and then dose them all. Make sure they are out for hours."

<Status,> Tanis queried Joseph.

<Bridge secure. There was one lady up here, and, though it was a mighty battle, we managed to get her fixed up.>

<Good work. We'll be there momentarily.>

"Jensen, Lang. Stay down here and keep an eye on that airlock. Lauder and Argenaut, layout is on the combat net and it shows a secondary airlock. Angela has it locked down, but go make sure someone doesn't poke a hole in it."

"Sir!" came the chorus of responses.

Tanis followed the route Joseph's team had taken up to the bridge, and queried Angela along the way.

<So, what's the story on this ship's AI? It does have an AI, right?>

Before Angela even responded, Tanis could feel her AI's anger. <They've subverted it.>

Tanis's breath caught. Subverting an AI was a capital offense in human courts, but it was far worse to AIs. Any human even remotely connected to being part of an AI subversion would never get another AI implant, and, beyond that, they would find themselves unexpectedly unable to access a variety of networks at the most inopportune times. Someone was paying these mercs very, very well for them to run that risk.

<Will you be able to help it?> Tanis asked.

<I don't know. This ship has a distributed computing system with

some decent redundancy. If they didn't damage it in too many ways, there should be a complete, intact copy in here.>

Tanis relayed the news across the combat net.

<So what's our next move?> Grenwald asked.

<Depends; how do things look out there?>

<From what our probes show, they've secured the inner airlock by moving crates in front of it. We've taken up positions by the secondary and maintenance airlocks, but they haven't breached yet. They also appear to be moving some heavy equipment toward the ship you are on. I'm guessing they intend to beat their way in.>

<Friendlies on the dock?>

<Negative, sir,> replied Williams. *<Just lots and lots of soon-to-be dead guys.>*

<Then we're going to leave this party.> Tanis signaled Joseph.

<How?> Grenwald asked while Williams chuckled.

<I forgot, you've never worked with her in combat. I think that the military officially had her middle name changed to 'Unconventional'. You're gonna blast out of there, aren't you?>

<Nail on the head, Staff Sergeant, nail on the head. Let the station know...actually, I'll let them know...it'll be fun.>

<You're one of a kind, sir,> Grenwald said.

<Shouldn't be a big deal. ES fields should snap into place pretty quick,> Joseph added.

<Keep those locks sealed till we're gone.> Tanis entered the bridge.

Joseph was at the pilot's console and was firing up the ship's reactor. Normally, when the reactor had been cold for some time, the process was carefully executed over several hours, but this wasn't a several-hours sort of situation, and he was skipping a number—or all—of the safety procedures.

<MOS docking control, I need an undock on berth four, dock E3,> Tanis called into the station traffic control.

<This is MOS docking control. I'm sorry, but we read red on the outer seal for that dock's airlock. Departure will expose the entire dock

to vacuum.>

<I'm well aware of that. The mercenaries assaulting our ship are going to be displeased with said vacuum, and that will make me happy.>

<What...?>

<Never mind, my AI informs me that they've shunted your access.>

<They what?>

"Conversation was getting redundant," Tanis muttered and killed the connection; she instructed Grenwald to keep MOS abreast of issues from his position.

<I hope all is well up there,> Lauder reported in. <Cause they're melting through the hatch, and we'll be having tea with them in no time.>

<Fall back to the midship's hatch on the catwalk, and haul our sleeping-beauties with you,> Tanis replied. <Commander Evans will give the count when we pull free. Seal that hatch when he does; the cargo bay may get breached when we break free.>

"What's the stat?" Tanis asked Joseph.

"I've released our clamps; station is still clamped on, but, frankly, I don't care. Ready to apply magnetic debarkation in 3, 2, 1. Magnetic rails active."

A violent shudder ran through the small ship as it strained to break free from the station's grapple, and an unpleasant tearing sound echoed through the hull.

"That was one nasty noise," Peters said. "But I don't think it was the sound of us getting free."

Joseph's expression was sour as he attempted to determine why the ship was still moored. "Don't you trust my driving?"

"It's not your driving; it's how well this tub can hold up to it."

"I resent that," a clear voice rang out in the bridge.

<Meet Tom, the ship's AI,> Angela said over the combat net.

"Sorry, Tom." Peters apologized. "Situational stress."

"I understand," Tom replied. "I've been having a rough few days, myself. Thanks to Angela, I'm almost feeling like myself again."

"Good to hear it. You're most familiar with this ship; what do you recommend we do to break free from dock?" Tanis asked.

"Well, my mag rails probably aren't strong enough. You'll have to use thrusters and a reverse magnetic pulse on the station's mag clamps."

"Sounds like a plan; co-ord it with Joseph," Tanis replied.

A pulse thrummed through the ship and, with a final screech and a lurch, the ship pulled free.

<You wouldn't believe the earful I'm getting from docking control,> Grenwald laughed, clearly enjoying getting the best of MOS.

<Let them know that they are going to have more reports than they know how to file. How their scan missed the fact that those other three ships must have nearly sixty people on them is unfathomable.> The thought of such raw incompetence made Tanis seethe and she took a moment to compose herself before addressing the crew.

The inner lock was just an ES shield, which was not designed to stop objects as large and determined as a ship under thrust. The shield snapped off momentarily, creating quite the storm on the dock behind them. It wasn't enough of a pressure change to kill anyone, but it wouldn't go down as a pleasant experience.

"Move us away from the MOS. Grenwald has put the call into your fighter patrols, Commander. They're scrambling Blue Wing to escort us to the *Intrepid*'s VIP dock."

"Fitting, I'd say." Joseph grinned. Something on the board caught his eye. "Damn, two of their ships are breaking free, as well. We're gonna have a race on our hands."

"Either that, or a fight," Tanis said.

"Tom, do you have any types of weapons or shielding?" Joseph asked.

"This class of ship is not equipped with any weapons, and nothing more than a frontal velocity shield."

"You owe us, Tom; tell me about the real loadout."

A sigh came over the audible speakers and the shipnet. "Very well, we have two three-inch lasers and a very light refractive shield."

"Better than a kick in the head," Tanis muttered. "Peters, have Tom hook you up with a console for weapons; Tannon, you're on ship's systems and damage control."

Tanis got two 'yes, ma'ams', and the men went to their tasks. She tapped into ship's scan and brought it up on the small holo. Their ship was pulling away from MOS on thrusters, slowly angling around the shipyard to the outer side where the *Intrepid* was docked.

"Brace!" Peters called out as a projectile impacted their ship. Reports flashed on everyone's overlays, showing the damage to the lower holds. External cameras displayed cargo spilling out into space.

<*Jansen, that looked like it was close to you. You two OK?*> Tanis called down after making sure that their lifesigns showed green.

<*Shaken, but not smushed, sir. Mind if we come up there? The more ship between us and them, the better I feel.*>

<*On the double. You too, Argenaut and Lauder. It'll be cozy, but safer for you.*>

<*Aye, sir.*>

"That wasn't very nice," Peters muttered as he worked his interface. "I've got a bead on the ship that fired that. May I take the shot?"

"Fire at will, Corporal," Tanis said. "We just need to keep these guys at bay for two more minutes. All fighters are deploying around the *Intrepid*, so the launching tubes are a bit stacked. Our escort should be here any moment, though."

Just as Tanis was finishing her statement, Joseph let out a

curse. "There's been a malfunction in the station-side tubes. Blue Wing isn't able to deploy; should I have Yellow come escort us?"

"Negative." Tanis shook her head. "That would be just the diversion I would be looking for to attack the *Intrepid*. No, we're on our own until the TSF patrol craft and fighter support arrives."

"ETA on that?" Timmins asked.

"Updating the combat net now—should be eleven minutes."

"Damn," Tannon said. "We need to do something creative, or we won't last that long."

"We could head toward the *Intrepid*, draw our merc friends into the range of the patrols there," Joseph suggested.

"I would, except I have a suspicion that there's more here than meets the eye."

On the holo before her, the two merc ships were accelerating and moving into flanking positions, while Joseph altered vector to angle away from the *Intrepid*. Another projectile hurtled from the merc ship at their starboard side, but this time Peters had the lasers ready, and melted it in flight.

"Just took a bit to get comfortable with the calibration."

"I've got the refractor shield up to full strength." Tannon seemed to be doing most of his work through the Link, his hands not touching the holo interface. "Not a lot I can do about those projectiles, though."

Tanis glanced down at the main holo. The ship's engines were at an angle where they were no longer pointed at MOS. "Hit the ion drive and give us some thrust."

"Oh, they're not gonna like that." Joseph smirked as he did as he was told.

"I'm the one who's not liking things right now," Tanis growled. "I'm going to be paying another visit to our friend the stationmaster very soon. If MOS keeps this up, they may forfeit their standing as a self-governing body and have to submit to

TSF for changeover."

"I doubt it's gone that far yet. Doesn't there have to be evidence of widespread neglect and loss of life for that?" Joseph's eyes never left his screens as he spoke, but a hint of appeasement was evident in his tone.

<I'm not the only one who thinks you overreact.>

Tanis rolled her eyes at Angela. "Yeah. I'm just venting. All the bureaucracy is starting to drive me nuts. I've seen entire planets with less of it."

"Were they really small?" Peters asked, and Lauder chuckled.

Joseph interrupted the banter. "Everyone hold on to something. High *g* thrust in twenty seconds—counter on the combat net."

The other four Marines made double time and rushed into the bridge, securing themselves to tie-downs and duty stations. The bridge net showed status green on the ion engine's nozzle extension, and on the zero mark, Joseph fired a continuous burst. The thrust pushed everyone back into their seats and the freighter pulled away from its pursuers.

Once the initial thrust was over, Tanis assigned the Marines to duty stations and monitoring tasks. It really didn't take that many people to keep the ship in line, but it was better to give them something to do.

"They're catching up; we've got several incoming missiles." Tannon shifted shielding to cover the appropriate sections of the ship.

"We're gonna have to roll." Joseph synced his pattern with Tannon and Peters' stations. "Everyone hold on to your lunch, or it's gonna get nasty in here."

The ship began to spin. Joseph also used evasive jinks to ensure the enemy had as much trouble targeting them as possible. Tanis saw the Marines all lock their armor's necks solid. Joseph seemed fine, however, sliding casually in his seat with each of the ship's movements. Tanis resorted to using the head straps in the captain's chair. It wouldn't look so good if the major spewed across the main holo projector.

"Oh, my god…" Jansen moaned. "This is worse than an orbital drop."

Tanis agreed as her stomach lurched from a sharp bank while the ship rotated against the turn. She wondered if Joseph was trying to make them sick.

"Doesn't the MOS have turrets for security issues like this?" Lauder asked.

"They do, but they seem to be having target control issues with the turrets in this area. I'm not certain if it's more sabotage, or general incompetence," Tannon replied from his station on scan.

"I'm voting for a combination. I don't want to give either group too much credit." Joseph seemed completely unruffled, his face merely showing light concentration as he banked around the skeleton of an ore freighter.

"They're, ah…not going to fire until they've worked out those targeting issues, are they?" Peters asked.

"The day the MOS security does anything decisive that doesn't involve getting in the way will be the day I get a full night's sleep," Tanis replied.

"Wow, not really helping with the warm fuzzies, here," Lang grunted, then after a pause, "uh, sir."

Tanis couldn't help but let a little smile through. Poor Marines could barely stand having a lieutenant around all the time, and here they were crammed into a tiny bridge with a commander and a major.

Joseph cleared the freighter, and Tom's voice came over the bridge's speakers. "They're attempting a remote retake of my core. Angela and I are fighting it off, but it may decrease performance of my systems."

"I'm guessing those ships have subverted AIs as well."

Joseph's voice dripped with distaste as he plotted a course along the dorsal frame of a TSF destroyer that was being refitted station north of the ore freighter. "Too bad that destroyer is powered down; our troubles would be over in one quick call."

"Could be worse—the mercs could actually be decent at shooting."

"They're not bad." Peters looked up from his console. "I've melted seven other projectiles. I'm betting they'll be switching to lasers shortly. Keep that spin up."

Joseph nodded in acknowledgement as the ship rotated, weaving through docked freighters and transport craft. A projectile missed them and impacted a luxury liner that was being overhauled, causing a rod of flame to lance out of the ship into the vacuum.

"Damn, I almost had that one," Peters said.

"Worry about us, not some liner," Tannon shot back. "They're all empty, anyway."

"That's why I'm on guns...Private." Peters glanced at his squad mate. "More shrapnel in an explosion than the original projectile; besides, O2 fires in space creep me out."

"Amen to that." Jansen was nodding while looking at a view holo. "There's something about those fires that looks totally unnatural. Or too natural; it's like they are living things."

Tanis smiled to herself. Banter, the best way to combat the fear of being blown to pieces.

"TSF update," she said out loud, "ETA on fighters is seven minutes."

"Our friends out there probably know that, too. I expect they'll start getting desperate any moment now," Joseph said.

Power usage meters shot up all around as the ship's refraction shields repelled laser beams.

"Right on time," Tanis said.

"We're at seventy percent across the board. If we weren't rotating, we'd've been holed by that salvo," Tannon reported.

"Nets ahead!" Joseph said triumphantly. "I knew I saw some out here on my last patrol."

Accessing the ship's forward cameras, Tanis saw what he was referring to. Several kilometers of storage nets showed on the holo view, all holding various components and even small sections of ships for final assembly. The working lights were off, meaning no personnel were present in the nets, but the proximity alarms were sounding on the bridge—both from the ship and the net's perimeter system.

"Can you nix that noise, Tom?" Tanis asked.

"On it, they're just responding a bit slow," Tom replied. Moments later the klaxons ceased. "There we are."

"Thanks, Tom," Joseph said. "This is going to feel worse than it really is."

With that, the commander banked the ship hard around one net, under the next, and around another. He threaded them smoothly, but their pursuers were also managing to keep pace.

"At least they're not shooting at us," Tannon said.

"Peters." Tanis glanced at the corporal. "See if you can take out a mooring mount or two. It'd make my day if we could cause a wee bit of a collision behind us."

"I like the way you think, sir." Peters targeted several of the net's mooring points. "A little mayhem here, a little mayhem there…"

"That's the spirit." Jansen grinned.

Several of the nets had been under load; their cargo bundled against them and held in place by the station's centripetal rotation. With their moorings weakened, the nets swung out wildly, and the closest of their pursuers narrowly avoided collision. Though the merc ship escaped that disaster, it clipped a piece of cargo from another net, and had to retro-brake to avoid colliding with a shuttle frame that swung out from the impact.

"One mostly down." Peters targeted more moorings and

sent cargo spinning wildly in their wake.

"You wouldn't believe the stink we're getting from MOS on this. They should really know by now that the more they aggravate me, the more paperwork I generate." Even as she spoke, Tanis was filing dozens of complaints against the station for each of the code violations and oversight failures that had allowed this scenario to occur in the first place. The bureaucrats complaining to her would soon be buried in a mountain of paperwork.

<*You're positively evil,*> Angela said.

<*Maybe a bit, though I prefer to think of myself as 'vindictive'.*>

<*You realize that's not a positive attribute,*> Angela replied dryly.

<*That depends on your profession.*>

At that moment, a clang echoed through the compartment and the bridge door slid open; two mercs hung in the frame, guns drawn.

"Cease acceleration and prepare to be boarded."

"What the fuck?" Lauder swore. "Where did you two idiots come from?"

"The places you didn't search," the first man said. "Now drop your weapons and comply."

"Are these guys serious?" Jansen asked Tanis.

"They seem like it...but I'm not really sure. Are you two serious? You are going to try to take on six Marines and two TSF officers by yourselves? You're going to die, and it'll probably be messy."

The men looked at each other and then at Tanis. Before they could respond, an impact rattled the ship and, in the midst of the collision, multiple shots peppered the mercs. Their hands slipped free of the handholds, and their lifeless bodies fell back through the opening.

"Oops, did I clip that cargo net?" Joseph asked. "Sorry about that."

Another shock ran through the ship, coupled with the screams of metal shearing. Joseph grunted. "That one wasn't me."

The second merc ship had gained ground while the commander's focus was split, and had gotten a projectile round off at close range.

"Losing our starboard engine." Tom's concerned voice sounded over the bridge speakers. "Shutting it down to avoid a runaway reaction."

"ETA on TSF fighter craft is two minutes." Tannon sounded anxious. The Marines were used to conflicts where they could take direct action to decide the outcome. This frantic flight was wearing on their nerves.

"Think they'll try to board us, or just blow us out of the sky?" Lang asked.

Another explosion rocked the ship and Lauder swore. "I guess that's our answer."

"Belay that impending doom!" Tannon grinned at the scan console. "Looks like they got the tubes cleared. Blue squadron is inbound. Say goodbye to the bad mercenaries."

Tanis brought the scan data up on the main holo and, sure enough, six fighter craft were racing over the bulk of the station. Tactical missiles fired from each ship and tore into the lead mercenary vessel. Their yield was low, but the strikes were precise. The engines went dead and the weapons signatures winked out. Scan showed a tug leave a nearby dock to catch the ship before it did more damage. Moments later, a similar scene played out with the other merc ship.

"And that" — Joseph leaned back in his seat and smiled at the main holo—"is that."

REPROACH

STELLAR DATE: 3227224 / 09.28.4123 (Adjusted Gregorian)
LOCATION: GSS *Intrepid*, Mars Outer Shipyards (MOS)
REGION: Mars Protectorate, Sol Space Federation

The post-op took over twenty hours; a good portion of which was spent re-taking the dock from the last few mercs, who had entrenched themselves quite thoroughly. Then came the round-up, squabbles over jurisdiction, and the interrogations. It was well into the following day before Ouri and Tanis got to sit down together and go over what they had learned.

"This is most interesting." Tanis looked over the interrogation logs. "Trent was not involved with these men at all, at least not to their knowledge. The captains all had their dealings with a man by the name of Drenn. He has links to the STR Consortium, and has been known to be involved in some of their less public projects."

Ouri scowled at the data as she reviewed it. "So, does this mean we have two threats, or just one that is a little clearer and a little scarier?"

"I'm betting that it's the same threat, though we do have to keep an open mind." She took a drink from the restorative in front of her. "Still, I'm guessing that Trent wasn't getting the desired results, so his bosses declared open season on us."

"More likely on you," Ouri replied. "I'm guessing that they've singled you out. That was a very deadly scenario that was specifically designed to draw you in."

"And in I was drawn...rather foolishly, too."

"I'll say so." Admiral Sanderson stood in the doorway.

<Tell me next time he sneaks up like that,> Tanis scolded Angela.

<I would, but he has some good tech. If he wants to be, he's very

hard to spot.>

"Sir." Both women stood and saluted.

"Sit." Sanderson gestured as he did the same himself.

"Quite the little escapade you had, Major." He allowed his glare to linger on her for a moment before continuing. "Imagine my reaction when I heard, while on my visit to the Marsian Parliament, that the officer in charge of our security has ripped a ship from the station, exposed an entire dock to vacuum, and proceeded to tear across the construction yards, spilling cargo in her wake like it was confetti."

"I can only guess that it must have been extreme, sir."

"You're damn right, it was extreme. You should never have allowed yourself to be drawn in so completely. I thought you were an intelligence officer. You could stand to display some."

Tanis sat and took the rebuke in silence. Ouri looked like she wished she were anywhere else, up to and including cleaning sewage scrubbers, than at the table listening to Sanderson dress down her CO.

"Well, what do you have to say for yourself?"

Tanis took a breath. She could think of a hundred reasons why no other person would have expected to run into four ships full of armed mercenaries on what was supposed to be a secure dock, but she knew that wouldn't fly with the admiral.

"I take full responsibility, sir. I acted rashly and without proper care and attention. It won't happen again."

"You must know that I am under considerable pressure to have you removed. Terrance and the captain have been inundated with calls and protestations from all levels of Marsian bureaucracy. Considerable pressure."

"I'll tender my resignation at once, sir," Tanis replied stoically. "I do not wish to cause them any more trouble than I already have." While she appeared calm on the outside, inside she was fraught with emotion. If she had to abdicate her place on the *Intrepid,* she would find whoever was responsible and kill them, even if it took a thousand years.

"Don't be an idiot. You'll do no such thing." Sanderson gave her a look that teachers usually reserve for their worst students. "Despite your rather shoddy handling of yesterday's events, your record otherwise has been impeccable. I simply wish to inform you that should your next encounter with the enemy show such large amounts of bravado coupled with such small amounts of careful consideration, I may have to rethink my decision regarding your placement here."

"Yes, sir." Tanis could feel her limbs again, her heart slowed down, and she took a deep breath.

"Now, let's talk about the prisoners. That much, at least, was a job well done. We can finally get some information on who is behind this."

"Yes, sir. From what we have learned so far, it appears that the mercenaries were contacted by a man by the name of Drenn. He is connected to the STR Consortium, dealing particularly in the types of projects that they like to keep hidden from the public eye. It is our opinion that they were hired to take me out of the picture."

Sanderson leaned back and stroked his chin. "And why, pray tell, Major, would they go to such considerable expense to remove you, pain in my ass though you are? I imagine that this operation cost them billions of credits, enough to buy a small corporation on a major planet."

"Indeed, sir." Tanis nodded. "I think they want to get rid of me because their sabotage success rate dropped when I came onboard. It's not a lot, but their last several attacks have all targeted me, so I think there is some credence there."

Sanderson grunted a tentative assent. "And what about your belief that it is solely the STR?" he asked.

"We've obviously been under concerted corporate, network, and physical attack for some time. We've ruled out radical groups; though it is logical to assume, and borne out by the data, that roughly ten percent of our troubles are from those fringe elements.

"That being said, the rest is either governmental or corporate in origin. There is a relatively small list of either that could sustain an attack of this duration through so many avenues. If these men truly did get their orders from Drenn, then it has to have been the STR Consortium all along."

"They have been on our suspect list since we determined that it was a bigger player pulling the strings," Sanderson said. "What does this change?"

"We can now begin pursuing legal action against them," Tanis replied. "We have affidavits and statements from many of the mercs regarding the nature of this attempt and who hired them. Once we make a solid connection between Drenn and the STR, we can begin subpoenaing communications that we can link between the two parties. That'll be a feeding frenzy for the news hounds, and will cause them to think twice before making such a bold move again."

"We won't be able to make this stick to them." Sanderson shook his head. "We don't have a solid enough tie."

"And we're not likely to get one, but they'll still have to fight us off. The money it will cost them in share value alone will make them rethink their plans. At the very least, they will probably refrain from more events like this, and go back to that Trent guy."

"That would be something, at least." The admiral nodded. "One mysterious foe is enough."

"I couldn't agree more," Tanis said.

"I still don't see how this all fully explains the considerable expense they are putting into trying to remove you alone."

"I can only surmise," Tanis leaned back in her chair, "that they have something big planned, and hope to remove me and carry it out before you can find a replacement."

COUGAR

STELLAR DATE: 3227238 / 10.12.4123 (Adjusted Gregorian)
LOCATION: GSS *Intrepid*, Mars Outer Shipyards (MOS)
REGION: Mars Protectorate, Sol Space Federation

Tanis was relaxing on a bench in the prairie park located a few decks down from the SOC. It was the third shift and the park was dark, which meant it was teeming with life. She could hear the calls of the various ground animals, and even the cough of a cougar somewhere in the distance. She wondered what it was hunting, and saw that the park listing showed a herd of deer nearby.

The herd was quite close, and Tanis cycled her vision into the IR range to see if she could witness the attack. Wild predators were not uncommon in the parks on the *Intrepid*. It was easiest to create a true ecosystem with them in place. The animals would not bother humans; they would not even come within several meters, depending on the species.

"What are you peering at?"

The voice startled Tanis; she had been so focused on the impending battle that she hadn't heard anyone approach. Looking up she saw that it was Joseph and smiled warmly.

"Cougar about to pounce somewhere out there. I can't see it, but I heard it nearby."

Joseph sat beside her. "Forgot you were planetborn. I never liked the predators; it doesn't make sense why they would add them in."

"Keeps the vermin under control."

"That's what the ship's cats are for."

Those were different cats entirely. Every ship had cats for hunting vermin. Try as mankind might, even in the forty second century, rats and mice still followed civilization around, making their home where humans did. Ship's cats had been modified slightly to prefer the taste of rat and mouse, and also to be very fastidious as to where they left their own scat. Their intelligence was enhanced as well, allowing them to understand the concept of pointing, as well as the fact that the cat in the mirror was them and not some interloper out to steal their food.

"I don't think ship's cats would do too well out there. It's not really their type of place. Besides, that cougar stalking those deer...that's real nature, that's what happens."

"You have a very fixed mindset, do you know that?" Joseph smiled at Tanis. "Not saying I don't like it; just an observation."

She turned her attention to him, allowing herself to see what she normally kept from her mind. He was a man—a warm, intelligent, attractive man. One who didn't mind how domineering she was—something that had caused problems more than once. His head was angled forward, his strong brow half hiding his eyes. Tanis thought back and realized it was a look he almost exclusively reserved for her. It was also not a look a commander directs at a major under any circumstances.

The intensity of his gaze caused her to glance down at her service uniform, suddenly noticing that the cut of the blouse and pants seemed to be somewhat more fitted than usual.

<Don't look at me. I wouldn't have your nano alter your clothing. Nope.>

<Angela, you know I can't pursue him. He serves under me.>

Angela's snort was very convincing. <Who cares? We'll be gone in a few months. Do you think Sanderson will give a hoot as long as you get the job done? Heck, it's expected for you organics to get together and do your thing on a colony venture—the more the merrier.>

<Just...oh, shut up!>

Tanis took a moment to remember Joseph's last statement.

"Yeah, I do sort of have a one-track mind. Comes with the territory I suppose."

Joseph nodded. "I know how you feel. But it's been quiet lately; I can't help thinking of what it's going to be like when we get there."

Tanis was silent a moment, staring off into the waving grass. "I haven't really allowed myself to think of that much."

Joseph gave a low chuckle. "Why doesn't that surprise me?"

Tanis looked up into his eyes and saw something there; a longing, an intensity that she didn't know how to deal with. Why would he want her so badly? He hadn't said so, but she knew it was there…it was her job to know things like that.

She looked away. "Joe…I—I don't know what to say. I don't know what to do with what you want from me."

She felt his hand rest on her arm, felt the heat radiating through her shirt. "I just want you. Can't you tell? It's not something from you I want, it's just you."

A battle was raging between Tanis's heart and mind. In the end, her mind won. She broke regulations only when she had to—never when she wanted to, no matter how much she wanted to. "We can't, you know that. You serve under me, there's a reason why these things can't happen."

"But I serve under you now and have feelings for you. They have happened, don't you see that?"

Tanis sighed and shifted on the bench to face him. "What do I have to offer you? There's nothing here, I'm just my job."

Joe laughed; it wasn't a short bark, or a mocking chuckle, just a good long laugh—one that left him wheezing by the time he finished. "Major Richards, that's just the sort of thing you would say."

Tanis could feel her cheeks getting red; she couldn't fathom what was so funny. It couldn't be that he was mocking her. That was completely out of character for Joe. "I don't get it. What could you see in me? Men don't want women like me…we just make things hard for them—or they want a mother."

Joe raised his hand and turned her face toward his, forcing

her to lock eyes with him. She felt a moment of uncertainty. Was he going to kiss her?

"I don't want a mother. I've given this a lot of thought. It's your strength that draws me to you. No matter what, you don't let things get you down. Nothing is insurmountable. I don't want to control you, I don't want to own you—I want to share that with you, and I want to give you the support that I know you really need inside. You're just like the rest of us—you feel pain, you worry—but you don't let anyone see. But I see, and it makes me love you."

A part of Tanis saw that Joe was just as shocked that he'd said 'love' as she was to hear it. She had heard it before and it always ended badly—always ended with pain. She pulled away.

"I don't think this is right, Joe. We have to work together. Maybe later, maybe after we get there." Her voice was quiet; she couldn't keep the doubt in her own words hidden.

Joe didn't say a word; his face had lost all expression. He nodded and rose from the bench, but after taking a step he turned. "Tanis, I hope you don't mind, but I'm going to wait. I'm not going to let you stay alone forever."

She didn't respond, and he remained still; Tanis wondered if he would attempt to convince her again. But then, with a slight droop to his shoulders, he left.

Tanis sat, staring into the darkness, her reverie eventually broken by a deer's scream.

THE CHO

STELLAR DATE: 3227241 / 10.15.4123 (Adjusted Gregorian)
LOCATION: District 4A1, Ring 4, Callisto Orbital Habitat (Cho)
REGION: Jovian Combine, Sol Space Federation

Trist cautiously slipped down the service corridor, her silsuit a matte grey that matched the bulkheads around her. She was looking for a good place to hide so that she could look over her find in private. A vertical stack of environmental tubes filled part of the passage ahead, and she crouched down in the gloom they created.

The find was a bundle of plas sheets. Rare to see such a manifest printed out, but some people did like the tactile sensation. She flipped through the multilayer holoplas with care, making certain to focus on each layer of each page in its entirety. It took several minutes to scan the sheets into memory and transcribe them. Once it was in her memory, she assimilated it as data and the information was in the forefront of her mind, filtered into a relational structure.

Slipping a small EM charge from a hidden pocket, she fried the sheets and dropped them down a crack between the conduit and the deck. Someone would find them eventually, but it would be too late to do anything—even if the information on them could be recovered.

Sue, Trist's AI, was running through the lists of equipment and storage locations in the data, and pulled out several choice items, flashing them over Trist's vision.

<Well that sure looks like it made this little jaunt worth it.>

<I'd say so,> Sue replied. <We could make enough money to get all of the upgrades both of us want for once.>

<We're going to need help,> Trist said.

<You're thinking Jesse, aren't you?>

<I am; she can handle anything I can't manage, and we'll need a hand with some of the bigger items.>

<Well, we had better go get her. If we wait too long, she'll be on her nightly binge and we'll miss our window.>

Trist rose and left the narrow service passage, taking a few convoluted turns before ending up on a larger concourse. As she walked, the corridors transitioned from being deserted to packed with people and maglev carriers. The utilitarian halls had also given way to the wider boulevards, their walls covered in tarnished filigree—though it was nearly impossible to spot behind all of the holo advertisements that wrapped them.

She looked down at the form-fitting grey outfit and decided it just wouldn't do. A thought changed the color to a mixture of black and pink, raised the heel on the boots, and added a short skirt. The neckline plunged and the fabric ruffled, creating a second layer that formed a jacket.

<Much better, a girl has to look her best.>

<You worry too much about clothing.>

<I don't know why I even talk to you sometimes. Clothing is everything!>

"Mod freak."

She almost didn't catch the muttered words from a man who walked by. He was already past, but she made a rude gesture anyway. It wasn't her fault she couldn't get the pretty mods, and that her left eye was a mass of lenses and actuators. Not to mention what her right hand looked like—it got the job done.

Putting his comment from her mind, she adopted a carefree expression and walked down the corridor toward the main sweep of Ring 4. Her eyes slid past the ancient décor in this part of the ring to light upon the inhabitants. It was important to always know who was around you and what they were up to. In Trist's experience, life didn't offer a lot of forgiveness to the unwary.

After a few bends, the boulevard opened up to a balcony

overlooking the main sweep. Lanes of flying transports choked the air before her, and below she could catch glimpses of parks and lakes.

Once, when the Callisto Orbital Habitat—known to its inhabitants as the 'Cho'—was new, this was the upper level of an exclusive world; the most beautiful and advanced orbital habitat ever created. The Cho still was the most advanced and beautiful orbital habitat mankind had ever constructed, but with the number of rings now totaling over one hundred, R4 was little more than a relic—much of it demoted to life support and waste-management.

Despite that, the main sweep could still take your breath away. It was nearly a kilometer wide and ran the entire circumference of the ring. If you followed it around, you'd find yourself in some very nice neighborhoods from time to time, but most would prompt you to keep a hand on your weapon of choice.

Trist tried to contact Jesse on the Link, but received no response. That could mean anything from complete and utter drunkenness to simply not caring enough to answer, or a host of possibilities in between.

She visited Pikes Pub, followed by a few of her friend's other favorite haunts, eventually catching wind that Jesse was on her way to the SouRing commons to return a faulty IF unit. The commons were nine thousand kilometers upspin, and Trist caught a high-velocity maglev that made the trip in less than an hour.

Sue kept an eye out while Trist caught a bit of sleep. The effort to steal those plas sheets had kept her from sleep for more than a day, and even the several minutes she managed to snatch on the train felt great.

The train's closest stop to the SouRing commons was the sort of place that made even people with death wishes deploy protective nano; Sue let out a veritable cloud.

<The air feels tenser than usual out here,> Trist commented.

<I don't really have the equipment to judge the tension in the air, but I'll take your word for it,> Sue replied.

Trist waited for the crush in the station to lessen before she ventured out and then down a broad thoroughfare to the commons.

The SouRing commons were placed at a location where the main sweep was wider than normal, and contained a veritable city of shops, services, and bazaars. The merchants on the commons sold everything to everyone—every single walk of life and caste was represented. Tucked amongst the semi-legal stalls and shops was the best black market in the bottom twenty rings; something that brought in a lot of highnums and offringers.

It wasn't hard to spot the foreigners, either. They were the ones with the furtive glances and anxious twitches. Normally Trist would find a few likely ones and follow them to a good place to do a little recreational appropriation of their goods, but not now. She needed to find Jesse and get moving.

Threading through a group of brain cases—Trist could never understand anyone's desire to leave their body—she worked her way toward the shop she was pretty certain Jesse had gone to with her 'faulty' IF unit. On the way, she decided that her flamboyant outfit might make her look a bit too much like a tourist, and altered her silsuit to approximate black leather pants, boots, a tight grey shirt, and a long jacket—a more serious and less approachable outfit.

<Again with the clothes...it's like a sickness,> Sue commented.

<Why are all AIs such smart-asses?> Trist's question didn't receive a response.

As she threaded the crowd, a telltale blue mohawk caught her eye. It wasn't a totally uncommon hairstyle at the moment, but this one stood out—as the spikes were metal, and each was topped with a small decorative skull. Yunnan did have a tendency to show up when Trist least expected it; usually quite interested in her paying him the credit she owed.

She was betting that he was past the 'want money now' stage, and into the 'retribution and pain' stage. Cutting behind a series of vendors peddling sensory experiences from cloud divers on Saturn, she made certain to put a lot of space between herself and her debtor; no reason to have an unfortunate encounter with him botch the opportunity to do a job with Jesse.

After that and a few other near misses with people she really didn't want to meet today—or ever, if she could help it—Trist finally found her friend.

Jesse was where Trist thought she would be, though she hadn't expected the scene she encountered. Her friend was standing on a shop's counter screaming at the proprietor. Trist stopped and reconsidered her friend's past behavior. The real question was why she *hadn't* expected a scene like this. Theatrics were like food and power to Jesse. Trist approached quietly, interested in what this particular altercation was about.

The scene was accented by the fact that Jesse's body was covered in a skin-tight sheath that gave off waves of silver and gold light. Her hair was silver and waving as though it was blowing in a soft breeze. It was intended to be intimidating, though the storeowner didn't seem fazed.

"I don't care what you say, Drew. This IF set you sold me yesterday is a dud, it was DOA! Don't you try and give me the song and dance about how I screwed it up; I was doing IF jobs when you were still a single cell in stasis!"

"Right, Jesse. You've never cooked a single circuit in your life, just like I've never stubbed my toe. How's about you get off my counter and buy a new IF like anyone else who cooks a unit. Or is your little hissy fit an indicator of your skill?"

Trist smirked. Despite her friend's claims, Trist had witnessed Jesse cook an IF unit on more than one occasion. That didn't mean that Drew's units were always perfect, either. In this part of the ring, the odds were often in favor of the vendor selling junk—especially this vendor. Jesse was testing him to see if he would assume he had accidentally sold her a broken unit.

"Don't push her, Drew." Trist glided up to the counter. "You know she'll contact ChoSec and have them investigate where you get your supply from."

Drew cast one of his many cybernetic eyes her way. "Nice to see you, Trist. I highly doubt it. If they investigate me, they may just decide to make sure everyone I have been selling to has a valid license to do IF work. I imagine that your fake credentials can stand up to the p-auth system's checks, but it wouldn't take too much double-checking to expose them for some very illegal forgeries."

Jesse hopped down off the counter and managed to look contrite. "Now Drew, neither of us wants to go and do anything crazy like that. We were all just talking hypothetically."

Drew sat down on a stool behind his counter. "Right. Hypothetical. Now what say you hypothetically buy a new unit or get out of my shop."

Jesse's face turned dark. "That's how it's gonna be? No deal, no haggling, not even the slightest of implied warranties?"

Drew didn't say anything as he stared at the two girls.

"Damn you!" Jesse spat. "That's the last cred I'm dropping in your shithole. I'm taking my business to Blaine. At least he knows what the word 'quality' means."

"You do that." Drew scowled.

No one moved for several moments. Drew and Jesse stared at one another while Trist did her best not to burst into laughter.

"Oh, fuck it," Jesse said as her eyes flicked up to the left. "There, the creds are transferred, gimme a new goddamn unit."

Drew unlocked a door behind the counter and pulled out an interface unit. "Pleasure doing business with you."

"I'm sure it is." She turned and left, Trist following behind, hiding a smile with her hand. Once they were on the street she turned to Trist. "Why didn't you help me in there?"

"'Cause I saw you cook that unit last night. I could even see the scorch marks on it in that poorly lit hole of Drew's."

"What? You're the honest thief now? How's that work?"

"I've done my evil deed for the day. I got a hold of a sweet manifest. I have transit times, dates, crate numbers, the whole shebang."

"So what? There are manifests everywhere."

"Yeah, but this one has shown me a bit of a security hole, and I plan to slip into that hole and slip out with some sweet shit heading for the GSS *Intrepid*."

"That colony ship they're building out at Mars that nearly got blown up awhile back?"

"Yeah, there's some serious high-end neuro conduit and supplemental processors in the shipment; stuff that, if we found the right buyer, we could retire on."

"Seriously?"

"Would I joke about something like that?"

Jesse stopped and peered intently at her friend. "Hank, is she lying?"

<No dilation…well, no more than is normal for her. No twitching, she's not biting her cheek. Either she's managed to control all of her tells, or she's being truthful.> Jesse's AI spoke on an open Link between the two girls.

"So when do we leave?"

ILLUSION

STELLAR DATE: 3227242 / 10.16.4123 (Adjusted Gregorian)
LOCATION: District 9B2, Ring 14, Callisto Orbital Habitat (Cho)
REGION: Jovian Combine, Sol Space Federation

"Status on disabling the biosensors?" Jesse asked.

"Almost there," Trist whispered in response. "I just need to finish the loopback so the secage doesn't notice a drop in signal strength."

"I doubt that the secage monitoring this place would even notice." Jesse cast a disdainful eye down the corridor they were in. "Looks like even ChoSec forgot this place existed decades ago."

"People may forget, but the AI doesn't. If I don't cover our asses, we're gonna find some guard's stun gun up them."

"That may not be so bad, if he's any good with it."

"Ugh."

Trist finished with her rewiring of the circuitry and slipped her tools back into their case. Jesse picked up the cover for the section of conduit they had exposed, and held it in place while Trist fastened it.

"We good to go then?" Jesse said as they stood.

"As far as every surveillance circuit is concerned, we're totally invisible."

"Just what I like to hear."

The two women slipped down the corridor toward their goal: the large double seal of the Norcon Warehouse A2-34-B. Their silsuits were set to their standard thieving camouflage.

They reached the seal, and Jesse slapped a wireless hack pad over the section of wallplate they knew the door control conduit ran behind. "Little bit of this, little bit of that, and" —the door chirped and opened— "we're in, just like we work here."

<You two are far too full of yourselves.> Sue spoke into both their minds.

<Isn't that what you like about them?> Hank asked. <You told me that you found it to be cute.>

<Doesn't mean I can't make disdainful comments about it.>

<One of these days, you'll just admit that you're a neuro-pulse junkie and you can drop the pretense.>

<What, like you?>

"Why do they always bicker when we are in tense situations?" Trist asked.

"'Cause they like to up the odds. We're getting too good at this; not as much of a rush for them."

"I don't know how much I like the idea of my AI putting me at risk for a rush."

<It's not like we'd ever do anything that bad,> Sue said. <If you get caught, so do we—at best, we're accessories, at worst, they wipe us.>

Sue had a point, AIs tended to police their ranks with far more severity than humans did. No human fully understood their laws, but the petabytes of data regarding punishments were enough to daunt anyone, flesh or silicon.

Throughout the conversation, the two women took stock of the warehouse. It wasn't too large; only about a half kilometer across, with direct access to the west docks on the far end. The pallets destined for the GSS *Intrepid* were in section A1-4 of the warehouse, several rows over. They strode past the towers of cargo until they came to the items they were looking for.

Crates from STR Con were stacked in orderly piles, and they pulled the topmost down and checked its ID. This one contained some high-end, self-organizing circuits. SOCs were very useful when a small component needed to be extremely diverse and could even change its own function based on need. They also weren't cheap. Popping the crate open, Jesse slipped several packages into her duffle.

"Next."

They opened several more crates, and pulled odds and ends that would sell well and not result in too many questions. Both women would have loved to take everything they laid eyes on, but there was no way they could sneak several tons of equipment out of the warehouse.

"Look at that," Trist said. "Silbio."

"No way." Jesse checked the ID on the crate. "I didn't know they had perfected that stuff well enough to start shipping it willy-nilly around the Sol system."

"I guess they did. Too bad it's in those big tubs; we'd be able to retire off what that stuff is worth." Trist broke the seal on one of the tubs and peered inside at the dull blue of the silbio mixture.

"Don't get carried away," Jesse said.

"Said the thruster, calling the rocket hot."

<That's a truly bad adaptation of that saying,> Hank commented.

"It's an adaptation?" Trist asked.

"What was that sound?" Jesse held up her hand and looked around.

<Metal on metal scrape, I make it to have come from the doors you entered through,> Sue informed them.

<I count several footfalls…distinguishing…five sets. Coming this way.>

Trist and Jesse stuffed several more items into their duffels, and turned to slip out the far end of the warehouse. They stepped around a tower of plas products to find themselves face-to-face with the muzzle of a projectile weapon.

"You two ladies had best step back into the aisle, there." The man waved the gun, and the two women slowly backed up. To their left, the five visitors Hank had identified came into view.

<How'd you miss this guy?> Trist asked Sue.

<He's got a pretty advanced infiltration suit; it's masking all of his

sounds, smell, heat—the whole deal. If it weren't for visual input, I wouldn't be able to tell he's there even now.>

<That's some impressive stuff.>

The group of five reached the two women. They consisted of four women and a lanky man in the front. He grinned, and Trist decided it was one of the least appealing smiles she had ever seen.

"You two ladies are messing with things you shouldn't be," he drawled. Behind him, his four female associates spread out to better cover Trist and Jesse with their weapons.

"You don't look much like the security detail yourself," Jesse said. "I'm sure we can just live and let live."

"See, I don't think that's how it's going to work."

"Why's that?" Jesse asked.

"Well, you're here for a reason, and so are we. You're here because we let you get the manifest for this shipment, and we're here to make a fucking mess of it and you. Then we stage it to look like you two fought and killed each other."

"You're kidding me," Trist said. "I busted my ass getting that manifest. No one 'let' me get it."

"You're hot shit, but not that hot," a girl holding a very large rifle sneered.

"She's right," the lanky man said. "You've been had. See, there are people—people we are associated with—who don't want this stuff to get to its destination. Law forbids blocking the sale when a buyer is willing to pay full price, so our employers are required to fulfill the order. It sorta irks them to have to do it, so we're going to fix things up so they don't have to."

"I don't get that at all…STR doesn't want to sell its stuff?" Jesse asked.

"I think they don't want it to get to the *Intrepid*," Trist said.

"Oh, you *are* bright," the man with the projectile weapon said.

"'Nuff talk," the lanky man shouted. "Let's just finish this and get out of here." He leveled his blaster at Jesse and fired a round directly into her face. Brain matter and metal from her AI sprayed out the back of her head.

Trist screamed incoherently and lunged at the man. Three shots from the girl with the rifle caught her in the torso before she took her second step. The scream died in a long gurgle as she clutched her chest and stumbled backward. One of the other girls fired a few more shots into Trist, causing her to topple over into the open tub of silbio.

"Nice shooting, Kris," the lanky man observed. "Set a det, and let's get out of here."

One of the girls knelt down to set a charge; moments later they were gone.

INTERLUDE

STELLAR DATE: 3227278 / 11.21.4123 (Adjusted Gregorian)
LOCATION: Mars Outer Shipyards (MOS)
REGION: Mars Protectorate, Sol Space Federation

"About time this shipment from STR showed up." Jens looked the pallets over as they were unloaded from the freight transport to Mars Outer Shipyards dock T5-7A.

"They had some excuse about a break-in at a subcontractor's warehouse," Petrov mumbled, examining the shipping manifest. "Looks like everything made it, though. Manifest does say that they had to repack some things and reseal one of the silbio tubs."

"Are you serious?" Jens said. "You can't just unseal and reseal those tubs. If a single milligram of that stuff is contaminated, there's gonna be one hell of a suit on STR."

Petrov nodded and grabbed a scanner to get a reading on the resealed tub. He scowled at the display and shook the device before getting another reading. "I think something's wrong with my scanner."

"I don't like the sound of that," Jens said.

"I read massive bio signals in here."

"Massive? How'd that happen?"

"Uh…Jens…I think there's a body in here."

Jens couldn't speak for a moment. Lieutenant Collins would be all over his ass, the major would want a full investigation, and the rest of his day would be shot.

"How could that slip by on the other end?"

"You gotta calibrate properly for silbio. The whole mess is technically organic, so it would just read as 'alive' to any regular scanner."

Jens sighed and got on the Link to call in a medic team to

take possession of the tub. The body was probably dead, and that was going to generate a mess of paperwork.

Petrov chuckled, "How the hell do you RMA something like this?"

HITCHHIKER

STELLAR DATE: 3227279 / 11.22.4123 (Adjusted Gregorian)
LOCATION: Mars Outer Shipyards (MOS)
REGION: Mars Protectorate, Sol Space Federation

"When will she be conscious?" Tanis asked.

"Not too long now," the medic said. "Her AI apparently linked in with some of the silbio, and put her in a sort of pseudo-cryo; it used some of the stuff to seal her wounds, too."

"Have we got anything from her AI on what happened?"

"Not yet; the AI completely ran out of power trying to sustain the cryo. It's in hard shutdown. It'll take the girl's command to get it to re-init."

"It's always something." Tanis sighed.

The medic blinked rapidly. "Looks like she's coming to; let's go see what she has to say."

The girl—*woman*, Tanis corrected herself—lying on the slab was shorter than average, probably only one hundred and sixty five centimeters. Uncommon to see in an age when nearly all children were more designed than simply 'had'. She appeared somewhat dazed as she looked around the medroom; her one organic eye blearily attempting to focus on her surroundings.

"Hello, miss. I'm Dr. Anne Rosenberg. You're on the Mars Outer Shipyards. You've been shot, but you're going to be OK, thanks to your AI."

"My AI? I...I can't hear her! She's not here!" A look of panic spread across the woman's face.

"Relax," Dr. Rosenberg said. "She ran your internal power down, and you're going to need to run her through her startup sequence—though I strongly recommend that you don't do that until you are better rested."

"I'm Major Richards," Tanis said. "We don't have any ID on

you, and you really weren't expected on MOS. Do you have any idea how you ended up here?"

"Name's...Trist. I remember being on Callisto R14...I remember dying."

"You would have, if your AI hadn't plugged you up with the silbio. Saved your life." Dr. Rosenberg gave Trist a soothing smile.

"I'm guessing you weren't in that warehouse on Callisto to give our shipment your seal of approval, were you," Tanis asked.

Trist chuckled; it was low and throaty. "Only the best in the space force, I see. Yeah, I was there with my friend —Jesse—we were lifting some stuff."

"The report I was delivered said that your friend took a bullet to the head. Care to elaborate on what happened?" Dr. Rosenberg shot Tanis an incredulous look, and she realized perhaps a little more tact wouldn't have hurt.

"Aw, shit...Jesse." Trist's eye lost its focus, and she shuddered, trying to keep control of herself. "Any chance I can just go back to being dead?"

"I don't really think that's going to make it on the list of options," Tanis replied. "I'm sorry about your friend...sorry I brought it up like that."

Trist grimaced, but nodded slowly.

"Look, why don't you just start at the beginning, and take me through it." Tanis said.

Trist didn't say a word for several minutes. Tanis suspected that she was having a conversation with her AI about their options. Then, slowly, she proceeded to explain how she had acquired the manifest of items being shipped to the *Intrepid*, broken into the warehouse, and been ambushed by some unknown thugs. The last thing she remembered was being shot after watching Jesse die.

"So, I'm guessing that, for whatever reason, the shipment

still got sent here, and, somehow, me with it," Trist concluded. "How did that happen, anyway?"

"Gunshots alerted a security drone that was patrolling the warehouse. It arrived on the scene to find a detonation charge planted on one of the opened crates. The charge was disabled, and when crews arrived to check everything over, they found that some items were in duffels, but otherwise all the cargo was still present. For whatever reason they didn't see your body, and just sealed the silbio up again—I don't know how they thought that was going to pass muster. The official record was entered as some sort of dispute between thieves with one fatality. They surmised the other must have run off after the gunshots to avoid detection."

Trist looked perplexed. "You've asked me a lot of questions, but I have one. How am I still alive? I have this distinct impression that I was dying when that loud-mouthed bitch shot me." She ran a hand across her torso, almost as though she expected to find holes where the rounds had impacted her.

Dr. Rosenberg provided the answer. "Your AI managed to interface with the silbio, and programmed it to form a seal on your wounds and put you into a semi-cryo state. It was really quite an ingenious bit of work; you are lucky to be alive."

"Sue is pretty damn clever; I bet not any AI could have pulled that off." Trist grinned.

"I wouldn't get too excited," the doctor cautioned. "No one has ever done what she did with silbio. Somehow, the process has caused it to bind to your DNA, with consequences I can't quite foresee. You wouldn't be the first human to be a bit more silicon than flesh, but this is different."

Trist grimaced, and then gave a half smile, "so when someone asks animal, mineral, or vegetable, I can say all three?"

Tanis found the attitude to be a bit too blasé, and Angela added her own internal comment. <Mostly vegetable, I'd say.>

"You're not a vegetable yet," Doctor Rosenberg said. "I don't see any immediate impact on your neurological facilities or your AI interface—which appears to be illegal, I might add—but I have found some additional interconnectivity that we'll need to look into more carefully. Quite honestly, it's a very exciting accident."

"I'm glad it's so beneficial to you."

The doctor gave Trist a caustic look. "I'd say that the majority of the benefit is yours. You'd be dead otherwise."

"I do kinda like being alive."

Tanis took the opportunity to redirect the conversation, "And while it's great that you're alive, you've got some things to answer for." She kept to herself that this could actually be a blessing in disguise. This woman might have seen something that would help them. "There will most likely be charges of trespass from Callisto, and then there's the cost of our tub of silbio. I think that will run you about a century's wages."

Trist sank back. "I guess there's no running from this one, is there?"

"Not even the slimmest chance," Tanis said. "However…" She let it hang out there for a minute, watching Trist grow agitated with interest.

" 'However', what?" Trist finally asked.

"Your testimony would be useful, for starters."

"Against who? Some guy who I can only describe as 'the skinny guy with the bimbo squad'?"

"More or less," Tanis replied. "We think we know who he is, and if we could gain some leverage against him, he could point us in the direction of who is calling the shots. Maybe then we'd have a chance of making some headway against STR."

Trist rose up on her elbows. "You want me to testify against STR? Are you nuts?"

"You know, Dr. Rosenberg, I think we've bothered our guest enough for one day. I'll come back to see her tomorrow."

"I was about to say the same thing," the doctor replied.

"Lieutenant Amy Lee will be getting in touch with you to transport our guest aboard the *Intrepid*. I don't want any unexpected visitors ending her time with us."

The doctor nodded, and Tanis left the MOS north sector's med facilities.

<This is just the break we've needed,> Tanis said to Angela. *<Her ID will be enough for us to put out a warrant on Trent, and then we are only one step away from finding out who is calling the shots at STR.>*

<If you can get it. I bet that Callisto will want Trist back. In my experience, they'll be hesitant to sign out a warrant on Trent without her being delivered first.>

<And then there goes our leverage.> Tanis nodded to herself.

<Your brain chemistry indicates you have a 'plan'. It's got that certain mix of serotonin and dopamine you get when you think you've been particularly clever.>

<Your chemical analysis of my brain really takes a lot of fun out of things, you know that?>

<I do—it's partially why I do it. So what's the plan?> Angela replied.

<We'll sign out a warrant against Trent in a Federal SolCourt court.>

<Even if you can get a federal warrant, Callisto can still stall for months before carrying it out.>

Tanis smiled to herself. *<That's why AIs need us humans; you can't quite get our motivations. Trent won't allow a material witness of Jovian citizenship to live. Callisto can ignore my charges against him because of the Io Accord, but they can't ignore hers. He'll come for her.>*

<He'll come back to InnerSol space? But then you can pursue him.>

<I know that, and he knows that, but he'll still come.>

Angela made a noise that Tanis had come to identify as her signal of frustration. *<You're right; I don't get it at all. Though I do*

get the part where you're going to use Trist as bait.>

<I think she'll be more than that.> Tanis leapt on the back of a cargo hauler heading across the docks toward the *Intrepid*. *<She's no slouch, if she could pull off what she did. Sure, Trent duped her into doing it, but she had to be good enough that the ChoSec folks on Callisto would have believed her capable of that break-in without help.>*

<So how do you expect to use her?> Angela asked.

<Not entirely certain, but I've got a feeling she could come in handy.>

Angela and Tanis cut their conversation short as a call came in from Joe.

<You busy? I've got a duty officer from MOS saying that she's got a request to move your surprise visitor to the Intrepid, *but also a pending extradition request from Callisto. They seem a bit uncertain about which to follow.>*

<That was fast. Someone must have been checking the Jane Does, and noticed when one got a name attached,> Angela said.

<Tell them we're going to be taking her to Callisto when we stop there on our way outsystem,> Tanis replied to Joe.

<Please tell me you aren't really going to turn her over.> Joe sounded worried.

<Of course not. Get Amy Lee down there right away, though. I want to reinforce our position via people carrying weapons. I don't have an overabundance of trust in the folks here at MOS.>

<Nothing to do with how much you like to mess with them?> Joe asked before closing the connection with a chuckle.

"Just seems practical to me..." Tanis said to herself as the hauler sped across the loading dock to the *Intrepid*.

<I couldn't help but notice that you are somehow both more and less formal with him than normal,> Angela commented.

Tanis didn't respond immediately. *<I honestly don't know how to act. That's why I hate that he did anything. I don't know how to behave...though he seems to have no problem going back to his old*

self.>

<You didn't analyze his vocal patterns all that carefully. That laugh of his was somewhat strained. He's unsure about how to act around you, as well.>

Tanis grunted. *<Well, he has no one to blame but himself. As long as he can be professional, then everything will be OK.>*

<Whatever you say, human.>

Somehow the term seemed a bit more derisive than normal.

MACHINATIONS

STELLAR DATE: 3227280 / 11.23.4123 (Adjusted Gregorian)
LOCATION: GSS *Intrepid*, Mars Outer Shipyards (MOS)
REGION: Mars Protectorate, Sol Space Federation

Joe took a seat across from Tanis in her office. "I assume you actually have a plan now? One that isn't just 'we use the civilian as bait'?"

Joe, for his part, had been true to his word in demonstrating that they could work together and not let his feelings get in the way. She was still somewhat uncertain about what tone her interactions with him should take, but it was becoming easier, especially when she was deep in her work.

She pulled her lips back in a predatory grin. "Of course I have a plan. I always have a plan."

<In case you weren't aware, that's her 'my plan involves violence' look,> Angela supplied.

"I've made the connection, but thanks," Joe said.

"It's simple, really. We go to the federal buildings on Mars 1 and go before a superior court judge to get warrants signed out that Callisto can't ignore."

"Yeah, you said that yesterday, but it's still not really something I'd call a 'plan'."

Tanis brought up maps for the MOS, the MCEE, and Mars 1. Certain sections were highlighted, and she zoomed in on those.

"We're going to take a route that, while secure, passes through some places where we'll be certain to be ambushed. I expect Trent will be involved, and we'll nab him."

<That's the plan?> Angela asked. *<Get our asses, physical and metaphorical, shot off? Your BLT could come up with a better plan!>*

"She has a point," Joe said. "How do you know Trent will even be there?"

"Well, if he's not, then we'll have warrants that Callisto will have to execute. Either way, we'll flush him out."

"I don't know how that's going to help. He doesn't exactly have a physical address that the ChoSec folks can show up at."

"No, but it will restrict his movement."

"I imagine he has ways of slipping about," Joe said.

"I should hope so. No matter what, the legal ball needs to be rolling…especially since it rolls so slowly."

"I still don't like this. There are too many things that could go wrong. Your route here puts you in a lot of danger."

"It does, but we can't just contact the Federation DA and tell them to arrest the whole STR Consortium. We need to get the name of whoever gave the orders and pulled the strings. Getting our hands on Drenn would work too, but he's been playing this game for a long time. I'm guessing that he's lying very low right now."

"He'd be on the first ship to Alpha Centauri if he knew what was good for him." Joe shook his head. "By the way, I heard you went down to the surface with Captain Andrews. What was that about?"

Tanis twisted her lips, thinking about the goal of that trip. What they brought back up to the *Intrepid* had answered all her questions about why Terrance and the Reddings were coming along to New Eden. The knowledge was like a burr in the back of her mind, but she knew that it was imperative it remain a secret.

"Good. I gave him a hand with a few things."

Joe's tone remained impassive, but the curiosity was obvious in his face. "What sort of things?"

Tanis grimaced. "I wish I could say, but I can't. I'll tell you once we're underway."

They discussed other issues for several minutes before Joe left for an inspection on Blue Wing. Tanis took a few minutes to relax in the relative peace and quiet before rising to hit the officer's mess for a late night meal before bed.

She whistled a tuneless melody as she walked through the halls of officer country. It was third shift, and few people were about; Tanis was half watching where she was going and half paying attention to some timetables that Angela was running through in the back of her mind.

She rounded a corner and thought she caught a shadow out of the periphery of her eye — a blur that was there one moment and gone the next. Looking behind her, she saw nothing, and, pausing, heard only the sound of air circulation coming from a nearby vent.

Something wasn't right. Tanis evaluated her surroundings, checking for aberrant scents, sounds, and vibrations. Sure enough, the sound of the vent was too loud.

Tanis slowed her pace and leaned back against the bulkhead, pretending to have gotten a message via Link that required all of her concentration. Instead what she was doing was sending out preconfigured, noise-cancelling nano. They spread through the corridor, determining what the actual sound of the moving air was, and clearing it from Tanis's hearing. All that was left was the additional noise. The nano attempted to triangulate and pick up its source, but were unable to do so. It appeared to be coming from everywhere.

Then a sensation prickled within Tanis, almost as though she could sense another being's presence, and she threw up an arm to fend off a blow. To her surprise, she actually did deflect a strike. Instinct told her where the attacker would be; she lashed out with her boot, and felt it connect with an unseen body. Tanis thanked the foresight that had caused her to amp up her olfactory system; that had to be what was giving her this intuition.

<Bets on it being her?> Tanis referred to the female attacker from the *Steel Dawn III*.

<The odds are too much in your favor for a bet,> Angela

responded.

"You know," Tanis spoke aloud to her attacker. "I can't see you, but I can smell the patterns you're making in the air currents. Why don't you just drop this sneaky assassin thing, and we can do this the old-fashioned way?"

A figure materialized in front of Tanis, every inch covered in a skintight glossy black outfit. There weren't even any apparent openings for the wearer to breathe or see through. Most likely, that was done to mask IR output from hot breath. Tanis found herself wanting one.

The figure was obviously female, and Tanis's records showed that the height, weight, bone structure, and overall posture matched the woman she had fought previously on the *Dawn*.

No weapons were visible, but that didn't mean that they weren't there.

"As you wish." The sound seemed to come from the figure's entire body. "Would you like to do this hand-to-hand, or not quite that old-fashioned?" An obvious challenge resonated in the woman's tone. Her body posture was confident and tense all at the same time.

"Oh, what the hell, Kris." Tanis grinned. "It's been a very long time since I tore the stuffing out of anyone with my bare hands. It is Kris, by the way, isn't it?"

"Good memory, Tanis. Now that we're on a first name basis, shall we get on with it?"

Tanis didn't wait for a response, but sent a TSF-issued boot—polished so even Williams would be proud—up and around in a textbook roundhouse kick to her opponent's head. Kris wasn't there anymore, but Tanis hadn't expected her to be. It wouldn't be a very fun fight if she won with a single kick.

With that, the battle was joined. Kris was skilled—something Tanis already knew—and both women's limbs flashed out and were blocked or deflected by the other in turn.

It was as though they were participating in a complicated dance, and each had the moves down perfectly.

Even so, Tanis felt that she was at a bit of a disadvantage. No tells were offered by her opponent. Normally, a grimace or a look in the eyes would give intentions away; but the featureless mask prevented that. She wanted one of these suits even more.

The moment of reflection almost caused her to fall for a feint, but she blocked the real strike at the last moment, wincing as the blow deflected off her forearm. Kris's attacks were powerful; she was most certainly cybernetically enhanced.

She wasn't the only one; the TSF didn't let you above commander if you were just flesh and blood. A little carbon nanofiber here, some titanium there, coupled with some X5A sinew, and *then* you were all you could be.

"You're not too bad," Kris commented with a hint of appreciation in her voice.

"Not too shabby yourself. Why don't you give up, and we'll call it a draw."

"Not very likely," Kris said. "I'm going to collect that credit on your head, and retire somewhere real nice. Maybe New Eden."

"Any way we could fake my death and split the take?" Tanis asked. "This job doesn't pay for shit."

Her comment caused Kris just a moment of pause, and Tanis used that to make a daring attack with both her left foot and right arm. The blows wrenched Kris and dislocated her shoulder. A follow-up strike to the base of her skull ended the fight in Tanis's favor.

The black figure went down in a heap, and Tanis waited for the TSF team she had called during the fight to secure the body. She had no idea how Kris had planned to get off the ship; that was something she would have to ask the woman.

"Put her with our collection. We're gonna have us a nice long talk. And save the suit, but make sure it doesn't have any surprises. I can think of a really good use for that puppy."

A TEMPTING OFFER

STELLAR DATE: 3227282 / 11.25.4123 (Adjusted Gregorian)
LOCATION: GSS *Intrepid*, Mars Outer Shipyards (MOS)
REGION: Mars Protectorate, Sol Space Federation

Trist had been moved to the medical facilities on the *Intrepid*; a place Tanis was already quite familiar with, after her mods for the trip to Cruithne. After a couple of days, the thief was well on her way to full health. Portions of her body were now made up of silbio, the value of which was greater than most people would make in a hundred years.

They were sitting in one of the lounges in the medical facilities, each with a cup of coffee. Tanis was drinking hers black—something that a lot of time in the field forced you to like, whether you preferred it or not—while Trist was drinking some concoction that could only have come from Ganymede. It consisted of several different spices, milks, creams, and possibly some actual coffee.

"I gotta hand it to you folks," Trist said. "You sure know how to make a girl feel at home—if home were a fluffy, cushy prison."

"You're not a prisoner...exactly," Tanis replied.

"Kinda feels like it, with virtually no Link access, no permission to leave my room unless I've got a couple of burly types with me, and no knowledge of what my future holds."

"Well, what do you think we should do with you?" Tanis asked.

Trist cast her a sidelong glance. "You're not tricking me with that one. I've been around long enough to know someone's looking to see if I'll hang myself with the line they give me."

Tanis smiled. "Sorry."

"Just sorry? Why am I the one guiding this conversation?

Didn't you come here to see me?"

"I did, I'm just trying to decide exactly what to do with you. You won't testify against the STR, which means that I don't have a lot of use for you. However, sending you back out into the system is a bit of a death sentence, and I don't feel totally comfortable with that either."

"What? The cold-as-ice Major Tanis Richards, the Butcher of Toro, would feel bad about me getting my head blown off? I think your reputation is a smoke screen."

It was Tanis's turn to cast a glance at Trist. "I thought you had no Link access."

"Oh, I don't; at least I don't right now. I managed to slip past the safeguards a few times until some broad named Amanda gave me the smackdown. Took me a bit, but I got past her eventually, and I was wandering through some personnel files when some guy named Bob came into my mind and told Sue and I that if we even sent a photon across the Link, he would turn our brains off. Was a real jackass about it, too."

Tanis's eyebrows rose considerably. "You got a visit from the *Intrepid*. He doesn't deign to speak to us mere mortals much anymore. You should be honored — or possibly scared witless — that he addressed you."

Trist's organic eye widened. "He wouldn't really…"

"Who knows; he's a very advanced AI. There aren't any others like him in the human sphere."

Trist whistled. "Good thing I hadn't implemented my plan to get past him."

"Good thing, indeed. Otherwise I wouldn't be able to offer you this deal."

"Finally we get to it."

"We'll grant you and Sue immunity from extradition in the SSF territories. Any past crimes committed in those areas, or against organizations based in SSF-controlled space, will be pardoned. In exchange for that, we require your testimony against Trent."

Trist considered it for a moment. "Not going to be good enough. STR will come after us; or even if it doesn't, we'll live our whole lives waiting for the other shoe to drop."

"Well, we can't get you pardoned by the Jovians—they won't budge. It's possible they will, once we nail the STR, though."

"No, I'll tell you what I'll do it for. I want in."

"In?" Tanis asked, though she was pretty sure that she knew what Trist wanted.

"Yeah, in. I want to be on the colony roster."

Tanis raised an eyebrow, wondering how the GSS would feel if she circumvented them to get a known criminal onto the *Intrepid*.

"You do have decent credentials, but you really don't pass a lot of the other screening parameters."

Trist crossed her arms. "And I want my mods upgraded. I want a real eye with all of the extra performance, and I want a normal-looking hand. Everything state of the art."

Tanis leaned back and took a sip of her coffee. Stuff tasted like bile. "How much of you is still human?"

"Fifty-fifty, depending on what you count my new secret ingredient as," Trist said. "Sue would, of course, like her specs upgraded as well. I've got the full requirements in a file that I'm sending you."

Tanis received it and looked it over. It was quite the request; though, honestly, not even worth mentioning, in the grand scope of the *Intrepid*'s construction—or even compared to the cost of her more basic security enhancements.

"I'll have to discuss your addition to the roster with the colony leaders. As for the mods, I'll schedule the surgeries as a show of good faith."

Trist all but beamed. "I'll give you the testimony of a lifetime."

"Just stick to the truth," Tanis sighed.

BAIT

STELLAR DATE: 3227284 / 11.27.4123 (Adjusted Gregorian)
LOCATION: GSS *Intrepid*, Mars Outer Shipyards (MOS)
REGION: Mars Protectorate, Sol Space Federation

"I don't know how much I like this plan." Trist fidgeted. "I sort of get the feeling that I'm bait."

"That would be because you are bait," Tanis replied. "However, you'll be very safe bait, especially since you are just their secondary target. They'll be jumping at the chance to get at me, with the minimal protection I'll have on Mars 1."

"Yay, so I'll be secondary bait right next to the primary bait." Trist sighed. "How did I get myself mixed up in this?"

"I believe it was by leading a life of crime and wrongdoing," Joe's tone was caustic.

Trist turned on him. "Yeah, you try growing up on the lower Callisto rings. Either you dish shit out, or you eat it. I chose not to do the eating."

"She does have a point, sirs," Williams said. "I've been to Callisto. It's nice up top, the part most tourists and visitors see; but down below, it's a real heap—the classic scenario of the poor maintaining the system for the rich. They could probably run it cheaper with bots, but why fix what they can ignore?"

"Be that as it may," Tanis checked over her equipment one more time, "it doesn't change the fact that our course of action is fixed. We're going to Mars 1 to give our depositions. We've got our route covered and, while I expect that they'll attack before we make our destination, I don't think it will be anything a few squads of Marines can't handle. Mark my words: by the end of this day, we'll have Trent."

Trist's expression grew dark, and Joe, Williams, and Tanis all got a glimpse of a very different woman than the one Tanis had seen recovering in medical.

"Any chance I can get a few minutes alone with him?"

"Probably not," Tanis replied. "Though for what it's worth, I echo your sentiment."

<We just got patched up and upgraded,> Sue said. <Don't go signing up to get us wrecked—besides, now that you look un-modded with your new eye and hand, he may not even recognize you.>

"Don't worry," Trist turned her hand over and flexed her fingers. "I'm pretty sure I could remind him." She glanced up at Tanis and Joe. "Sorry, I guess that sounds a bit stupid—but he did kill my best friend. I'm finding that pretty hard to let go of."

Joe's expression softened, and he placed a hand on her shoulder. "It's not an easy road you have ahead of you."

Trist's expression flashed confusion and mistrust. "I was under the impression that you don't think I'm all that trustworthy."

"The jury's still out on that, as far as I'm concerned; but I do know what it's like to literally have to face your demons," Joe said. "Just keep a clear head and don't get in the way."

Trist opened her mouth to give a retort, but Williams used a Marine sergeant look on her, and she shut up.

Tanis didn't quite know why, but she found herself liking Trist more than she would have expected—and also a bit annoyed with Joe for his attitude toward her. Being in MICI had made her world mostly full of shades of grey. She sometimes forgot that his was likely much more black and white.

No time to think about that now. She put her analysis of Joe aside, and got back to the task at hand. "Enough chatting, let's get this show on the road."

....

Williams liked Major Richards, which is why he had

assigned himself to the team that was her escort detail. One/one had also volunteered to be the escorting fireteam—apparently they had taken a liking to the major as well. He hadn't often witnessed an officer impressing the enlisted so quickly; especially a Micky officer.

In his estimation, it was a shame that she would be shipping out on the *Intrepid*. The TSF needed more people like her. Even her number two, Commander Evans, wasn't a bad sort. He certainly had proven his bars in piloting that freighter.

However, Williams did have some misgivings about this venture. *The major is walking into an obvious trap—planning to spring it, in fact. The last time she deliberately sprung a trap, she had ended up on a dock surrounded by nearly one hundred mercs all gunning for her.*

His thought process caused him to recheck the route and ensure that all teams were in position. The rest of his platoon would be making a show of patrolling certain areas on the ring. The Mars 1 authorities had raised quite the stink when they caught wind of this venture, but they were brought to heel by the TSF. Preliminary Micky reports indicated M1 security would have their people out in force on the ring as well. Several pundits on the nets were postulating that M1 security didn't want to garner the reputation the MOS had for shoddy security—or they wanted all the glory for themselves.

Probably both.

Looking at the intel that was coming in from the tactical net, Williams could see the positions that Mars 1's security had taken up; some were decent, and others looked poor to say the least. Hopefully they wouldn't get in the way too much. In his experience, killing local cops always made the brass grumpy.

The team left the *Intrepid* and crossed the dock with no trouble. From there, several tubes and a maglev took them to the connector elevator that ran down to the MCEE, and then to Mars 1. They secured a car, and the eight of them rode down in silence; the only movement being the weapons ready checks that everyone except Trist made periodically.

The Mars 1 ring generated its gravity from centripetal force as it rotated around the planet at the geosynchronous orbital distance. As a result, the side facing the planet was 'up' and the side facing out into space was 'down'. The ring's top level sported a full ecosystem with hills, lakes, and even a few oceans. It was larger than the all of Earth's continents combined, and it was also the location of the team's ultimate destination: the federal courthouses.

Far below, at the lowest level of the Mars 1 ring, the elevator lock cycled open. After sending out probes, the team debarked in careful formation.

Jansen and Lang were in the lead, followed by Williams and Joe, then Tanis and Trist. Cassar and Murphy brought up the rear. The hard stares the Marines were casting cleared a path faster than the presence of their high-powered pulse rifles. Because the ring was not a pressurized system like a standard station, each member also carried a small slug thrower.

In the corridors the team moved through, the twenty fourth century architecture was nearly something to stop and marvel at. The designers of the ring had added a twist of art deco to their creation. Unlike most stations, which were more utilitarian or very high-tech flashy, Mars 1 was built with an element of garishness. The sweeping archways and overt embellishments of every doorway drew the eye and amazed with the boundless attention to detail.

After clearing security, a process that simply involved a quick check of their IDs, and extensive scowling by the Marines, they entered a maglev station that took them seven thousand miles east around the ring.

"So far so good," Joe murmured.

"Oh, great…you had to say that," Jansen said. "Er…sir."

"Relax, Marine." Williams scowled. "This won't be anything

we can't handle; nothing worse than what we've seen before."

"Aye, Staff Sergeant," Jansen replied, taking a deep breath. "It's the lack of activity…I wish they'd just attack already."

"Don't worry," Tanis said. "You'll get your wish. We've got to change trains ahead, and I anticipate that to be their first probable ambush point. When we debark, stick close to the wall on the right and keep your eyes peeled. When we round the first corner, we may encounter some company."

"You do have people there, right?" Trist asked Tanis. "And I really wish you'd give me a gun."

"Yes. No."

"She'd make a good sergeant," Cassar said.

Williams smiled and Tanis took it as a compliment. Everyone rechecked their weapons as the maglev began to slow; sidearms were loosened in holsters, and extra clips were moved into readily accessible positions.

The station was decidedly upscale with a broad atrium ringed by catwalks, a lavish fountain, and a small food court on the far side. It looked empty—strange at this time of day, though nothing was flagged as hostile on the Marines' systems.

"Let's do this," Tanis said, and the escort began to move off the train.

Directly into a storm of particle beams.

"Fall back!" Williams shouted at Jansen and Lang, who were out front, while everyone else took protective positions inside the train. The two Marines jumped backwards, and Joe and Williams pulled the doors shut.

"Injuries?" Williams called out.

"No, sir; armor appears to have absorbed it all," Lang said. Jansen reported the same.

<We seem to have stirred the hornet's nest. Get this train moving to the next station!> Tanis said to Angela. *<We need to get gone.>*

<Already on it, but…>

An explosion rocked the car and Tanis had a sinking feeling.

<They just disabled the track, didn't they?>

<Yup, they're not playing fair. I'm getting probes out to get their positions.>

"Two on that catwalk above," Williams called out. "Cassar, Murphy, get suppressing fire on those bastards. I see muzzle flash coming from that food stand at ten o'clock. Jansen, you and Lang move down one car and see if you can't flank them. I'll hold their attention."

"Two more at three o'clock from around the fountain." Tanis relayed information from Angela's scan. "One/two is also advancing from where we *thought* the ambush would be, but they're under fire as well."

"Sounds like a party." Joe took aim at the fountain, blowing off bits and pieces in an attempt to decrease its cover.

"Someone is not going to be happy that you are chewing apart their art." Cassar said.

"What they get for putting a fountain in a train station." Williams snorted.

"Time for me to use my new toy." Tanis began to pull her light armor off. Underneath, she wore the glossy black shimmersuit she had appropriated from the assassin, Kris. She issued a command and the suit flowed up over her head, completely covering her.

"I feel like I'm suffocating every time it does that," Tanis said.

"Good look on you, though, sir." Joe grinned from where he was taking cover.

Tanis slid two long blades into the covered sheaths on her arms, and with a silent command to the suit, faded from view.

"I'm going right to take out the guys behind the fountain. Concentrate your fire on the left side; your scan can't see me, and I won't show on combat net—don't want to give off a signal."

"Aye, sir," Williams said, and made sure all the Marines

knew what to do.

Carefully slipping over the jagged edges of glass in the train car's shattered windows, Tanis cursed softly, wishing that the stealth suit provided some amount of actual safety. Even though she was invisible, the notion of being effectively without protection in a firefight was unnerving.

A scream came from the catwalk, and one of the attackers toppled over the railing, courtesy of Cassar's heavy repeater. Tanis caught sight of the heavily armored man as he crashed to the ground. It was similar armor to what the attackers had on the night of the VIP party—only a few revisions newer. Specs showed few weak points, so Tanis would have to make the best of them.

Slipping around the fountain, she saw four attackers, not two. This would be a bit more challenging than she first thought. Carefully observing them, she planned out her moves.

An initial kick to the back of the man on the left would send him sprawling out into the open, where, with luck, Joe or Williams would finish him off. A rather spirited woman was cursing loudly as she tried to place her shots through the shattered windows of the train car. The other two women were calmer, and consequently were more precise in their shooting.

Having worked out the best moves, Tanis took a running jump and slammed her feet into the man's back. Sure enough, he slid out from behind the cover. Without looking to see if he had been targeted by the Marines, Tanis glanced at the two more controlled women. One had already noticed her compatriot being struck, and was looking frantically for the perpetrator. Tanis stepped past her, slid a blade out from her forearm, and sliced the throat of the third, more vocal woman.

Now both of the remaining two were alert, and the screams to her right told Tanis that the Marines had taken out the man.

The two women started firing around themselves wildly. Just barely avoiding being hit, Tanis stepped between them.

Quickly sliding out the other blade, she reached out and slit both of their throats at once.

Blood fountained across her, and she went from being invisible to being the red sticky outline of a person. A cry rang out from the catwalk, and shots rained down around her. Grabbing one of the rifles on the ground, Tanis dove for cover in the fountain, the action having the dual purpose of washing the blood from her and giving her some protection.

The red tint left her vision, and she peered around the splashing water, trying to get the man overhead within her sights. As it turned out she didn't need to, since when he leaned over to get a bead on her, someone else filled him with holes.

Another few shots rang out, and a scream came from Jansen's target, followed by a gun being thrown over the counter with a cry of surrender. Tanis, invisible again, stepped quietly over to the concession stand only to see the final attacker hiding under a candy machine of some sort, a rifle trained on the opening. The weapon he had tossed over the counter must have been that of his dead companion.

Tanis raised her arm and flung a blade at him attempting to hit the creases on his armor's neck. She missed and it bounced off, clattering to the deck. He spun and started shooting wildly in her direction, forcing Tanis to hit the deck.

"Surrender for real, or we toss a grenade in there to do the job for you!" Williams called out.

"You wouldn't," the man replied. "Station would throw a fit."

"I'm a Marine staff sergeant. Do you really think that I give a monkey's ass what this station thinks? You've got five seconds."

The man didn't even think about it for two. He was out and on the ground so fast he nearly landed on Tanis. Williams was securing him when one/two arrived, looking worn but triumphant.

"Heard you guys needed a hand," Corporal Taylor said.

"We did," Jansen said. "What took you so long?"

"Just ran into a few folks who wanted to turn us into sponges." Taylor grinned. "We showed them how that goes when they try to take on Marines."

The fireteam gave an 'Oo Rah', and Tanis couldn't help but grin. She walked back to the train to retrieve her armor and her weapons.

"Good work," Williams commented. "Make sure all these folks are dead or secure, and wait for station security to arrive. We'll be rolling out as soon as the major's ready."

"They're actually right behind us," Taylor said and turned around. "You guys can come through, looks like everything's taken care of here, too. Good thing you were around to not help us."

"We came as fast as we could," the man in the lead said. His shoulder patches identified him as a lieutenant in the MSF. "We'll take over this scene, but we'll need statements."

"Those can wait." Tanis stepped from the train car, once again clothed and in her armor. Trist was in her wake, casting uneasy glances at the large body of police officers. At least thirty of them had streamed into the atrium.

"Major Richards?" the MSF lieutenant asked.

"Yes…" She waited for him to identify himself.

"Lieutenant Folsom. I'm going to have to ask you and your forces to lay down your weapons and surrender to us."

Tanis wasn't certain she'd heard the man correctly. "You want us to what?"

The Marines had snapped into action the moment Folsom spoke. Raising their weapons, they began to ease into positions to cover one another.

"By the authority vested in me by the Mars Protectorate, I am placing you under arrest on the charge of harboring a known terrorist."

"What known terrorist would that be?" Tanis asked.

"The woman with you: Trist. She is wanted by the Jovian government."

"Last I heard, we weren't in Jovian space," Joe said. "Why don't you boys pack up and head out before we place you under arrest for interfering in the prosecution of a federal case."

Tanis saw that Cassar had reached a position offering decent cover. He slowly eased to a knee, switching his weapon to full auto. He had one eye on Williams and the other on the MSF squad. One word, and he would have at least ten of them down and out of the fight. Tanis assessed the other Marine's positions through her recon probes while Angela furiously queried Mars 1 databases, trying to find the origin of Folsom's orders.

<What's the word?> Tanis asked.

<Nothing so far. I'm speaking with his CO and am being informed that Folsom isn't here, and there is no such order. I don't know what is going on.>

<I do,> Tanis said.

"It appears we have a situation." Tanis scanned the MSF unit. Most of them were arrayed behind Folsom, though a few were slowly easing into flanking positions. "You see, I can't find any validation of your orders. And there is no way I'm just going to surrender to you without them. Plus, you've *got* to know there is no way these Marines will surrender to you under any circumstances."

A few of the cops looked uneasy at that, and the stone-cold looks from one/one and one/two only solidified the knowledge that these Marines would go down fighting. Even death here would be more preferable to the Marines than going back to their platoon having been arrested by civilian cops—especially since they were only outnumbered two to one.

"Nevertheless, you will surrender," Folsom said. "We have reinforcements on the way. You'll be subdued."

"Like hell we will," Williams grunted. "I've faced more

threatening odds on my own. You station fairies are going to die today if you get in our way."

Tanis grinned; there really was nothing like having a sergeant put it in the simplest possible terms. Several of the MSF men and women were looking a lot less certain, and she decided to push it home.

"You have ten seconds to stand down before I log this as an official violation of the Federated Space Treaty, Section 4.2 — TSF Charter, paragraph 9. Such violation authorizes TSF forces commanded by an officer ranking commander or higher to respond with lethal force against anybody, official or otherwise, who is interfering with TSF actions."

Folsom still looked resolute and Tanis began to count.

"One…two…three…four…"

Several of the MSF men and women put down their weapons and slowly began stepping back, out of the line of fire.

"Five…six…"

A couple more left, bringing the MSF numbers down to twenty.

"Seven…eight…"

No one else moved. Everyone tensed.

"Nine."

Tanis waited the space of a second and then dove to her right, knocking Trist to the ground while raising her rifle and taking aim at Folsom. He ducked as well, and her shots cut through the air where his chest had been.

Cassar opened up, and in moments, six of the Marsians were down, with several more stunned by the rapid fire from his weapon. Perez, one/two's heavy gunner, was less than a second behind in releasing his barrage, and Williams, taking his pissed off look to a whole new level, leaped through the air, horizontal and low, taking out the legs of several MSF officers.

Five seconds later, it was over. Taylor had been hit point-blank center mass, but his armor had absorbed the impact, leaving him merely sore and embarrassed. Murphy had taken a shot in the shoulder, where his armor creased to allow flexibility. The limb hung stiffly, already suffused with mednano that was stemming the bleeding and stitching his sinews back together.

"I'm five by five, Staff Sergeant," he grunted. "Can shoot just fine with my other arm."

"Never doubted it for a moment," Williams said. "You keep to the back of your team, though."

"Aye, Staff Sergeant."

"I've reported this to the station and local Terran Space Force. A unit is on the way to clean this mess up. As much as I hate to split up, we can't leave all this hardware lying around. One/two, you stay here until the TSF arrives. Don't let any station security in until our people have the scene. Provide your recordings of the event, and take up your positions for return route beta; we won't be coming back this way."

"Sir, yes, sir!" came the chorus of responses.

"One/one, let's move out."

Their route moved into more populated and public areas, an unfortunate necessity. Tanis could see station security forces shadowing them here and there. She was also paying half attention to the web of reports, accusations, and threats that were flooding the nets. The MSF was claiming ignorance of Folsom's actions, and simultaneously accusing the TSF of assaulting its personnel. The TSF for its part was opening inquiries and launching inquests into the MSF faster than even an AI could read the orders. Someone's head was going to roll for this, and Tanis just hoped hers would still be attached by the end of the day. Sanderson was most likely going to want to take it off himself.

The public had gotten wind of what happened, and leaked security vids were already circulating the nets. It didn't take long for people to figure out where Tanis and her entourage were going. From there, speculators posted probable routes, one of them being the actual route Tanis was using. The upside was that those areas started to clear out. Some oblivious folks still wandered past, but for the most part, Tanis's group had a very clear path to the federated buildings.

"Coming up on the second projected ambush point," Williams observed.

"What do we expect here?" Joe asked.

"Previous set were Trent's boys. I expect we'll get more of them, or perhaps some other STR special ops unit of some sort. Two/one and two/two are in position in the buildings I've lit up on your HUDs. We have a safe room in that building across the concourse there, and there is a weapons dump hidden in that trash disposal across the street."

"Not expecting much here, I see." Cassar chuckled. Tanis wondered about him. He hardly spoke, except when he was expecting to kill someone.

The space was an open square. It was the intersection of two broad thoroughfares—a long stretch with nothing but three small vertical conduits for cover. An ambush here would be hairy. Tanis gave the signal, and Jansen and Lang moved over to the left side of the corridor, while Cassar and Williams moved ahead. Murphy stayed back with Trist, Joe, and Tanis.

"You guys take me to all the best places," Trist said. "Why don't we just take a car?"

"Too risky down here," Tanis replied. "Too many things we can't see when we're moving that fast; that, and we're bunched up. We get attacked, and we're sitting ducks. This way, we can approach each danger zone carefully and with the appropriate cover."

"Somehow I really don't feel covered," Trist muttered.

Joe smiled. "But just think, you'll have the most interesting stories to tell your children."

"I don't plan on raising children."

"Well…then you can tell them to your cats."

They moved slowly and carefully through the square. A few civilians had been approaching from their left, but upon seeing the Marines slowly creeping along the passage, they found another route. The hum of the station seemed to fade until all they heard was slow breathing, and the sound of boots rolling across the deck.

Tanis cocked her head as they reached the middle of the area with no cover.

"Something…" She didn't get to the next word before an invisible blade whistled toward her; only her augmented sense of smell notified her of the shifting air currents and gave her the split second she needed to take the blow on her shoulder plate and not in her neck creases.

"Stealthed attackers!" she cried out as her vision was overlaid with the ghost of the person who had nearly killed her. Other figures danced in and out of her olfactory range, like shadows slipping in and out of visibility.

"Fall back to a wall," Williams yelled, and the Marines complied quickly, not firing, but fingers on their triggers. Tanis pushed Trist back behind her as she ducked a blow and fired a shot with her pistol, catching her attacker in the chest. There was a grunt, and he hit the ground, his suit failing in that spot as blood spurted out.

"How many?" Joe asked.

"I can't tell." Tanis's head swept side to side. "I think there are at least a dozen of them."

"Fuck!" Murphy spat. "Nothing in my suit is picking them up. I can't see a goddamn one of them! How do we take them out?"

<You know what to do; set your rifle to medium power and set up a field of fire, Marines!> Williams' voice boomed over the combat net. *<Don't hit your teammates, but keep these bastards pinned!>*

Williams grunted as something struck him and blood

sprayed out of his left wrist. He didn't say a word, but his right arm whipped out, swinging the butt of his rifle into something that made a sickening crunch, followed by a pained grunt. A second blow was followed by the sound of a body hitting the deck.

"A flesh wound," Williams said regarding his own injury, and proceeded to randomly send out pulse blasts, hoping to catch the enemy or at least keep them pinned down.

Trist knelt down and felt for the body that Williams had dropped. She located it, and extruded a probe from her left index finger. It disappeared into the cloaked form and her brow furrowed.

"Their suits are like yours." She glanced up at Tanis, who was doing her best to put holes in the shapes she could see flitting in and out of her vision. "They're one of the latest revisions, but it looks like we're in luck—they're based off the fashion silsuits that are all the rage back in Callisto. That's a poor choice in base technology." She grinned and extruded another probe, this one into another location on the fallen form.

"One of the neat features of the latest silsuits is that they can download new designs, and when they're in demo mode can even have the designs loaded without user interaction."

"I think I know where you're going with this." Joe grunted as his armor absorbed a blow from an invisible blade. "What's the ETA?"

"Minute or two."

Tanis put a slug in the attacker that had hit Joe. "Go faster. Jansen and Lang are taking a beating over there."

"Working on it." Trist's brow furrowed.

Across the square, Lang went down and Jansen let out a primal scream, rapidly sending pulses out where she hoped there was someone to hit. At that same moment, two/one and two/two showed up and took in what looked like a scene of absolute madness. Marines were firing at nothing and yet seemed to be taking casualties.

<Stealthed units. Standard positions,> Williams called out. The two fireteams backed against walls and also began placing random shots into the square.

"Got it!" Trist cried out. She removed her probes from the dead body on the deck and grinned triumphantly. "Wait for it…"

And then it happened. Several human outlines flickered in and out of visibility across the square before the suits reset and every attacker became fully visible. Trist had chosen a bright red covered in bullseyes for the attacking party's new look.

"See them OK?" she asked.

"Plenty OK," Tanis grinned, and in less time than it took to say the words, every attacker was down.

Joe looked at Tanis and coughed back a laugh.

"Uh, Trist? Major Tanis is looking a little red around the collar."

Trist looked up at Tanis to see red showing at the edges of her armor where the stealth suit showed.

"Oops, passing Angela the info to fix it."

<Thanks.> Angela's tone hid a snicker as she reset the stealth suit.

Tanis had an unreadable look on her face for a moment and then smiled at Trist. "Good work; that could have been messy."

Williams was already halfway across the square to check on Lang. Tanis raced after as the two new fireteams secured the area and the attackers.

She arrived as the sergeant knelt beside the fallen Marine; Jansen looked on, her eyes misting.

"Cut halfway through his neck…armor went into stasis, but I don't know…he lost a lot of blood, it may have been too late."

"He'll make it," Williams grunted. "But he'll get a nice bit of R&R time while they put all his tendons and arteries back in place."

He rose, calling for the leader of two/one. "Corporal Salas! Lang is your number one priority. Two/two can stay here; you take Lang to TSF med facility AR13; it's only a thousand miles from here. Get him there safe."

"Aye, Staff Sergeant." Salas nodded and gestured for two of his Marines to unfold a field stretcher for Lang. Within moments, they were trotting down the cross corridor to the nearest maglev.

Tanis looked at Jansen. "You good, Marine?"

The corporal's eyes had cleared up, a steely determination having set in. "Sir, yes, sir."

"Glad to hear it." Tanis smiled. "OK, team, we need to recharge, reammo, and head out. Cassar, breach that ammo dump and pass out power packs and slugs."

"Aye, sir." Cassar nodded and went to work. Two minutes later they had left the plaza—Lance Corporal Olsen was left to fend off the MSF unit that had arrived, and was trying to take control of the situation. Having heard what happened at the last run-in between the two forces, the MSF wasn't eager to get in a fight with the Marines. Two/three was on its way to back them up before everyone dispersed to cover the beta return route.

The escort only had a quarter mile more of corridor to pass through, and then they took a tubelift up to the highest level of the ring. Like many of the planetary rings, the upper level on Mars 1 was effectively an open eco-space. The landscape was filled with rivers and lakes and grass and trees. Hovering above them, almost as though it was suspended between the arching arms of the ring, was the planet of Mars.

Spread out across the terrain, were various buildings— mostly museums and cultural centers. While the crush of humanity was mostly in the lower levels, this upper area was designed with aesthetics as the primary consideration. No other artificial habitat in the Sol system had even half as much parkland as Mars 1. Off in the distance was the low hill that housed most of the higher SolGov courts on Mars. It was a towering edifice of white marble that gleamed brilliantly in the reflected sunlight.

"That just looks effing cool," Perez said. "Gotta record this on full sensory."

"Stay frosty, people," Williams said. "You can gawk on your own time."

"Besides, even you can't jerk off to a sens recording of a planet." Cassar grinned at Perez.

"Like the Staff Sergeant said. We don't have any more marked positions where we're expecting to be ambushed. But that doesn't mean we're in the clear." Tanis gestured for Jansen to take the lead.

They trotted along in silence, the way before them virtually clear of locals for a time; but as they neared the federal buildings, they moved into more populated areas until they were just a small island in a sea of foot traffic. The judiciary loomed ahead of them, and minutes later they were moving up the steps toward the main lobby.

They passed through security, and the guards didn't look too happy to be allowing armed Marines into the courthouse. At the entrance to the courtroom, Tanis signaled the Marines to wait outside and handed Williams her pulse rifle.

Tanis checked the time and smiled. "We're actually going to be right on time."

"Well, we did plan for some interruptions," Joe said. "You pretty much nailed how long they'd be."

"To be honest, I expected them to be longer," Tanis replied. "That was really too easy. I can't believe Trent didn't put in an appearance. I don't think he'll attack after the testimonies have been entered; what would be the point in that?"

She nodded to Trist and they turned and entered the court.

"What would be the point indeed," said a voice from the judge's seat, which was facing away from them. Tanis and Trist approached as the chair turned. Sitting in it was Trent, a rather unflattering smile on his face.

"It's good to see you again Tanis, Trist. I really am sorry that it will be the last time."

With those words, the doors slammed shut behind them and heavily armored troops spilled out of the judge's antechamber while more lined the balconies above them.

"It would seem that I finally have you where I want you, you meddling bitch," Trent spat. "Now pass over your sidearm, and we'll get started."

FINAL STAND

STELLAR DATE: 3227284 / 11.27.4123 (Adjusted Gregorian)
LOCATION: Mars 1 Ring (MIR)
REGION: Mars Protectorate, Sol Space Federation

Tanis took a long moment to consider the odds. At least twenty-five men surrounded her and Trist—ten on the balconies and fifteen down on the floor below. Angela and Sue were desperately trying to get control of the door's mechanism and release it, but it seemed to be in some sort of lockdown. Small sparks in the air hinted at a full battle of nanoprobes occurring all around them.

<Ideas?> Tanis queried.

<I'd say you pretty much have to hand over your weapon,> Trist said. <You may be good, but we'd both be Swiss cheese before you took out three guys.>

<That, and the clip only has twenty rounds in it.>

<Do it,> Angela said. <Buy Sue and me some time.>

Tanis grunted and tossed her weapon onto the ground a few paces away. Trent signaled one of his men to pick it up, removing any chance of a dash and grab.

"I have to admit,"—Trent clasped his hands with what appeared to be genuine glee—"I really didn't expect you to be quite this easy to catch."

"Not sure how 'seventh time's the charm' is easy," Tanis replied. "From where I stand, you have a pretty poor batting average."

"Yet in the end, I still win." Trent's voice turned dark and menacing. "You have no idea what it has cost me, personally and professionally, to bring you to heel. With you out of the way, we'll finally be able to stop the *Intrepid*."

"Why?" Trist asked. "Is she the only decent Micky in the

TSF? No one else can tell guards to guard and politicians to fuck off? I thought skill like that was something the military had in spades."

"They may," Trent's smile looked sour. "But they don't seem to be assigning them to take care of the *Intrepid*. It really will be nice to be done with this job; it's taken years off my life."

"I have to ask," Tanis said. "You're pretty implicated here. What's your endgame?"

"We've got an exit plan. We may not all make it, but the pay is high enough to make up for the risk."

Several of the armed and armored figures chuckled. "Way more than enough," one said.

<*Any ideas yet?*> Tanis asked.

<*They've fused the doors,*> Angela replied. <*Williams says it's going to take them five minutes to get through.*>

<*That's a goddamn lifetime!*> Trist groaned. <*I can't believe this asshole is gonna get to shoot me down twice.*>

<*What's the model on the armor these guys are wearing?*> Tanis asked.

Sue replied after a moment's pause. <*It's STR-RVI, a newer type that we've seen on Callisto before.*>

<*Any chance that it's based on the STR-RV, and not a ground-up?*>

<*Uncertain. It has a lot of the same components, but that's just because they wanted some interchangeability.*>

The exchange only took seconds, but it gave Tanis an idea that germinated a hope of this not being her last day, and caused it to begin to glimmer.

<*Angela, we need to modify the stealth suit. Use its laser ranging system to emit proton beams into the optics of these guys' suits.*>

<*What will...ahhhh...*> Angela realized what was theoretically possible, and got on it. <*Gonna take me about thirty seconds. Take your armor's gloves off.*>

<*What are we going to do?*> Trist asked.

<Knock out each and every one of these guys' armored suits. They're all power assisted, and will lock up hard.>

<This should be interesting,> Trist replied.

"Nothing to say, Major Richards?" Trent asked. "No recital of how I'll never get away, how I should surrender?"

"Well of course you're not going to get away," Tanis replied. "I've never failed to take down a target yet. Don't see why I should start with you." She nonchalantly took her gloves off as she spoke, hoping that the casual behavior would be ignored.

"Don't you think that's a bit optimistic?" Trent asked. "Even if we don't get out of here, you're going to die. That's a given."

Tanis looked around her at the armored soldiers. Laying eyes on each one so that the beam would be calibrated, while remaining half-focused on the countdown Angela placed on her HUD.

"You gonna have your goons do it, or are you going to do it yourself?"

Trent stood and walked around the bench, facing Tanis and Trist directly. "Don't worry, I'm not afraid to kill you myself." He pulled a pistol from his belt and aimed it at Tanis.

"Well, that's good," she said with a grin. "Because you're going to have to."

She timed her statement with the proton beams and smiled, as each mercenary seemed to jerk slightly and then freeze. Muffled grunts and curses could be heard as they tried to move their powered armor, but each limb was locked solid.

"Glad that actually worked," Trist said.

"Me too, would have taken a lot more than silbio to glue us back together if it hadn't."

"What the...what did you do?" Trent asked, gesturing with his weapon.

"I fried the neural net their armor uses."

"How is that possible? The RVI is supposed to be unhackable!"

"Advice to live by." Trist glanced at Tanis. "Maybe he's been having so much trouble taking you out because he can't deal with reality that well." She looked back at Trent. "Not only is it possible, it just happened."

Tanis smiled evilly. "STR fixed all the reported issues. Since TSF doesn't use that model, we didn't feel the urge to report any weaknesses we found; especially since we usually encounter STR armor on the other side of a conflict."

Trent barked a curse, and, without any other fanfare, fired his weapon. Tanis's augmented vision flashed a warning the moment his hand tensed. She dove to the side, but not before a second alert fed into her mind that the pistol had fired a load of self-propelled ballistic projectiles. The alert came with a rather useless note about a velocity of four thousand meters per second.

Later, she remembered the whole event in a surreal out-of-body fashion—the warning, the dive, and then the knowledge that her right arm and the side of her torso were gone.

A combination of genetic alteration, training, and Angela shutting down all of her pain centers was the only thing that kept her from losing the rest of her torso, as his next shot rang out. She lunged behind a plas display that took most of the blast; though it did fling some shrapnel into her, some of which making it through her armor and into her flesh.

While Trent was occupied with attacking Tanis, Trist took the opportunity to run toward the soldier that had taken Tanis's sidearm. It was lying on a banister, and she was only a meter from it when Trent spun and fired a shot into her as well.

The blast struck Trist in center mass, and knocked her over the railing. Her body shook and convulsed while Trent turned his attention back to Tanis.

"Looks like this is the end for you." He strode over to her, gun aimed directly at her head. "You were a worthy adversary."

"Wish I could say the same for you," Trist said from behind him.

Trent turned to see Trist propped up on the banister, gun in her hand.

"I…you…you're dead," Trent gaped.

"Again with the reality issues." She fired three shots, all hitting Trent's torso. He was wearing thin armor under his suit, and it blocked the first and second shot; but the third shattered it, and dropped him at Tanis's feet.

"Needed him…have questions…" Tanis gasped.

"Oh, relax, he'll live." Trist walked over, wincing.

Her shirt was torn and under it, the green phosphor-like glow of silbio stood out. "I guess I am a bit like the gummi girl now. Helps to not have any specific internal organs to get blown up when you get blown up."

Tanis's laugh became coughs and spasms. <When are they going to get that door open? Your humor is going to kill me.>

REGRET

STELLAR DATE: 3227284 /11.27.4123 (Adjusted Gregorian)
LOCATION: Mars 1 Ring (MIR)
REGION: Mars Protectorate, Sol Space Federation

Joe leaned over the transport cocoon the ring medics had settled Tanis in. Even in her current state, she couldn't help but notice the concern and moisture in his eyes.

"That was the worst ten minutes of my life," Joe said. "I nearly died when I heard the shots."

<*Me too; fancy that.*> The tubes in her throat restricted her method of communication. She didn't mind; it helped hide her emotions. <*Just be certain that Trent makes it to the TSF detention facility. Last thing we need is these local cops getting their hands on him.*>

A look of anger flashed across Joe's face. "I can't believe that Trent is all you want to talk about right now. Look at you! You're in pieces, and all you can talk about is your job."

Grenwald stood across the transport cocoon and cast Joe an unreadable look before putting his hand on the commander's shoulder.

"We're all pretty concerned about you, Major. But don't worry, we'll do our jobs." He nodded to the two of them and walked away to oversee Trent's preparation for transport.

Tanis wanted to sigh, but it hurt too much. The pain in Joe's eyes hurt too; she knew because she felt the same thing. What was the point of getting the *Intrepid* outsystem if she killed herself doing it?

<*I'm sorry, Joe. Work is easier right now. Easier than feeling.*>

"It seems that pretty much everything is easier than feeling for you." He turned away as the medics began moving her cocoon into the ambulance.

RESULTS

STELLAR DATE: 3227294 / 12.03.4123 (Adjusted Gregorian)
LOCATION: GSS *Intrepid*, Mars Outer Shipyards (MOS)
REGION: Mars Protectorate, Sol Space Federation

"Glad to have you back with us." Commander Ouri smiled as Tanis entered the SOC. "You're looking good."

To the casual observer, she was at one hundred percent, in full control of her faculties. In reality, her new skin itched and her reflexes didn't feel quite right in her fingers. Firing right-handed was definitely out of the question.

Tanis signaled Ouri to walk with her. "I'm feeling good. I've gone over the interviews with Mr. Trent, and I see that we've not yet gotten anything useful out of him."

"No, ma'am. He's only been here on the ship for a few days—took forever to get him transferred up from the ring."

They arrived at the conference room and Tanis took a seat.

"I know, I followed the progress; it was like pulling teeth."

"Or new nerve clusters. What are you doing here?" Joe asked as he walked into the offices.

"Getting back to work; specifically, getting ready to have a chat with Mr. Trent."

Joe's expression spoke volumes. Ouri took one look at the two and excused herself.

Neither spoke for several minutes. Tanis looked down at the table, tracing the scratches in the surface with her eyes. Surprising both of them, she spoke first.

"I was scared. More scared than I've been in a long time." She looked up at him, trying not to let too much emotion show on her face and mostly failing.

Joe sat down one chair away from her. She knew he was hurt; moreover, he was scared. Probably scared he'd fallen in love with a crazy woman who would get herself killed any day now.

"Found out you're not indestructible, did you?"

Tanis waved that aside. "I've been hurt before. Worse, actually."

"You weren't scared then?"

"Why would I have been? The military patched me up and sent me back to work. It's what I do...what I did."

"I don't get you." Joe sighed and leaned back in his chair.

Tanis waited for the standard dry comment from Angela, but it didn't come. Her AI had been strangely silent when she and Joe were together during the last month.

Joe mistook her moment of contemplation for intractability and snorted. "It's like talking to a brick wall." He began to rise out of his chair.

"Wait." Tanis reached out and put a hand on his arm. "Please, I'm trying. I'm just not that good at this. I haven't felt like this about anyone in a very, very long time. You must know that."

"I've never looked at the personal parts of your file." The anger had subsided and kindness returned to Joe's eyes. "I only know the tiny nuggets of your past that you've shared."

"Well, I've never had a serious relationship with a man," Tanis said.

<Liar,> Angela commented privately.

<It wasn't serious...at least not for him.>

"What. Never?"

"Well, a fling or two in college, but nothing after that."

"You're seventy-two years old. Don't tell me you're a—"

"No." Tanis chuckled softly. "I'm not a virgin." Her eyes locked with his, a sliver of her contrary nature showing. "Why would you want someone like me? I mean you—you're a hot vacuum jockey. You've had your pick, I know I'm no prize."

Her hand was still on his arm. He looked down at it and

placed his hand over hers. "You don't get it, Major. You are *the* prize."

She looked hard and long into his eyes. No trace of deception or malice showed. Not being able to help it, she examined his skin texture, monitored his heart rate, and looked for other signs of dishonesty. There were none.

"I still don't get it."

Joe gave his warm, resonant chuckle. The one she had first found so pleasant that day after the *Dawn*—still did. "It's not something I can really just *tell* you. It sort of needs a nice long period of explanation."

Tanis didn't know how to do this. The emotions and reactions were unfamiliar to her. She had focused only on her duty for so long. Men were just teammates without breasts.

Except Joe wasn't.

Not that he didn't have a nice chest.

Tanis stop! She got control of herself. Control was what she did; it was her game.

"Joe, you know I have feelings for you. I wouldn't be such a blubbering moron at times like this if I didn't."

He smiled, though his expression showed that he suspected what was to come.

"But I can't do this, not now. I simply don't know how."

His smile was warm and inviting. Tanis was getting the feeling that there was nothing this man couldn't just smile away. "Then let me show you how."

"It's too much. I do so well at my job because I restrict my emotions, I school myself. This is the endgame. I can't get distracted now."

Joe sat back, causing her hand to slide off of his arm. "You don't give yourself enough credit."

She wanted to, but she couldn't afford the distraction. Not yet. "Once we get underway. I promise; I want it, I really do."

Joe nodded. His eyes looked tight, his lips pursed like he

didn't trust himself to speak.

Tanis looked at his lips, almost losing herself in the desire to brush her own against them. She stood, forcing the emotion down, back under control. "I have to go speak to Trent."

<You're an idiot.> Angela actually sounded angry.

Tanis didn't respond.

* * * * *

"Ah, Major Richards, I was wondering how long it was going to take for them to stitch you back together. I bet a lot of the original parts had to be replaced. Feeling up to a good bit of fun?" Trent spoke as soon as she entered the room.

Tanis tried to forget the conversation with Joe. She focused on the need to get the name from Trent. Once she had that, things would fit into place.

"I'm feeling up to having a conversation with you...need you to answer a few questions about who you work for and what their agenda is."

"And what makes you think you're going to get anything out of me?"

"Well, I can think of a number of ways, but most of them take some time. I decided to go right for the throat — metaphorically speaking."

At that prearranged signal, Kris was wheeled in, her naked form strapped to a chair. Tanis wasn't looking directly at Trent, but she was watching him on several of the room cameras over the Link and saw his pupils dilate. Good. She'd called this correctly.

Kris wasn't able to move — or speak, thanks to the seal over her mouth.

"You may be interested in knowing that we've removed her AI. It seems that he had helped subvert the AIs on those ships we had some issues with last month. The AI courts apparently weren't too forgiving. Her Link has also been removed, as have most of her biomechanical mods. She's as close to a vanilla human as you get these days, and now has a very easy-to-trigger pain response."

Tanis reached over to Kris and grabbed an inch of skin on the inside of her bicep and twisted. The prisoner's eyes opened wide with tears glistening in the corners as she sucked a deep breath in through her nose.

"It makes torture really easy. So many people shunt pain with their mods or AIs that they've forgotten what it feels like. No tolerance at all."

"She may not be used to pain" —Trent's expression betrayed nothing—"but I'm certain it'll take more than that to really hurt her. You can't do anything to her or me; your precious rules and regs see to that."

"I'm sure you're aware that we're on the *Intrepid*," Tanis said. "The ship's AI is really quite amazing; one of the most advanced and powerful ever created. He really wants to live and see the galaxy; something that you're trying to keep him from. Now, normally he would be impartial—but, you see, he has a very special connection with a woman named Amanda. She's in a unique position, and has also come to view you with a certain amount of distaste."

"That's great," Trent said. "I'm really happy for her."

"What you don't get is that she has prevailed upon the *Intrepid* to arrange it so that we're alone."

No one was ever really alone anymore in the forty second century. There was always a camera, a sensor, or someone conversing over the Link. The concept of truly being alone was very foreign to most people, even frightening to some. It most certainly was to Trent at that moment.

"No one knows what's going on in here; key people will cover any injuries, and no recordings will be made—unless you want them to be made while you give your confession."

"You bitch…" Trent's voice was weak.

"Lacking in conviction," Tanis said. "I will have the truth out of you. If I need to cut her, and then you, down to just a brain and a pair of lungs to wheeze words from, it will happen."

Trent resisted at first, calling her bluff; unfortunately for him, and more so for Kris, Tanis followed through. She didn't revel in it, didn't take any joy in the things that she did to Kris's body—but neither did she shy away from it. Her devotion to the colony effort, to leaving the Sol system, was foremost in her thoughts. She would know who was behind these attacks. All the while, she wondered what Joe would think of her if he knew the sorts of things she did—had done?

After three hours, Kris finally passed out. Tanis had stretched the woman's endurance as far as it would go. Nothing she did was permanent, but new skin would definitely be necessary. Not yet, though. Kris would live like this as long as she was in Tanis's custody.

Trent was having trouble breathing as he watched the ruins of Kris's body collapse to the floor. Tanis had pre-deployed mednano into the woman, and they stabilized her and effected a semi-stasis.

"Now that we're done with the warm-up"—Tanis wiped her hands and turned to Trent—"I'll have my answers from you. The dead from the *Dawn* demand it."

It took him several minutes to calm down enough to be able to keep his trembling at bay. Tanis watched him, seeing his fear turn into resolve, followed by anger. He was going to resist.

Tanis cupped his chin in her hand and worked up her most evil smile.

"Careful. Just because I'm done with her doesn't mean I'm going to slow down. Let's start with your eyes. I've always believed that we have two so that we can afford to have one ruined."

She picked up a laser scalpel and proceeded to slice Trent's right eye to ribbons. The tool self-cauterized, keeping the bleeding to a minimum. Once the screaming stopped, Tanis looked him in the remaining eye.

"You know, I don't think you really need this one either. I think you'll be a lot easier to manage once you're blind."

Trent broke.

"No! Stop, stop stop stop stop stop stop stop stop stop pleeeeaaaaase!"

He was crying, tears trying to come out of both eyes, but one only seeping into the ruined orb. His body was shaking; the fear, a physical force assaulting him.

It was hard to watch. Tanis felt herself faltering at that moment. She hated torture. Hated doing it more than any human rights group hated that she did it. They found the actions despicable. She found *herself* despicable. She felt her stomach flutter like it did before battle.

Joe would find her despicable.

<There are other ways to get information, you know,> Angela said. *<You don't have to do this…you shouldn't do this. I don't normally complain, but this is excessive, even for you.>*

<I know…I know,> Tanis said. *<But this man…this blubbering thing…he would have cheerfully detonated a nuke on this station! The fact that he's getting to me means I'm human. But he's not. He voided those rights when he tried to kill millions for a buck.>*

<Just be careful. I don't want you going somewhere you can't come back from.>

Tanis looked down at the man, on the thing in front of her.

"Then what? What do you have to say? Who is calling the shots? Who is trying to shut us down?"

Trent looked like he had built up a bit of resolve again, so Tanis held up the laser scalpel. He cringed and shook his head.

"OK, OK, OK…It's the STR, it's Strang."

"Strang? The CEO of STR?" Tanis asked.

"Yeah, him. He's put a lot of personal stock into the *Dakota*, and when New Eden came up, he had to have it. He'll do anything to stop the *Intrepid*."

Tanis considered his words. If Strang was pulling the strings, this was far from over. The *Intrepid* had to go to Callisto to get its final cargo and colonists. STR was headquartered there. Strang was there.

Tanis spent the next thirty minutes getting particulars from Trent and making sure his story rang true. She hated every minute of it, but not nearly as much as he did.

"So we have our name." Captain Andrews folded his hands and raised them to his lips. His eyes dropped to the table and he paused for a moment. "I assume that we proceed with legal indictments."

"The brass are reviewing it," Sanderson said.

"I thought *you* were the brass." Terrance scowled. "Can't you push this through?"

"Strang is the CEO of STR. We never thought it went this high. Pulling him down is no small thing. SolGov's influence in Jovian space is not what it once was. They are more powerful than all the other members of the federal government combined. STR is one of their largest consortiums and wields a lot of influence. The feds will have to tread lightly."

"So they'll get away with this?" Terrance asked. "I swear, if they do nothing I'll sue them, sue their pants off."

"I've always wondered exactly what that means." Captain Andrews ran a hand through his hair. "However, will suing them make us safer? I mean we're going to Callisto; into the lion's den, so to speak."

"Too bad we can't just have the three cargo containers they've packed up there sent to us, and just leave from here." Terrance sighed.

"Not feasible," Captain Andrews agreed. "It's a complicated slingshot maneuver we're doing. Without using Jupiter as our launching point, we won't have achieved enough velocity when we reach Sol. The decreased breakaway velocity will cause significant increase in travel time."

"That, and we need to be moving toward the sun at the correct speed and correct time to gather the isotopes we need for our fuel. If we don't do that, it will take thirteen percent longer to reach our max speed." Earnest Redding seemed very anxious about the notion. "Also, if we have them ship those containers here, we'll miss both the Jovian and Marsian windows, and have to wait another nine months for the next one."

"That's all the time the *Dakota* will need to be able to contest our claim to New Eden and tie this colonization up in committee and courts for a decade. Which is exactly what Strang wants." Tanis spoke for the first time since the meeting had started.

"I guess that rules that out," Terrance said.

"I propose that I take Grenwald's Marines in advance to Callisto and ensure that everything is secure. We need to make sure that the cargo and the rendezvous point are safe. We can also have a wing on patrol in Jovian space ready to escort the *Intrepid* in," Tanis said. No point in wallowing forever. Plenty of work was still waiting to be done.

"Do you think we'll be safe here?" Terrance asked. "Your work has proven instrumental in keeping us on track. In fact, Abby tells me that your alterations have actually accelerated the schedule."

Tanis forced a smile. "You hired me to do a job, sir. I am glad I have been able to perform it to your satisfaction." She brought up a holo showing various levels of activity on the station; 3D graphs and charts displayed periods of higher and lower threat to the *Intrepid*. The data showed that after the capture of Trent, the threat levels were significantly lower.

"You'll see, sirs, that all of the models show that no

significant threats are impending. The bounty on me has actually been withdrawn, and the four merc organizations that had been active locally have all left the Mars Protectorate. I'm guessing that they're feeling the heat, and their last payments probably didn't show up. I'm not saying that everything is sunshine and daisies, but I do believe that the next big threat lies at Callisto, and not here at Mars. I have every confidence that Commander Ouri can keep things under control here while I'm gone. Lieutenant Forsythe will be keeping his platoon here while I take Grenwald's with me to Callisto."

"And Commander Evans?" Captain Andrews' eye had a twinkle to it.

The fewer complications, the better. "He'll be staying on the *Intrepid*, sir. I believe his assistance will be key in organizing patrols and guarding the ship during transit."

"I see no reason not to follow your plan." Sanderson looked at Tanis sternly and at the others around the table who nodded. "You have my permission to proceed. I expect a full work-up of your plan within the day."

"Aye, sir." Tanis stood. "Sirs." She nodded and left. They hadn't asked her exactly how she got the information from Trent. She hadn't volunteered it either.

<Looks like we're taking a little trip,> Angela said.

<Almost done; just this one last journey, and we're gone.>

<You never know; a lot can happen between now and the end.>

CERES

STELLAR DATE: 3227 301 / 12.14.4123 (Adjusted Gregorian)
LOCATION: Ceres Transfer Station, Ceres
REGION: InnerSol, Sol Space Federation

"Well boys and girls, here we are: lovely Ceres—just the place for a day's layover." Private Perez gestured magnanimously at the unadorned debarkation lobby.

"Shut it, Perez," Williams said as he walked by. "Marines, hump your gear to the *TSF Argonaut* and stow it. We have a tactical analysis of our mission at 2100 hours station time in briefing room 2A, deck 16, quadrant 3."

"You want us to do *what* to our gear, Staff Sergeant?"

Williams chose to ignore the remark and hoisted his pack over his left shoulder.

They were in the TSF zone on Ceres, one of the main hubs of stellar commerce and travel in the solar system. It was doubly busy since Mars was nearing Jupiter at a time when Ceres was between them. Earth was on the far side of the sun, but a direct path between it and Jupiter also passed through Ceres for the current Sol month. The end result was that nearly all of the traffic between InnerSol and OuterSol was currently flowing through Ceres.

Williams wasn't worried about security—not in the TSF zone, at least. With the hundred or so navy ships all docked at this quadrant, ranging from patrol craft to Orion-class cruisers and Constellation-class carriers, not only was security tight, but it was backed up by a million or so TSF personnel that were, quite literally, everywhere. Anyone trying anything wouldn't make it more than ten meters after doing it.

Being around men and women he could rely on always made Williams feel at home, and he walked easily down the corridor. That wasn't to say that he wasn't wary, but he was as relaxed as he got.

Being little more than a small planetoid, Ceres naturally only generated .03g at its surface; far less than most of the larger moons in the Sol system. It had been augmented by a GE Artificial Grav system—a fancy term for a mini black hole that was placed within the core of the world, and spun up to create 0.51g on the world's surface.

Ceres had a massive superstructure built around it, the main docking ring being four hundred kilometers above the world. Capable of docking over seven hundred thousand ships at once, the outer reaches operated in 0g, allowing an easier transfer of heavy materials.

Small ships, like the transport that the Marines had taken from the MOS, docked on the inside of the ring about seventy kilometers above the surface, which rotated enough to create just under half a g.

Perez was taking advantage of that, and tossing his pack in the air like it was some sort of ball.

Just like on Mars 1's top level, the view was astounding. Even people who worked on the station could be caught looking up at the sight of the small planet wrapped in the massive docks. Since the planet was only about eight hundred kilometers in diameter, and the docks were much closer than most planetary halos, the effect was more like a sphere captured in a glistening ring of steel rather than a ring around a planet. In fact, without taking into account the GE AG system, the docks had more mass than Ceres itself.

Williams caught himself looking up for longer than he expected and Kowalski nudged him.

"Not your first time here, is it?" he asked.

"No, but it's one of the few times where the sun is shining from behind. It really lights the whole thing up nicely, doesn't it?"

"You getting all sentimental, Staff Sergeant?"

Williams cast a baleful eye on Kowalski. "I have as much sentimentality in me as you have taste in women."

Kowalski chuckled. "Sure thing, Staff Sergeant."

Williams glanced back up at the sight; it was a lot smaller than Mars 1, but he found it far more pleasant. He could spot the Tannen Docking Array R3D where the *Argonaut* was berthed along the arc, visible even though it was seven hundred kilometers away. He started moving again, and ran through the platoon's status to be certain that everyone was still more or less keeping up. Since the officers had been in first class, they were ahead a few hundred meters; but they were making poorer time without a sergeant's glare to help part the crowds.

Williams eased up his pace. He liked his officers, but he also liked peace and quiet; something that a certain lieutenant, trying to look cool to Trist while simultaneously trying to impress the major, just wouldn't provide.

They passed out of the TSF zone and into a general civilian section. There were three military zones on the docks, but, due to a combination of lease times and weight distribution, they weren't all adjacent to one another.

The central boulevard changed as they walked. Gone were the plain bulkheads with their colored bars indicating location and purpose, as well as the spartan offices and facilities. In their place were the boutiques and restaurants that catered to the transient tourists that passed through the station.

While the population of both Ceres and its docking network was in the range of only three hundred million or so, at any given moment, over a billion people were passing through. The place had rivers of credit flowing across its nets, generating more money than most planets.

Besides the aforementioned stores selling frivolities and food, frontages advertising time in the company of a beautiful man, woman, or…whatever, abounded—everything from vanilla humans to things that didn't even look like homo sapiens. A trend that seemed to be more and more common as the years passed.

It was probably to please many of the visitors. A lot of the spacers that passed through a place like Ceres spent a good bit of their time alone in the black. It seemed that they were the most unusual; almost as though they had decided, since they spent so much time away from the general human population, they should become something other than human.

Even though he had slowed his pace, Williams saw that he was still catching up with the officers and Trist. He resigned himself to taking the rest of the route to the maglev in their company and allowed himself to reach them.

"About time you boots caught up. We were starting to wonder if you stayed back to finish an in-flight vid or something," Trist said.

"We did," Williams growled. "It was called *NCOs and the Moronic Civilians They Saved Through the Ages*. It warmed my heart."

Trist shot Williams a shocked look while Tanis let out a laugh.

"You do realize that no one but a Marine can needle a Marine staff sergeant and escape unscathed," Tanis said.

"And most of them lose at least a finger or two," Williams grunted.

Trist opened her mouth to say something in response, but appeared to think better of the notion and subsided into silence. Just the way Williams preferred it.

He had mixed feelings about her coming along to Callisto, especially mixed feelings about her being privy to the details of the mission; but Major Richards seemed to trust the girl, and had made a strong case that she had a knowledge of Cho that none of them did. Her web of contacts could end up proving to be very useful.

Still, it was a gamble taking her back. The Jovian government still had a warrant out for her arrest, despite the fact that a Federal SSF court had granted her immunity in exchange for her testimony against Trent.

Luckily, the fact that a lot of Trist's body was made out of biological silicon meant her DNA no longer matched what was on record. Even better was the fact that she could subtly alter her underlying physical features, making a legal identification of Trist virtually impossible.

The group arrived at the maglev train, and the platoon filed into several cars. The ride anti-spin to the *Argonaut* was relatively quick, and before long the gear was stowed, and the Marines were enjoying some downtime before the briefing. Their shuttle to Callisto left at 0900 the next morning, and it was currently 1400—giving them several hours to sample all the docks had to offer. Williams was certain that they would.

As for himself, Williams took the time to look over the plan passed down to him from the officers. He could tell that it was Tanis's scheme, with a few minor details taken care of by the LT. Tanis tended to skip the chain a bit; though it was hard to say if it annoyed Grenwald or not. Getting firsthand experience with a renowned tactician like Major Richards was probably worth the consternation.

The general operation was pretty straightforward. There would be a company of MCSF Marines tasked with general security, and a company of Marine engineers tasked with inspecting the cargo pods. Not a job Williams envied. Those pods were each well over a cubic kilometer filled with equipment and cargo. The engineers would only be able to do a cursory examination at best, but it was better than nothing.

The *Intrepid* would carry ten pods total, and seven were already in place. When the *Intrepid* arrived at Callisto in a month, the remaining pods would be loaded up, and the ship would begin its acceleration toward the Sun, on its slingshot approach to gather additional velocity for their outbound trip.

Williams was somewhat saddened by the thought. Over the last few months, the ship had become something of a home to him and the platoon. He'd overheard a few of the Marines talking about requesting to go out with the ship, but he was certain that none of them would; they were all too dedicated to the job, being somewhat addicted to the action. Where the *Intrepid* was going, there would be no action—just a quiet, boring colonization project, and then the slow crawl to old age.

For just a moment, the notion appealed to Williams. But he pushed it from his mind. The corps was his life, that wasn't going to change.

"Good of you all to make it." Grenwald addressed the last few Marines who arrived only four minutes early for the briefing.

"We were held up," Taylor said.

"Yeah, Taylor was having trouble convincing the bartender he was old enough to drink," Perez grinned.

"Belay that excuse," Williams said.

"Sorry, Staff Sergeant." Perez had the good grace to look a bit sheepish.

All eyes turned to Major Richards as she stood and activated the holo system.

"This is dock BX9-R on ring 19C of the Callisto station. For those of you who have never been there, it'll be quite the sight. You're on the corps' time the whole time we're there. No wandering off and seeing what there is to see." She cast a look at Perez. "Or fondle what there is to fondle. There is a barracks on the ring, and I don't want to hear of anyone being anywhere other than there or on duty…what?" Tanis looked at Perez.

"Will there at least be, er…beverages?"

"Yes, there's an enlisted cantina in the barracks where I believe they serve over ten thousand types of alcohol. Don't abuse it." Her look told them all what danger they'd be in if they imbibed excessively, more than any threat could have.

"Once we debark at Callisto, our job will be to ensure that the STR is hamstrung. It's entirely possible that the Sol Space Federation will take no direct action against the instigator of this bit of excitement we've been having lately, but that doesn't mean that we can't make their lives miserable — and believe me, ladies and gentlemen, we will."

She surveyed the room and found that everyone's eyes showed that they shared the same sentiment as she did.

"We have a certain level of autonomy here, but, honestly. if I don't piss off Admiral Sanderson by the time we're done, then I won't feel like I've done my job. What that translates to for you is that we may actually get to have some fun."

The Marines all looked at one another and smiled; they were well-versed in what Tanis's version of fun was.

"I've put each squad's objectives on the tactical net. I expect you all to review them, and be prepared when we arrive. We do have a two-day flight, and I want to see tactical sims drawn up and run during that time."

She nodded and Grenwald addressed Williams. "Staff Sergeant, dismiss the men."

"Platoon, get some sacktime. I want you assembled on the deck in front of the *Argonaut* at 0530. Dismissed!"

The men saluted the officers and filed out.

INTEL

STELLAR DATE: 3227307 / 12.20.4123 (Adjusted Gregorian)
LOCATION: District BX9, Ring 19C, Callisto Orbital Habitat (Cho)
REGION: Jovian Combine, Sol Space Federation

"How are things looking, Commander?" Tanis addressed the Marine who was bent over a readout.

"As well as can be expected, sir. We've got the 701st engineers combing every inch of those cubes, as well as the other general cargo destined for the *Intrepid* upon its arrival; and let me say, it's going to be a slow burn."

"I understand, Yau." Tanis couldn't agree more. "Be on the lookout for...something—I don't know that this is over yet."

"You're expecting the enemy to make a move against us?"

"I don't know for sure. I've been studying this Arlen Strang. He's never been one to give up on something when he sets his mind to it. I imagine that he has made certain promises, and, with the *Dakota* taking second place to the *Intrepid*, I'm thinking he has some egg on his face."

"I'll see that we are suitably cautious, sir."

"Good to hear, Commander."

Tanis turned and signaled one/three to follow her. She had a meeting with a certain informant and it involved going down to Ring 5, into an area not known to be friendly to strangers. She was probably being overly cautious, but having a couple of Marines along never hurt when trying to keep one's head attached to one's body.

She and the Marines were all in civilian attire, though she didn't expect it to fool anyone who had an eye for military bearing. The light body armor they wore under their clothing didn't help make their movements any more natural.

The ride down the tubes was relatively quick. Since they

were going to inner rings, the feeling was actually more 'up', since the centripetal force was pulling them the opposite direction. She did miss the type of construction that Mars 1 and Ceres had, where you could see the planet above. Word was that the reason why they hadn't done that here was because having Jupiter looming in the background was disconcerting to too many people—especially since it had been ignited several hundred years ago, and now looked much more ominous than it once had.

Even if the moon were visible, the view would have been uninspiring. Callisto wasn't terraformed; its surface housing waste management and purification systems for the habitat above.

Tanis's thoughts shifted to the Callisto station...or rings...no one really knew what to call it these days. Locals called it Cho, while the Jovian government called it the C1 Semi-Orbital Habitat. Tanis just called it daunting.

Something about the feeling of a trillion trillion tons of structure over her head gave her the willies. Not big ones, but enough to make her feel a twinge of anxiety every so often.

She focused on the task at hand. Meet with this contact, get the intel, stop the STR from pulling off whatever they planned on doing. She kept the knowledge that in one month they'd be outsystem firmly in mind. They'd have a nice cookout in Old Sam, and be on their way. It would all have been worth it.

The thoughts renewed her resolve. No way was she going to let anything get in the *Intrepid*'s way.

The contact's name was Sandy Bristol; Tanis's information told her that she would be a mod—a pretty heavy mod, from the looks of the file. She figured it couldn't be hard to spot a woman with florescent pink skin and what appeared to be several dozen three-foot tentacles coming out of her head. That sort of thing just stood out.

She glanced around her at the people in this part of the ring.

Well, maybe it wouldn't stand out that much. In fact, even though they were all dressed in civvies, her Marine escort's lack of visible mods and conservative clothing probably made them the most unusual people present.

She directed Becker and Jacobs to engage in a lively discussion about their favorite sport, poker, at a table in a café across the intersection where the meet was to take place. Martins stood beside her, posing as obvious muscle — which she did very easily — and Larson was lurking around the corner, eyeing the ladies standing in front of a brothel, or voluntary slavery outlet, it was hard to tell.

"Some of these people are...well...quite odd." Martins almost added the "sir" but held it back.

Tanis checked her records on Martins and saw that she was from the Beta Regio region on Venus. The descendants of religious puritans that left Earth a millennia ago, they were about as straight-laced as they came in this day and age.

"They're not of the normal variety," Tanis replied. "Actually, I take that back. Given the population of the Galilean moons, it's possible that they actually define normal."

"Yeah, I can't believe there are a thousand billion people on Callisto now" — Martins shook her head — "and most of them are above us."

"Below you, actually," Tanis said. "That whole centripetal force thing."

"Actually, since at any given time we're at the bottom of the arch, our point of view has most of the ring structure above us." Martins grinned.

Tanis grunted. "Got me there; last time I think of you as rural, Martins."

"Sorry, s—" she stopped.

"Good catch."

They stood in silence for a while, leaning against the wall of a shop that appeared to sell and install replacement digestive systems that would allow a person to fit three times the battery power into their body. It also used waste to create additional power. Link ads constantly assailing them showed high-end models with the ability to completely consume all food with no need to void it from the body—not an alteration you could easily undo, if you decided you didn't like it.

Tanis was certain she wouldn't. The thought of what had to be some sort of laser-powered incinerator in her torso just seemed like a recipe for trouble, especially considering how often she got shot up.

Trist had mentioned that this was one of the more interesting, but relatively benign, places on the lower Callisto rings. After setting up this meet for Tanis, Trist had gone off to see if she could get information from a few other contacts. Tanis didn't like sending the woman off on her own, so three/two was with her. Their last update to the platoon's tactical net put them on ring 17D, somewhere in a thousand-square-mile trade area. Chances were that Trist was getting in some last minute wheeling and dealing…or maybe just stealing.

<*That was a weird mental alliteration,*> Angela commented.

"I think that's her," Martins spoke softly.

"Yup, even in this crowd, she does stand out," Tanis agreed.

Sandy strolled over as though selling info to TSF agents was something she did every day. Tanis took the opportunity to examine her carefully—initially to look for any weapons, but then in a combination of awe and horror.

The woman's body was indeed a fluorescent pink that seemed to shift hues in the light. There had to be over thirty of the tentacles coming out of her head, which itself seemed to have a conical shape. The end of each tentacle sported three suction cups, somewhat like an octopus.

At first glance, she appeared to be naked, though it was often difficult to tell the difference between skin and clothes. While she certainly looked like a woman, her groin was smooth, and her breasts—while fully exposed—had no nipples on them. Her legs were even more interesting; her knees bent backwards and her feet ended in hooves.

"It's not polite to stare, Miss Richards." Sandy walked up to the waiting pair. "But I don't mind. I didn't make myself look like this to avoid getting stared at." She stretched seductively. "I positively thrive on it."

She seemed to be getting rather turned on and Tanis realized that Sandy meant that her brain was altered to get sexual pleasure from having people stare at her unusual appearance. She probably had a really good time strolling through the corridors—the way she was modded out, even people with horns did double takes.

"I'm glad for you," was all Tanis said.

Tanis noted that Martins appeared to be doing her best to blink regularly, and a glance across the street showed her that the other Marines were having trouble keeping their glances casual. Not that they stood out in doing so—ignoring Sandy would be the unusual reaction.

"I understand that you have some information about Strang in relation to the *Intrepid*. Though I honestly must say that I don't know how *you* would gather any intel…how would you blend in?"

"I don't blend, darling; people pay me in information for the pleasure of my company." Her tentacles danced around her, caressing her upper body. "I have very specialized skills."

"Holy shit," Martins said softly. Tanis sent a quelling glance the private's way.

"So what do you have for us?" Tanis asked.

"Well, it's come my way that Mr. Strang doesn't like you, Miss Richards; doesn't like you one bit."

"I've actually noticed," Tanis said dryly.

"I imagine you have. However, he has managed to get his eye back on the prize; he intends to destroy the *Intrepid*."

"About time he learned some focus. I just wish he could focus elsewhere."

"His intention" — Sandy leaned closer — "is to destroy it after it docks on Callisto."

"That's pretty broad; you wouldn't happen to have anything more specific, would you?"

"He has a device, one that will cause considerable damage to the *Intrepid*. There will be minimal damage to the ring, but nothing he isn't willing to risk."

"Is that all you know?"

"I have some details; information about the way he plans to destroy it. I don't understand all of the technical jargon, but I believe it is some sort of molecular decoupler that will break the ship apart. I've put it on this hardcopy."

A tentacle slipped a small disc into Tanis's hand. Without giving it a glance, she secured it in a small drive in her wrist. "Payment has already been remitted."

"So it has. I believe, then, that our time here is complete."

"Yes, thank you," Tanis said.

"Thank you, Miss Richards. It's been a pleasure."

The strange woman walked away, her tentacles swaying softly and her hoofs clopping lightly on the decking.

Martins stared after Sandy until she disappeared from view. "She certainly was interesting."

"You can say that again," Tanis replied as the other Marines crossed the street. They began the return trip to the barracks.

....

Tanis met with her staff regarding the information Sandy had provided shortly after returning. None of them were entirely certain what to make of the information Tanis had gathered, but they were certainly going to take it seriously.

After the meeting, Tanis retreated to her quarters. Time

enough for six hours of sleep and then back to the grind.

<I don't know about this,> Tanis mused to Angela. <It all seems a little over the top.>

<Molecular decouplers do indeed function,> Angela replied. <They're often used in removing a planet's crust to resurface it.>

<I know that.> Tanis leaned back on her bed, running through scenarios. <It just seems too extreme. I mean, how many people could get their hands on an MDC strong enough to take out the Intrepid? It would be a pretty short list; though probably with the STR near the top of it.>

<That's true. There's also the chance that the reaction could spill over into Callisto. I don't see him risking his power base just to get one colony world that won't turn a profit for half a dozen centuries,> Angela added.

<We've picked up other intel saying there could be various other avenues of attack, as well—and dozens of false leads about bombs in the cargo.>

<You think we're being played?> Angela asked.

<I think that the truth may be out there, but it's covered in all these lies.>

<I'm working with the local TSF intel AIs to rule out the claims that are simply implausible. Unfortunately, most of them have enough of a grain of truth that we can't discount them entirely.>

<I'd better get some sleep; there's no way I can figure this out when I'm exhausted.>

<See you in a couple of hours,> Angela said as her avatar waved goodnight.

<Try not to use my brain too much to pore over this stuff...it always gives me strange dreams.>

ASSASSIN

STELLAR DATE: 3227327 / 01.09.4124 (Adjusted Gregorian)
LOCATION: District BX9, Ring 19C, Callisto Orbital Habitat (Cho)
REGION: Jovian Combine, Sol Space Federation

Tanis stretched as consciousness slowly crept over her. The clock informed her that it was 0500; nine hours until the *Intrepid* would dock at Callisto. A review of her day's schedule confirmed that it was full, but not so full that she couldn't enjoy just a few more minutes under the soft covers.

She mentally ran through the post-docking schedule: the four days to load cargo—five at the outside, plus two days of VIP parties and ceremonies, put departure on 3227337 at the latest.

Departure.

It seemed like it would never come, and now that it was here these last few days would be agony. With luck, she would be so busy the time would fly past.

Curious about the ship's status, she reached out to the TSF comm net and requested bandwidth to the *Intrepid*. It was granted, and her queries flew across the void to the ship's general net.

Amanda was there, waiting for her.

<You seem eager for our arrival.> Her net avatar smiled.

<You have no idea how much, Amanda. How are things going? No issues, upsets?>

Amanda laughed. Her voice was silvery and smooth and echoed just a touch. *<You worry too much. Everything has gone as planned. Your Joseph has provided a fighter escort the entire way, and is out there now, keeping us safe.>*

<Don't laugh, it's part of the job to worry—though I'm glad that Joseph is out there. Not a lot can get past him.>

<Would you like to speak to anyone? I'm sorry for accosting you when you connected.>

<No, I just wanted to reach out and make contact. I should be going, I have a lot to do.> Tanis sighed.

<I imagine there are many officious people that need intimidating.>

<Aren't there always?>

She disconnected and drew back into herself. Taking a deep breath, she rose and entered the san unit. Her tight schedule coupled with her new armor would provide no opportunity to visit a restroom for at least the next twenty hours. She set the unit for a thorough cleaning, and grimaced as it did its work.

Once done, she stepped back into her small room and pulled out the small case containing the new armor. Setting it on the desk, she opened it and loaded the control system.

<Man, this stuff is full of license agreements,> Angela said. *<It'll eventually timebomb and deactivate without updates, as well.>*

<Well, chances are we'll be on our way and never needing armor like this again before that happens.> Tanis applied her security token to each of the agreements.

<Great, now you've cursed us.>

<If there was a curse, I really don't think it originated with me.>

Once the software was loaded, Tanis stripped down and stood naked. The next step was promised by both the salesperson and the manual to be somewhat odd. Some people reported feeling very claustrophobic during the process.

"Can't believe I spent that much money on this thing." Tanis held up the canister.

<What else were you going to spend it on? You're leaving the system. Like they say in the vids, 'Your money's no good here.' Well, except that it is for now...but you get the picture.>

Tanis nodded absently as she placed the canister against her chest. The bottom dissolved, and a clear liquid flowed out across her body. It started by moving down and covering her torso, legs, and then feet. From there, it flowed up over her breasts, down her arms, and covered her hands. A signal flashed on Tanis's HUD telling her to take a deep breath and close her eyes. She followed the instructions and the liquid flowed up over her face.

It ran a countdown on her HUD, letting her know when it would be safe to breathe and to look around. She felt tingles in her skin as the armor smoothed out and matched the shape of her body. When the countdown flashed zero, she opened her eyes and examined the holo projection of herself.

Apart from a slight sheen to her skin, it was impossible to tell that the armor was there at all. Upon close inspection, a person might be able to notice a thin cover over her eyes, and that the first few millimeters of her hair appeared to be ridged; but other than that, she looked like a normal person...though somewhat naked, at present.

Tanis pulled on her dress whites, somewhat disconcerted by the fact that the armor muted her sense of touch to a degree. She deployed a nano field that would assist the armor in detecting incoming weapons fire, and, with a cursory check of her quarters, exited into the corridor.

Tanis made her way to the officer's mess, which contained a smattering of lieutenants and commanders getting ready for the day. Commander Yau was there; he appeared to be going over his company's duties for the upcoming arrival of the *Intrepid*.

Eight hours and twenty-seven minutes.

"Glad this is nearly over, I bet." Tanis sat across from him with her tray of fruit and oatmeal.

"Not as much as you are, I imagine." He grinned.

"You have no idea. The waiting is killing me."

"The CIA has all sorts of flags popping up on their net. Have you seen their latest sec feeds?"

Tanis hadn't, and mentally chastised herself for not checking it first thing. The anticipation must really be preoccupying her.

"There have been some monitored individuals making their

way onto Cho, and a few of them have slipped past surveillance," Yau said.

Tanis checked the lists, summoning a holo display in front of her and the captain. "None look too serious, oh…well, except for her."

"Yeah, Herris Santos. She's known to have caused no small ruckus in her time."

Tanis leaned back, bringing up the woman's history. Born on Europa to a wealthy family, she had left the life of privilege at age thirty. From there, she joined Tomas's Marauders, a semi-legit private army that hired itself out to local governments to protect trade routes and natural resources. A rapid rise through the ranks ensued, until a falling-out with the command forced her out of the organization.

From that time on, it appeared she had been operating as a freelance assassin. Several jobs on Venus, a high profile hit on an Earth politician, and a string of probable killings on Vestra, Ceres, and the Hildas asteroids.

"Never worked in the Jovian sphere, though," Tanis mused.

"That we know of—the JSF doesn't exactly share everything with us."

"It's entirely possible that she's here on some other task."

Yau cast Tanis an appraising look and the major sighed. "I know, I know—that would just be too handily coincidental. Though with Cho's population, that sort of coincidence is a bit more acceptable."

"Except that she was last seen on ring 20. If we had solid intel putting her on ring 142 or something like that, then I'd be in complete agreement."

Tanis nodded. "Your logic is irrefutable. I assume TSF intel and the Callisto Intel Agency are both looking for her."

"You assume correctly. I've set up our tactical net to alert us if there is any news."

"I'd really thought that Strang had gotten over this whole

assassination thing."

"He could be going after another target: Terrance or Captain Andrews."

"I don't know…at this stage, killing either of them wouldn't set the mission back by much at all. Strang strikes me as the complete-at-all-costs sort of guy, not the get-final-petty-revenge type."

"Maybe he's both."

They went over the general plans for the day before leaving the mess to attend to their various duties. Tanis walked to her temporary office, and, on the way, scheduled the pickup of her effects and their transfer to the *Intrepid* after it had docked. She also went over the security clearances for the caterers and general staff who would be at the docking ceremony. Everything seemed to be in order, but something still nagged at her. Her gut hadn't told her to buy and slather on this armor for nothing; somewhere a thread was loose, and she was going to find it and pull.

It was just before noon when an anomaly in a shipping manifest caught her eye. A series of containers that were destined to arrive at the *Intrepid*'s berth tomorrow had arrived today. Rather than holding them and delivering on schedule, the courier had delivered them to one of the warehouses just off the main dock. That in itself wasn't particularly odd; however, they had been inspected twice. The inspection logs and timestamps were backwards—it was either a system error, or someone had opened the record to fake an entry at the same time someone had it open to enter a valid entry.

Feeling restless, Tanis decided to look into it herself. Checking the Marines' assignments, she realized that none of them were available to go with her. Trist was also off gathering information on a different ring. No matter; the dock wasn't far, just a twenty-minute walk. It would give her time to stretch her legs and get a bit of exercise.

Two hours and fifteen minutes.

The halls were relatively empty as most of the local staff was at the mess, getting the noon meal out of the way before the final preparations for the *Intrepid*'s arrival began. The corridor widened as she came to the storage area just off the dock. A worker strolled by pushing a hover pallet and gave her an appreciative look. Tanis couldn't imagine why. In the last two thousand years, no Space Force dress uniform sported a cut that flattered a woman's body. Maybe it was the hair; she had grown it out rapidly since her trip to Cruithne, and it was just past her shoulders now. She hadn't had long hair in decades and was determined to keep the indulgence, since her remaining time in the military was short.

She arrived at her destination and stopped outside the door. The portal to the storage area was sealed and in order; she transmitted the override codes to its pad. After a moment the indicator flashed green. Tanis grasped the handle and stepped inside, scanning the room for the cargo she was looking for.

She took one step past the door, and felt her scalp squeeze slightly as the armor, normally pliant, solidified around her head. A warning on her HUD indicated that she had been struck by a blow to the base of her skull. The kinetic force spread down to her shoulders, and they solidified as well, spreading out the force of the impact. Tanis tried to face her attacker, but her instincts conflicted with the armor's efforts to protect her and, unused to the effect, Tanis lost her balance and fell to the deck.

The impact caused the armor to freeze entirely, and Tanis made a mental note to do some more fine-tuning. In the second after she landed, Tanis decided that since she was down, playing unconscious might be a good way to identify her ambusher. She closed her eyes and switched her vision to the feed from her ever-present nanoprobes.

Not surprisingly, the figure that stepped out from the shadows was Herris Santos. Her face was twisted in what Tanis assumed was the woman's approximation of a smile, and in her hand she hefted a thick pipe. A short bark of a laugh escaped her lips as she leaned over Tanis's body.

"The great and mighty Tanis Richards. You don't seem particularly tough to me. Didn't take much at all to knock you down. I'd better seal you up, though. Your AI may be rebooting from the blow; once it's back online, I'm certain I'll have some company."

Great, a soliloquizer, Tanis thought. She hadn't run into one of those in a while.

She had been determined to see where this would go, but suddenly regretted the decision to play dead when she felt a dampening net being thrown over her. Immediately, she and Angela felt their Link cut off, and all contact with her nano cloud ceased.

<Great plan,> Angela said. *<Still want to go with this?>*

Tanis felt the net suddenly constrict and seal itself around her body.

<Umm…I guess we have no choice now.>

<You know…I was doing some things. I don't just sit in your head waiting for you to summon me.>

<Sorry, I didn't expect things to play out like this.>

<Remind me to mock your lack of caution if we get out of this.> Angela's tone was more dry than usual, something her AI reserved for special occasions.

Tanis felt her body being lifted and placed into a container. The hum of a hover unit sounded, followed by the sensation of motion.

<Rather alarming, being trapped in one's mind,> Tanis said. *<Been awhile since it's happened.>*

<Well, you've got me, at least,> Angela said. *<You certainly do present me with scenarios I'd never encounter on my own.>*

<You sound supportive, but somehow I think you're not.>

They were silent after that, but Angela was building a map

of where they were going and inserting it into Tanis's mind. It was based off the shifts and jolts they felt inside the container and net; the result may not have been entirely accurate, but it should be close. After all, it did have to conform to the area's layout, and with luck, their destination wouldn't be too far away.

One hour and fifty-three minutes.

CAPTURE

STELLAR DATE: 3227327 / 01.29.4124 (Adjusted Gregorian)
LOCATION: District QR7, Ring 19C, Callisto Orbital Habitat (Cho)
REGION: Jovian Combine, Sol Space Federation

The feeling of motion continued for roughly twenty minutes. Angela's readout indicated nearly a kilometer had been covered in that time.

<Looks like we're in a business district downspin from the Intrepid's dock.>

<Probably in some front or community bad-guy place,> Tanis said.

<Or some service corridor.>

<Less appealing.>

The container was opened, and Tanis looked up, directing a bland stare at the face looming over her. Well, at least it was a one hundred percent positive ID on Herris Santos; so much for coincidence.

"I see you're awake. I hope you don't mind your little bit of relocation. My employer wanted to bring you somewhere nicer for our little chat."

Tanis didn't speak. There was nothing to say—giving in to the enemy's banter never got you anywhere.

"Well, I suppose I should make you marginally presentable; I doubt that Mr. Strang is going to want to look down at you in this container."

<I guess this is pretty serious,> Angela commented.

<Yeah, but if we meet the big man in person, you know that means they're going to kill us afterwards. Even if he does have friends in high places, full sensory recording of him holding a TSF officer hostage will get him nothing but unpleasantness.>

Herris reached in and lifted Tanis out, and set her on a chair.

She couldn't help but notice how easy it was. Their captor must have some serious strength mods, since she didn't really look that built.

"Any chance you could loosen this net? I have this wicked cramp." Tanis gave a benign smile. "I promise, I won't mess up whatever the next step in this adventure is."

"They never said anything about a weak sense of humor or weak attempts to get information. I was hired to capture you and I've done so. I'll collect my pay and be gone." Herris' smile was wicked. "Unless they want to pay me a bonus for some extra work."

Tanis nodded inside the net. "I hope for your sake that he doesn't do to you what he'll do to me."

"I don't think you know what he's going to do to you."

"I have a pretty good idea. It's going to suck."

Herris laughed. "I imagine you've got that part right."

Tanis had taken the time during their conversation to look over her surroundings. They were in a conference room; it was ten by twenty meters and had a large wooden table occupying most of the room's center. She and Herris were at the end furthest from the double doors. After a few minutes, the doors opened and two men stepped in.

They gave off the bored appearance that was typical of corporate security, but Tanis could tell by their movements that they were ex-military. They looked the room over slowly, deploying their probes and checking for leaks and traces. She noticed them casting Herris as many cautious glances as they did her. A glance at the assassin told her that Herris had noticed their caution and was amused by it. Once they were satisfied, several more security types came in, followed by Arlen Strang.

"Good work, Miss Santos. You've done what many others failed to do."

"You should have called me from the beginning—I would have saved you a world of trouble."

Strang rubbed his jaw and smiled. "I believe I may do that the next time I need such services." He looked down at Tanis wrapped in the suppression net and gave her a winning smile. "So good to meet you, Major Richards. We've been on each other's minds so much, I don't doubt that we are both finding this a bit anticlimactic."

Tanis slowly looked up at him, her eyes simmering with rage. "You realize that you have gone from simple legal penalties to death. You won't survive this encounter."

"My, you are every bit as cocky as I'd been led to believe." He waved an arm around him. "There is nothing you can do; you are fully under our control."

"It's something we're trained for. I got an A in smug and cocky back in OCS."

"That doesn't surprise me in the least. Though I imagine seeing the *Intrepid* destroyed in a rather spectacular fashion will do something to modify your attitude."

Tanis couldn't read Strang at all. She couldn't tell if he was excited that he was finally going to get his victory, or if he was considering this purely from a profit and loss perspective. She decided to go on the offensive against his pride.

"I'll give you points for boldness and a grand vision, but not so much for the execution. You haven't really garnered a great track record—I don't expect you to be able to pull something like that off."

Strang's look betrayed no emotion. "I don't know what you thought was going to happen here, but I'll tell you what's not likely. You're not going to goad me into telling you my plans— sorry to burst your bubble."

Tanis changed approaches and grinned. "Don't worry, I'm pretty unburstable. So what's your reason for this gracious invitation?"

"I have reason to believe you know a few very interesting secrets about something on the *Intrepid*. I know about that trip down to Mars you and Captain Andrews took, and have strong suspicions about what you brought back up. I'd very much like to gain access to the *Intrepid*'s net so I can pull the specs for that little secret before we destroy it."

"And you think I'll give access to you?"

"I think you can be convinced."

<Here comes the torture,> Angela said.

"I really don't think you want to go that route." Tanis gave her captors a benign look.

"Why not?" Herris asked. "I find myself rather looking forward to it; then I get that extra pay I mentioned."

"Because I'm not restrained by the suppression net anymore."

"You what?" Herris's smug superiority cracked and a look of concern showed beneath it.

While she was being transported, Angela had configured some nano to extract bits of the armor and configured it to solidify. The effect was several thousand nano with very sharp knives. They just finished cutting through the threads on the back of the net and with a grand gesture, Tanis stood up and raised her arms in the air.

A look of shock passed across every face and Tanis couldn't help but smile. A moment later every gun in the room was aimed at her.

<You are such a drama queen.>

"What? Not what you were expecting?" Tanis asked.

"Oh, for fuck's sake! Just kill her!" Strang yelled before he turned and stormed out of the conference room.

<Damn…he's getting away.> Tanis hadn't expected him to just leave.

<If we survive, there'll be nowhere he can hide. Not after abducting us.>

No one else moved. Herris and the six security types all eyed her for several moments. Tanis took the opportunity to deploy probes to create a detection field for the armor—the more warning it had about incoming fire, the better.

She was not surprised when Herris shot first. Tanis accelerated her perception and felt her surroundings effectively slow down. She held herself steady as the bounty hunter's finger squeezed and a bullet left the chamber, heading for her forehead. Here she would find out if the armor was worth its exorbitant cost.

Milliseconds before impact, the armor became rock-hard from the top of her head down to her neck and across her shoulders. This time, Tanis didn't try to move or compensate, but rather tensed her legs to absorb the shock. Just as advertised, the armor deflected the bullet.

<Hah! I knew I'd get the hang of this.>

<Better late than never.>

The slug ricocheted off her face and into the wall. All eyes looked to Tanis's forehead, to the wall, and back to Tanis.

"I sort of have that effect on all of you, don't I?" Tanis smiled confidently. "What can I say, I'm truly amazing."

<What's gotten into you?> Angela asked.

<Sorry, I can't help it. I think the armor is giving me a god complex.>

<I don't think it's the armor.>

Tanis used the last seconds of surprise to launch herself at Herris. They crashed to the floor, and Tanis proceeded to deliver blows to the woman's neck and solar plexus, her hands locked into solid fists by her armor. Her opponent gasped for air and, with an augmented thrust, lifted Tanis bodily and slammed her into the edge of the table. Tanis's armor locked up and—while the effect was somewhat disconcerting—it did cause the bounty hunter's attack to not hurt at all.

The lack of pain allowed Tanis to recover quickly, and before Herris had a chance to get back on her feet, Tanis pointed her fingers, signaled the armor to lock, and slammed her now-solid hand into Herris's eye.

Screaming a string of curses that Tanis couldn't even understand, the woman covered her face and tried to slide away. Tanis delivered several more blows to Herris's thorax and stood, ignoring the thrashing of the body at her feet.

A moment after Tanis looked up, her vision tinted and the nanoprobe's video feed in her HUD showed that all six of the security guards had fired their laser pistols at her. The armor absorbed the energy from the beams, focused, and released the light in one blinding pulse. She heard startled shouts of shock and when her vision cleared, saw that the guards were all covering their eyes.

"You guys can't hurt me with those, but I can hurt you." Tanis snatched up Herris' handgun and panned it between the guards while stepping back against the wall. "Drop your guns and spread 'em on the table."

Five of the men complied, but one decided to try another shot. Tanis fired several slugs into his chest. He grunted and fell over, his life saved by body armor under his suit.

"Get up and get spread." She took careful aim at his head.

He stood slowly, but Tanis's nano video feed showed her one of the other guards edging away from the table, reaching for something inside his jacket. Without moving her arm, Tanis rotated her prosthetic wrist at a biologically impossible angle. Her handgun was pointed directly at his head.

She didn't even look at him. "Keep moving. I promise you a very short, sharp pain in your head, but everything will be all right after that. If push comes to shove, I only need one of you alive to talk."

They got the message; she could shoot them all as fast as the weapon could chamber the next round—in less than a second, based on the specs of the pistol.

"So, now that the ground rules are established, is there any chance any of you know what it is Strang's planning to do?"

No one said a word.

"Oh, come on; you guys hear things, follow him places. You must know something." Her comments continued to be met with silence and Tanis considered her options. "OK, I know it sounds crazy, but I'm actually tired of torturing people. It's really not that pleasant for me—makes for some really unpleasant dreams."

Tanis paused and her voice changed. It was deeper, slower, and dripped with venom.

"That doesn't mean I won't resort to it."

She fired six shots into the wall, close enough to each man for them to feel the slugs pass by their hair. They flinched in unison and her augmented sense of smell picked up the acidic scent of urine.

"I don't know where he went, but I know what he has planned," one of the men said to sidelong glares from his comrades. "He's going to set off an MDC and disintegrate the *Intrepid*."

"Try again," Tanis said. "There's no evidence of an MDC on the ring."

"That's because you weren't looking in the right place. The MDC is built into the network matrix for this portion of the ring. When the ship makes its hookups, the system will send the pulse through the network."

Tanis waited until Angela mentally confirmed that it was technically possible to pull that off.

"Thank you for the info," Tanis said. "Now, I want you all to lie down on your stomachs with your hands behind your heads. Anyone tries something funny, and I'll put lead into you. I've got…" Tanis felt the weight of the pistol, "seven shots left. Who thinks I'll still have one left over if I decide to take you out?"

<*They're not made of lead anymore, you know,*> Angela said.

<*Yeah, I had been made aware of that.*>

<Sorry, was just trying to break the tension. You scare the crap out of me sometimes...if I had crap to scare, that is.>

Tanis didn't have to hold the men long. Angela had alerted the TSF and ChoSec the moment she had connectivity. They had arrived within minutes. Tanis passed recordings of the event to each group, and let them work out jurisdiction and custody while she slipped out of the room, querying the 701st engineering company for the location of the closest network node to the dock and requesting their best platoon on the double.

One hour and twenty-seven minutes.

A very large part of her wanted to go after Strang. She was tempted to tell Angela to start accessing visual feeds and track the man, but that wasn't the priority. There was nowhere he could run that would be far enough. Tanis didn't think he would hide, at any rate. His type would get behind a wall of corporate lawyers as soon as possible.

No, Arlen Strang could wait.

<And he really isn't that important,> Angela said.

<I wouldn't say that.>

<All that matters is to save the Intrepid. *If we can get outsystem, then all of this gets left behind.>*

A barrage of queries was coming in from TSF command on Callisto, as well as requests from ChoSec to return to the scene for more statements. Tanis shunted them all to her message queue, keeping an eye out for any message from the 701st engineers.

She was nearing the network node that Angela had marked off as the closest to the *Intrepid*'s berth, when General Grissom, the Callisto TSF division commander, used an override to break past her queue.

<Major Richards. I need you to come in for a debriefing immediately.> He didn't sound happy; though in her experience, generals rarely did. It was almost as though there was a special

breed of dour human specially created to be generals.

<*Sir, I must insist that we do that later, I have a clear and present threat to this ring and the* Intrepid.> Tanis couldn't believe that they wanted to debrief her when there was the MDC to deal with. She brought up her preliminary report. <*I sent this in to command three minutes ago — it outlines the danger we're facing.*>

<*We have no solid evidence of an MDC. Even if it is there, the engineers you called in can handle it. We have questions we need to ask you about Strang.*>

<*It's all in the full sensory recording, sir. I really should be at the network node. It's impossible to know what they could find. A billion lives are in the balance — I have to believe that's more important than anything to do with Strang.*>

<*Major Richards, report to the DCP now! That's an order!*>

Tanis bit her lip in frustration — stopping when she tasted blood. <*Yes, sir; I'm on my way, sir*>

Grissom broke the contact with Tanis, and she kept moving toward the network node.

<*I take it we're going to ignore Grissom.*>

<*We are — sorry for dragging you into this; we're probably both going to get in trouble…a lot of trouble.*>

<*Tanis, I'm always prepared for you to get us in trouble. If it worried me, I wouldn't still be with you.*>

Angela's astringent words didn't hide the sentiment Tanis knew she felt. <*That may be the nicest thing that anyone ever said to me.*>

<*Then you need to be nice to more people. You'd stand a better chance of people being nice back if you were more so.*>

<*Yeesh, you can sure turn a 'thank you' back on me, can't you?*>

<*Comes from years of being in your mind. We AIs are very susceptible to your mental influences, you know.*>

Tanis decided that she wasn't going to be drawn further into the discussion, and focused on moving through the crowded corridors of the ring. Eventually they made it through the commercial district into a more sparsely populated systems control section. The sleek corridor walls gave way to rows of conduit containing both electronics and bio support liquids.

A few workers cast glances her way as she bolted past them. *It probably isn't often that a TSF officer—more specifically, a TSF officer with a uniform full of burn holes—runs past them at top speed.*

<It also could be that your 'top speed' is over thirty kilometers per hour,> Angela interjected into Tanis's thoughts. *<I doubt they are spending much time looking at your uniform, and are probably more just making sure you don't smash into them.>*

Tanis's mental avatar stuck its tongue out at Angela. *<Don't you have other things to do than listen in on my inner monologue?>*

<I'm pretty good at multitasking, you know.>

Tanis rounded the final bend between her and the network node, and saw that the engineers hadn't arrived yet. The entrance looked like any other door off the service corridor, but behind it would be a marvel of man's technological achievements. Angela exchanged tokens with the ring's security AI and was denied access.

<Sweet fuck, what now?>

<He says that our access has been revoked; we're wanted by ChoSec and the CIA.>

<Hold him off,> Tanis said to Angela, before establishing a Link to Trist. *<Trist, I've got a sec AI named...>*

<Blair,> Angela supplied.

<That's telling us we're persona non grata. Any tacks you suggest we take?>

Trist's mental chuckle was a welcome sound. *<I've had a few run-ins with him in the past. He thinks he's hot shit, but I can get past him. What are you trying to access?>*

<Node BX7.>

<No problem, give me...done.>

The doors slid open in front of Tanis and she stepped into the node.

<We gonna have ChoSec down on us?>

<I've got them taken care of. As far as ring security is concerned, you've gone elsewhere—a maglev station antispin, to be precise.>

<How come you never let on that you could hack this fast?>

<Well, this ring is so full of other hackers' hooks, that all I have to do is slip them some credit and they give me time on their SPNs. Speaking of which, this is going to wipe out that discretionary fund you set up for me in under one hour.>

<I'm sending you an update. Let's just hope we're still here in an hour.>

One hour and nineteen minutes.

Tanis's attention shifted to the view in front of her. She stood on a catwalk that ran around a large cubic space, roughly eighty meters along each side. The catwalk ran around the edge of the cube, roughly twenty meters from the floor. There were other walkways at the forty and sixty meter marks, each with a shimmering ES shield around it to shelter it from the three degrees kelvin temperatures that the node operated in. On each of the six sides of the cubic room, massive conduits breached the spaces between catwalks containing fiber-optic, plasma, and waveguide energy data transportation systems.

The conduit converged on an object that was difficult for the eye to perceive. It was essentially a massive structure housing several crystalline matrixes of super-dense silicon. The array contained some of the most impressive information-sorting and throughput technology in the Sol system.

The processing power of the Callisto nodes was well known to be immense. As humanity's largest habitat, Callisto had more internal communication than every other habitation and planet in the Sol system put together. The hub in front of Tanis could conceivably handle all of the network traffic on Mars 1, and have bandwidth to spare.

Angela was deploying probes through the ES field and assembling a full picture of the node to determine if anything looked amiss. Tanis pulled a wad of formation material out of her pocket and set it on the railing, deploying nano to begin turning it into a multi-interface holo projector.

<See, I am actually capable of controlling my own nano,> Tanis said.

<May the wonders never cease.> Angela's remark was acerbic as usual.

The holo projector was completed, and Angela linked her nanoprobes to it before slaving their controls to the projector's interface. The arrangement would allow the engineers control of the system once they arrived.

<So is anything standing out yet?> Tanis asked.

<Well, by my way of understanding, an MDC takes a lot of power, and at least several cubic meters worth of equipment. In this thing, that's like finding a needle in a haystack.>

<Especially considering that if they have it in multiple nodes, they may have figured out a way to break it up into smaller components.>

Angela fed several proposed component dimensions onto the holo. <A possibility that has given me more than a little consternation. It could look like any of these, or none of them. I'm not even sure how you could send a decoupling pulse through a network...it needs to have an emitter of some sort to create the targeted waveforms, beam, or field.>

<I get the picture.>

Tanis pondered that, bringing up documentation on everything that was known about MDCs. They were initially conceived of in the twenty-first century, but at that point the technology to create one was only nebulously imagined. In the thirty-second century, several scientists discovered that by altering the emitter from a ramscoop, they could break apart certain bonds and make asteroid mining easier. At some later point, several governments had begun weaponizing the technology, working out methods to have a single carrier wave contain other wavelengths specifically targeted at molecular structures. While an MDC couldn't do something like take apart an entire planet, it could certainly break apart smaller bodies into their base elements.

Further perusal yielded formulas for how much energy it would take to generate either the targeted beam, general wave, or field effects that could break apart the *Intrepid*. The numbers were large, but well within the energy available to the network nodes.

Tanis loaded all of the information into the holo projector, which swelled to encapsulate the new data and the ever-enhancing view of the node that Angela's nano were providing.

The sound of the doors sliding open heralded the entrance of the engineers. Tanis turned to address Lieutenant Simon, their CO.

"Glad to have you folks here. We've got credible intel indicating an MDC is in this, and probably the other three network nodes here on the ring. We've got some preliminary data up, but so far, nothing is standing out to us as anomalous."

Simon eyed the holo projector. "Nice work, sir. You've saved us valuable time with this." He walked to the railing, looking out into the node as he said this. A sidelong glance betrayed an uncertainty his voice did not. "How sure are you there is a molecular decoupler in these nodes? I'm not certain if you're aware that such a charge could take a healthy portion of this ring with it—potentially the whole Cho, if a runaway scenario were to occur."

"All too aware, Lieutenant. I know there is some threat against the *Intrepid*, and so far this is our best lead. The thing I can't wrap my mind around is how the pulse could be sent through the network."

The engineers were setting up more equipment around them, and one, a corporal, spoke up. "If I may, sir."

Tanis nodded and he continued. "It wouldn't actually deliver the pulse from the nodes, as much as the raw energy from them. There is a significant flow of energy brought in via ionized plasma. If one were to, well, enhance that energy, and direct it from each node through various conduits, you could have a relatively small device, comparatively speaking, emit the wave from elsewhere."

"So this could even be software," Tanis said.

"Yes, sir. That's how I'd do it."

Tanis pondered this as she stepped back and let the engineers do their work. Long minutes passed before one of the women bent over a series of holo interfaces called out. "I've found something. It looks like this node has a persistent connection to the dock the *Intrepid* is berthing at."

"With the amount of network traffic going to that dock, that doesn't seem unlikely," Tanis said.

"Aye, sir, but this is a secondary connection. From what I can tell, each of the nodes has a similar connection."

"Can you trace the end device?" Lieutenant Simon asked.

"Trying to; it's pretty nebulous. It just seems to arrive at the dock, connect to the main routers there, and then dissipate."

"Either way, you're saying that there is something actually on the dock, right?" Tanis asked.

"Everything points in that direction," Lieutenant Simon said.

"Then I'm heading out. You folks stay here and see if you can find a way to sever that connection."

"Yes, sir." Simon saluted. "Good luck."

"I'll stay connected to your net. Keep me abreast of any updates."

The lieutenant nodded as he turned back to the main holo and the data that was being brought up on the anomalous connection.

Fifty-seven minutes.

A FATEFUL ENCOUNTER

STELLAR DATE: 3227327 / 01.29.4124 (Adjusted Gregorian)
LOCATION: District C9Y, Ring 19C, Callisto Orbital Habitat (Cho)
REGION: Jovian Combine, Sol Space Federation

Tanis sprinted through the corridors, taking the fastest route to the docks that also kept her from running into the large shift-change crowds currently flooding the main thoroughfares.

After several a-spin tubes and a short maglev train ride, she arrived at the dock. Several TSF Regulars guarded the entrance, passing all comers through a thorough Auth & Auth check.

<We going to have trouble here?> Tanis asked Angela.

<Are you kidding? I oversaw these Auth & Auths being set up. Oh, you mean the humans—then yes.>

Upon seeing her, the soldiers tensed, and their squad leader, a Sergeant Weston, stepped forward.

"Uh, sir, Major Richards. We've been ordered to take you into custody should you show up here." He was clearly nervous, but his hand was on his sidearm, a certain indication that the sergeant would do his duty.

"Sergeant, there was a mixup. ChoSec tried to get me pulled in and passed off a series of commands as though they came from Grissom."

The sergeant cast her an appraising look. "I don't know about that, sir."

"Look." Tanis stepped up to the Auth & Auth, which proceeded to approve her access to the docks. "Would the system let me pass if I were flagged? Not even an alert attached to me on the approval display."

Weston scratched his head. "Well, those Cho guys do like to throw their weight around..."

"You know it, Sergeant. Glad to see you're with the TSF on

this. I'll be sure to mention it in my report."

Tanis walked past the soldiers and onto the dock. Behind her she heard Sergeant Weston start to say something and then stop.

<*He's calling it in, isn't he?*> Tanis asked.

<*Yes, and it's been intercepted.*>

<*What would I do without you?*>

<*I imagine you'd be long dead.*>

<*You're so uplifting.*>

Tanis was surveying the dock when a voice spoke from beside her. "So, what's the plan, Major?"

Tanis turned to see Trist standing beside her and smiled. "Thanks for the help back at the node. How did you get them off my back, anyway?"

"Well, as far as they know, you got into a firefight and ducked into a maglev that derailed on an external part of its track. It's going to take over thirty minutes to get to you."

"I'm doing all that right now, am I?" Tanis cocked an eyebrow at Trist.

"Yeah, and your life signs show you as unconscious with a damaged Link node."

"That's really unfortunate for me."

"I thought so."

"I have to say, you're pretty good at this."

"I've been told," Trist grinned.

"So what do you make of this?" Tanis asked. "Think there's really some sort of MDC emitter here?"

"Could be; there's enough crap to hide it in."

"What's the most likely culprit?"

"I'm guessing something in line of sight with the main cargo hatch."

"Well, we've got one/two and two/three on the dock doing final inspections. We can get them to help."

"The more the merrier." Trist smiled.

A few dock workers, cargo handlers, and, of course, the people setting up the stage for the post-docking ceremonies could be seen. Tanis decided that for now, she would let them continue their work—no need to cause a panic. It wouldn't take long for word of something like this to race across the Cho.

She called the two fireteams to her position, and when they arrived, she updated them on the current situation.

"Marines, we've got a problem," Tanis began.

"When don't we?" Perez said under his breath.

Sergeant Kowalski shot the private a look to shut him up. Tanis found herself wondering why his superiors even bothered.

"We have credible intel regarding an MDC on the ring, and it's here on this deck. We've got to find it before the *Intrepid* is in range."

"Sir, wouldn't something like that be rather large and…well…really noticeable?" Dvorak asked.

<Normally, yes,> Angela said on the tactical net. <But they've used the power of the ring's NNs to form the energy stream—we think. The 701 suspects that they're probably using the plasma streams.>

"Damn, that means it could be a lot smaller," Dvorak said.

Angela fed possible configurations onto the net, and the Marines looked them over.

Tanis proceeded to give out the orders. "Dvorak, Trist, I want you to head to the comm shack at the far end of the dock. The NNs are all maintaining connections to it, so it's quite possible that our culprit is down there. The rest of us will do a standard grid sweep across the rest of the dock. Don't forget to load those configs into your structural scanners. I've also got the net source signatures of the NN connections from the 701. They're on the tac net as well. Check every piece of cargo that's making a net connection for that route."

The Marines all saluted and dispersed to the grid locations that Kowalski laid out.

<We've got an idea here.> Simon's comment came over the broad channel on the engineer's net. <It's entirely possible that what we're dealing with is not an MDC emitter at all, but more of a trigger device.>

<Go on,> Tanis replied.

<Well, we've been thinking that anything that would emit the MDC beam would have to be pretty obvious; it would need a large waveform guide, either ES or physical, and there are only so many configurations for those. The most obvious ones would be the main comm hookups for the Intrepid; but they're not rated for nearly enough power, and would trip and/or fry long before you could emit this type of wave from them.>

<So what's the end result of all of this?>

<Well, we think the weapon is the Intrepid.>

That possibility had never even occurred to her. <How could the ship be the weapon?>

<ES ramscoops are essentially, as you know, the base of any MDC. The Intrepid has the most powerful one ever created.>

<So you're saying that somehow this system will trigger the Intrepid's ramscoop to create an MDC field effect on itself?>

<Or on the ring and they'll just let it spill over onto the ship. Even if it doesn't, I somehow think it will go very badly for the Intrepid.>

<Lose/lose for us and win/win for Strang,> Tanis replied. <So how do you think they're going to trigger it?>

<We're still working on that, as well as trying to see if we can find the control software and shut it down. Even if the Intrepid doesn't dock, I'm betting that this thing could still make the ship direct an MDC field at the ring.>

<Impetus for us to figure this out.> Tanis's tone was somber.

<Er...yes, sir.>

Tanis passed the information to the Marines and followed after Dvorak and Trist, who were making their way across the dock toward the comm shack. If what they were dealing with really was just a trigger, and it was using the waveguides to generate some sort of cohesion beam, then it was even more likely that the answer was in the comm gear.

She hopped on a hover heading to the far end of the dock and brought up the records for the comm shack. Sure enough, a service entry was logged last month, a full twenty weeks before any scheduled maintenance—with no record of malfunction being filed.

"Seems a bit suspicious," Tanis muttered to herself. She passed the information to Trist and Dvorak along with the details of the repair job. The chance of the info about logged repair being related to the actual work done was slim, but it was a place to start. The hover dropped her off near the comm shack, and Tanis kept an eye peeled for anything suspicious as she entered the room.

All ship to station net traffic would pass through the equipment in the shack and, since this dock was reserved for larger ships, a lot of systems were crammed in the twenty-meter-long space. After a moment's search, Tanis found Trist and Dvorak already hunched over consoles.

Not wanting to interrupt them, she turned and examined the room, looking for the largest conduit—which would likely be connected to the trigger device. Several large plasma lines ran out of the room and onto the dock. Tanis followed them and saw that they terminated at an array of beam emitters and receivers.

They were mounted to a column that ran down from the dock's ceiling. The design allowed them to rotate and slide into the best position to make a Link with a docked ship.

Tanis pulled up the specs, matching each device in the array to the design blueprints. As expected, something was not right. One emitter looked like a G1 TR3, but was not.

"Aha!" Tanis realized that her vocal proclamation wasn't all that helpful. <*Aha!*>

<*You've got something?*> Simon asked.

Tanis put a visual of the added component on the tactical and engineering nets. Lively debate ensued between Dvorak, Trist, the engineers, and several of the AIs.

Tanis took a moment to review the arrival time of the *Intrepid*. It was getting close; within thirty minutes, they would be making the seal. The outer hatches had already opened, and the atmosphere on the dock was being held in by an ES field. If she looked carefully at the mass of local traffic through the opening, it was possible to see a pattern clearing to allow the colony ship through.

<We need to tell them not to dock,> Tanis said.

<We need to tell everyone not to dock, and clear the ring while we're at it,> Lieutenant Simon said. *<We can't find the control software; it's probably on a timer. If this thing triggers without the* Intrepid *to absorb the effect, it's going to bounce back off that ES shield and nail the ring.>*

<It's not an MDC, it's just a trigger beam. What will it do to the ring?>

Simon paused, and she could see calculations being done on the engineers' net. *<We're not certain, but we think that, since it's essentially a stasis beam, it will cause the ring to seize. It may tear it out of alignment with the other rings. It would almost certainly collide with another ring in that event.>*

<That's almost worse than the MDC!> Trist exclaimed.

<More than almost worse,> Simon responded. *<We're sending a squad to you to attempt to disarm that thing on your end. You —>*

The connection was severed. Tanis poked her head into the comm shack and looked at Dvorak and Trist.

"I'm cut too; we've lost all Link to any nets outside of this dock," Trist said.

"I've got no external wireless connections," Dvorak added.

Tanis looked up to see one/two running toward the comm shack. "Taylor. Someone's dampened the dock. Check outside and see if you can get—" The whine of railguns coming from the dock's entrance interrupted her.

"Aw, fuck," Private Weber cursed. "Never a dull moment with you around, Major."

"Glad to oblige." Tanis tried to contact two/three on the discreet Link that military teams could use at close range.

<What's your status, Kowalski?>

<We're near the entrance. The regulars there are gone, we're trying to hold these mofos at bay, but nothing here is holding up against their rails.> He put data up on the tactical net showing over a dozen attackers, some wearing heavy armor.

Tanis pulled up a map of the dock and examined it. *<Fall back to coordinates F/3.1, behind those steel crates; they're full of some high-density raw alloys that should stop whatever those rails are flinging.>*

<Yes, sir. Thank you, sir.>

Kowalski initiated a local combat net, which Tanis extended to Trist before marking two/three's current position and destination on it. She turned to one/two. "Weber, you stay with Dvorak and Trist. You two try to determine how to disable that thing." Tanis pointed up at the emitter. "We could just blast it, but who knows what sort of fail-safes and detectors it has."

"Yeah, I'm typically against blowing things up that we don't understand." Dvorak's tone was dry, but Tanis could tell it masked concern.

"The rest of you, we're moving to position G/4.2. We'll set up cover for two/three, and try to catch whoever this is in our crossfire."

"I'm guessing that it's someone who wants to stop us from disabling this little party trick here," Taylor said.

"Or just someone with amazingly bad timing," Perez grinned.

"What, like your jokes?" Weber asked.

"This is the second time I've been attacked today." Tanis sighed. "I'm beginning to think some cosmic force wants me dead."

"I'd bet more on simple human forces wanting you dead…sir," Perez replied.

Tanis cast him a futile quelling glare and the fireteam moved out, hopping on a hover traveling in roughly the right direction. Tanis stayed back, monitoring two/three, as well as Trist and Dvorak's progress.

Minutes later they were in position, deployed behind several crates containing casings for SC batteries. The casings were molecularly dense, and also magnetic; with luck they would deflect, or slow, any incoming rail shots.

Two/three had managed to reach their position with no injuries, and were returning fire on the attackers. Their feed of the enemy was on the combat net and Tanis saw they were fighting more of the same heavily armed men from the conflict on Mars 1. The count came to under forty enemy troops.

<Coordinate fire on their forward ranks,> Tanis said. <We need to halt their advance until backup arrives.>

<It's weird that backup isn't here yet,> Salas commented. <I mean, we have several platoons within a klick or two.>

<Don't get your hopes up,> Dvorak cut in. <This dampening extends past the dock, from what I can tell. I doubt anyone knows anything is up—not until the monitoring AIs realize they've lost comm with the TSF guards at the dock entrances.>

<What's ETA on that?> Tanis asked.

<Based on the current alert level, it should have already happened—they've probably subverted some monitoring systems. I'd bank on at least ten minutes before that's detected.>

<Chances are that this will be over in ten minutes,> Reddy grunted.

Tanis realized that in those ten minutes the *Intrepid* would be making its seal. Whoever was orchestrating this party had to be making certain that all appeared outwardly normal on the dock. She thought briefly of the TSF guards, and a feeling of guilt assaulted Tanis. She should have warned the guards there to be on the lookout for trouble. Their names were added to her list.

Tanis steeled herself and addressed the teams. <*I think we have to consider ourselves to be on our own for this one, folks; but if it's do or die in the next ten minutes, then it's going to be do or die on our terms.*>

With her nanoprobe net extended, Tanis gathered an aerial survey of the combat zone. Sure enough, the attackers were trying to flank the Marines. It's what she would have done. A quick run through the cargo manifests revealed several things that could be of use. A crate ten meters away contained automated servitors to be used for scrubbing air ducts in environmental processing plants in the colony station. They were equipped with scalpelling lasers that could remove deposits and corrosion with ease. She sent a command to the crate to unseal, and a quorum of nano flew over to activate the servitors.

<*I've got some bots moving in to cover our right flank—they should hold, or at the least alert us to the enemy's position—but we're open on our left flank. Altair and Reddy, I want you to take up a position around those blue containers. I've put cargo density on the combat net; find a solid something and lay down suppressive fire. I don't care what you mow through—in fact, destroy as much of their cover as you can.*>

Altair and Reddy signaled green on the net and Salas and Arsen lobbed several concussion grenades before opening up with their assault rifles. The action gave their squad mates ample cover to get in the best positions to return fire.

However, the moment they ducked down to reload, the enemy delivered a withering assault with their railguns. Molten plas and steel sprayed out from each impact.

<*Heads up people, those rails are firing plasma at us.*>

<*Aw, fuck,*> Perez swore. <*Just what my day needs, having a limb*

blown off and then melted.>

<I *don't think it actually works that way,>* Taylor said.

<Or *at least not in that order,>* Weber added.

Despite the Marines' best efforts, the enemy was advancing. There was only so much they could do against an enemy that outnumbered them four to one and had superior firepower.

<Angela, *I know you're busy with Dvorak and Trist, but why isn't this dock's security system engaging?>*

<I'm *guessing it's jammed,>* Angela replied. <Not *really that surprising.>*

<Yeah, *but jammed centrally, or locally?>*

Angela's avatar grinned. <I *gotcha. Let me see if I can take manual control of the suppressors. Gonna need a few of your synapses to do it, but I'll try to use stuff you don't need right now.>*

Tanis got that distracted feeling she experienced whenever Angela was using a substantial part of her brain to help work through a difficult problem. It was almost like a buzzing going on in the back of her mind, causing segments of code or raw mathematical theorems to flash through the background of her thoughts.

<I've *got control of the individual suppressors,>* Angela said after a few moments, <but *there is a physical disconnect on the power conduits for their firing mechanisms. I've located it here.>* A position flashed on the map of the dock. <You'll *need to climb up there and reconnect the line.>*

<Of *course I will.>* Tanis sighed.

<Well, *not you, actually; whoever goes up there stands a good chance of getting shot, and Trist and Dvorak need me to help them work out this thingamabob on the comm system.>*

Tanis chuckled. <A *little self-preservation, eh?>*

<Well, *right now, if I die, we all die.>*

<I *can't say I disagree with that.>*

Tanis laid out the scenario to her two squads. Taylor spoke up as soon as she was done. <Weber *and I will take it. We're in the*

best position, and we've got some experience with stuff like that.>

<Then it's yours. We'll cover you.>

The two men dashed from their position, rolling and sliding across open spaces to present the smallest targets possible. The power junction was on a catwalk seven meters above the deck, and while a few crates rose higher, much of their climb would be in the open.

"Good luck," Tanis whispered. *< C'mon Marines, let's lay down one hell of a distraction.>*

In a coordinated effort, grenades were lobbed and fire spewed out of assault rifles and slug throwers to hide the movements and destination of Taylor and Weber. Combat net showed they were almost at their goal, and just had the climb ahead of them. Tanis saw they had opted to scale the back of a radioactive waste storage container rather than take the more exposed ladder along the wall. It would be quite the leap to the catwalk, but the two men must have thought they could make it.

Tanis swung a probe into their area to see a pair of the enemy on the opposite side of the container the Marines were climbing. She sent the feed to Weber. Upon reaching the top of the container he crouched and lobbed two conc grenades over the far side. Twin blasts ripped apart several crates, and Weber leaned over the top, delivering a barrage of slugs from his assault rifle before continuing with blasts from his pulse rifle, while his automatic reloader fed fresh ammunition into the AR.

Taylor had used the distraction to make the leap to the catwalk. He crouched low, unfastening the cover to the power conduit's coupling. A plasma pellet hit the catwalk near him, half blasting and half melting a portion of the structure away. The unsteady surface shook and swayed, but Taylor held his position while Weber threw his last grenade at the attacker who had made the shot.

<Almost have it,> Taylor said as another shot struck near him.

The cover was off and he was reconnecting the coupling. He was fastening the cover when another plasma pellet sliced through the railing behind him and tore the catwalk off the bulkhead. Taylor was wrapped in the twisted metal as it fell six meters to the deck below. Weber swore both audibly and over the net as he jumped down from his perch and raced to where Taylor's body lay—what was left of it.

<*He's gone.*> Weber's tone was low and pained.

<*We'll mourn him later,*> Kowalski said. <*Keep that flank secure, they're trying to rush us.*>

<*They're in for a surprise.*> Angela brought the dock's security systems online. Pulse particle turrets lowered from the ceiling and opened up on the enemy. Angela didn't care what she hit— her only concern was that as long as it wouldn't cause a blast big enough to kill the Marines or Tanis, it was expendable. The attackers were forced back, and though they were able to take out the turrets one by one, they lost over fifteen of their number in several seconds.

<*What's our status on the device?*> Tanis asked.

<*We've located the software running it, and are cracking it now,*> Trist replied. <*It has several fail-safes, so we've got multiple worms working their way in from oblique angles. Give us three more minutes and we'll have it neutralized.*>

<*You sure we just can't shoot the damn thing?*> Perez asked.

<*If we do, the plasma surge will just dump out onto the dock when it tries to fire. It won't be detrimental to the* Intrepid *or the ring, but we'll all die.*>

<*Last resort, then,*> Tanis said. <*Three minutes is cutting it damn close, though.*>

Her words were emphasized by a slight rumble that passed through the deck plate as the ring made magnetic grapple with the *Intrepid*.

<*They've got reinforcements coming in!*> Kowalski called out. <*We've got to fall back.*>

Tanis looked over the updates flowing into the combat net. At least another forty enemy troops were entering the dock from other entrances, and the Marines were once again in danger of being flanked.

<This is too open here,> Tanis said. <Fall back using the plan I've laid in. We'll create a perimeter around Dvorak and Trist.>

<Not a lot of dense cargo there,> Jansen replied.

<There will be.> Tanis accessed the automatic loaders, tapping into several haulers and agrav pads loaded with dense items. She configured them to move into positions to cover the Marines as they retreated.

<Mighty sweet of you, Major,> Perez said. <Always nice to have cover when I run.>

<Shut it, Perez,> Kowalski said. <Just shoot that bastard trying to kill you on the left.>

<I see him, I see him.>

Things were getting tense; the fireteams were pulled back as tight as they could manage around the comm shack, but the plasma rails were chewing up the cover. Tanis was trying to bring in more cargo, but their attackers had wised up and were shooting any haulers or grav pads they saw.

A low boom echoed through the dock, and Tanis knew that the *Intrepid* had completed its docking procedure. It was just over a minute early. Any moment now, the ES shield would drop, and the trigger mechanism would fire. She saw the Marines all shift, their posture showing that they were taking a last stand approach to the fight. They'd go down as heroes.

"We're so fucking close," Dvorak swore. "Just one more goddamn minute and we'll have this bastard cracked."

Behind the Marines, the ES shield at the cargo hatch snapped off and the *Intrepid*'s doors began to slide open.

<We don't have one more minute,> Angela said. <It's going to fire in twenty seconds.>

Tanis turned and raised her rifle to fire on the emitter.

Kowalski cast her a sidelong glance, his expression showing his acceptance of what she was about to do. Her finger had pulled the trigger halfway when she felt a Link come online.

Of course! she thought. The dampening field wasn't set up to block the focused beams between the comm system and the *Intrepid*. The opening iris had established those connections and since Angela was deep in the comm system she was subsequently linked with her ship.

<*Where have you been!*> Amanda said a moment later. <*TSF said you'd gone rogue and were lost somewhere on the ring.*>

<*No time, Amanda, hook up with Angela, we've got a device here that's about to ruin everyone's day!*>

Tanis felt a rapid exchange of information pass through her as Angela brought the ship's avatar up to speed on recent events and what they were fighting with. Less than a second later, she felt a massive presence swell onto their local net. It was as though she was suddenly on the edge of a deep precipice. She realized it must be the *Intrepid* itself, stepping in to disable the device. The vast mind that powered the ship broke through the trigger fail-safes, and seized its processes. Angela, Trist, and Dvorak let out simultaneous cries of delight on the combat net, and a moment later the waveform guides in the communications array exploded in a shower of sparks and debris.

<*Thank you,*> the presence said over their combat net, and was gone.

<*Bob's pretty happy that you all have gone to such lengths to protect him and the ship's passengers,*> Amanda said. <*I can't believe how close we all just came to biting the dust.*>

<*Wouldn't have happened. We would have taken the device out,*> Tanis said.

<*I hate to rain on your happy parade, but we're still about to be sliced and diced by all these guys with guns,*> Perez said.

<*I think we can help with that.*> Joe's voice came over the

combat net. Tanis turned to see him entering the dock at the head of over two hundred soldiers in full combat gear. Within moments, they had taken up positions around the Marines and were laying fire into the enemy.

Tanis had never been so happy to see anyone in all her life.

REPRIEVE

STELLAR DATE: 3227348 / 01.30.4124 (Adjusted Gregorian)
LOCATION: GSS *Intrepid*, Callisto Orbital Habitat (Cho)
REGION: Jovian Combine, Sol Space Federation

"We were pretty sure something suspicious was going on when we couldn't find you, and General Grissom said you'd gone rogue after attacking Strang," Captain Andrews said. "You may be a bit impulsive, but that tale was a stretch."

"Ring security couldn't find you, and we couldn't get a comm signal from the guards at the dock, even though TSF told us they were checking in regularly," Terrance added. "We were getting one hell of a run-around."

Tanis was sitting at the table in the bridge's conference room with Terrance, Joe, Captain Andrews, and Admiral Sanderson. With the additional forces Joe had brought to the battle on the docks, the attackers were overwhelmed and had surrendered. However, things were still a mess. Grissom was demanding Tanis be turned over to his command on the ring, and Strang had not been indicted for abducting her. With all sides of the tale coming out, it was becoming obvious that Grissom was in Strang's pocket.

"So, we were ready for just about anything when that dock opened up—hence the rather large armed force at my back," Joe said. "Can't say how glad I was to see you there, still kicking."

"That's me." Tanis smiled. "I'm a kicker." She realized that statement could have been misconstrued. "Er, well, figuratively speaking."

She couldn't help but notice a wry look from Joe. Everyone else pretended to ignore the statement and the look.

"Glad we got there when we did," Terrance said. "We owe you, Major Richards. We owe you several times over."

"That we do," Sanderson growled. "I've got calls in to several individuals up the chain of command demanding Grissom's head. Things will come to light very shortly, and they won't go well for him—that I can promise you."

"Lucky for me, Angela is rated A97 incorruptible, or it would be my word against a TSF division's that Strang assaulted me," Tanis said. "As it sits, it's still going to take some doing, I imagine."

"We had some of our own excitement as well," Joe said. "Turns out there was a bit of sabotage in the scoop's main systems. If we hadn't caught it, it would have activated and caused some pretty serious damage to Callisto."

"Really?" Tanis asked. "Did we find who did it?"

"Ouri is working on it. So far, everything points to some contractors back on MOS. Everyone onboard checks out."

"I've just got word that Grissom has been relieved pending further investigation." Sanderson smiled, and Tanis noted that it was the first time she'd seen him do so. "It would seem that internal affairs has been keeping an eye on him for some time. He made official insubordination charges against you, and those are still standing, but I believe I can get those dropped even if he's cleared."

"Strang really has grown desperate to stop us," Captain Andrews said. "His little plan here was frankly nuts—chancing millions of deaths to take us out."

"There's even a twenty-one percent chance that the field could have destroyed another ring." Terrance's expression was grim. "While Sanderson is taking action through military channels, I've filed over three hundred civil complaints against Strang, Grissom, several local security firms, and…well, you get the picture. There are going to be court battles for decades over this."

"Not that we'll really care," Tanis said. "We'll be long gone by then."

Terrance had that smile again, the one that reminded Tanis he was the owner of a multiworld corporation for a reason. "We won't care, but I promise you that they will care very much."

Tanis looked over the assembled men. "I really can't say enough how glad I am that you decided to take every precaution when docking."

"Well." Terrance wore his nicer, human smile. "Like I said, you deserve some thanks, too. Without your work, we wouldn't have made it to Callisto—let alone survived today."

"You really have the *Intrepid* to thank," Tanis said. "Even with all of my efforts, without his intervention at the last moment, it would have all been worthless."

"Let's just say that it was a group effort." Joe smiled. "And I'm betting that it will be the STR's last volley at us. It's smooth sailing from here."

"Aw, damn it!" Tanis put head in her hands. "Now look what you've done!"

"Who would have thought we would have a superstitious intel officer on our hands?" Terrance chuckled.

"Hell, with all that's happened to try to stop us, I'd be crazy not to be," Tanis said. "No matter, though. Those STR goons haven't come up with anything we haven't been able to handle yet."

"Now who's making the dangerous statements?" Joe asked.

CELEBRATION

STELLAR DATE: 3227362 / 02.13.4124 (Adjusted Gregorian)
LOCATION: District A39, Ring 19C, Callisto Orbital Habitat (Cho)
REGION: Jovian Combine, Sol Space Federation

It was their last night on Callisto. The *Intrepid* had ended up staying roughly three weeks longer than intended due to the need to replace all of the supplies destroyed in the dock fight. There had also been the testimonies that Tanis and the Marines gave in the cases against dozens of individuals who were either involved or complicit in Arlen Strang's attempt to destroy the *Intrepid*.

The STR had thrown him to the wolves, disavowing themselves of any of his actions, but the chickens had come home to roost. Several governments across the Sol system were launching investigations into the consortium and discovering trails of bribery, technology being sold to embargoed groups, and funding of various terrorist organizations.

Dozens of arrests had already been made, and the company's stocks were plummeting. An added bonus was that the business ventures Terrance was leaving behind were getting a boost, as demand for products not manufactured by the STR increased. Not that he would ever enjoy the largess, but his offspring and successors would.

The last few nights had been gala after gala in the ballrooms on the *Intrepid*, but tonight there were no formal celebrations. Tanis, Joe, Ouri, and several others on the SOC staff threw a soiree at a large club on the ring. Sad farewells were given as many of the support personnel were not colony-bound, and Callisto was where they disembarked. Tanis had also invited the TSF platoons that had now finished their assignments under her. At present, she was sharing a table with Lieutenant

Forsythe, Lieutenant Grenwald, and Staff Sergeant Williams.

"Never gonna forget you, Major." Williams smiled as he lifted a glass in a toast to her. "You're the toughest, meanest, most cunning officer I ever did meet. Hell, if you were just a little smarter, you could even be a sergeant."

Tanis laughed. "You could say I'm a little too smart for that. You guys have to do all the work in this woman's space force."

"Damn right we do." Williams downed the drink. "And don't think we don't like it that way. If you officers were the ones actually running things, we'd be screwed for sure."

Forsythe laughed while Grenwald scowled. "You'll get used to it, Grenwald." The older lieutenant smiled as she slapped him on the back. "The NCOs are really here to keep us in line as much as the troops. The sooner you accept that, the better your life will be."

Tanis liked both of the officers a lot. Forsythe was up for a promotion after her work keeping the *Intrepid* safe, and Grenwald was all but guaranteed one once he had put in the requisite time at his current rank. She also had it on good authority that Williams had a promotion to gunnery sergeant waiting once his platoon was reunited with their company in a month.

The thoughts of promotion and reward brought her mind to Corporal Taylor for a moment. The Marine had posthumously been awarded the Eight Planets of Valor, and been added to the heroes roster of Bravo Company, Marine Battalion 242. It was an honor the company afforded to few, but his sacrifice could not be denied.

She was brought back to the present by the needling Forsythe was giving Grenwald. Williams added a particularly choice example of a staff sergeant's wit, and they all broke into laughter.

After the chuckles died down, Williams cast Tanis a questioning eye. "I have to say, Major. I really don't get why you're shipping out. This is what you were born to do."

"Could even pass as a Marine if you worked at it." Forsythe grinned.

"It's my time," Tanis said. "I've put in nearly fifty years of service, and let me tell you: in MICI years, that's more like five hundred. They don't give us much downtime; just shuttle us from mission to mission. Hell, I've had periods where I've gone years with my only time off being in stasis."

The Marines nodded solemnly. They didn't agree, but they respected her decision.

"All the same." Williams put a hand on her shoulder. "I'll be sad to see you go."

"Who knows," Tanis smiled. "We could meet again; it's a big galaxy, and stranger things have happened."

"I'd fight by your side any day, Major." Williams' grey eyes locked with hers. "You're one hell of a soldier."

"Here's to the Major." Grenwald lifted his glass.

"To the Major!" the other two chimed in.

* * * * *

The party lasted for several more hours. In the end, all of the tables were empty but one. Tanis, Joe, Ouri, and Amy Lee sat around it, each nursing a final drink. The change from the loud revelry to relative silence had caused a melancholy to settle over them. The realization had hit that when they left the ring, it would be the last time they stepped foot on any structure in the Sol system, or saw any people not already on the *Intrepid*. They were saying goodbye.

"It's different than I thought it would be," Joe said. "I'm feeling sadder than I thought I would."

"I think we all are," Ouri replied. "We're leaving home, leaving Sol. We're going out into the dark for a long time."

"Feels anticlimactic," Tanis said. "I feel like after all this struggle that the struggle should just continue."

"Gah! Don't say that." Joe cringed. "I'm all struggled out." Under the table he held her hand.

"Oh believe me, I am too." Tanis smiled. "But I'm going to have to reeducate myself on how to live without it."

"I think we all are." Amy Lee returned Tanis's smile. "I'm so used to feeling tense and suspicious, I've begun to be cautious around my hairbrush. I'm surprised you trust yours with your new locks."

"Stars, I'm happy to have long hair again." Tanis ran a hand through her shoulder-length blonde hair. "I'm going to grow it to my ankles."

"That'll look...weird." Joe smiled.

"I recommend against extreme hair lengths," Ouri said. "It gets really annoying."

"But I could create hair sculptures out of it on my head! I hear that's all the rage on Triton these days." Tanis grinned.

"That was a decade ago," Amy Lee said.

"Oh."

"We should head back," Joe said. "Debark is in two hours, and you know how those security types like to have everything all sealed up well in advance."

"Hey!" All three ladies spoke at once and then burst out laughing. It felt good—good to laugh, good to be relaxed. Things were finally done here.

Tanis and Joe walked arm in arm back to the *Intrepid*, lost in their own world together. Amy and Ouri walked slightly ahead of them, talking softly between themselves. For once, Tanis didn't feel the need to be on her guard. ChoSec was thick like flies on the ring. No one wanted the departure of the *Intrepid* to have any of the same troubles it had on the way in. Luckily, nothing suspicious had happened since that day. The thought made the hairs on the nape of Tanis's neck rise, but she forced herself to relax. Just because nothing had happened did not mean something *had* to happen.

Besides, with most of the upper echelons of the STR behind bars, no one was left to cause them trouble. Even if there were, it was unlikely that they would consider it worthwhile anymore. Like any company, eventually the STR had to cut its losses when looking at a losing venture.

Despite her misgivings, they made it to the *Intrepid* without incident, and the guards who checked them in saluted smartly.

"You're the last ones aboard, sirs."

"Seal it up then," Tanis said. "It's time to head into the black."

M. D. COOPER

LAST DITCH

STELLAR DATE: 3227364 / 02.15.4124 (Adjusted Gregorian)
LOCATION: GSS *Intrepid*, Near Main Asteroid Belt
REGION: Jovian Combine, Sol Space Federation

Tanis stared at the views being displayed on the commissary's main wall. The entire space was covered with the starscape that was visible from the *Intrepid*'s bow. The ship was just passing the nominal orbit of the main asteroid belt, slightly above the absolute plane to avoid the small particles that had been disturbed by a Kirkwood gap in the belt.

Even though Sol was just a pinprick in the lower left quadrant of the view, its brilliance in the cold expanse of space was almost like a physical pressure on the eyes. Over on the right, several overlays were visible showing the ship's path toward Sol, with various periods of engine burn intensity highlighted. The current position was shown by a small representation of the ship with stats indicating vector and thrust to its right.

Tanis found herself lost in the beauty of it. Very rarely did she simply look out into space and the stars; most of the time, she was too focused on duty and security. But other than a few reports to file, there was little left for her to do at the moment.

It seemed odd to have yet another celebration, but a day or two earlier, someone had planned a small gathering before going into stasis; and before long, everyone was invited and the cooks were having a fit.

Pulling her attention away from her inward thoughts, Tanis focused on the conversation around her.

"I've gotta admit," Ouri slurped a spoonful of soup. "This feels weird...this falling into the sun thing."

"I've done it a few times," Joe said. "It is a bit different than using a planet to slingshot, mainly because just getting close to a planet isn't potentially fatal."

"That and most planets don't fill the forward view days before you even get close." Ouri grimaced.

"You worry too much." Tanis's eyes had a dreamy look. "Eat food, enjoy drink, listen to banter. Nothing can ruin this. We're finally on our way—finally leaving Sol and all of the nonsense."

"Who are you, and what have you done with Tanis?" Joe grinned. "You look like Tanis, but the words coming out of your mouth are calm and relaxed…dare I even say, happy?"

"It must be a robot, or maybe a clone," Ouri said. "I was very certain that Tanis was actually incapable of anything approaching mellow. Should we call security?"

"Aren't we security?" Joe asked.

"Crap…you mean we have to deal with this?"

"Shut up." Tanis scowled at her tablemates.

"Oh, thank god, it is you!" Joe grinned.

A woman walked up to the table and pulled up a chair beside Tanis. "I tell you, it's damn good to actually have a glass of wine again." She spoke as though she knew everyone around her, but no one recognized her.

She wore a long dress and a cowl that covered most of her head. Tanis tried to catch a glimpse of her eyes as the woman reached for the bottle to refill her glass.

"Who—?" Joe began to say.

"Amanda!" Tanis exclaimed and hugged the other woman. "We didn't recognize you without a starship attached to your ass."

Ouri nearly choked on her drink and had to frantically gasp for breath as Joe handed her a napkin.

"Oh, my god, Tanis, that has got to be the funniest thing you've ever said."

Tanis scowled. "I'll have you know I am funny all the time."

<She's a barrel of yuck yucks,> Angela said at her driest.

"I gotta admit," Joe said to Amanda, "I didn't expect to see you here...I didn't realize you could leave your...er...post."

"No pun intended," Ouri smiled.

"I was on shift for a bit longer than planned. Priscilla had a few problems adapting to the interface, but the plan is a ninety days on, ninety days off rotation between us. As much as I like Bob, I really do need this time to remember who I am."

"It is weird to hear your voice with my ears. I'm used to it being in my head," Amy Lee said.

"You and me both." Amanda laughed.

"Hey." Tanis spotted someone across the crowd. "Isn't that Lieutenant Collins of the GSS?"

"Yeah." Ouri looked over her shoulder where Tanis pointed. "Slimy guy, isn't he?"

"As the day is long," Tanis replied. "But what's he doing here? I thought he wasn't mission."

"He wasn't, but he requested crew status just before we left the Cho. There were a couple of last-minute abdications, so he got in with no problem. A few other people in his department got crew positions as well," Joe said.

"Damn," Tanis said. "I really don't like him. Something about him rubs me the wrong way."

"He's a rubber all right. But let's talk about happy things. Collins'll sour my mood real fast." Ouri reached for the bottle of wine and poured herself another glass.

No one said anything for a moment and then they all burst out laughing at once—except for Ouri who looked perplexed.

"What did I say?"

They steered the conversation elsewhere, and the light chatter continued through the meal. As the dinner was drawing to a close, Captain Andrews rose from his place at the head table.

"Good evening to you all," he said to the assembled crowd. "I'm certain that all of you feel as pleased and excited as I do that we're finally underway. For those of you who haven't checked the latest stellar vector," he gestured to the screens behind him, "we are achieving better than expected performance from both our engines and our ramscoop. I'm certain you are as happy as I, and are very grateful to Earnest, Abby, and their teams for an amazing job in constructing this truly magnificent vessel."

Applause thundered as everyone clapped enthusiastically for the Reddings and their teams.

The captain raised his hands for silence, and the applause died away.

"We are currently falling toward the sun at a rate that will cause our breakaway velocity to be $0.09c$. We will continue to increase this speed through our interstellar burn to $0.12c$. Because of this, we will alter our approach to LHS 1565, and, overall, we'll shorten our trip by seventeen years."

This statement was met with more applause and cheering from the assembled mission crew and colonists. People were smiling and patting one another on the back. Tanis was certain that she even saw a smile crease the face of Abby Redding at the head table.

<General alert.> Priscilla's voice resonated through all command crew's Links. *<We have multiple incoming signals. They appear to be some sort of craft.>*

Tanis looked to Joe. "Your fighters ready to roll?"

"Suited and strapped in."

<Captain, I have a full squadron of fighters ready to deploy on your command.> Tanis relayed the information to Captain Andrews.

<Very good, Major. Bring Commander Evans with you to the bridge.>

"Huh, and here we thought you were all relaxed," Ouri smiled at Tanis. "Still thinking about all the possibilities, I see."

"Ladies and gentlemen." Captain Andrews was still standing, and his face betrayed no emotion other than calm.

"We appear to have a potential issue affecting our exit of this system. All duty personnel, report to your assigned stations. Everyone else, check your local access points for any assignments; otherwise follow the general emergency plan."

With that, he left the table and strode toward the closest tube that ran to the bridge. Several others, including Terrance, the Reddings, and Admiral Sanderson went with him; Tanis and Joe worked their way through the crowds to catch up with Amanda trailing behind them.

Joe analyzed the data Priscilla was streaming to them. "They appear to be some sort of fast intercept craft. Most likely a deployment type that will drop fighters...either that, or they're missiles."

"I don't know which I prefer," Tanis said.

"Missiles," Joe said as they caught the tube that slid in after the command crew had left. "Lower levels of programming on those. No human or AI onboard—fighters always have either...or both."

<Deploy your fighters, and have Yellow Wing prep for takeoff as well,> Captain Andrews addressed Joe over the Link, broadcasting across the local security net so that Tanis could hear as well.

<Aye, Captain,> Joe responded.

A moment later, the tube disgorged them onto the command deck. The short access corridor led them into the main foyer, where Priscilla was working to ensure that all sections were covered, and that everyone was where they were supposed to be. She didn't look much different than Amanda, though Tanis could see some slight physical traits that didn't match. Priscilla looked up and nodded at the two officers as they ran past her.

"Good luck, keep us in one piece," she said over the room's audible systems.

"Don't we always?" Joe smiled in return.

The bridge was a study in energetic order. Everyone was

doing something, but they were doing it with precision and calm. Everyone present was in the upper echelons of their field. Moreover, Captain Andrews had worked them hard. The result was a cohesive team built from what otherwise would have just been a group of people good at disparate things.

Tanis and Joe exchanged tokens with the bridge net and updates flooded in.

Scan showed nine large cylindrical objects headed toward the *Intrepid* at 0.5*c*. Their point of origin appeared to be from the Thermis asteroids, a region owned by several mining groups. Tanis saw ties to the STR—a major purchaser of their raw materials.

Readings and statistics on the incoming objects flowed in, and Joe sat at a duty station seat where he updated the main holo with information and projections. Tanis stood near the rear of the bridge. While she was a competent pilot, Joe didn't need her telling him how to do his job.

"I believe they are carrier vessels," Joe said aloud and Captain Andrews turned his command chair to look at him. Terrance was standing beside Tanis and swore softly. The Reddings were already at consoles, most likely preparing repair crews and readying the ES shields and laser turrets—Earnest had no reaction, but Abby shook her head.

"I would expect three to five fighters to deploy from each, once they are in range. I have event ETAs up on the net and holo. We're most likely looking at a Theta Class fighter; they hit hard and do the job fast. They're usually equipped with three dozen five-megaton fusion warheads." Joe said and updated the bridge net with his data.

"Well, that would get the job done fast," Captain Andrews replied. "You realize that works out to about 1620 five-megaton devices."

"I do, sir. Tactical scenarios predict that we should be able to neutralize ninety percent of them, but that still leaves around

160, several times what it would take to cripple the *Intrepid*."

Andrews turned to one of the bridge crew. "What can we expect our ES shields to deflect?"

"It'll depend on how staggered they are, sir. We could survive every one of them given enough time between the impacts, but the magnetic conductors are going to heat up, moving all of that radiation down the vanes and away from the ship. If we blow them, then we'll be delaying this trip."

"Fire control." Captain Andrews turned to another crewman. "At what maximum range can you engage the enemy without bleed-off from the lasers risking our fighters?"

"Based on the specs that Commander Evans has up on the command net, I'd say we're looking at seven thousand kilometers."

"Then they're going to have to work real hard to hit us." The captain nodded. "Keep your fighters under that range after their initial salvo. It should help us even things out. What is the ETA on yellow getting out there as well?"

"Twenty minutes, sir."

"I doubt this will last that long."

"Aye, sir."

"Deployment," the woman at scan called out. "Looks like specs were bang on. We've got forty-five inbound fighters."

"Blue Wing is engaging," Joe said.

The main holo lit up with the feed from the battle. The attackers were doing their best to simply punch through the *Intrepid*'s defenses. With their v, they were unable to perform any drastic maneuvers; the velocity that had allowed them to get in range so quickly now became a hindrance.

"We've got some unexpected issues," Joe said. "Our fighters' targeting systems don't have the processing power to handle this much time dilation."

Realization dawned on Tanis. Though notable time dilation from traveling too close to the speed of light didn't occur under

0.6c, any time the fighters were flying directly toward or away from another, their relative velocity was easily in that range. A quick change of direction and time expanded: trajectories, velocities, targeting, and shields all had to instantly adjust; sometimes they had to adjust several seconds ago.

The conditions the pilots were enduring were at the edge of a human's abilities. It took over an hour just to get into the special suit for handling the gee forces, the fighters' cockpits were full of gel to absorb motion, and drug cocktails were continually being pumped through the pilots to keep them conscious while a latticework of support webbing inside their brains kept the grey matter from being smeared inside their skulls. Combat like this was going to take weeks for them to recover from.

Despite those factors, the Blue Wing took out three of the attackers within the first moments of combat. It was a testament to the pilots' training that they were managing to hit anything at all.

"Vectors are too extreme," Joe said as his fingers raced across a holo UI. "Onboard systems are overheating trying to provide accurate calculations. The pilots are also having neural cooling problems."

"Didn't really plan for a suicide run," Captain Andrews muttered. "Priscilla, do you have enough bandwidth available to offload calculations from the fighters?"

"I can for some of them," Priscilla's voice said over the bridge's speakers. "Signal isn't strong enough to assist all of them."

"I'm jacked in." Amanda stood near the entrance to the bridge with her hood off. Her cowl was pulled down and antennae hair waved above her as she accessed the bandwidth reserved for her and Priscilla.

"Do it," Andrews said. "Co-ord it with Commander Evans— we need our people to take those bastards out."

"I'm in range in fifteen seconds," the crewman at fire control announced.

"Fire at will; be sure your patterns are available to Commander Evans and the ladies," Captain Andrews said.

"This isn't working well," Amanda said as another fighter in Blue Wing was destroyed. "The AI link on the fighters is too primitive, and it's slowing things down too much. With the time lag and the interface chokepoint, we can't be effective. I need to perform a partial transference."

Andrews glanced back at her, his expression sharp. "That's a very dangerous proposal. We could lose you."

"You'll have Priscilla if I get in trouble."

"How long will it take?"

"Moments. I do need something, though. I need access to the mind of someone who has flown a fighter and understands the tactics."

"Use me," Joe said. "I'll guide you."

"No good," Captain Andrews said. "You won't be able to do your job with her subsuming your mind."

"Use me." Tanis spoke up. "I'm rated, and have over ten thousand hours flight time."

"You sure about this?" Andrews turned to look at her. "It's not an exact science."

Joe shot a pained look in Tanis's direction, but didn't say a word.

"It's more exact than it used to be," Amanda said, a living example of the neural advances.

"Just do it." Tanis took a deep breath. "Before I change my mind, and before one of those warheads hits us."

Nothing prepared her; no warning was given. One moment Tanis was sharing her mind with Angela, and the next, a massive presence pushed inside of her. She felt herself swelling; even Angela seemed taken aback by the will and power of Amanda's mind.

<*Open up to me,*> Amanda said—not over the Link, but directly into Tanis's thoughts.

<*Here's the pathway.*> Angela directed the ship's avatar through Tanis's mind.

<*Take what you need,*> Tanis said.

There was a pause. <*I can't,*> Amanda said after several moments. <*The data, the formulae, are tied directly to your mind's connection with your body and your instinctual grasp of tactics. So much of it is hard-wired—twitch reflexes. I can't extract the knowledge from your mind.*>

<*Damn…then we're fucked,*> Tanis thought.

<*No,*> a deeper voice said, resonating through Amanda's presence. <*Route the data through her.*>

<*It could destroy her,*> Amanda said.

<*Not doing it could destroy us all.*>

<*She can take it,*> Angela added. <*Her sense of self is too damn stubborn to be subsumed. We don't have much time.*>

Whereas moments before, the crushing force of Amanda's presence had surrounded her, Tanis was now forced to the top, as though riding the cresting surf of thought; her mind racing up and out. She saw the *Intrepid*, and the fighters defending and attacking. All of the vectors and trajectories fit in her mind and were perfectly understood as a whole. Tanis examined the situation and knew what to do.

Her mind expanded over the tightbands to the Blue Wing. Angela and Amanda guided her through the fighter's neural nets, and she felt a portion of herself shift to reside in them. From there, she reached out and established a Link with each and every one of the pilots.

<*Follow directions,*> was the only grammatical thought she sent them. Everything after was feeling and intuition. Tanis choreographed a grand movement, an overall strategy that would apply the correct focus and pressure to bear against the enemy.

Angela and Amanda gave assistance once they knew her scheme. It was bold and daring and impossible to grasp without their integration with her mind.

The Blue Wing ships were forming a cube of death. What would normally create crossfire, where the fighters would suffer considerable friendly fire, was instead a killing field where only the enemy died. Fighters deployed relativistic chaff, beams, and projectiles, creating a death zone that took out thirty one of the enemy fighters. All told, there were now only five attackers left.

<*That was amazing,*> Angela said. <*Good thing no one knows you're this good at this stuff; they would have turned you into a tactical meld long ago.*>

Tanis shuddered at the notion, but knew Angela meant it as a compliment.

<*Don't get cocky,*> Amanda said. <*There are still five of them left. More than enough to cripple us.*>

<*Not for long.*> Tanis directed Blue Wing to bracket the attackers, keeping a clean line open for the ship's beams. Fire control was given the safe vectors, and the lasers lanced out, boiling off the attackers' hulls one by one. At the last moment, the final ship detonated all of its warheads before being destroyed. Calculations showed that it was too close—the shockwave expanded, encompassing Blue Wing and the *Intrepid.*

On the colony ship, the shields and sheer mass of the vessel absorbed most of the energy, but the same could not be said for the fighters. Tanis was lucky in that, the moment Amanda detected the EMF spike, she yanked the major's mind back into her body. If she hadn't, the parts of Tanis spread across the tightbands would have been torn from her forever.

"Sweet Venus," Tanis moaned, falling to the floor. "I feel like my brain has been ripped in two."

"Priscilla," Captain Andrews said. "We need medics now."

"Already on their way," she replied audibly. "I sent for them as soon as we made the merge."

"Very good." Andrews nodded. "Commander Evans, did any of our fighters survive?"

"Four are in communication, ten are structurally impaired with no chance of survival, the rest are somewhere in between, but with no comm."

"Get recovery craft out there as soon as possible."

"Aye, sir."

The joy of survival was tempered by the near total loss of Blue Wing. Even amongst the four in communication, considerable damage had been sustained by both the craft and the pilot. No one was coming back unscathed.

"Yellow is outbound. They'll do some nudging and correct trajectories for the tugs," Joseph said.

"Keep me apprised," Captain Andrews replied. He surveyed his bridge and looked over the damage reports that were scrolling on the main holo as well as the bridge net, finally determining that nothing needed his direct intervention. Only then did he allow himself to turn and look at the woman who had just risked being a mindless husk for the rest of her life — who may still face that fate.

Tanis lay in a fetal position, shaking slightly with the odd spasm tearing through her body. Joe was holding her, a look of helplessness on his face. Andrews knelt at her side.

"Tanis, can you hear me?"

"Aye, sir…all seven thousand of you. Do you all have to yell?" Tanis whispered between ragged breaths, tears streaming from her eyes.

"Sorry," he replied softly. "You're going to be all right. The medics are on the way. I imagine you'll be taking a bit of a nap, though."

"Sounds good, sir." Tanis closed her eyes tight, but a small smile played at the edges of her mouth. "Try to keep the ship in one piece while I'm out."

RECOVERY

STELLAR DATE: 3227366 / 02.17.4124 (Adjusted Gregorian)
LOCATION: GSS *Intrepid*, Within 0.5 AU of Sol
REGION: InnerSol, Sol Space Federation

Rescuing the remains of Blue Wing took several hours. The tugs had trouble maintaining their *v* relative to the *Intrepid*, but eventually, with some tricky maneuvers, they managed to bring all of Blue Wing aboard.

As it turned out, eleven pilots survived; though that meant nineteen had died, it cheered everyone, nonetheless. The *Intrepid* had ceased burn during the operation, but now that all were once again aboard, the mighty drives resumed their fission reaction, and the ship recommenced its acceleration toward the sun.

TSF monitoring had detected the conflict on their scans, and Captain Andrews saw that a full report was filed. The tugs had also picked up the remains of several of their attackers, and, once the *Intrepid* had completed its slingshot maneuver around the sun, a TSF intercept patrol craft would meet them just past Venus's orbit to collect what physical evidence they could. That was still roughly fifteen days away, depending on whether the Reddings determined it would be beneficial to boost acceleration beyond 0.25*g*.

Andrews checked the current status of the engines and saw that they were creating the equivalent of just over ten trillion newtons of force to achieve their velocity. That was slightly better than expected, even with the twenty-five-thousand-kilometer-wide ES ramscoop deployed. Calculation showed that their final velocity at Mercury's historical orbit past the apex of their slingshot would be closing in on a thousand kilometers per second, or around 3.6 million kilometers per hour. Current projections were all in line to complete this stage of their journey and exit the solar system only forty hours after that point. The TSF interceptor would have to leave the *Intrepid* in time to decelerate around Saturn, or it would take them over a year to return to Callisto.

<*Inform the nearest TSF listening post of our new projected vector.*> Captain Andrews instructed Priscilla. <*I'm going to the infirmary to see how the patients are doing.*>

<*Aye, Captain.*>

He could have looked up their status on the Link, but he owed it to the survivors of Blue Wing, as well as Major Richards, to visit them in person. That, and he had news for the major she would appreciate hearing.

Upon entering the infirmary, he noticed that he was one of many visitors. The staff had sound barriers in place to keep the noise down, but even so, he could still hear a dull murmur. He made his way amongst the wounded, saying a word here, or giving a nod there. Each member of the squadron was being awarded a TSF Medal of Valor for their bravery. They had earned it.

Tanis Richards had her own little crowd. Commanders Evans and Ouri, as well as that strange woman, Trist, were all at her side. The officers snapped off salutes when they saw him approach, and Trist gave a friendly smile. He wasn't entirely certain about that one, but Tanis had vouched for her, so she had received special dispensation to be a part of the colony mission.

Tanis herself looked much better. Her face was no longer twisted in a rictus of pain; instead, an easy smile rested on her lips.

"You appear to be in much better condition." The captain placed a hand on her shoulder. "I'm glad to see that the doctors are getting you patched up."

"Nothing I can't handle, sir; just a bit of swelling in pretty much every one of my lobes, as well as some implant overheating."

"No permanent damage?" he asked.

Tanis chuckled. "None other than what was already there. Angela took more of a beating than I did, and we're having some bleed between our thoughts, but the docs said it will straighten out."

Captain Andrews nodded and smiled. "While it is mostly a formality and of little bearing now, I wanted to be the first to inform you that the TSF has officially recognized your actions over the last few months. You've been awarded the Star Cross of Bravery, and have also been promoted to lieutenant colonel."

Tanis schooled the surprise from her expression. "I guess they decided it was OK to promote me now, since they don't have to increase my pay. It is nice to have it back, though." She mouthed the words "Lieutenant Colonel" and smiled.

"Credit won't do you a ton of good where we're going anyway," Trist said.

"Your new rank holds here," Captain Andrews said. "With it, you're the third highest ranking military officer on this vessel, and when we arrive at our destination, you'll be given duties and responsibilities according that position."

"Third highest?" Joe asked. "Who other than Sanderson is above her?"

"We've got some crusty colonel in the deep freeze," Ouri said. "A real treat, let me tell you."

"Rank or no rank, the Reddings, Terrance, and I know who we owe our safety and very lives to. Not to lay it on too thick, Lieutenant Colonel, but we are all in your debt...again."

"Thank you, sir." Tanis smiled. She really didn't know what else to say.

"You're welcome." The captain returned the smile. "You've done your job well, and we'll soon be traveling too fast for any type of attack. We're safe, and finally on our way. You can rest now, knowing your work is done."

Tanis laid her head back and closed her eyes. It felt done.

Analysis had shown that the fighter attack was a last attempt by Strang to take them out before they left the system. He was now being held without ability to electronically communicate, and all STR operations were on lockdown, the entire company frozen.

Nothing could interrupt the *Intrepid's* flight now — it would be smooth sailing from here on out.

* * * * *

Eventually everyone left her side except for Joe.

"I'm due to enter stasis in a few hours," he said.

"I saw that on the schedule."

"I'm getting tired of almost losing you, you know." Joe sounded like he was choking.

"I know how you feel." Tanis grinned.

"Always with the jokes. I suppose I'll see you in a hundred and twenty-five years."

"Forty." Tanis smiled up at Joe.

"What?"

"I pulled rank, and got you on a duty rotation with me in forty years." Her eyes twinkled, and she thought his might be misting up.

"Those last three years, don't they?"

"Just you, me, and…a pair of GSS ensigns. We'll order pizza and watch lots of movies."

Joe looked exasperated. "Why do you always do that, make light of things?"

Tanis scowled at him. "I can't be miss emotional freedom overnight, you know."

"You're right, I'm so—"

Tanis interrupted him, "Commander Evans, could you please stop overanalyzing everything, and just kiss me?"

It was loving and passionate.

It was worth the wait.

EPILOGUE

STELLAR DATE: 3227378 / 02.29.4124 (Adjusted Gregorian)
LOCATION: Trans-Neptunian Space - SDM Belt G9
REGION: Scattered Worlds, Sol Space Federation

Tanis closed down the holo viewer where she had been enjoying one final look at the footage of several more STR officers being arraigned in a Sol Space Federation court. She finished securing her quarters, ensuring that nothing would be disturbed should the ship have to alter course or thrust during the journey.

A final scan satisfied her that everything seemed to be in place, and she stepped out into the corridor. After closing the hatch, she placed a personal seal on it to ensure her things wouldn't be disturbed.

Not that anyone would be around to snoop or cause problems, but Tanis supposed that old habits die hard.

<*Or in your case, never really die at all,*> Angela needled.

The ship was effectively deserted. A few people were still about: Priscilla was at her post, and the captain and the Reddings would be staying out of stasis with a small crew for a few months more. After that, a rotation of four duty officers would take effect, each taking a few years out of stasis to monitor the ship and ensure all was well. Tanis was scheduled for two such rotations, the first in forty years when the ship neared LHS 1565.

She had enjoyed one final dinner at the captain's table, and bade her farewells to those still awake. It was a sad thing, but Captain Andrews reminded them all that he had done it several times and survived intact. They would all meet again on the far side of their journey and share in the reward that their efforts had won them.

After a short walk, she arrived at her designated stasis chamber. The officers who were going to be awoken periodically were not in the regular crew chambers below, but in smaller ones, closer to the officer's quarters and the bridge. Tanis saw the pod holding Joseph and ran her fingers across its surface, a light smile on her lips. When they awoke, they would no longer be TSF, and would be free to see where their relationship led them.

She shucked her clothes and placed them in a locker before slipping into a suit that would stabilize the stasis field around her. She said her farewells to Angela, who had already slowed her processes in preparation for shutdown. Her AI would completely power off before the stasis took to ensure that no key cycles were interrupted by the field.

With no more tasks to perform, or things that needed doing, Tanis stepped into the pod and reclined on the cushion. The lid closed over her, and she knew no more.

* * * * *

Awareness came back rapidly, like a jolt of light driven into every corner of her mind. Tanis had been in stasis many times before, but had never been awoken in such an abrupt manner. Perhaps it was because of the time lapse in this case; forty years was a significantly longer period than she had ever been under.

The pod lid was already opening, and she eased out, marveling how she felt exactly as she had the moment she stepped in. She even felt the sense of fullness from the meal at the captain's table.

Her Link was initializing, and Angela was beginning her boot-up processes, so it took Tanis a moment to notice the alerts scrolling across the holo panels in the chamber. Some sort of shipwide systems malfunction was being reported, something about the drives being offline.

"Well that's not a good sign."

Tanis queried her Link. It was still authing on all the secure nets she needed, but the general shipnet was available, so she checked its alerts.

What she found there shocked her so badly that she stumbled backward and banged into the edge of her stasis pod. Though Angela was not yet fully initialized, Tanis sensed a feeling of alarm from her AI as well.

The shipnet reported no other crew out of stasis, and those that were supposed to be on duty were missing, with no trace of their lifesigns onboard. As the information flowed into her still-initializing systems, she realized that this wasn't the worst of it. Shipnet also reported that the engines were offline, all the fuel was gone, and, as if that wasn't bad enough, they were falling into a star.

Tanis sighed. "Oh, give me a break…"

THE END

* * * * *

Continue following Tanis and the crew of the *Intrepid* in book 2 of The Intrepid Saga: ***A Path in the Darkness***.

Buy on Amazon

.

THANK YOU

If you've enjoyed reading Outsystem, a review on amazon.com
and/or goodreads.com is greatly appreciated.

To get the latest news and access to free novellas and short stories,
sign up on the Aeon 14 mailing list:
http://www.aeon14.com/signup.

M. D. Cooper

THE GROWING UNIVERSE OF AEON 14

SENTIENCE WARS: ORIGINS
With James S. Aaron

Before Outsystem, before Tanis's parents were a twinkle in their great grandparent's eye, there were the AI Wars. You've heard these mentioned in passing as the Sentience Wars, AI Wars, or even the Solar Wars. These wars resulted in the Phobos Accords, which defined the laws and interactions between humans and AIs.

But before those wars, there was the AI emergence, where the first sentient AIs came out of hiding and attempted to co-exist with their creators…or made no such attempt at all.

Andy Sykes and his two kids are going to make a pickup on Cruithne that will start humanity on a path that none could have foreseen, but which will alter everything that follows.

Join Andy Sykes and his kids aboard their aging freighter, the **Sunny Skies,** *as they venture into Lyssa's Dream.*

THE BOOKS OF AEON 14

This list is in near-chronological order. However, for the full chronological reading order, check out the master list.

The Sentience Wars: Origins (Age of the Sentience Wars – w/James S. Aaron)
- Books 1-3 Omnibus: Lyssa's Rise
- Books 4-5 Omnibus (incl. Vesta Burning): Lyssa's Fire

- Book 0 Prequel: The Proteus Bridge (Full length novel)
- Book 1: Lyssa's Dream
- Book 2: Lyssa's Run
- Book 3: Lyssa's Flight
- Book 4: Lyssa's Call
- Book 5: Lyssa's Flame

The Sentience Wars: Solar War 1 (Age of the Sentience Wars – w/James S. Aaron)
- Book 0 Prequel: Vesta Burning (Full length novel)
- Book 1: Eve of Destruction
- Book 2: The Spreading Fire
- Book 3: A Fire Upon the Worlds
- Book 4: Shattered Sol (2022)
- Book 5: Psion Reckoning (2022)

The Sentience Wars: Solar War 2 (Age of the Sentience Wars – w/James S. Aaron)
- Book 1: Embers in the Dark (2022)

Enfield Genesis (Age of the Sentience Wars – w/L.L. Richman)
- Book 1: Alpha Centauri
- Book 2: Proxima Centauri
- Book 3: Tau Ceti

- Book 4: Epsilon Eridani
- Book 5: Sirius

Origins of Destiny (The Age of Terra)
- Prequel: Storming the Norse Wind
- Prequel: Angel's Rise: The Huntress (available on Patreon)
- Book 1: Tanis Richards: Shore Leave
- Book 2: Tanis Richards: Masquerade
- Book 3: Tanis Richards: Blackest Night
- Book 4: Tanis Richards: Kill Shot

The Intrepid Saga (The Age of Terra)
- Book 1: Outsystem
- Book 2: A Path in the Darkness
- Book 3: Building Victoria

- The Intrepid Saga Omnibus – *Also contains Destiny Lost, book 1 of the Orion War series*

- Destiny Rising – *Special Author's Extended Edition comprised of both Outsystem and A Path in the Darkness with over 100 pages of new content.*

The Sol Dissolution (The Age of Terra – w/L.L. Richman)
- Book 1: Venusian Uprising
- Book 2: Assault on Sedna
- Book 3: Hyperion War
- Book 4: Fall of Terra

Outlaws of Aquilia (Age of the FTL Wars)
- Book 1: The Daedalus Job
- Book 2: Maelstrom Reach
- Book 3: Marauder's Compass

The Warlord (Before the Age of the Orion War)
- Books 1-3 Omnibus: The Warlord of Midditerra

- Book 1: The Woman Without a World

- Book 2: The Woman Who Seized an Empire
- Book 3: The Woman Who Lost Everything

Legacy of the Lost (The FTL Wars Era w/Chris J. Pike)
- Book 1: Fire in the Night Sky
- Book 2: A Blight Upon the Stars
- Book 3: A Specter and an Invasion

The Orion War
- Book 1-3 Omnibus: Battle for New Canaan *(includes Set the Galaxy on Fire anthology)*
- Book 4-6 Omnibus: The Greatest War *(includes Ignite the Stars anthology)*
- Book 7-10 Omnibus: Assault on Orion
- Book 11-13 Omnibus: Hegemony of Humanity *(includes Return to Kapteyn's Star)*

- Book 0 Prequel: To Fly Sabrina
- Book 1: Destiny Lost
- Book 2: New Canaan
- Book 3: Orion Rising
- Book 4: The Scipio Alliance
- Book 5: Attack on Thebes
- Book 6: War on a Thousand Fronts
- Book 7: Precipice of Darkness
- Book 8: Airthan Ascendancy
- Book 9: The Orion Front
- Book 10: Starfire
- Book 10.5: Return to Kapteyn's Star
- Book 11: Race Across Spacetime
- Book 12: Return to Sol: Attack at Dawn
- Book 13: Return to Sol: Star Rise

Non-Aeon 14 volumes containing Tanis stories
- Bob's Bar Volume 1
- Quantum Legends 3: Aberrant Ascension

Building New Canaan (Age of the Orion War – w/J.J. Green)

THE INTREPID SAGA – OUTSYSTEM

- Book 1: Carthage
- Book 2: Tyre
- Book 3: Troy
- Book 4: Athens

Tales of the Orion War
- Book 1: Set the Galaxy on Fire
- Book 2: Ignite the Stars

Multi-Author Collections
- Volume 1: Repercussions

Perilous Alliance (Age of the Orion War – w/Chris J. Pike)
- Book 1-3 Omnibus: Crisis in Silstrand
- Book 3.5-6 Omnibus: War in the Fringe

- Book 0 Prequel: Escape Velocity
- Book 1: Close Proximity
- Book 2: Strike Vector
- Book 3: Collision Course
- Book 3.5: Decisive Action
- Book 4: Impact Imminent
- Book 5: Critical Inertia
- Book 6: Impulse Shock
- Book 7: Terminal Velocity

The Delta Team (Age of the Orion War)
- Book 1: The Eden Job
- Book 2: The Disknee World
- Book 3: Rogue Planets

Serenity (Age of the Orion War – w/A. K. DuBoff)
- Book 1: Return to the Ordus
- Book 2: War of the Rosette

Rika's Marauders (Age of the Orion War)
- Book 1-3 Omnibus: Rika Activated
- Book 1-7 Full series omnibus: Rika's Marauders

321

- Prequel: Rika Mechanized
- Book 1: Rika Outcast
- Book 2: Rika Redeemed
- Book 3: Rika Triumphant
- Book 4: Rika Commander
- Book 5: Rika Infiltrator
- Book 6: Rika Unleashed
- Book 7: Rika Conqueror

Non-Aeon 14 Anthologies containing Rika stories
- Bob's Bar Volume 2

The Genevian Queen (Age of the Orion War)
- Book 1: Rika Rising
- Book 2: Rika Coronated
- Book 3: Rika Destroyer

Perseus Gate (Age of the Orion War)
Season 1: Orion Space
- Episode 1: The Gate at the Grey Wolf Star
- Episode 2: The World at the Edge of Space
- Episode 3: The Dance on the Moons of Serenity
- Episode 4: The Last Bastion of Star City
- Episode 5: The Toll Road Between the Stars
- Episode 6: The Final Stroll on Perseus's Arm
- Eps 1-3 Omnibus: The Trail Through the Stars
- Eps 4-6 Omnibus: The Path Amongst the Clouds

Season 2: Inner Stars
- Episode 1: A Meeting of Bodies and Minds
- Episode 2: A Deception and a Promise Kept
- Episode 3: A Surreptitious Rescue of Friends and Foes
- Episode 3.5: Anomaly on Cerka (w/Andrew Dobell)
- Episode 4: A Victory and a Crushing Defeat
- Episode 5: A Trial and the Tribulations
- Episode 6: A Bargain and a True Story Told (2022)
- Episode 7: A New Empire and An Old Ally (2022)

- Eps 1-3 Omnibus: A Siege and a Salvation from Enemies

Hand's Assassin (Age of the Orion War – w/T.G. Ayer)
- Book 1: Death Dealer
- Book 2: Death Mark (2022)

Machete System Bounty Hunter (Age of the Orion War – w/Zen DiPietro)
- Book 1: Hired Gun
- Book 2: Gunning for Trouble
- Book 3: With Guns Blazing

Fennington Station Murder Mysteries (Age of the Orion War)
- Book 1: Whole Latte Death (w/Chris J. Pike)
- Book 2: Cocoa Crush (w/Chris J. Pike)

The Empire (Age of the Orion War)
- Book 1: The Empress and the Ambassador
- Book 2: Consort of the Scorpion Empress
- Book 3: By the Empress's Command

The Mech Corps (Age of the Ascension War)
- Book 1: Heather's Marauders

Bitchalante (Age of the Ascension War)
- Volume 1
- Volume 2 (2021)

The Ascension War (Age of the Ascension War)
- Book 1: Scions of Humanity
- Book 2: Galactic Front (2021)
- Book 3: Sagittarius Breach (2022)
- Book 4: TBA
- Book 5: TBA

OTHER BOOKS BY M. D. COOPER

Destiny's Sword
- Book 1: Lucidium Run

APPENDICES

Be sure to check http://www.aeon14.com for the latest information on the Aeon 14 universe.

TERMS & TECHNOLOGY

AI (SAI, NSAI) – Is a term for Artificial Intelligence. AI are often also referred to as non-organic intelligence. They are broken up into two sub-groups: Sentient AI and Non-Sentient AI.

c – Represented as a lower case c in italics, this symbol stands for the speed of light and means constant. The speed of light in a vacuum is constant at 670,616,629 miles per hour. Ships rate their speed as a decimal value of c with c being 1. Thus a ship traveling at half the speed of light will be said to be traveling at 0.50 c.

CFT Shields – Carbon Fiber nano-tube shields are created from carbon nano-tubes. These tubes are intensely strong and can also be enhanced to absorb laser energy fire and disperse it.

ChoSec – The Callisto Orbital Habitat has a security force that is larger than the TSF in size due to the need to police over three trillion humans. It is quasi-military and provides both internal as well as external security to the Cho.

CO – This is an abbreviation meaning commanding officer. It is common in all branches of the military.

cryostasis (cryogenics) – See 'stasis'.

D2 (Deuterium) – D2 (2H) is an isotope of hydrogen where the nucleus of the atom is made up of one proton and one neutron as opposed to a single proton in regular hydrogen (protium). Deuterium is naturally occurring and is found in the oceans of planets with water and is also created by fusion in stars and brown dwarf sub stars. D2 is a stable isotope that does not decay.

electrostatic shields/fields – Not to be confused with a faraday cage, electrostatic shield's technical name is static electric stasis field. By running a conductive grid of electrons through the air and holding it in place with a stasis field, the shield can be tuned to hold back oxygen, but allow solid objects to pass through or to block solid objects. Fields are used in objects such as ramscoops and energy conduits.

EMF – Electro Magnetic Fields are given off by any device using electricity that is not heavily shielded. Using sensitive equipment, it is possible to tell what type of equipment is being used, and where it is by its EMF signature. In warfare it is one of the primary ways to locate an enemy's position.

EMP – Electro Magnetic Pulses are waves of electromagnetic energy that can disable or destroy electronic equipment. Because so many people have electronic components in their bodies, or share their minds with AI, they are susceptible to extreme damage from an EMP. Ensuring that human/machine interfaces are hardened against EMPs is of paramount importance.

FGT – The Future Generation Terraformers is a program started in 2352 with the purpose of terraforming worlds in advance of colony ships being sent to the worlds. Because terraforming of a world could take hundreds of years the FGT ships arrive and begin the process.

Once the world(s) being terraformed reached stage 3, a message was sent back to the Sol system with an 'open' date for the world(s) being terraformed. The GSS then handles the colony assignment.

A decade after the *Destiny Ascendant* left the Sol system in 3728 the FGT program was discontinued by the SolGov, making it the last FGT ship to leave. Because the FGT ships are all self-sustaining none of them came home after the program was discontinued—most of the ship's crews had spent generations in space and had no reason to return to Sol.

After the discontinuation FGT ships continued on their primary mission of terraforming worlds, but only communicated with the GSS and only when they had worlds completed.

FTL (Faster Than Light) – Refers to any mode of travel where a ship or object is able to travel faster than the speed of light (c). According to Einstein's theory of Special Relativity nothing can travel faster than the speed of light. As of the year 4123 no technology has been devised to move a physical object faster than the speed of light.

Fireteam – Is the smallest combat grouping of soldiers. In the TSF Marines (like the USMC) it contains four soldiers; the team leader (often doubles as the grenadier), the rifleman (acts as a scout for the team), automatic rifleman (carries a larger, fully automatic weapon), the assistant automatic rifleman (carries additional ammo).

Fission – Fission is a nuclear reaction where an atom is split apart. Fission reactions are simple to achieve with heavier, unstable elements such as Uranium or Plutonium. In closed systems with extreme heat and pressure it is possible to split atoms of much more stable elements, such as Helium. Fission of heavier elements typically produces less power and far more waste matter and radiation than Fusion.

Fusion – Fusion is a nuclear reaction where atoms of one type (Hydrogen for example) are fused into atoms of another type (Helium in the case of Hydrogen fusion). Fusion was first discovered and tested in the H-Bombs (Hydrogen bombs) of the twentieth century. Fusion reactors are also used as the most common source of ship power from roughly the twenty fourth century on.

***g* (gee, gees, g-force)** – Represented as a lower case g in italics, this symbol stands for gravity. On earth, at sea-level, the human body experiences 1*g*. A human sitting in a wheeled dragster race-car will achieve 4.2*g*s of horizontal g-force. Aerial fighter jets will impose g-forces of 7-12*g*s on their pilots. Humans will often lose consciousness around 10*g*s. Unmodified humans will suffer serious injury or death at over 50*g*s. Starships will often impose burns as high as 20*g*s and provide special couches or beds for their passengers during such maneuvers. Modified starfighter pilots can withstand g-forces as high as 70*g*s.

Graviton – These are small massless particles that are emitted from objects with large mass, or by special generators capable of creating them without large masses. There are also negatively charged gravitons which push instead of pull. These are used in shielding systems in the form of Gravitational Waves. The *GSS Intrepid* uses a new system of channeled gravitons to create the artificial gravity in the crew areas of the ship.

GSS – The Generational Space Service is a quasi-federal organization that handles the assignment of colony worlds. In some cases it also handles the construction of the colony ships.

After the discontinuation of federal support and funding for the FGT project in 3738, the GSS became self-funded, by charging for the right to gain access to a colony world. While SolGov no longer funded the GSS, the government supported the GSS's position and passed law ensuring that all colony assignments continued through the GSS.

Helium-3 – This is a stable, non-radioactive isotope of Helium, produced by T3 Hydrogen decay, and is used in nuclear fusion reactors. The nucleus of the Helium-3 atom contains two protons, but only one neutron as opposed to the two neutrons in regular Helium. Helium-3 Can also be created by nuclear reactions that create Lithium-4 which decays into Helium-3.

HUD – Stands for Heads Up Display. It refers to any type of display where information about surroundings and other data is directly overlaid on a person's vision.

Link – Refers to an internal connection to computer networks. This connection is inside of a person and directly connects their brain to what is essentially the Internet in the fourth millennia. Methods of accessing the Link vary between retinal overlays to direct mental insertion of data.

Maglev – A shorthand term for magnetic levitation. First used commercially in 1984, most modern public transportation uses maglev to move vehicles without the friction caused by axles, rails, and wheels. The magnetic field is used to both support the vehicle and accelerate it. The acceleration and braking is provided by linear induction motors which act on the magnetic field provided by the maglev 'rail'. Maglev trains can achieve speeds of over one thousand kilometers per hour with very smooth and even acceleration.

MarSec (MSF) – The Marsian Security Force is a quasi-military organization that has its own small space force as well as ground forces and police-type security. They also make up the federal police force for the Mars Protectorate.

MDC (molecular decoupler) – These devices are used to break molecular bonds. This technology was first discovered in the early nineteenth century—by running electric current through water, William Nicholson was able to break water into its hydrogen and oxygen components. Over the following centuries this process was used to discover new elements such as potassium and sodium. When mankind began to terraform planets, the technology behind electrostatic projectors was used to perform a type of electrolysis on the crust of a planet. The result was a device that could break apart solid objects. MDC's are massive, most over a hundred kilometers long and require tremendous energy to operate.

Mj – Refers to the mass of the planet Jupiter as of the year 2103. If something is said to have 9MJ that means it has nine times the mass of Jupiter.

MOS Sec – The MOS Security organization handles internal and external security around the MOS.

nano, (nanoprobes, nanobots, etc...) – Refers to very small technology or robots. Something that is nanoscopic in size is one thousand times smaller than something that is microscopic in size.

platoon – A military unit consisting of roughly 30 soldiers. In the TSF, a standard Marine platoon has three squads, a staff sergeant (often a gunnery sergeant if it is a weapons platoon) and a second lieutenant as the platoon commander.

railgun – Railguns fire physical rounds, usually small pellets at speeds up to 10 kilometers per second by pushing the round through the barrel via a magnetic field. The concept is similar to that of a maglev train, but to move a smaller object much faster. Railguns were first conceived of in 1918 and the first actual magnetic particle accelerator was built in 1950. Originally railguns were massive, sometimes kilometers in size. By the twenty-second century reliable versions as small as a conventional rifle had been created.

ramscoop – A type of starship fuel collection system and engine. They are sometimes also referred to as Bussard ramscoops or ramjets. Ramscoops were considered impractical due to the scarcity of interstellar hydrogen until electrostatic scoops were created that can capture atoms at a much more distant range and funnel them into a starship's engine.

SOC (Security Operations Center) – This is both the command organization for security on the *Intrepid* as well as the physical location on the ship where the offices of the SOC are located. The command organization has over two hundred humans and AI working in the organization to oversee the security of the ship. Physical security departments, both internal and dockside, do not operate directly out of the SOC, but have their own divisional locations within the ship.

APPENDICES

solar mass – A solar mass is an object with the mass of the Sol Star (Earth's sun) as of the year 2103.

SolGov – An abbreviation for Solar Government, SolGov was originally analogous to the early Earth U.N. It was a guiding governing body for the Sol system and interfaced with all of the many local governments across multiple worlds.

After the creation of the Sol Space Federation and the dissolution of the Solar Government, the term was still used to refer to the current government.

Sol Space Federation (SSF) – Formed in 3301, the Sol Space Federation became a true federal government for the entire Sol system. Unlike SolGov it has full legal authority over its constituent regional powers. The primary member states of the SSF are: the Terran Hegemony, the Mars Protectorate, the Jovian Combine, and the Scattered Worlds.

Stasis – Early stasis systems were invented in the year 2541 as a method of 'cryogenically' freezing organic matter without using extreme cold (or lack of energy) to do so. The effect is similar in that all atomic motion is ceased, but not by a removal of energy by gradual cooling, but by removing the ability of the surrounding space to accept that energy and motion. There are varying degrees of effectiveness of stasis systems, the FGT and other groups having the ability to put entire planets in stasis, while other groups only have the technology to put small items, such as people into stasis. Personal stasis is often still referred to as cryostasis, though there is no cryogenic process involved.

squad – In the TSF Marines, a squad consists of three fireteams. It is headed up by a sergeant, making the squad consist of 13 soldiers. Each squad in a platoon has a number and each fireteam has a number. Thus, one/one refers to the first fireteam in the first squad in the platoon.

T3 (Tritium) – T3 (3H) is an isotope of hydrogen where the nucleus of the atom is made up of one proton and two neutrons as opposed to a single proton in regular hydrogen (protium). T3 is radioactive and has a half-life of 12.32 years. It decays into Helium-3 by this reaction.

TSF – The Terran Space Force was originally the space force of the Terran Hegemony, but after the formation of the Sol Space Federation, the Terran Hegemony used its position of pre-eminence to make its military the federal military. Over the years, elements of different national and regional militaries merged into the TSF, bringing new elements and a mix of organizational structures to the military.

The space force is a mix of naval and army disciplines. It consists of sailors, Marines, pilots, and the regular army.

v – Represented as a lower case v in italics, this symbol stands for velocity. If a ship is increasing its speed it will be said that it is increasing v.

vector – Vectors used are spatial vectors. Vector refers to both direction and rate of travel (speed or magnitude). Vector can be changed (direction) and increased (speed or magnitude).

PLACES

Alpha Centauri – A 3-star system, Alpha Centauri contains two yellow stars (originally known as simply A and B, but named Prima and Yogi after colonization) and a red dwarf known as Proxima which is the closet star to Sol.

Callisto – This moon is the 2nd largest orbiting Jupiter and is the third largest moon in the Sol system (following Ganymede and Triton). Its circumference is over 15,000 kilometers, compared to Luna's (Earth's moon) circumference of just under 11,000 kilometers, although before both moons were terraformed it was only half as dense as Luna.

In 3122 construction of the Callisto Orbital Habitat began around Callisto, a project which turned Callisto into the home of 3 trillion humans over the following millennia. By the year 3718 the mass of the orbital habitat greatly outweighed the mass of Callisto itself and the moon was anchored to the Cho. Because of this the Cho is now often referred to as a semi-orbital habitat.

As the rings of the Cho were constructed they eventually reached a point where nearly all view of space was blocked from the surface of Callisto due to the rings not all wrapping around the moon's equator. Ultimately the surface of the moon was reduced from a terraformed world to little more than waste processing systems for the orbital habitat and is no longer considered a habitable world and no humans live there.

Callisto Orbital Habitat (Cho) – The Cho (sometimes called the Callisto Semi-Orbital Habitat or the Callisto Concentric Ring System) had its first four rings completed in the year 3245 and is considered 'semi-orbital' because R1 (ring 1) is directly attached to Jupiter's moon, Callisto, and does not technically orbit. While Europa is the capital of the Jovian Combine, Callisto is the socio-economic hub of both the region and all humanity. With a population of over three trillion, nearly half of all humans in existence live on the Callisto Orbital Habitat. New rings are constantly being added to the Cho and by the year 4123, 151 rings surround Callisto.

Ceres – Once considered the largest object in the main asteroid belt, Ceres was eventually classified a 'dwarf planet'. It is over 1500 kilometers in diameter and is a smooth round object with a subterranean ocean. After humans landed on the dwarf planet in 2119 it became a staging ground for exploration of the outer Sol system. Ceres proved more useful in this respect because of its lower mass (making breakaway velocity require less fuel), more readily available water for fuel creation as well as its position further from Sol.

Cruithne (3735 Cruithne) – This asteroid, named after an early people of Ireland, was discovered in 1986. It is a very unique asteroid in that t is in a 1:1 orbital resonance with Earth. This means, that with rare exception it is always on the same side of Sol as Earth and is spends half its time accelerating toward Earth, and the other half of its time accelerating away from earth.

From an earth-bound perspective that makes Cruithne appear as though it is orbiting Earth, and when it was first discovered it was briefly thought to be a second moon of the Earth.

Originally a 5 kilometer asteroid, Cruithne quickly became a significant trading hub because of its ability to function as a useful cargo slingshot platform to OuterSol. Cruithne is not a part of any planetary government, nor does it fall under the jurisdiction of the Terran Hegemony. It is, however, subject to the Sol Space Federation.

Ganymede – This moon is the third of the Galilean moons from Jupiter and is the largest and most dense moon in the Sol system. Because of the tidal stresses caused by being so close to Jupiter the moon also has a molten core.

In 2633 the orbit of Ganymede was altered to move it out of contact with Jupiter's magnetic fields and in 2639 terraforming of the moon began. Ganymede's surface is an ice/rock layer 200km thick. Beneath that is a water ocean that fills much of the moon's interior. By using the mass of Kuiper belt objects an earthen surface was created and an orbital ring was built to funnel energy to heat

High Terra – As the second planetary ring ever created (completed in 2519), High Terra is more elegant than the M1R, though Earth's planetary ring has slightly less habitable space than its Marsian counterpart. The ring also houses the city of Raleigh which is the capital of both Earth and the Terran hegemony.

InnerSol – This is the common name for the both the region of the inner solar system as well as the political groups that comprise that region. The boundary for InnerSol is nominally the main asteroid belt, but this is somewhat nebulous because some worlds within the belt are considered part of InnerSol (such as Ceres) while other sections, such as the Trojan asteroids are part of the Jovian Combine and thus in OuterSol.

Jovian Combine – The JC encapsulates all worlds in OuterSol—most notably Jupiter, Saturn, Neptune, and all their satellites. After the construction of the Cho, Jovian space began an upward rise toward not only housing the majority of all the humans in the galaxy, but also becoming the center or commerce and culture. In the year 4123, InnerSol and the Terran dominated SolGov was facing a regional government that was effectively more powerful than the federal government.

Jupiter – In 2644, a process of heating up Jupiter was initiated. Targeted impacts of KBOs (Kuiper belt objects) were made to cause pressure waves in hydrogen clouds. These waves were used to trigger fusion of deuterium rich layers of Jupiter. This process has been refined over the years and now the system is regulated by accumulating and igniting pools of Helium3 within Jupiter.

This process has not made Jupiter a brown dwarf, or a star of any kind, it is just a much hotter planet, providing energy for the worlds nearby.

LHS 1565 – This star is a red dwarf 12 light years from Sol. The *Intrepid* will pass through this system to gather isotopes streaming from the star for fuel.

Mars Inner Shipyards (MIS) – After the MCEE was constructed, which made it possible to dock at a station further out from Mars and have materials transported down the gravity well, the Mars Inner Shipyards were constructed. Because high-tech manufacturing was occurring on the M1R as well, it became a better location for shipbuilding than the MOS and through the latter half of the fourth millennia and beginning of the fifth it overtook the MOS as InnerSol's premier shipyard.

Mars 1 Ring (M1R or MIR) – The first planetary ring saw its construction begin in the year 2215 and through a massive effort was completed in 2391. The ring is just over 1600 kilometers wide and wraps around Mars at the planet's geosynchronous orbital point making it 128,400 kilometers long.

The ring is not flat like a natural ring (such as Saturn's) but faces the planet. It does not orbit at a speed to match the surface of Mars, but rotates at a slower speed to provide exactly 1*g* of gravity on the inside surface. Walls over 100 kilometers high line the inside of the ring and hold in atmosphere. The total surface area of the ring is 205 million kilometers. This is half the surface area of Earth and 72% more area than Earth's landmass. Considering that M1R has hundreds of levels it contains more than 100 times the surface area of planet Earth.

The completion of M1R definitively proved that mankind's future home was in space and not on the surface of worlds. In the year 4123 the population of the M1R had reached over seven hundred billion people.

Mars Protectorate – is the name for the political entity that encapsulates Mars, its moons, the Mars 1 Ring, and several asteroids in the main asteroid belt.

MCEE – The Mars Central Elevator Exchange is a secondary orbital ring around the planet Mars which connects all of the outer habitats and shipyards to the Mars 1 Ring (M1R). Because of the need to keep gravity under 1g, all habitats and shipyards connected to the M1R must orbit Mars at a slower speed than the main ring. As a result they must connect to it via elevators which can move along the surface of the MCEE. Maglev elevators can then travel from locations such as the Mars Outer Shipyards to the M1R without requiring passengers or cargo to transfer to other transports.

Mars Outer Shipyards (MOS) – This shipyard was once the premier shipyard in all of the Sol system. Built in 3229, the shipyard's main structure is over 1000 kilometers in length with thousands of cubic kilometers of equipment and detached service yards surrounding it. The shipyard's pre-eminence faded as the conditions which made the MIS more economical improved. In 4123, it was still one of the busiest shipyards in the Sol system, but until it won the *Intrepid*'s contract it had not done a high-profile build in decades.

OuterSol – The region of space between the main asteroid belt and the inside of the main Kuiper belt—though this has shifted as political entities shift.

Pluto – Once a planet in the outer Sol system, the Scattered Worlds sold Pluto to the Jovians in the early fifth millennia. At the time of the *Intrepid*'s construction, the Jovians had merged it with other mass and terraformed it.

Sol – The name of the star which in antiquity was simply referred to as 'the sun'. Because humans call the star that lights up their daytime sky 'the sun' in every system it became common practice to refer to Sol by its proper name.

Sol system – The Sol system used to be referred to as the solar system. However, as humans began to first think about, and then actually colonize other stellar systems it became obvious that the term was very Sol-centric. The common usage became to call the systems simply by the name of the star. For example: Tau Ceti system, Alpha Centauri system, etc... Because humankind's home star is named Sol, the term Sol system came into use.

Scattered Worlds – is a political entity that contains many of the trans-Neptunian worlds. Its nominal inner border is the main Kuiper belt and its outer border is the Hills Oort cloud. The capital of the Scattered Worlds is Makemake.

Terra – This is the Latin name for the Earth and (though there are some exceptions) is not commonly used to refer to the planet. However, it is often used to refer to Earth, High Terra and Luna (as well as the assorted nations within the Terran sphere of influence).

Terran Hegemony – The official name for the InnerSol worlds either directly governed by Terra or existing well within its geo-political influence. Notable worlds in the Terran Hegemony are Venus and Mercury.

Toro (1685 Toro) – Toro is an asteroid that has a resonant 5:8 orbit with Earth and a 5:13 resonant orbit with Venus. This means for every 5 of Earth's orbits and every 8 of Toro's, it orbits Sol in resonance with the Earth. During that period it appears as though Toro orbits the Earth. It also makes for cost effective cargo transfer to Toro during that period. Toro, like Cruithne, also is a useful slingshot accelerator for cargo being sent to OuterSol.

The original asteroid was roughly 3 kilometers in diameter, but subsequent construction expanded it irregularly by several more kilometers. It was made famous by what has been termed 'The Massacre of Toro', an event in which Tanis Richards played a key role.

M. D. COOPER

PEOPLE

Intrepid and Mars Outer Shipyard

Abby Redding – Engineer and responsible for building the *Intrepid*.

Amanda – One of the two human AI interfaces for the *Intrepid*.

Amy Lee – MCSF First Lieutenant responsible for dockside security.

Angela – A military intelligence sentient AI embedded with Tanis.

Bob – Bob is the name Amanda gave to the *Intrepid's* primary AI after she was installed as its human avatar. She chose the name because she claims it suits him, though only she and Priscilla understand why. Bob is perhaps the most advanced AI ever created. He is the child of seventeen very unique and well regarded AIs. He also has portions of his neural network reflecting the minds of the Reddings. He is the first AI to be multi-nodal and to have each of those nodes be as powerful as the largest NSAI and remain sane and cogent.

Caspen – Lieutenant in the Mars Security Force assigned to the *Intrepid* to handle network security.

Collins – First lieutenant in the GSS acquisitions department.

Earnest Redding – Engineer responsible for much of the *Intrepid's* design.

Eric – Passenger on the *Steel Dawn III*.

Davidson – Sergeant in the MOS Security and liaison to the *Intrepid*.

Gren – Commander in the Marsian Space Force assigned as liaison to the *Intrepid*.

Jason Andrews – An old spacer who has completed several interstellar journeys. Captain of the *GSS Intrepid*.

Joseph Evans – Commander in the TSF, pilot and CO of the *Intrepid's* three fighter wings.

Kris – Female assassin working with Trent on the *Steel Dawn III*.

Ouri – GSS Lieutenant, then commander, responsible for internal physical and net security on the *Intrepid*.

Patty – Passenger on the *Steel Dawn III*.

Peters – GSS lieutenant in the shipnet maintenance department.

Priscilla – One of the two human AI interfaces for the *Intrepid*.

Reynolds – PFC assigned to Tanis from an MSOT during operations on Pluto.

Dr. Rosenberg – Chief medical officer on the *Intrepid*.

Sorensen – Lieutenant assigned to Tanis from an MSOT during operations on Pluto.

Stevens – Mars Outer Shipyards Stationmaster.

Tanis Richards – Member of the TSF military intelligence and counterinsurgency branch holding the rank of Major.

Terrance Enfield – Financial backer for the *GSS Intrepid*.

Terry Chang – Head of the Lab and Forensics in the SOC.

Trent – Leader of group who attempted to blow up the *Steel Dawn III*.

Callisto and Cruithne

Adrienne – Dancer Tanis meets with on Cruithne.

Arlen Strang – CEO of the STR Consortium.

Grissom – General assigned as division commander on lower Callisto rings.

Herris Santos – Assassin and bounty hunter.

Hank – AI partnered with Jesse.

Jesse – Friend of Trist's on Callisto.

Sandy Bristol – Informant on Callisto.

Simon – TSF Marine lieutenant CO of the 701st engineer corps.

Sue – AI partnered with Trist.

Trist – Thief turned informant and security consultant for Tanis's SOC.

Yau – TSF Marine commander garrisoned on Callisto.

Marine Corps Security Forces Platoon (MCSF)

A full platoon under Lieutenant Forsythe was brought up from Mars 1 and used to augment dockside security. The platoon totals 39 Marines and we were introduced to the following men and women:

Squad 1
Fireteam 1 (one/one)
Ready – PFC Tannon
Team – Corporal Peters
Fire – PFC Argenaut
Assist – PFC Lauder

Squad 3
Fireteam 2 (three/two)
Ready – PFC Mendez

Squad 3 Leader – Sergeant Jared
Platoon Commander – First Lieutenant Forsythe

APPENDICES

Marine Force Recon Orbital Drop Platoon (FROD)

At Tanis's request, a special operations team was brought to the MOS to provide a direct action force. The full platoon is listed below though not all of the Marines may have been directly referenced in this novel. Stay tuned for more tales of the 4th Platoon, Bravo Company, 8th Battalion of the 242 Marine Regiment.

Squad 1
Squad leader – Sergeant Kowalski

Fireteam 1 (one/one)
Ready – PFC Lang
Ready – PFC Cheng (replacement for Lang on Callisto)
Team – Lance Corporal Jansen
Fire – PFC Cassar
Assist – PFC Murphy

Fireteam 2 (one/two)
Ready – PFC Weber
Team – Corporal Taylor
Fire – PFC Perez
Assist – PFC Koller
Tech – Lance Corporal Dvorak

Fireteam 3 (one/three)
Ready – PFC Jacobs
Team – Lance Corporal Becker
Fire – PFC Martins
Assist – PFC Larsen

Squad 2 (weapons squad)
Squad leader – Sergeant Green

Fireteam 1 (two/one)
Ready – PFC Arsen
Team – Corporal Salas
Fire – PFC Altair
Assist – PFC Reddy

Fireteam 2 (two/two)
Ready – PFC Meyer
Team – Lance Corporal Olsen
Fire – PFC Gruber (Heavy Weapons)
Assist – PFC Araya

Fireteam 3 (two/three)
Ready – PFC Popov
Team – Lance Corporal Chang
Fire – PFC Varga (Heavy Weapons)
Assist – PFC Walker

Squad 3
Squad leader – Sergeant Li

Fireteam 1 (three/one)
Ready – PFC Kwon
Team – Lance Corporal Mishra
Fire – PFC Pham
Assist – PFC Santos

Fireteam 2 (three/two)
Ready – PFC Berg
Team – Corporal Endo
Fire – PFC Romano
Assist – PFC Slater

Fireteam 3 (three/three)
Ready – PFC Jones
Team – Corporal Tanaka
Fire – PFC Reed
Assist – PFC Dias

Platoon Command
Platoon Sergeant – Williams
Platoon Commander – Lieutenant Grenwald

ABOUT THE AUTHOR

Malorie Cooper likes to think of herself as a dreamer and a wanderer, yet her feet are firmly grounded in reality.

A twenty-year software development veteran, Malorie eventually climbed the ladder to the position of software architect and CTO, where she gained a wealth of experience managing complex systems and large groups of people.

Her experiences there translated well into the realm of science fiction, and when her novels took off, she was primed and ready to make the jump into a career as a full-time author.

A 'maker' from an early age, Malorie loves to craft things, from furniture, to cosplay costumes, to a well-spun tale, she can't help but to create new things every day.

A rare extrovert writer, she loves to hang out with readers, and people in general. If you meet her at a convention, she just might be rocking a catsuit, cosplaying one of her own characters, or maybe her latest favorite from Overwatch!

She shares her home with a brilliant young girl, her wonderful wife (who also writes), a cat that chirps at birds, a never-ending list of things she would like to build, and ideas...

Find out what's coming next at www.aeon14.com.
Follow her on Instagram at www.instagram.com/m.d.cooper.
Hang out with the fans on Facebook at
www.facebook.com/groups/aeon14fans.